PLAYING DIRTY

PLAYING
Dirty

....

Monkey Business Trio

C. L. PARKER

Bantam Books
New York

A Bantam Books Trade Paperback Original

Copyright © 2015 by C. L. Parker

Excerpt from *Getting Rough* by C. L. Parker
copyright © 2015 by C. L. Parker

Published in the United States by Bantam Books,
an imprint of Random House, a division of Penguin Random House LLC,
New York.

BANTAM BOOKS and the HOUSE colophon are registered
trademarks of Penguin Random House LLC.

This book contains an excerpt from the forthcoming book
Getting Rough by C. L. Parker. This excerpt has been
set for this edition only and may not reflect
the final content of the forthcoming edition.

LIBRARY OF CONGRESS CATALOGING-IN-PUBLICATION DATA

Parker, C. L.
Playing dirty: monkey business trio/C. L. Parker.
pages; cm
ISBN 978-1-101-88294-8
eBook ISBN 978-1-101-88295-5
I. Title.
PS3616.A74424P58 2015
813'.6—dc23   2015001383

Printed in the United States of America on acid-free paper

www.bantamdell.com

2 4 6 8 9 7 5 3 1

Book design by Elizabeth A. D. Eno

This book is dedicated to all the Shaws, Caseys, Landons, Chazs, and Denvers of my life.

They say artists draw inspiration from their environment. So for that, I should thank you for all the highs and lows you have put me through. If it weren't illegal (and slightly horrific, albeit justifiable), I'd get my Dr. Frankenstein on and take the best parts of each of you to put together the perfect man. I'm too pretty to go to prison, so I'll just continue to do it on paper. Thank the powers that be that I've found an outlet for all my crazy, because you sure as hell weren't helping matters.

PLAYING DIRTY

CHAPTER 1

Shaw

"So the goal here, people," Wade Price, CEO of Striker Sports Entertainment, said as he wrapped up—I hoped—his very long-winded pep talk, "is to wine and dine Rockford. Give him any and everything he wants. Romance him until he signs with this agency. Matthews, I'm counting on you and Whalen. And, since you're the best of the best, I'm sending both of you to meet with him. The decision I make regarding the partnership hinges on who is able to succeed. Simply put, whichever one of you gets me Rockford gets the position."

It figured.

Every agent employed by Striker Sports Entertainment was present at the weekly staff meeting to give witness to what was, undoubtedly, the biggest showdown between the most competitive agents in the city. And they just happened to be employed by the same agency. I was one of those agents, Shaw Matthews. The bane of my existence, Cassidy Whalen, was the other.

After Wade's partner, Monty Prather, retired, the vacant spot came up for grabs. Cassidy and I had been competing for the job since it had been announced, three months ago. I think Wade loved to watch us go at each other. I know the rest of the office did. We were both ruthless in our antics, unforgiving in our quest to secure the most coveted prizes, which were usually the same clients every other agent in the nation wanted. More often than not, we won. Combined, our haul was impressive, but it was small potatoes compared to what was in store. Cassidy and I had never gone head-to-head for the same client.

Until now.

It wasn't often that one of the most sought after athletes ditched their agent and publicly advertised that they were on the lookout for someone who could make them even more money than they were already making, which was an insane amount. Wade Price wanted a taste of that insanity, so he was unleashing his favorite pets and pitting us against each other. I had to hand it to him; it was a smart move. Tapping into our insatiable need to one-up each other guaranteed that Striker would bring home the win.

Our target was Denver "Rocket Man" Rockford, San Diego's star quarterback. Apparently, his former agent hadn't had the same vision as Denver for his future, so he got sacked (no pun intended), and Denver was on the hunt for new representation. And it just so happened his contract was up for renewal, with him coming off a more than stellar performance for the season and little time left before he needed to get back to training for the next. Fast decisions needed to be made, which meant fast talking and fast walking. Naturally, Wade felt Striker was the agency that could best negotiate the deal. And even though the payday was a nice bit of incentive, it was the notoriety of being Denver's agent that I craved most.

Cassidy stood in the way of that. I meant to plow her down, but she wasn't going to make it easy.

She was a real man-eater, the sort whose career meant more to her than enjoying the fruits of all that labor. She never missed a day of work, and she knew things about her clients they didn't even know about themselves. Cassidy Whalen was as worthy an opponent as I had ever come up against. In fact, her client list was every bit as impressive as mine. Not bad for a chick. She was good. She was also a bore. And a bitch.

She didn't like me very much, which was unusual, because most women did. Maybe she just needed to get laid. I doubted very seriously that anything like that was happening. I didn't really care, but I'd made it my business to know my enemy, so I'd paid attention to details. No ring on her finger meant she wasn't married or engaged. And around here, no gossip at the water cooler meant she also wasn't involved in any interoffice romances. Not that gossip equaled fact. There were plenty of stories circulating about me, but those were all wishful thinking without an ounce of truth.

My adversary's aversion to me, seemingly without a man to whom she was simply loyal, forced me to formulate my own theories in an attempt to reason it all out. The one at the top of my list was pretty clever, in my opinion. I was betting she was secretly a black widow, sucking the life out of men who dared get near her. Even if I'd hit the mark with that one, I wasn't the least bit intimidated. I could handle her. Admittedly, I was sort of curious to know if she was as much of a hellcat in the sack as she was in the boardroom. Lord knows she'd given me more than one hard-on while strutting her stuff like her shit didn't stink, mostly while taking shots at me.

"Sir, do we have anything on him?" Cassidy's glasses were perched on the end of her nose, and her long legs were crossed, with her hand poised to jot down any information he could provide on her next target. Somehow she even managed to make suck-up look sort of sexy. Not that she'd intended to.

She and I were alike in a lot of ways, but this wasn't one of them. I preferred the casual approach, leaning back in my chair and propping an elbow on the table to take it all in. For one thing, I was bored. For another, this meeting had already gone on far longer than necessary, and I had shit to do. I didn't bother with a pen or a pad of paper; I wasn't interested in taking notes. I didn't need to. I had the memory of an elephant and could recall details others missed even if they'd recorded the whole damn thing.

I chuckled under my breath, amused by Cassidy's eagerness. She must have heard me, because the spike of her heel found its way onto the top of my foot. And it felt none too pleasant. I shot up straight but covered my growl with a cough when Wade's eyes pinned me to my seat. Cassidy sat prim and proper beside me, like nothing had happened. Innocent, she was not.

I took the look of disapproval from Wade and kept my trap shut so he could answer her and this meeting could be over with already.

"I expect you to do your own digging for his personal details. Makes it more authentic. And you could use a challenge, Whalen."

Cassidy nodded. "Yes, sir. I look forward to it."

Suck. Up.

"I want a report from each of you first thing after your meeting. Now get your butts out of here. It's a madhouse out there, and I want to head home." Finally. He turned away, mumbling under his breath, "I hate rush-hour traffic."

As eager as I was for the meeting to adjourn, I was even more eager to mess with my nemesis. Maybe shake her foundation a bit. Any chance I had to do it, I pounced. So I took my time hauling myself out of the leather seat, which had nearly become glued to my ass, while the room cleared and Cassidy studiously gathered her things. No one needed that much crap for a staff meeting.

Once the room was empty, I leaned in. "Ever worry your nose

will get stuck in his ass and you'll have to have it surgically re-moved?"

Without so much as a pause in her actions or a look in my di-rection, she came back with "Ever worry you'll get lockjaw from sucking his cock?"

There she was. Cassidy Whalen had everyone else in the office fooled, but not me. I'd been on the receiving end of her mouth since the day I'd arrived, almost a year before. She was jealous, and she'd formulated her opinion of me before I'd even stepped foot back on American soil after my long tenure abroad.

"Nice, Whalen. Really nice. Do you kiss your mother with that mouth?"

"Who I kiss and with what is none of your concern."

"How about you pucker up and kiss my ass?"

Cassidy dropped her messenger bag and turned on me. "I am so sick of your crap, Matthews. Since the day you got here, you've acted like everything should be handed to you. And now you think you deserve the position I've been busting my butt for?"

"Oh, so you're the only person who's been busting their ass around here? I'm sure the rest of the staff would appreciate know-ing that."

"Don't put words into my mouth. You knew what I meant."

"I'm sorry, but I'm not fluent in bitch."

Her laugh was sarcastic, but the ire behind those green eyes was completely authentic. She was so cute when she was per-turbed.

"Listen up, golden boy." She leaned in, encroaching upon my personal space. "You might have been Monty Prather's pride and joy, but he's not here to pamper you anymore. Which means you might actually have to do some real work, because if you think for one second that I'm going to roll over and play dead to appease your sense of entitlement, you're even dumber than you look.

You want that partnership? You better get your act together, since I will not hesitate for one second to do whatever I need to in order to rip it out of your precious, perfectly manicured clutches."

Pfft . . . I did not get manicures. And she obviously didn't know a thing about me, other than how to piss me off. My chair shot back when I stood—not that I'd meant for it to happen, but the effect was cool. "I was going to take it easy on you, but just for that, now I'm going to bury you!"

No, it wasn't a zinger of a comeback, and I was disappointed in myself. It was like lying in bed with an exotic beauty and having nothing to offer but a limp cock. And no, that had never happened to me, either—the limp cock, not the exotic beauty. I knew Cassidy was quick on the draw, though, so I didn't stick around for her witty retort. Instead, I bolted out of the boardroom and slammed the door behind myself.

The woman infuriated me no end. I had never let anyone else get under my skin, and I was perplexed as to why she was able to do it so easily. Normally, I was pretty laid-back, cool as a cucumber, comfortable in any element, without a care in the world. But when Cassidy Whalen walked into the room, something inside me went haywire. She was the Achilles' heel to my composure, kryptonite to my self-confidence. I kept it together for the most part when she was around, not wanting to show my hand lest she use it to her advantage. I knew she would because I would do the same thing. But she wasn't going to win. I'd never concede victory to a woman. I just wasn't made up of the stuff that would allow me to utter those blasphemous words from my mouth.

My feet landed heavily on the trek back to my office to pull my shit together so I could get the hell out of there and find a tall cold one. I even blew past the gaggle of assistants and receptionists who liked to bat their lashes and show way too much cleavage;

I wasn't in the mood to flirt. Okay, I could've used the boost to my ego, so I probably should've made that stop, but I didn't.

When I reached my suite, my assistant snapped his head up from his desk and stared after me. "I take it the meeting went well?"

"Can it, Ben!" I barked. "Shit! Shit! Shit!"

"What happened?"

"I'll give you three guesses."

"And I only need one," he said in a tone that was much too jovial. That was Ben Durand. He believed the glass was always half full and that no matter how stormy the day or how late the hour, the sun would shine again. If he'd had curly red hair and freckles instead of blond hair and blue eyes, he would've made an excellent Little Orphan Annie. "How is the ice queen today?"

I couldn't help myself from sniggering at the nickname someone had bestowed upon her long before my first day at Striker.

"Her Highness is just peachy—warm and fuzzy as usual," I said from my office. "In fact, she and I have to share a meeting with Denver Rockford. No doubt, she'll try to make me look like an imbecile in front of him. Let's make sure we don't give her any ammunition. Find me anything you can on him. I want to know every little detail, down to what time of day the man takes a piss."

"Aye, aye, Captain." Ben was used to my abruptness after a run-in with Cassidy, so he never took it personally. The man was quite possibly a saint.

Inside the relative sanctuary of my office, I paced more than I accomplished anything. Cassidy Whalen and her high-and-mighty attitude. Cassidy Whalen and her insinuations that she deserved the position more than I just because she's been here longer. Cassidy Whalen and her smart-ass mouth and frigid disposition. Cassidy fucking Whalen!

I needed a plan. Some way to bring her down once and for all.

Maybe if I turned on the old Matthews charm, it would make the ice queen melt. Maybe bringing her to her knees meant literally getting her down on her knees. Sure, I could do that. She'd be unable to resist me. She'd fall all over herself to get into my bed, and I'd fuck her so senseless she wouldn't be able to think clearly by the time I was done. Thus, mistakes would be made, and I'd be there to swoop in and snatch her coveted title right out of her teeny, tiny hands.

One problem: I hated her. How was I going to stick my dick inside someone I despised? Besides, doing something like that went against my own rule of no hanky-panky in the workplace. But wooing those damn panties off her frigid ass was probably the best shot I had at sweeping her off her feet and then under the rug. Nothing else had worked up until now, and winning the Striker partnership would mean I could finally settle down in one place. I could do it for the greater good.

It wasn't like Cassidy was ugly. As much as I hated to admit it, she wasn't half bad to look at. I mean, she had a few things working for her. Like the legs of a runner and an ass any man would give his left nut to see bouncing up and down on his lap. There might have been more to her physically, but she kept it hidden with the whole librarian thing she had going on. The tailor-made suits, brown Wayfarer glasses, and rusty-colored hair, which she kept in a bun at the nape of her neck, were typical of someone who wanted to downplay her looks. I couldn't decide if that was her true intention, if she really was that reserved, or if she secretly knew how many men had sexy-librarian fantasies swimming around in their heads and she was trying to use it to take over the world.

A sexy librarian with a soft New England accent and those damn peep-toe pumps. Okay, so maybe she was hot.

But that accent could be annoying when she put some snark behind it, which she did more often than not when speaking to me. And those peep-toes grated on my last nerve when she gave them an incessant tap each time I stole the spotlight away from her.

It wasn't until I pictured those spiky heels that I noticed I'd been clenching my teeth as well as my fists. I could just see the smug look on her face when she presented Wade with a contract signed by Denver Rockford. The woman would make my life a living hell as my boss, and I simply couldn't let that happen. In fact, I'd stoop to an all-time low to ensure that it didn't. My mind was made up. I was going to seduce my mortal enemy.

"You're going down, Whalen."

Cassidy

Ally was hot on my heels the second I stomped into my office, catching the door I attempted to slam shut and closing it softly behind herself instead. Even when I didn't have the presence of mind to keep my cool, she did. My assistant had become an expert at detecting my moods, though it wouldn't take the dynamic duo of Holmes and Watson to solve the mystery today. It was always the same after I'd been anywhere within the vicinity of Shaw Matthews. I did my best not to let it show, since I had a reputation to uphold, but it took a lot of work. And grinding of teeth. I'd even bitten into my tongue a time or two.

I growled in frustration, feeling the familiar Irish temper surge through my veins to warm my skin. No doubt, my face was red. "That arrogant—"

"—son of a bitch," Ally finished, which, I admit, coaxed another growl from me. I didn't know if I was irked more by her insubordination or by my predictability. "You hate him. . . . He's just so . . . *Arrrgh!*"

Arrrgh? Am I a pirate now?

I spun around to face her, the messenger bag on my shoulder continuing with the momentum and nearly taking me with it. "No one likes a smart-ass, Coop."

My assistant's name was Ally Cooper, to be exact. Even though the surname hadn't been her parents', they'd been Alice Cooper roadies and fanatics, and thought giving the name to their daughter, legally, would be an appropriate homage. Ally suspected that her mother had been more than just a groupie—something her mother had never confirmed or denied. I was with Ally. She had the Father of Shock Rock's lean physique and raven hair, and she was even rocking the nose, though Ally wore it better. If his tour dates matched up with the timing of her birth, no way would it have been a coincidence.

Ally exaggerated a pout. "Sorry."

I didn't think she was sincere. Mostly because I knew she wasn't. Like I said, she was insubordinate. I'd fire her if she weren't so good at keeping up with me. Apparently, there was something in the water. That or everyone was in on some scheme to drive me bat-shit crazy. Including Wade Price. Naturally, it made me growly.

At twenty-eight, I was the youngest woman to make a name for myself in the business, but Shaw was a minor league big shot who had only joined the U.S. office less than a year before. And already he was a contender for partnership. Talk about it being a man's world. His wealth and unconscionable flirting had gotten him far. So had all the influential people he had in his pocket, the name-dropper. It was his charisma that romanced his clients, though. I hated to admit it, but he was a mastermind, a real smooth talker who made big promises and always delivered. Even if he had to take the money out of his own pocket to do it. Cheater, cheater, pumpkin eater.

"Can you believe I have to share a car with him?"

"Seriously? They expect two people to ride in the back of a limousine? What were they thinking?" She wasn't even trying to cover her sarcasm. No Christmas bonus for her.

"Exactly my point. I really don't think the both of us can fit in there, what with his big, stupid, egotistical head and all." I sounded more like a child throwing a tantrum than a grown woman with a client list talented enough to form their own major league *every sports* team. Thank God no one else could hear me. Especially Shaw.

"Just ignore him." As if that were even a possibility.

Shaw Matthews was one of *those* people. That person others naturally gravitated toward in order to bask in his presence and maybe siphon off even the tiniest bit of his energy. You'd think he was the sun or something. And because the universe had some sort of vendetta against me, he just had to be good-looking on top of all that: six foot two with the body of a cover model, a strong jawline set with confidence, and eyes so blue, so hypnotic, you dared not gaze directly into them. And that bedhead of October brown hair always made him look like he'd just stolen a minute or two in the supply closet with a random woman. If the rumors around the office were true, he probably had. Money, looks, savoir faire; he had it all. And now he wanted my job, too.

"Ignoring Shaw Matthews is a little easier said than done." I went to my desk and grabbed my purse from the bottom drawer, stuffing it into my bag. "He and I have a meeting scheduled with Denver Rockford tomorrow afternoon, so I'll have to endure the suffering. I know you've already been putting that talented little search engine of yours to work to find out any and everything you can about him." I stopped short. "Oh, yeah. That's how you manage to keep your job." Ally was the best of the best, my most accomplished protégée. Okay, so she was my only protégée.

"What?"

I shook my head to get back on track. "Nothing."

A knock sounded on my door, and I sighed in frustration. I just wanted this day to be over with already. But when the door opened without invitation and my boss walked in like he owned the place—in fact, he did—I put on my best smile.

"I know you're probably ready to leave, but I'd like a moment of your time," he said.

"Of course, Wade," I answered, nodding to Ally to excuse herself, which she did on cue. "Have a seat."

He waved my offer off. "It's not really necessary." His hands slipped into his pockets, and he rocked back on his heels as if trying to come up with his next words. "Cassidy, it's no secret that you've always been my favorite, preferential treatment be damned."

It was true, though he'd never handed me anything I hadn't earned.

"Just as it's no secret that Shaw was Monty's," he continued. "What no one else knows is that Monty had been grooming Matthews to take his place when he retired."

Oh. That was certainly news to me. It suddenly felt like the world had tilted on its axis, forcing me to inconspicuously grab the corner of my desk to balance myself. Talk about a punch to the gut.

"In fact, Monty had been ready to name him partner, until I convinced him otherwise."

"What do you mean, sir?" I was surprised that the tremble I felt in my bones hadn't made its way into my voice.

"Monty and I founded Striker together, and I insisted that we make the decision jointly. I wanted you, and he wanted Matthews.

We were at an impasse. We also knew we only had one shot at getting Rockford. Normally we wouldn't pit agent against agent, but we realized that by doing so, we'd broaden our chances from one shot to two. So, together, we came up with the idea of the competition.

"The way I saw it, at least then you'd have a chance at the partnership. Every single staff member knows you deserve it. Monty knows as well, so don't be upset with him, kiddo. But," he said with a finger in the air. "I want you to make sure you win."

"That's not going to be a problem, sir," I assured him, though I was confused as to why he needed assurance after all the major deals I'd secured for SSE.

Wade nodded and eased his hand back into his pocket. "It's not that I don't have faith in you, Whalen. It's quite the opposite, in fact. I know what you're capable of, so I've put my best against Monty's best. And I don't think I need to tell you that I hate to lose."

"No, sir, you do not."

"Good. That's why I'm going to stress this." He leveled a look at me that commanded attention. "Bring home that win. By *any* means necessary. Do you understand?"

I nodded, but that didn't seem to be good enough for my boss.

"Say it."

"I will bring home the win by any means necessary."

"*Any* means," he reiterated.

I wasn't dim. He meant even if I had to fight dirty.

Setting a determined chin, I nodded again. "Failure is never an option for me, sir."

He smiled, the tension in his frame easing. "I'm glad we had this talk, but I wouldn't want anyone else to know about it."

"Understood."

"Now get out of here, kid. I want you well rested for your meeting tomorrow." His wink was conspiratorial, every bit as inappropriate as if it had been flirtatious, but I didn't take offense.

Wade exited then, leaving the door open for me to follow, which I did after gathering my things again. Ally was still at her desk, and I felt bad about keeping her later than usual, but I knew she'd never go home before I did. Maybe she was a little sassy-mouth, but no other assistant could fill her shoes.

"Is everything okay?" she asked.

"Perfect." Even if she didn't believe me, she'd never press. "Email me everything you've got on Rockford, and I'll go over it during the car ride tomorrow afternoon. Maybe if I look busy, Matthews won't try to talk to me."

Ally snorted. Actually snorted. "Who are you kidding, Cass? The second the news broke that the marriage between Denver and his agent was on shaky ground, you knew everything there was to know about him. And you'll be poring over every single detail of it tonight, probably not getting a wink of sleep." She knew me well. "You work too hard."

"There's no such thing. Da and Ma worked their fingers to the bone to give me this opportunity. I'll not be squandering it."

The picture that sat on the corner of the desk caught my eye, and a familiar longing punched at my chest. My parents weren't the only ones who had been left behind. I hadn't had a lot of friends while growing up, but Casey was my absolute best. Not a day went by that I didn't think about him or wish he were there to tell me one of his lame jokes. No one understood me like he did, though I had some pretty terrific friends who came pretty close, and they were waiting for me at our spot.

"I need a drink. Have a good night, and I'll see you in the morning." With any luck, I'd survive the rest of the evening without having to look at Shaw's stupid face.

———

Lady Luck was a fickle bitch, and Irony was her sadistic sidekick.

Monkey Business was a neighborhood pub that had an old-world Irish feel, with the traditional emerald-green and gold trim, dark wood everything, and a menu that boasted a selection of ale even the most snooty of beer snobs could appreciate. It could've been on any street corner, but as it happened, it was halfway between the place where I made a living and the place where I laid my head at night. And it was more like a second home to me than my own apartment. Which was exactly the reason it irked me when I cracked the door only to hear *his* voice. Of all the taverns, pubs, and bars in San Diego, Shaw Matthews had to hang out in mine. I was convinced he did it on purpose, but I refused to let him run me off. After all, I had been there first.

"Hey, Cass! The usual?" Chaz, my bartender friend, asked as I made my way through the happy hour crowd to get to our table. A nod was all the answer he needed. And the follow-up eye roll when I spotted his buddy Shaw occupying the bar stool in front of him reaffirmed the fact that I still didn't approve of his choice of besties, to which he only smiled and shook his head.

Chaz was a chiseled mountain of a man with a perfectly rounded bald head, soft baby blues, and a pristine smile. For someone who didn't know him, the body ink and piercings might have been intimidating, but Chaz was an all-around good guy. Like a lot of bartenders, he had a worldly sort of wisdom about him, so I couldn't quite figure out why he kept the company of someone as superficial as Shaw. I could only assume that Shaw had said something similar yet different about me, because every now and then Chaz liked to remind me that he was Switzerland in this war that wasn't really a war.

On the far side of the room and near the left corner of the bar was a table of rich, dark wood with a glossy top. Four unmatched chairs sat in an arch so that none of their backs were to the crowd but, instead, each seat had a perfect view of the entire room. My friends and I liked to people-watch. We also liked to keep an eye on anyone who might be eavesdropping on our own conversations. The proximity to Chaz and the bar was another perk. At the beginning of his shift, our bartender friend always did us a solid by placing the Reserved sign on the table in the alcove to ensure that we would never have to kick anyone out of it. Well, Demi would probably be the one doing the physical work.

Demi Renée was as sweet as sweet could be, as long as she called you friend. Not that she was a royal bitch to strangers, but if someone rubbed her the wrong way, they'd soon wish they hadn't. Demi led self-defense classes for women, and she could take on just about any man who dared challenge her. You wouldn't know it by looking at her, though. She was a tall, leggy broad with platinum-blond hair that was cut short and spiked on top, Barbie's perfect figure, and lashes you'd swear were fake, but weren't. And she wasn't afraid to get her hands dirty. Unlike her best friend and ex–college roommate, Sasha.

Sasha Hale was spoiled rotten, a real girly girl. She had a heart of gold and would give strangers the shirt off her back, which of course meant she was left with far more heartache than any one person should have to endure. She was Demi's exact opposite, so they balanced each other. Not that Sasha was ugly, by any means. Her mixed ethnicity gave her all the best traits from her mother and her father. She was short and curvy, with a tiny waist framed by a bodacious chest and a voluptuous ass. Her caramel-colored skin was softer than any I'd ever felt. It was unnatural, but she swore she didn't have any sort of special skin-care regiment. I was convinced she was lying and had told her she would burn in hell for doing so. Her figure and angelic skin weren't the only parts of my friend I coveted. She also had these round doe eyes the color of dark honey, with thick lashes and perfectly arched eyebrows, and the natural pink tint on her lips was sickening. I hated her. No, I didn't. I loved her. Okay, so I loved to hate her.

Pushing through the last of the crowd, I finally plopped down into my chair. The ice-cold tall draft Chaz had poured and slid to the corner of the bar was just out of reach, so I waved my hand for whoever was closest to pass it over.

"Uh-uh! Girl, who do you think you are? Coming in here all late and then waving for somebody to do your bidding. They might call you the ice queen where you just came from, but you are not royalty here. You better get off your ass and fetch it yourself."

That would be Quinn, my nearest and dearest, though I couldn't feel the love at the moment. So I did the only thing I could do: I pouted.

Quinn's skin looked porcelain in contrast to his jet hair. He was well kempt, perfectly groomed, and dressed to impress no matter what the occasion. With his toned physique, he could've been a professional model for any twentysomething boutique, but he was just our Quinn. Though he had no problem calling us out when we weren't at our best. "Stop that. You do not look attractive," he said, grabbing my beer and sliding it over to me. The pout worked every time. "You need it for this toast, anyway."

I sighed, more mentally exhausted than physically. I was also breaking in a new pair of heels, so there was that. "What are we toasting?"

He sat tall and straight in his chair, with a smile so bright it could've been seen from Mars. Sasha and Demi were exhibiting the same smile and looked like they were about to burst into a cheerleading routine, complete with pom-poms and herkie jumps.

"Look what Daddy bought me!" He held his wrist out, and I

was nearly blinded by the bling that adorned it. A Breitling Bentley watch in yellow gold, leather, and—if I had to guess—fifteen or so carats of diamonds. It had to have cost a fortune.

Clearly he expected me to be every bit as excited as he was. And I was. Mostly. Sasha and Demi leaned back and out of his eyesight and started throwing out hand gestures that I was sure were meant to get me to not say what I really thought, because that was how we played the whole "Daddy" situation. Quinn could become quite defensive otherwise, and that was never a pretty thing.

Daddy was Quinn's sugar daddy. Quinn's gay-yet-not-out-of-the-closet sugar daddy. We were Quinn's best friends, and even we didn't know what the man's real name was. All we knew was that Daddy was an account holder at the bank where Quinn worked. A married account holder with lots and lots of money and influence who didn't believe it was in his best interest to let his wife, his constituents, or the general public become aware of his sexual preference. I thought it was stupid. Especially considering the leaps and bounds the world had been making in that regard. But it was his life, and Quinn accepted the hidden role he played in it. I loved my best friend, I really did, but I was quite sure the posh lifestyle Daddy was providing helped in keeping Quinn's mouth shut about their secret affair.

"What did you have to do for that, and did he at least let you wear kneepads?" I asked, deciding to keep it light and maybe even a little funny.

"Oh, hush. Jealous," he said, waving me off. I wasn't so sure it was a wave-off as much as an attempt to blind someone with the reflection of the lights off the diamonds.

Demi rolled her eyes. "You're going to get robbed the second you walk out of here if you keep flashing that thing around."

"Damn, Q," Chaz said from the bar. "You might want to get your bodyguard to walk you home. Huh, Demi?"

Demi giggled, the flirt. The chemistry between those two was off-the-charts hot, but Chaz had never made a move on her. The chemistry between me and Chaz's bestie, on the other hand . . . left a lot to be desired.

"Very nice," Shaw said, getting up to examine the piece for himself. He probably thought it was fake, that no one in our circle could afford such a thing. A circle in which he was forcibly included, which put quite the strain on the elasticity of the band that held it together.

Sasha elbowed me and cut a sharp glance toward my still frosty glass. I hadn't realized I'd been white-knuckling it. Not only that, but I'd also been biting the inside of my cheek. A barely perceptible chuckle from Shaw let me know he'd noticed. Damn it! I didn't want him to know how much he got to me. Though that ship had sailed the day we'd met, I was sure.

"Still slumming it, Matthews? All your posh friends have plans for the night?" I never could figure out why someone like Shaw Matthews, a.k.a. Richie Rich, chose to hang out in a pub rather than a La Petite Frou-Frou something or another.

"You really think you have me pegged, don't you?" When I smirked up at him, he shook his head and turned to slither back under the rock from which he'd come. Okay, so the rock was a bar stool.

Fighting to maintain what little bit of composure I had left, I decided I really needed that drink. So I lifted the glass to my lips and completely forgot I was a lady in a public place. It never failed; when that first taste of hops hit my tongue, I closed my eyes and was instantly transported back to the only hole-in-the-wall tavern in Stonington, Maine. My da and his crew would always stop by for a few nice cold ones after a long fishing trip to exchange their sea legs for a pair of drunken ones, which really wasn't much of a transformation. When he wasn't looking, I'd sneak a sip or two, mostly because I wanted to emulate everything that was my da.

I hadn't realized I'd chugged the entire glass until I opened my eyes and found my friends gaping at me. "What?"

"Jeez, Cass. Would you like a trough next time?" Sasha looked around, clearly embarrassed. Thankfully, Shaw was nowhere to be found.

"I swear to God, if you burp, I'm going to reach across this table and smack you." Quinn wouldn't really hit me, but I also wouldn't be that rude, and he knew it.

Demi beamed with pride and offered me a high five, which I accepted with a playful wink. I was a lady most of the time, but every now and then, it felt good to live wild and free. If Casey were there, he'd insist on it.

"Where did the superjerk go?" I asked, hoping he hadn't seen me.

Sasha gave me the look. That one people give the runner-up to some grand prize. "I take it the announcement was made today?"

Quinn threw his hands into the air. "I knew it. He got the partnership, didn't he? They didn't even give you a chance, the chauvinistic bastards."

"What? No!" My friends could be a little dramatic at times. I still didn't understand how they could possibly underestimate me so much. "We have to compete for it. Whoever gets Denver to sign will also get the partnership." I reached across the table and grabbed Demi's bottle of beer for a quick swig

"Well, that should be easy," she said.

I started to laugh, but then I saw that her brows were lifted like she expected me to understand words that hadn't and didn't need to be said out loud. She was serious about whatever point she was trying to make, but I obviously wasn't on the same page. Having all gone to college together, Demi, Sasha, and Quinn had been friends for far longer than I'd been in the picture. They could practically read one another's minds, and did a lot of the time. I was nearly there, but not quite. Whole conversations sometimes took place around me that left me oblivious, and this was shaping up to be one of those times.

I sat her beer bottle down. "What are you talking about?"

Sasha sighed. "Seduce him, dummy."

"What? I am not going to seduce the most sought after player in the National Football League. Not that it could be done even if I tried." Even if I wanted to sink so low, the man could, and did, have any woman he wanted.

Sasha merely pointed at my roommate. "Gaydar says?"

Quinn made a buzzer sound. "Not gay, but I'd sure like to try to change his mind about that."

"See? Not gay means it can be done, if done right. Totally seductable."

Demi snorted. "I don't think 'seductable' is a word."

"I said it, therefore it is." Sasha crossed her arms with a pretentious yet playful set of her chin.

Quinn was still in plotting mode; otherwise, he would've been all over her spoiled behavior. "You know, she could always skip the jock and go straight for the ball cutter. That way, if neither one of them lands the tight end—"

"Quarterback," Demi corrected.

"Hold on. Ball cutter?" Things were getting out of hand.

Sasha patted my arm. "Wait a minute, honey. The grown-ups are talking."

"Right. Quarterback. Whatever. They're all tight ends as far as I'm concerned. But like I was saying, *rudeness* . . . If neither of them lands the pigskin lover, she'll still have his balls in her purse."

I was being ignored. I didn't like being ignored. "Whose balls? What are you talking about?"

"Oh, yeah. Good idea! Why didn't we think of that before?" Sasha sat back, pleased with the result.

Demi followed suit. "*Brilliant* idea! Two birds. One stone."

Sasha nodded in agreement. "Yeah, she definitely needs to get laid."

"Of course it's brilliant. Hello? Queen of the balls, here." Quinn preened, proud of himself.

"Can I be part of this conversation, please? What just happened?"

Demi reached for her beer. "We just solved your problem."

I snatched the bottle away before it made it to her lips. "You did? Care to let me in on the secret?" It was still cold, so I decided on another sip for myself.

"Oh, sure thing. You're going to seduce Shaw."

I choked on the gulp I'd just taken, my eyes watering and the liquid going down what I was sure was the passageway to my lungs rather than to my stomach. Sasha started pounding on my back—as if that was going to help—while Demi lunged for the bottle, because clearly that was the culprit of my near-death experience.

Though I was still coughing incessantly, I couldn't let them go one more second thinking that was even a remote possibility. "Oh, no, I'm not!"

Sasha huffed. "Why not? He's good-looking."

Quinn guffawed as if insulted by her statement. I was glad some-one was on my side until he clarified himself with words: "Honey, that man is a piece of scrumptious wrapped up in good gawd!"

Demi laughed. "Right? So freakin' beautiful."

"And he knows it," I reminded them. "Besides, they say the Antichrist will be beautiful, too." Demi started to object but I cut her off before she could get a word out. "And I'm not going to screw Denver, either. I'm talented enough to get the partnership without having to stoop so low, but thank you for having so much faith in me."

I was disappointed in my friends. They knew I wasn't made up of the stuff that would allow me to do something like that. Maybe it was all in jest, but after the "by *any* means necessary" talk with Wade only minutes before, I wasn't feeling all that confident in my own words. I needed some distance. Picking up my bag, I stood up and made my way toward the door without saying goodbye.

My friends and I would meet in the same bar, at the same table, tomorrow. They knew it. I knew it. And Shaw Matthews would most likely be there, too. As if he could read my thoughts, he turned to look at me, the intensity in his gaze catching me off guard and nearly causing me to plow into a table full of frat brothers. I recovered well enough, but I could still feel him staring at me all the way to the door, the scorching heat of it dissipating only after I'd put brick and mortar between us. I was sure he wore a cocky grin at my expense, but I wouldn't lose any sleep over it. If all went well at the meeting with Denver, I'd wipe it off his face tomorrow.

CHAPTER 2
Cassidy

I threw my messenger bag over my shoulder and left the office, hoping to beat Shaw to the limousine so I could get situated before he got there. After all, being first had its advantages, the best of which was knowing it would piss him off.

I was sorely disappointed when I stepped out onto the sidewalk in front of Striker's big glass doors. The limousine was there, all right, but the impeccably dressed man with it wasn't the driver.

Shaw stood before the open door, basking in his small victory. "After you." He gestured toward the car with a gallant smile.

My feet felt heavy as they carried me forward, but I went anyway, though I didn't take him up on his offer. "You can stop with the whole chivalry routine, Matthews. I'm not one of your dumb bimbos who get all swoony just because you use good manners. *And* I'm not particularly keen on the thought of you ogling my ass, so manners aside, you can get in first."

The fake smile disappeared, as did Shaw when he climbed into the limousine. I slid in after him, situating myself as far away as I could get, which wasn't any farther than the bench behind the driver on the opposite side. Shaw huffed when I left the door for him to close, which might have pleased the little devil on my shoulder. He shut it harder than necessary, then tapped on the dividing window, signaling the chauffeur that we were ready to go.

When we finally pulled away from the curb, I decided to stick with my original plan of busying myself with my work in hopes of creating as little opportunity to interact with Shaw as I could. Plus, some last-minute brushing up on my Denver Rockford facts probably wouldn't hurt my cause. But wouldn't you just know it? Shaw wasn't the "suffer in silence" type.

"So, I was thinking about the reasoning behind Wade sending both of us to meet with Rockford at the same time instead of individually."

Shaw Matthews had had a thought. This could be comical. "Is that right? And what did your simple mind come up with?" I asked as I pulled my laptop out of my messenger bag.

"Simple." Shaw chuckled in that smart-ass sort of way. "You're so funny. Seriously, I think he wants us to double-team the guy. You know, to make sure he signs with SSE."

With the correct password entered, I was up and running and pulling up my next heavyweight client's folder. "Wade is aware that I work alone. And everyone in the universe knows you're a selfish prick, so I doubt very much he intended for us to work together. Teamwork does not a superstar athlete land."

"Oh, yeah? Well then, why do you think he sent us both?" As he relaxed into the plush leather, his body language reminded me of an informal visit with a friend rather than a competitive debate between two rivals.

Friends, we were not. And he was wrong.

"The answer is as obvious as the shit on the tip of your nose, Matthews. We've been playing this 'whose dick is bigger than whose' game for quite a while now. Today, we're going to find out."

Shaw feigned offense, and not well. "Well, I've never . . ."

"That's not what I heard," I said with an artificial smile.

"Ha ha! You know, if I wanted to play dirty, I could take you to HR for sexual harassment. You'd be fired, and that partnership would be mine for the taking."

"Ha!" My guffaw was loud enough to startle him. "You actually said that with a straight face. Like you wouldn't be joining me in the unemployment line. Just how many women in the office *have* you slept with?"

His bottom lip curled outward. "Aww, you're jealous."

"You disgust me."

"Yet you want to see my cock."

"I do not want to see your cock!"

"Come on. Just admit you're a little bit curious to know if all the rumors are true, and I'll show you."

I narrowed my eyes at him. "You're bluffing."

Shaw tilted his head with a quirk of his brow, as if to say, "Am I?" and that was when things started to go south really quickly. Or, rather, his hands went south.

I could feel his eyes on me even as mine stayed glued to the massive hands that were easing down the abdomen of his slumping body to slowly work his belt. Nimble fingers popped the leather loose of the buckle, and then an effortless tug did the same for the button of his pants, but I would never forget the amplified sound of the zipper as it lowered. With the separation of each metal tooth, my heart rate jumped another ten points higher.

Though every instinct screamed at me to turn away, to do anything other than let him continue, my brain simply wasn't getting with the program. This was wrong on so many levels; yet putting a stop to it wasn't going to happen. Shaw expected me to cry uncle, but I wanted him to keep going. He was right. I was curious, and I simply had to see what was going to happen next. Maybe my brain had taken a temporary leave of absence.

Shaw's brain, however, was present and fully functioning. There were no hiccups in his movements, no stifled sounds of protest, no indication at all that he wasn't in complete control of the situation. To him, this was no big deal. When his hand disappeared beneath the black cotton underwear and then reappeared, full of thick flesh, I swallowed the hard lump that had formed in the back of my throat. And then the stroking began. His long fingers delicately fondled the protrusion that had erected from his pants, an act I found particularly distracting, to make matters worse.

"Oh my God!" Those words finally breaking free felt like the top being blown off a pressure cooker; eventually, they had to find the way out.

"What's the matter? Never seen one before? Or do you have a little thing called penis envy going on, as I've suspected all along?" Shaw was obviously feeling particularly victorious that he'd been able to make me blush. And that would never do. It was just a penis, for Christ's sake.

It might have been a second later, or maybe an hour, but Shaw finally broke the awkward standoff with a reminder of the challenge I, myself, had issued. "You wanted to see whose cock was bigger than whose. Here's mine. Let's see yours."

My reservations were forgotten at the sound of the proverbial gauntlet hitting the floor. I snapped my head toward his, prepared to go the distance. "Are you seriously challenging me?"

He was. It was a contest I had no chance of winning. But I'd be damned if I'd ever back down from any he presented. Shaw knew that as well. What I found amusing was that he clearly thought I was a threat or he wouldn't have felt the need to take the small victory to make himself feel better. Well, we'd see about that.

With a smirk on his face and a wicked glint in his eye, he shrugged. "If you're scared, say you're scared."

I straightened up, put my laptop away, and secured the messenger bag under the seat, and then I pushed back my shoulders and set my chin in determination. "You don't claw your way up the ladder to get to where I am in this male-dominated industry by being scared." The material of my skirt slid up my thighs with finesse. "You might know something about that if you'd actually had to work a hard day in your life instead of having everything handed to you."

I was sure he thought I was bluffing. No way was the "ice queen" going to show all her goodies to the likes of him. Yes, I knew what the gossip brigade called me around the office, and I was fairly certain I knew its source. Shaw Matthews was about to find out just how steamy I could make things.

The lift of my skirt revealed the tops of my silky black thigh-highs, and he swallowed hard. The amateur hadn't been prepared for the possibility that I'd actually call his bluff, and it showed all over his face. His jaw dropped, his eyes widened, and his hand froze on his cock. And he couldn't look away.

"What's the matter, Matthews? Worried you're going to lose?" I asked with an air of smugness to match his.

"I swear to God, Whalen, if you're hiding a dick under that skirt . . ." His thought was cut short when I lifted my ass and revealed a dainty black thong to match my stockings.

"If I were a cross-dresser, I'm pretty sure these panties wouldn't be able to hide it." My fingers ghosted over the soft material between my legs.

Shaw cleared his throat and collected himself, still unwilling to back down. "That doesn't prove anything other than the fact that my dick really *is* bigger than yours."

True. "Oh, but mine's so much prettier."

"That remains to be seen, now, doesn't it?" He wasn't going to back down, either. "Show me."

I didn't hesitate. Shaw had upped the stakes in our competition, and I had no intention of letting him win. Showing the goods wasn't something I was ashamed to do. It was just flesh, nothing he'd never seen before. Not mine, of course, but still. Besides, I really was finding our little standoff to be quite erotic—of *that* I *was* ashamed. I'd deal with the consequences later.

Slipping two fingers beneath the fabric at the inside of my thigh, I slowly pulled back my panties. My eyes were trained on Shaw's face. His were trained on my semi-naked crotch. When his tongue flicked out to lick his lips, I knew I had him right where I wanted.

"And it tastes as delicious as it looks," I said, hoping to seduce him to his knees. The fingers of my other hand slipped between the folds and then pulled back the skin at the apex of my pussy, giving him a fantastic look at the hidden treasure that resided there. "Here's mine," I said, rubbing my fingertip over my clit. "Like I said, not as big, but a whole hell of a lot prettier."

I heard the words coming out of my mouth, but it was like I was having an out-of-body experience and wasn't in control of them. Any of them. Not even when I said, "Suck my dick, Matthews."

Shaw didn't seem surprised in the least. In fact, he nodded toward his lap and his insanely engorged cock. "Ladies first. Unless you don't know *how* to . . ."

It was another challenge. Challenges and I did not make a good combination. I was obsessed with rising above and winning any that were laid at my feet. It was a serious problem, and an unhealthy side effect was that I forgot who I was in the process.

I laughed. "Oh, baby, I'd have you whimpering like a scared little boy."

"I seriously doubt that."

My frown turned into a scowl. "Do you always have to be so

stubborn?" I asked even as I knelt to the floor. "I'm just going to make you look stupid again."

"How about if you shut up and put your money where your mouth is?"

I sighed. "Have it your way. I do enjoy the look of defeat on your smug face."

I crawled across the small space between us until I was between his legs, and Shaw jumped when I yanked his cock out of his hand.

"You're a real bitch, do you know that?"

"We'll see who's the bitch." I wrapped my tongue around the head of his cock before engulfing it with my hot, wet mouth. He smelled good, freshly showered with a manly fragrance, and his soft skin was stretched smooth over the rigid muscle beneath. The veins in his cock were taut and pulsing with his blood. And I'd have ventured a guess that it was pumping pretty hard right about then.

Shaw sucked in a breath through his teeth as his head fell back, and I couldn't help but notice the way his fists clenched on the seat at his sides with each bit of suction I applied on the upstroke of my mouth. Needless to say, I felt quite vindicated. He could've just sat back and enjoyed what was probably the best blow job of his life, but that wasn't good enough for Shaw Matthews. Nope. Apparently, he wanted to enjoy the show, because he somehow managed to lift his head so he could watch.

"Jesus . . . I like your mouth so much better with my dick stuck in it."

I let my teeth scrape along his flesh in retaliation for the comment, but he groaned in pleasure instead of pain. The guttural sound went straight to my naughty parts, and I could feel the wetness against my thighs, which really kind of pissed me off. I didn't want to be attracted to the man I openly loathed, but my body apparently had a mind of its own.

"Take your skirt off, but leave the shoes on." Shaw pulled the pins out of my hair and let it tumble free of its confines.

"Fuck you," I said when I released his dick from my mouth, all while unzipping my skirt and letting it slide down my thighs. *Dammit, since when did I like him telling me what to do?*

"If you're lucky, I just might let you." He smirked while shoving his pants down his legs as well. "Come here and finish sucking me off." He grabbed me by the back of the head and forced it toward his lap. I went willingly, giving him the death glare all the way, but I wanted it every bit as much as he did.

"Mmm . . . You like to suck cock, don't you? And all this time I thought you were either a virgin or a lesbian," he said, fisting my hair as I bobbed up and down in his lap. "Turns out, you're a bad little girl who likes to suck cock in the back of a limousine."

I hummed in answer. He'd found my weakness: I loved the dirty talk. All that prim and proper I had to live through all day, every day, had no place whatsoever in my sex life. I liked it rough. I liked it hard. And I liked it dirty. And even though I hated the man I was blowing, I loved his thick cock in my mouth.

"You know what bad little girls get, don't you?" Shaw gripped the hair on the back of my head to hold me in place and leaned forward. "They get spanked." His hand sliced through the air and landed hard on the cheek of my ass.

I moaned at the contact, and he pulled my head up and pushed it back down again. I grabbed his legs, giving him complete control—something I'd never do in any other setting—and he moved me as fast and as deep as he liked.

"God, yes . . . Suck my cock." He moaned and then spanked me again and again, because each time he did, I took him a little bit deeper. He was aggressive with his actions, but I was just as aggressive with my nails digging into his calf muscles and the death grip my mouth had on his dick.

The wet suction sounds and moans of pleasure from both of us were testament to how greedy we'd both suddenly become for each other. Finally, we were working together toward a common goal. The underlying competition was still there—we were both trying to make the other submit faster—but the journey was being taken together, each reaping the reward.

When I grabbed his hips and buried my head in his lap, taking in as much of him as I possibly could, he stilled. His jaw went slack and he breathed through his mouth, watching me work him. I could feel him all the way at the back of my throat and even a little bit farther. I stopped to look up at him, smirking around the cock lodged between my lips. And then I swallowed, the back of my throat giving the head a tight squeeze.

Shaw whimpered at the sensation, and I winked. Like a scared little boy. To my credit, I'd earned the right to gloat.

Shaw's ego must have been bruised, because he growled, "Fuck that" and pushed me back so that I was forced to release his dick.

I fell back onto the floor of the limousine, a triumphant giggle bubbling up and into the air. "Oh my God! The look on your face was priceless." I laughed hard. "I tried to warn you, but you were the one who chose not to take me seriously."

"If I were you, I wouldn't laugh, Whalen." Shaw loosened his tie and positioned himself on the floor at my raised knees. With a swift, hard yank, my panties were ripped from my body. "My turn." He smirked down at me and then grabbed both of my knees, spreading them before lifting the lower half of my body to hook my legs over his shoulders.

Holding on to my thighs, he quickly buried his face in my

center, licking and sucking at my pussy like a fat man lapping the remnants of grease from his fingers after gobbling down a bucket of fried chicken.

I gasped, caught off guard. "Oh . . . God!"

Shaw lifted his head to look down at me, a smirk crossing his face after he licked his lips languidly. "Mmm, you were right. It does taste as delicious as it looks."

He buried his face again, his tongue sweeping maddeningly fast over every inch of my drenched flesh. Words that not even I could've deciphered spilled from my lips, joining the wet sounds of Shaw's greedy mouth devouring me. The feelings he evoked in the pit of my stomach were unmatched by anything I'd ever felt before. My heart leapt from my chest, as if taking the plunge from the climax of a roller coaster. He grunted, he growled, he fed from me. It was the single sexiest thing I'd ever seen, felt, or heard.

And I hated him even more for it.

I bucked my hips toward Shaw's mouth, but he wanted to torture me for making him whimper. So he lifted his face, allowing his lips to barely ghost over my center, hovering and refusing what I wanted most.

"I don't believe I hear you laughing now, Miss Whalen. The landing strip is a nice touch, by the way. I pegged you for full-on bush." His warm breath cast a wave of heated sensation over my pleasure spot. "I could make you come, you know. But what would be in it for me?"

My chest rose and fell frantically as I searched my thoughts to find a desirable solution. Desperation to have my release threw my normally analytical side out of balance, and the need to satiate my primal urges took control. It was blatant mutiny, but I didn't care. I wanted him.

"Fuck me," I whispered.

"I'm sorry, what?" Shaw was an asshole to the most extreme degree. Either that, or he was an idiot.

"I want you to *fuck* me," I said, as if I were talking to someone who didn't understand the English language. You know, just in case the idiot part was the true story. "Stick your dick inside my pussy and fuck the shit out of me. Or can't you handle that? Surely all those rumors the girls at the office spread about you hold at least a fraction of truth."

Shaw released my legs and hovered over my body until we were face-to-face. His cock slid against my wetness, doing unspeakable things to my self-control.

"If we do this . . ." he started, but he had to stop when I lifted my hips to gain more friction. "If we do this, we do not speak a word about it to anyone else. I know it will be hard for you not to brag about it, but I don't want everyone to know I've had my dick inside the biggest bitch in the office."

"You are so full of yourself."

He bit down on his bottom lip, a cocky grin managing to peek through nevertheless. And then he undulated over me. "Wouldn't you like to be full of me?"

God, yes.

I rolled my eyes even though I was already locking my legs around his hips, but I wouldn't acknowledge his last question. The first statement was easy enough, though. "Believe me, the feeling is quite mutual. And I trust that, even though you're a whoremonger, your self-adoration means you've made sure you're not carrying any diseases?" *We must be very clear on that, mustn't we?*

"I'm clean. What about you? Are you on birth control?" he asked as he rolled his hips again.

Much more of that and all coherencies would be out the door.

Who was I kidding? I'd already lost my mind, hence the whorishness. "As if I'd want to give birth to your spawn and be single-handedly responsible for bringing life to the Antichrist."

Shaw chuckled facetiously. "That's . . . that's really funny. And here I thought you didn't have a sense of humor."

"Whatever, dickhead." My fingers traveled under the collar of his shirt. "I'm on the pill, and *this* has to go."

I quickly unbuttoned the first four buttons of his shirt, revealing a magnificently sculpted pair of pecs and an abdomen you could do your laundry on. My hands swept over his heated skin, feeling the contours of muscle and smooth flesh, until I spread my fingers over his back and pulled him to me. I lifted my head and sucked on the skin at the place where his neck met his shoulder. He smelled so delicious—a mixture of soap, a light cologne, and just plain *man*.

"Trying to mark me, Whalen? I don't do hickeys," he warned before he sat up and began to work the buttons on my blouse loose. He stopped when he'd uncovered enough to divulge the secrets that lay beneath. Hooking his fingers into the cups of my bra, he pulled them down and then pushed up so that my breasts spilled from their confines.

"Fucking great tits," he murmured, and then he dipped his head and captured the peak of one breast with his mouth while his hand kneaded the other. His tongue flicked back and forth, and I arched my back and threaded my fingers through his thick hair to bring him closer still. Shaw worshipped my chest before moving to the inside of the swell of my cleavage, where he proceeded to suck. Hard.

"Cheater." My distaste for his double standard wasn't at all convincing. That might have been because I was moaning even as I pushed and pulled at his head, not really trying to make him stop. As my punishment, the suction grew stronger and stronger, until he finally let my skin go with a wet pop. And then the smug bastard sat back to admire his work.

A self-satisfied grin spread across his face. It was irritating and gorgeous at the same time. "If you're going to give a hickey, put it where it won't be seen."

"How do you know it won't be seen there?" I asked with a grin of my own.

"Are you telling me you're a slut?"

"No more than you."

Shaw quirked an eyebrow at me. "Is that so? Well, then by all means, let me give you what you really want."

He lined himself up with my entrance, his fingers working my clit while he teased my opening with the head of his dick. His lips parted as he watched with rapt fascination. In and out he pushed into me, never giving me more than the tip. "Jesus, you're fucking tight."

I couldn't resist the opening he'd handed me. "Wow, that's it? You looked so much bigger than that. I've gotta say, I'm a bit disappointed."

Shaw stopped his motions and looked up at me. He was not amused. I thought he was about to retort with a smart comment of his own, but he merely winked at me and thrust his hips forward. Hard. My back arched off the floor and I sucked in a deep breath.

"I'm sorry, what was that?" he asked with a grin.

I smacked his chest. "Christ, Matthews! A little warning would have been nice before you attempted to gut me!"

"Yeah, I am pretty ginormous, aren't I? Maybe if you'd learn to keep that fuckable little mouth of yours closed . . ."

"Shut up and fuck me." I had no problem whatsoever using

his body for my own guilty pleasure, but I could do without his arrogance.

Shaw pulled almost all the way out and then slowly pushed back in again, both of us moaning at the sensation. And then he rolled his hips into me, the expression on his face a dead giveaway to the fact that he was savoring the hot wetness that encompassed his cock. When I closed my eyes and bit down on my bottom lip, Shaw did the unthinkable. He leaned forward and captured my lips with his own, actually kissing the woman he'd considered a pariah, his enemy, a coldhearted bitch who'd just as soon spit on his grave as look his direction.

And I kissed him back. Jesus, that man had a talented mouth.

After that, things really started to heat up. So much so that I had to grab the cheeks of his ass and dig my nails into his skin to hold on when his thrusts became faster and more urgent.

I came alive beneath him, losing myself to the long, thick cock that filled me so completely. Never had I felt so hungry, so willing to be consumed by a man. And he knew, without experimentation, how to move his hips, rotating them so that he brushed against my clit with the perfect amount of pressure to drive me to the edge. But he wasn't talking, and I'd loved the filth that had come out of his mouth while I was sucking on his massive cock.

"I hate you," I mumbled between heated kisses. "You're a whoremonger, and I can't believe I let you stick your dick in me, but God, it feels so good."

"Well, if I'm a whoremonger, that makes you a whore." He groaned. "A whore with a tight pussy who likes to be fucked hard and fast."

With that, Shaw intensified his thrusts, his hips slapping against my thighs as he slammed his cock into me.

"Oh, God. Yes," I moaned. "Fuck me, Shaw. Fuck me harder."

Obviously, I liked to be talked to as roughly as I liked to be fucked, which seemed to be right up his alley. Shaw pulled at my legs, situating them so that the heels of my shoes were pressed into his shoulders. Then he grabbed my hips and gave me what I wanted.

"You like that, huh? You like being fucked by the man that you despise?"

"Yes . . . More." As if what he was doing wasn't enough, my hand traveled down my stomach until I was touching myself.

"Son of a bitch." Someone liked what they were seeing, and I wasn't above letting him see more of it. Especially when he said dirty, dirty things to me. I worked my clit with two fingertips, frantically moving them back and forth before I stopped to press down hard and then slap at it.

"That's it. Work that sweet little pussy. Do what feels good, but you're not allowed to make yourself come. Your orgasm belongs to me. Do you hear me? It's mine."

I raised my hand, showing him the slickness that glistened on my fingertips. "God, I'm so wet."

A feral growl sounded from Shaw's chest, and in a flash, he lunged forward, my legs forced to hook over his shoulders again as his hands slammed down on the floor beside my head and he lay on top of me so that he could capture my fingers with his mouth. He was so much deeper at that angle, and I wasn't the least bit uncomfortable. Not that he cared. A hard fucking was what I wanted, and a hard fucking was exactly what he gave me.

He hummed around my fingers, his tongue working to gather all the juices, the greedy bastard. Skin smacked against skin as he fucked me. I couldn't tell if he was doing what felt good to him or if he actually gave a damn about what felt good to me. Though I was pretty sure we were both on the winning team. I tried not to make his fat head even fatter by my cries of pleasure, but trying to remain silent would have been expecting way too much from myself. All of my inhibitions were orbiting somewhere completely out of reach, and I might not ever be able to wrangle them back in. At the moment, I couldn't care less.

Shaw's greed proved to be too much for him—he pulled out of me and pushed my knees up so that my hips were forced off the floor. Once again, he buried his face in my pussy, lapping up all my wetness. When he thrust his tongue inside me, I cried out, my orgasm catching me unaware. He didn't stop there. *Thank you, Jesus, for not letting him be a selfish prick.* He kept licking and sucking at my skin until he'd captured every last drop I had to give. And then my body went limp.

"Uh-uh. No fucking way," he said sternly. "We're not done yet. Sit up here and taste yourself on my cock."

There were no arguments from me. I wasn't done yet, either. I wanted it—wanted him—more than I'd ever wanted a man. Clearly, he'd fucked my brains out, because not a single thought that made sense remained.

Shaw pulled me up by my arms and shoved my head toward his groin until his cock was fully lodged in my mouth. I could feel the sting of my hair being pulled by the roots, but it only fueled my inner fire more. I took control then, greedily sucking him, tasting myself while he pushed and pulled at my head. I moaned and hummed at the offering while Shaw's head fell back and he allowed himself to take pleasure in the sin we'd both indulged in.

"Christ, you suck a mean cock, woman." But he still wasn't finished with me yet. "Get on your knees. I'm going to fuck you like you want to be fucked. Like the kinky little slut you are but pretend not to be."

I sat back and wiped the wetness from my mouth with the back of my hand. "Promises, promises," I taunted him as I scrambled to get into position, wanting what he apparently thought was a threat but was exactly what I craved.

"Lean over the seat," he ordered me, and it felt good. "This is going to be hard. This is going to be quick. And this is going to be the best fucking you've ever had in your life. Try not to get *too* attached."

He impaled me with his cock, thrusting hard and without warning. My back concaved and my head was thrown back as I cried out. It was a sweet torture that I thoroughly enjoyed, and I knew that if I kept antagonizing him, there would be so much more where that came from.

"Oh, God! You bastard!" I half-moaned, half-growled through clenched teeth.

"You love it, and you know it." Shaw pushed the side of my face into the seat and slammed into me again. "This is how women who pretend to be in control but secretly want to *be* controlled get fucked, Cassidy. From behind, pinned down so that you have no choice but to take it."

He hovered, his hot breath cascading over my ear with each sultry pant for air. His hips rolled against my backside, the muscles in his thighs flexing and relaxing with each thrust, the rest of him straining to maintain control and hold my squirming body in place.

"Is this how you like it?" His husky voice growled into my ear between punishing thrusts. "You pretend to have it all together, to not need the help of any man. You are woman, hear you roar, right? But we both know you really want to be dominated—to let go of the façade, the carefully orchestrated control—and to be fucked into submission."

Shaw bit down on my shoulder as if he were claiming me with his last word. His fingertips dug into my hip when he pushed as far into me as he could go. Given the size of his cock, that was pretty damn deep from that angle. He angled his hips, forcing gurgled moans of pleasure from me, his grunted thrusts short and quick. I retaliated by doing the only thing I could do in my position: by squeezing my walls around him in a pulsating cycle.

"Christ! Fuck! I'm going to . . ." His words were cut off by a gruff moan.

"That's right, asshole! Who's in control now?" I didn't want the control, but I wasn't going to give it up without a fight, either. "Feels good, doesn't it? You can't hold on any longer. You want to come so hard. You want to let it go. Give into it, Shaw. Come inside my pussy."

Shaw's grip tightened, and I knew he was right there. I pushed back into him, unwilling to let him stop himself from giving me what I'd worked so hard for.

"God! No, not . . . yet."

I snapped out of his grip, the residual sting and burn a promise of a bruise by morning. I spun around before Shaw could register what I was doing and took his cock into my mouth. I sucked and licked, my teeth scraping as I cupped his balls and coaxed his release from its confines.

"Swallow it! Don't you dare spit it out!" Shaw thrust forward until the head of his cock was at the back of my throat, and then growled out his release. Hot, molten liquid shot out in spurts as his body stiffened and I stroked him with my mouth and hand, taking and accepting all he had to give.

When he was done, I looked up at him with a satisfied smirk on my face and wiped the corners of my mouth. "Mmm, tasty."

A loud shrieking sound rang through my head, and I sat straight up to reach over and slap at the source of the annoyance, as had become my routine. My head was pounding. Not only that, but my vision was blurry and my thoughts wouldn't quite come together. "Confusion" wasn't even the word for it.

Where was I? I looked around, the familiar surroundings of my bedroom coming into focus. I was alone.

Something wet at the corner of my mouth got my attention, and a memory that didn't seem quite so distant made me cringe. I wiped at the wetness with an "Oh, ew, ew, ew!"

False alarm. It wasn't Shaw's death sperm. It was just drool.

"What the . . . ?" I fought to regain my bearings, and then I realized what my conscious mind was trying damn hard to suppress. "Nooooo!" I groaned to myself as I fell back down to my bed and covered my head with a pillow. "No, no, no, no, noooo!"

I'd just had a very hot, very erotic dream about my mortal enemy. And it was the best sex of my life.

Kill me now . . .

CHAPTER 3

It was six-thirty in the morning, *Gilligan's Island* was blaring from the television set in my bedroom, and my dick was aching. I had no idea why. About my achy dick, not *Gilligan's Island*. I'd fallen asleep with the TV on again, but rarely had sitcoms from the sixties caused the problem I was having down below.

I was horny and hard. So hard I thought the skin barely containing my rigidity might split to give the fucker some relief. The real issue was how the hell I could possibly still be that horny and that hard after the night I'd spent with Yvonne. Or was it Yvette? Either way, it was apparent that my cock had found her just as forgettable as my brain had her name. Not that it mattered. She had been a means to an end, though not as favorable an end as I'd hoped to find when I'd left Monkey Business in the wake of yet another round with the she-devil.

You'd think I'd be used to the assumptions Cassidy made about me. I shouldn't care. I mean I *really* shouldn't, but there was something parasitic about that woman that managed to wedge itself beneath my fingernails to get under my skin and slither its way up my arm to my brain and then to my friggin' eyeballs to make me see red. I was sure it was the same parasite that made my eye twitch every now and then when she was in the same room. So it was a puzzle that her smart mouth was all I'd thought about since my little buddy had roused me from slumber to bid me a good morning.

Ha, little buddy. I supposed my cock's personality was a lot like Gilligan's in that eager-to-please sort of way. But its size was all Skipper, just as robust and every bit as stout. Everybody knew that both of them had a thing for Ginger. So maybe the fact that Cassidy *was* a ginger had put some sort of TV Land–infused Freudian twist on my subconscious mind.

Or maybe the parasite had taken a different route this time.

With a squinted eye, I lifted the tented sheet, half-expecting to see something grotesque attempting an Alien-like escape from the head of my cock. I breathed a sigh of relief when I found nothing out of the ordinary. Well, besides the extraordinarily rigid fatty that was screaming for attention.

Fine. Skippigan would win this round. I wasn't about to risk getting coconut juice on my clean sheets, though, so I got my naked ass out of the bed to hit the shower to do his bidding. Not that I was pleased by the fact that Cassidy and her librarian glasses were calling the shots.

That wasn't the only way my mind had decided to fuck with me, it seemed. When I crossed my bedroom and opened the door to the bathroom, I was instantly struck with the memory of my first day at SSE, upon the return from my internship at the company's U.K. branch. I remembered walking through the door to the conference room with the staff meeting already in full swing before I was introduced as the newest member of the team. I'd been confident, but new adventures always played a little mischievous ditty on my nerves. Nevertheless, when the door opened and Monty Prather beamed from the other side, I pushed my shoulders back and strode in like I held the world in the palm of my hand.

Though it pained me to admit it now, I'd thought Cassidy Whalen's beauty was one of the most understated I'd ever seen. Hers was natural, the kind other women caked on the makeup in order to achieve, and I'd very much looked forward to working closely with her. But then she had to go and open her mouth.

Once all the attention had shifted from the shiny new bauble to the up-and-coming college recruits Striker was watching for possible procurement, Cassidy had only slightly angled her chair in my direction. From over the rim of her glasses, she'd looked me up and down and whispered, "Welcome aboard. I'm sure you'll do very well with the female clients." It had all been very matter-of-fact, and then she'd turned back around like that had been a normal type of greeting.

"What's that supposed to mean?" Shock from her insinuation had caused my voice to be louder than intended, so I'd had to wait until the rubberneckers returned their focus to the front of the room before repeating the question in a whisper: "What's that supposed to mean?"

"Don't be offended. We all have our part to play."

"Is that so? And what's your part?"

She'd set her pert nose a little higher in the air. "I bring in the moneymakers."

I'd almost laughed out loud, but I hadn't wanted to draw further attention to myself for being disruptive during a staff meeting on the first day. "And you don't think I can?"

She'd shrugged. "If they're wearing a skirt, sure."

Now I yanked my shower door open, a little pissed at myself. Not only because I'd let her get to me then, but also because it'd been nearly a year ago and I still hadn't gotten over it.

"God, her mouth!" I said out loud as I stepped into the shower.

Rotating the faucet handle with a little more force than was necessary, I shoved up with my palm, not that it made me feel any better. A rush of hot water shot out of the showerhead and pelted my face and chest until I was forced to turn around. My apartment had great water pressure. Maybe even too great. Not so strong that I could use it in lieu of renting a power washer, but it certainly rivaled the intensity of Cassidy's smart mouth. As well as my hard-on's insistence.

"Still slumming it, Matthews? All your posh friends have plans for the night?"

I grabbed the bottle of shampoo and squeezed it too hard, making a mess. "Fuck her!" I said, slamming it back down on the shelf, which then took a tumble to the floor of the tub. With a frustrated growl, I slapped the shampoo into my hair and lathered it up.

"Since the day you got here, you've acted like everything should be handed to you."

That wasn't true. I'd worked damn hard. Harder than I had anywhere else. And all because she'd thrown the stupid gauntlet on the floor that first day with the insinuation that I could only bring in clients if they were female. Talk about reverse chauvinism. I'd more than proven myself, but that hadn't shut her up, had it? Nope. She slammed me every single chance she got.

". . . rip it out of your precious, perfectly manicured clutches."

I scoffed to myself when I popped the top of the body wash. I didn't give a rat's ass about that kind of stuff—I was no girly man. Squirting a generous amount of soap into my hand, I rubbed my palms together and went to work on scrubbing my face, then my chest, pits, and arms.

". . . your sense of entitlement."

"Entitlement, my ass." She was way off the mark on that one.

My abs were next, and then lower, to that stupid hard-on.

"Ever worry you'll get lockjaw from sucking his cock?"

If she would just . . . shut . . . *up*. I gripped my erection and squeezed, not hating the temporary relief I felt. I'd show her lockjaw. That was probably the only way to keep her from talking. She needed a nice, thick cock in her mouth.

I closed my eyes and imagined fisting her hair and forcing her to crane her neck. The fat head of my cock was at her lips, pressing forward and demanding that she open up and let it in. The second she started to say something else, I capitalized and shoved my cock into her mouth to keep her from spouting off any further. It worked. I couldn't hear her anymore, but I could damn sure feel and see her. She was on her knees, where she belonged, her mouth barely able to stretch around my cock. Her nails scraped at my abdomen, but not to push me away. She was drawing me closer, wanting more even as she looked up at me with eyes the color of grass trapped beneath a canopy of shade on a forest floor. Cassidy was pissed, yet craving the taste of my cock and loving that she was at my mercy. I had none to give.

"Oh, that's so much better," I said, reveling in the quietness.

I began a series of short quick thrusts into my hand, keeping my eyes closed and the vision of fucking Cassidy Whalen's mouth forefront in my mind. The water pummeled my back, and I braced a foot on the edge of the bathtub to open myself up further to all the ways I could make my affliction put her trap to better use.

I pulled my cock out of Cassidy's mouth but only allowed her a quick breath before making her dip her head lower. With my free hand, I cupped my balls, stroking them the same way I imagined Cassidy doing with her tongue and lips. Next I angled her head, dropping one side into her mouth for her to gently suck, then the other.

"Nice and easy . . ." I said, feeling some of the tension leave my shoulders. "Christ, that feels good."

Her hands were on the insides of my thighs and she was going to town, sucking and licking and trying to put them both in at the same time. She was enjoying it too much, so I used my imaginary grip on her hair to pull her back and then pushed my cock into her mouth again. The scraping of her teeth must have been her idea of punishment, but I liked it.

I shouldn't have.

"Fuck!" I opened my eyes to see the strained muscles and tendons of my forearm and the bulging veins that carried the flow of blood, ushered by my erratic heartbeat. The death grip I had on my erection wasn't normal. Neither was the angry red tip that appeared and then disappeared again with each punishing stroke of my cock.

I didn't want to think about her. I just wanted her to shut up, for Christ's sake.

When I closed my eyes again, she was still there, and I had no choice but to finish the deed. Cassidy's luscious red lips moved back and forth over my cock, the thin skin over the rigid muscle tinged from the abuse of her scraping teeth. I bit down on my lip and threw my head back as I pumped even faster in and out of her mouth. I couldn't hear her anymore. In fact, I couldn't hear anything over the thunderous spray of water that was pounding at the top of my head.

My balls drew up as that familiar feeling gathered in the pit of my abdomen, a rush of blood cells pushing and shoving their way to a central location. My head dropped forward and my mouth fell open with a groaning grunt when the momentum that had been building came to a climax and rocketed toward the nearest exit.

I came. Damn hard. And I kept coming, each release easing the tension in my body just a little bit more, until I was completely spent. A couple more calming strokes to my cock was all I needed to make up for the torture I'd put us both through.

And then I let my head hang. I could've fixed the morning-wood incident with a cold shower. I didn't have to stoop as low as I had. I didn't have to let her win. Again.

What really pissed me off, though, was that I felt more satisfied after giving myself a hand job to thoughts of Cassidy Whalen then I had while fucking Yvonne three times mere hours before. Something was very wrong with this picture.

As my shower grew cold, droplets of water fell from the tips of my hair, and I watched as they joined the larger streams flowing down my arm. Rivulets forked into opposing directions, like uncovered veins showing the secret to the manna that flowed within, only to merge again before continuing the journey. Funny how something as harsh as pressure created by man ultimately yielded to the delicate design of nature.

I had no idea why I'd made that observation, but it somehow seemed important.

Cassidy

Something was horribly wrong with me. Yesterday, I'd been relatively normal, or so I'd thought, but today? Today, I was a masochistic pervert.

This was all Shaw's fault. Somehow, that sneaky bastard had found a way to drug me with some dream rape potion. Or he'd paid a voodoo priestess to put a hex on me that involved chicken bones, the hair of a bitch in heat, and spit from a cuckoo bird. Or maybe it was a mad scientist who'd broken into my apartment and Frankenstein-fried my brain while I slept. However it had been managed, I couldn't stop thinking about Shaw in highly inappropriate ways.

Showering this morning had been a terror. An enjoyable terror, but a terror nonetheless. What started out as my normal bathing routine ended with an unexpected orgasm. And an unsuccessful attempt to pump shampoo into my ear to scour the nasty from my brain. And it hadn't stopped there.

While I was waiting in line at the coffee shop where I stopped every morning on my way to work, I checked the apologetic texts from my incredibly rude friends. Those three were going to pay for this later. Through careful deduction, I'd come to the conclusion that their suggestion from the night before that I seduce Shaw was the seed that had called forth the incubus demon in the first place.

That was when I heard the nightmare weaver's voice. Naturally, my head snapped up, and sure enough, there he was. Shaw Matthews.

What was his freaking deal? First it was my job, then my pub, my friends, and now my coffee shop? I was beginning to think maybe I should consider paying a visit to the local boys in blue, to press criminal stalker charges. I mean, dang! Were my sloppy leftovers really that hot a commodity?

The way too young for him barista handed Shaw a cup with his name scrawled down the side, along with what I knew to be her name, Tiff (the *i* dotted with a heart), and a phone number. "Try it," she said, with a flirtatious smile and a forward lean to show off her cleavage.

Shaw took a careful sip, then licked the foam from his lips. "Mmm, you were right. It does taste as delicious as it looks."

Holy déjà vu, Batman! He'd said the same thing in my dream, right after he'd gone down on me. With my mission for coffee effectively aborted, I made a mad dash for the door, but not before accidentally bumping into a breast-feeding mother at the table behind me, inadvertently jarring the baby from her tit and interrupting his breakfast, which of course caused him to cry. I threw out the sincerest apology I could muster in my rush—without questioning why a breast-feeding mother was loading up on caffeine—and then got the hell out of there before Shaw could spot me.

There was no rhyme or reason to my actions. In hindsight, I was aware that he had no way of knowing what I'd dreamed, but I was convinced he'd see it all over my face. As if a feisty little devil was going to appear on my shoulder and say, "Boyfrieeeeend, you should've seen the dream this woman had about you last night. Whew!"

I saw no sense in risking it, so I opted for a coffeehouse that was a little out of the way but was guaranteed to be a Shaw-free zone. At least for that morning.

My detour caused me to run behind, which frustrated me. Punctuality was a compulsion with me. I was always early for everything, because in my book, if I was on time, I was late. Any deviation from my regular schedule made the whole day seem off, and I couldn't afford "off" with the all-too-important meeting I had after lunch. So when it was time for my midday break, I decided that a walk might help clear my head. Only, the muckery in my noggin became even more befuddled.

I must have passed five limousines during my walk. A limousine in the heart of downtown San Diego wasn't an uncommon thing. But five limousines in the span of fifteen minutes? Not likely. What didn't seem so unlikely, but carried an air of WTF-ery nonetheless, was the couple I passed, both of them sporting matching hickeys. I heard his voice then, Shaw's:

If you're going to give a hickey, put it where it won't be seen.

Shivers trickled down my spine, which was a textbook reaction to the effect his voice had always had on me, only this shiver wasn't from disgust. This one was infused with something lusty, and that something lusty was causing my breasts to swell and my nipples to render useless the very expensive bra in which they were housed.

When I was a young girl, Casey had bestowed upon me a handmade membership card inducting me into the Itty Bitty Tittie Committee. Once puberty had hit, I'd set it on fire. I wasn't *Debbie Does Dallas*–endowed, but my breasts certainly fell under the "more than a handful" category. At the moment, I felt overexposed, and that was never a comfortable feeling. Even more uncomfortable was the sensation that surged through me when my walk was over and I rounded the corner to the busy sidewalk that lined the front of Striker Sports Entertainment.

Crap!

Shaw was leaning against the black stretch limousine that would take us to our destination, with his legs crossed at the ankles and a cellphone at his ear. His navy blue suit was perfectly fitted to his frame, as of course it would be. Shaw must have had the best tailor in San Diego on standby to make sure he always looked good. He hadn't even noticed my approach. Whomever he was speaking with must have said something that tickled his funny bone, because his head fell back with a hearty laugh that revealed his pearly whites and the crinkles at the corners of his eyes. He looked more human than I'd ever given him credit for. For some reason, I pulled up the camera on my cellphone and captured the moment.

Oh, my God! What was *wrong* with me? I was definitely going to have to delete that picture before my phone self-destructed, but now was not the time. Quickly setting the phone back to my home screen, I dropped it into my messenger bag before I could do something stupid like ask him to undo a couple of buttons on his shirt and give me the bedroom eyes.

"Hello? Did you even hear what I said?"

It wasn't until then that I realized I'd stopped in front of him and had been staring directly into those bedroom eyes. And he smelled good. Like cologne mixed with Zest fully clean, and . . . and sex. The same aroma from my dream, in fact.

I should have known then that this was only the beginning of what would become the big game changer, where it all would go wrong, the end of life as I knew it. But I was too busy trying to tamp down the sound of my groan when the object of what was apparently my kamikaze brain's newest obsession licked the inside of his bottom lip and tilted his head to regard me with a curious glint in his eyes. Striking eyes the color of a twilight sky on the edge of a summer storm caged by an obsidian ring that hinted at both the ominous and the divine.

Whoa! Something pulsed inside me, a single shock wave rushing toward and then deliberately slowing down to tease the naughtiest part of me before continuing down my thighs and then disappearing like a not so distant memory. When one corner of his mouth lifted in a devious grin, I thought for sure he'd done something on purpose. Maybe he did indeed possess some sort of sinister power that caused women's panties to drop on the spot. That, or he'd been reading my mind and knew exactly what I'd been thinking.

"Having issues?" Shaw nodded slightly toward my crotch. Holy cheese sauce, he *did* know what I was thinking!

Only when I looked down, expecting to see that my panties were in fact on the ground, I found that my subconscious mind had decided to work after all and had forced my hands to grab the top of said panties through my skirt to keep them from obeying his unspoken command. I looked like an idiot. And Shaw Matthews was eating it up. I couldn't very well let that continue, now, could I?

"Just trying to make sure none of your STDs or creepy crawlies find their way past the defensive mechanisms I put into place this morning to keep them out." I had to smile at that; it was a nice save on my part. Witty, too.

Shaw failed to see the humor in it. I failed to care. And into the car I went. I almost laughed out loud when he got in behind me and slammed the door, but then he tapped on the divider to signal the driver—only for me, it signaled something completely different. Realization.

I was alone in the back of a car with the man from my very wet dream.

Jeez, it was crowded in the confined space. But it smelled good. Like Shaw. "Dammit!" I muttered with a shake of my head, hoping to clear it.

"Did you say something?"

"Nope." I wondered if he was as well endowed in real life as he had been in my dream.

Stop it, Cassidy Rose!

"So, I was thinking about the reasoning behind Wade sending both of us to meet with Rockford at the same time instead of individually."

Thank God one of us was able to think straight, though I had to admit I was shocked to high heavens that it was the pretty boy instead of me. "Is that right? And what did your simple mind come up with?" I asked as I pulled my laptop out of my messenger bag.

"Simple." Shaw chuckled in that smart-ass sort of way. "You're so funny. Seriously, I think he wants us to double-team the guy. You know, to make sure he signs with SSE."

Where had I heard that before? "Wade is aware that I work alone. And everyone in the universe knows you're a selfish prick, so I doubt very much that he intended for us to work together. Teamwork does not a superstar athlete land."

"Oh, yeah? Well, then why do you think he sent us both?"

"The answer is as obvious as the shit on the tip of your nose, Matthews." I stopped. Not for dramatic pause or because I didn't have the follow-up but because I was experiencing one of the most intense feelings of "been there, done that" ever. This entire conversation had happened before.

"Well? What is it?"

I looked at Shaw. Then down at his crotch. Then at his hands, one of which was attached to the arm he had draped over the back of the seat and the other appropriately placed on his own thigh and not stroking his cock. That was it. This was the conversation that had started it all in my dream. Was I a freaking psychic? Had a lightning bolt struck me while I slept? Because, hello? What were the odds?

The way I figured it, I had two choices: I could either continue the natural progression of the conversation and see if magic really did exist, or I could take a detour and avoid making the worst mistake of my life.

Shaw dipped his head so that I'd have to look at him and that stupid way his brows were lifted, like he was waiting for me to come up with an answer. And even though I wanted to whimper when his tongue made a completely normal sweep of his bottom lip to moisten it, I knew what had to be done. "Figure it out on your own."

Anticlimactic and disappointing, judging by his expression. He'd deploy countermeasures in three, two, one . . .

"Pfft. Was that the best you could come up with?" Count on Shaw to gloat and *try* to make me feel stupid.

Maybe he had a point. Maybe the asinine thoughts I'd been having, including the dream, were my brain's way of telling me it needed a break, that it was dumbing down for the sake of self-preservation. Forty-three national league clients, including Olympic athletes, each wanting a bigger slice of the pie, one-on-one attention, and high-paying endorsements could take a toll on a person. I was overworked. That was all. But there was no rest for the clinically insane, and if I wanted that partnership, I had to give it my all.

And just like that, I was over it. To think I'd been avoiding him all day, when I should've done the exact opposite. The real Shaw was nowhere near as dreamy as my mind had tried to trick me into believing. He was an egotistical jerk served up on a cold platter with a heaping helping of sarcasm on the side. He needed only to open his mouth for the remnants of the fire that had been smoldering in my nether regions to be completely doused. If all else failed, I could certainly depend on his grating personality to snap me back to reality.

I ignored Shaw's question and sat back with my laptop, refusing to engage him any further for the remainder of the ride. He pouted like a teenage girl, and I let out a breath I hadn't realized I'd been holding.

Game face, on.

CHAPTER 4

Shaw

Denver Rockford loved to be seen, and at six foot four and 235 pounds of come-get-you-some, he was hard to miss. Especially when he was center stage at a karaoke bar, belting an off-key rendition of U2's "I Still Haven't Found What I'm Looking For." Now a small hole-in-the-wall establishment that probably never saw a full house was brimming with Denver's family, friends, fans, and probably some groupies. But the handful of camera-carrying vultures looking for that perfect shot were forced to circle the building and steal glances through the tinted windows.

Movie stars, rock stars, and star athletes might have glamorous lives, but that didn't mean those lives were anywhere near normal. With fame came a lack of privacy, and everything they did in the public eye was subject to scrutiny. Some had mastered an understanding of the beast and used it to their advantage, while others rode it like a mechanical bull set to giddy-up-off-of-me.

And then there were the paparazzi. The paparazzi were more than willing to make the famous even more famous. Exploitation: it didn't matter if it was in a positive or a negative light as long as someone was cutting the check for the fish-bowl look into the private life of a fellow human being.

What about the fans? How readily did they excuse bad behavior? When a star from music, television, or the big screen tumbled from on high, it affected their fans personally, and so the decline in their following was a guarantee. In sports, however, a stumble by one player could cost the whole team. Sports fans were some of the most dedicated and forgiving in the world, and most felt it was partly their responsibility to protect the team, much like a mother protects her children. The whole team shouldn't be made to suffer just because one player "made a mistake." And so it seemed that a suitable penance for a felony crime, in the fans' eyes, required nothing more than a swift apology and another win. After all, winning wasn't everything; it was the only thing.

My job as an agent wasn't limited to making the deals. A client's image helped sell them, so I had a particular interest in their representation. It had nothing at all to do with the direct reflection their behavior had on me, or on my perceived ability to do the job. Anyone in the business knew there was only so much advice you could give to someone with enough money to pay attorneys to get them out of whatever unfavorable or illegal situation they'd found themselves in. And as sad as it was, oftentimes, the more hype around an athlete, the more the fans were going to pay to see them. It was nearly impossible to convince a client to dial it back when their raucous behavior was making them enough money to pay the penalty tab and then some.

Denver "Rocket Man" Rockford wasn't off the rails . . . yet. Though he did like to throw his money around and was obnoxiously loud while doing so. The man drew far too much attention, which meant everyone was always watching him. Case in point: the slightly drunken spectacle he was making of himself at the moment, literally throwing money into the crowd while camera flashes lit up the room like fireworks on the Fourth of July.

Yep, he was a show-off, but he was also a fan favorite. And

not only because of his generosity or the fact that he knew how to have a good time. Denver had earned the name "Rocket Man" during his sophomore year at Arizona, after launching a Hail Mary eighty-four yards down the field, hitting his targeted receiver dead center in the chest and winning the championship game. He hadn't thrown that far since, but his stats were still off the charts. Having thrown for over five thousand yards and forty-eight touchdowns this past season alone, he was a superstar quarterback to rival the likes of Peyton Manning, Tom Brady, and Drew Brees. If he kept on the same trajectory, there'd be nothing to stop him from surpassing all of them. Plus, the Hall of Fame was a no-brainer at this point.

He was worth millions, and I wanted him. Not in a dude-on-dude sort of way, but damn straight I wanted to add him to my client roster.

The behemoth stopped in the middle of the lyrics he'd been butchering when he glanced toward the door. He pointed a meaty finger right at me. "Shaw Matthews in the flesh, people. Give that man some respect! Whoo!" He jumped down from the stage and came right at me.

"Rocket! I had no idea crooner was part of your repertoire," I said with my million-dollar smile and an offered hand, which he batted away.

"Man, don't give me that crap. You're family to Nate, and Nate's family to me, so bring it in." He grabbed my shoulders and crushed them with a mammoth hug instead.

He knew he was dead center on my radar and that I'd deploy any method necessary to sign him. Even if that method was frowned upon. That also proved I'd go to any length for him as well, so it was a win in my book. The fish-out-of-water stare I got from Cassidy meant she'd just caught on to what was happening.

Nate Hutchins was one of my guys. My number one guy. He

was also a world champion skateboarder and snowboarder who'd medaled gold in both the Summer and Winter X Games and the Olympic Winter Games. As it happened, he was a native of Aspen, Colorado. Same as my prospective client. And with the promise that I'd keep him my number one, he'd agreed to play the go-between and say a few nice things about me. There was no "I" in "team," after all.

With a hard clap on the back, Denver pushed me away, a playful expression lighting up his face. "Nate's shown so much love for you, I'm beginning to think he's got a schoolboy crush. You're a pretty good-looking guy, though, so maybe he's got reason." He laughed. "You planning on stepping out on your main man with me?"

I turned on the Shaw Matthews charm and went to work. Slipping into a character to match his own, I laughed. "Nah, it's not like that. Just thought I'd see if you'd be interested in a slow dance or two, see where it goes from there." And then I winked. It wasn't a flirtatious wink. Okay, I suppose it sort of was. I was trying to woo him into bed with me; it was just a different sort of bed. I'd have him hook, line, and sinker in a matter of minutes.

My very rude colleague wasn't content to sit back and watch me reel him in, though. Stepping forward and angling her body in front of mine, she introduced herself; she knew damn well I wasn't about to give her an opening. "Hi, Cassidy Whalen. I'm also with SSE. It's nice to finally meet you." She offered Denver a handshake, which he didn't take, because his arm was still draped over my shoulders.

"Cassidy Whalen. I've heard some pretty impressive things about you, little lady."

Little lady. Cassidy wouldn't like that one bit. The slight set of her shoulders and tilt of her chin proved me right, though Denver wouldn't have noticed. I was sure she'd bury herself if given the opportunity, but so far she was holding it together better than I'd thought she would.

Cassidy flashed him a confident smile and softened. "So tell me. What is it that you're looking for?" When he gave her a blank look, she nodded toward the stage.

Furrowed brows melted into an expression I'd mastered all too well myself. He surveyed her from head to toe and said, "I think I just found it."

If I didn't know Cassidy Whalen to be the ice queen she was, I would have been worried at that point. She could've done a little shimmy and pulled the pins from her hair to take home the win, though I would've put money on it that she had no clue what kind of power she held. That was a plus for me. I had some work to do if I was going to persuade Denver that my game was better than her gams.

"Is that your family?" I asked, hoping to distract him.

"Yep! I like to think of them as my blood, sweat, and tears," he said, pointing to his parents, lackeys, and groupies, respectively. He laughed at his own joke. I had to admit it was pretty clever.

"The girls are locals, but they know a winner when they see one. Especially if he's a *bread*winner. You know how it is." He laughed again. "Now, I ain't sayin' she a gold digger," he sang. "Am I right?" The elbow check he gave me might have cracked a couple of ribs, but I smiled right through the searing pain. "Mama Rocket doesn't approve. Still thinks her baby boy is innocent." He leaned toward Cassidy, conspiratorially. "I'm not," he assured her with a wink.

I laughed and clapped him on the back while turning him in the direction of his table, targets two and three acquired. No one had more influence over an unmarried man than the people who'd brought him into the world in the first place. It was my goal to get them aboard the Shaw Matthews Express, which would be easy enough to do.

Parents really liked me. Probably because the richer I made their kids, the fatter they got to live. If I was lucky, Mama Rocket would have a little cougar in her that I could finesse. Just a little, though. During the course of my career, I'd found myself in more mama drama than I cared to recount, and I had no desire to go back there. Papa Rocket, on the other hand, would be a lot easier to deal with. A man's ego was always his downfall. It didn't matter how true the words you spoke, as long as the stroke was just right.

Mama and Papa sat at the head of the table, and Denver shooed the occupants of three of the chairs next to them away before grabbing one for himself. I'd take my seat, but not before a proper introduction and warm invitation to do so was made. Mothers especially liked that kind of stuff. Denver's mom noticed my good manners and smiled up at me.

"It's so very nice to meet you, Mrs. Rockford." I bent to kiss her hand, but to my utter shock, she pulled it free. Not because she was offended. Nope. It was because her attention was elsewhere. Like over my shoulder. Standing, she reached between her son and me for the one person I'd been trying to block. Mental warfare, an attempt to make my rival feel excluded. Clearly, my attempt had failed.

The short, bulbous woman gave a smile to my rival that was much larger and more genuine. "Well, it's about time we get to meet face-to-face, Cassidy Whalen!" She pulled her in for the sort of hug a mother gives her child. "I want to thank you again for the interview and all the free advice you gave my followers. So generous of you!"

"Oh, you're very welcome, Mrs. Rockford. I was honored to have been included."

"Interview? What interview is that?" I asked.

Mrs. Rockford ignored my question and sat, offering the seat beside her to Cassidy. Dammit. "What's with all the formality? Call me Delilah. After all, we're practically old friends now."

Old friends? I looked around for a film crew, thinking that surely I'd been cast unawares in an episode of *The Twilight Zone*.

"Only if you call me Cassidy."

Who cared who called whom what? Obviously, there was fuckery afoot, and I wanted to get to the bottom of it. I played it cool, though, kept that Shaw Matthews smile in place even though I was about two seconds away from losing my composure from all the niceties being thrown around. "So do the rest of us get to know about this interview?"

"Oh, it was nothing."

Well, then in that case . . . What was that supposed to mean? Nothing? It had to be something if it was important enough to be brought up now.

Mama Rocket threw her hands into the air. "Nothing, she says. So modest, this one."

"She is, isn't she?" I turned to glare at Cassidy, who had the gall to flash a not so innocent smile in my direction.

"Mrs. Rockford . . ." Cassidy paused to cross her long legs—a move Denver didn't miss—and gave Mama Rocket an apologetic smile. "*Delilah* writes a blog for sports moms. Sort of a 'what to expect when your expected goes pro.' A couple of years back, she interviewed me for a spotlight on agents." She shrugged as if it was no big deal. "She's quite talented at what she does. You should check it out, Shaw. Maybe you'll learn a thing or two about your job." She laughed. In my face. In front of Denver "Rocket Man" Rockford and his frickin' father. And then *they* laughed.

That did it for me. The gloves were off.

The best way to remedy a situation where you're the odd man

out is to blend in, be on the level, and learn to laugh at yourself. So I did just that. "Oh, I have zero doubt she can school me. Though, lucky for her son, I know enough about my job to get him the best contract out there. I can also sweeten the pot by landing her baby boy more national ads than any other player on the field. Because instead of giving free advice, I'd be out there making him money. That's the sort of game I play. Am I right, Mr. Rockford?"

Denver's father dropped the wing he'd been gnawing on to give me a "Hell yeah!" and a nod of approval. Bull's-eye.

Boulder Rockford was a blue-jeans-and-leather-vest sort of guy with a chain wallet and biker boots. He kept his head shaved, his solid white goatee in a rubber band, and a silver hoop in his earlobe. If he hadn't been on vacation with his family, I was sure there would've been a chromed-out Harley with a skull headlight in the parking lot.

Apart from the cliché, Boulder was a man of business. It was all about the bottom line for his boy, and he didn't trust anybody, so he kept a keen eye on the numbers. A badass with a business plan wasn't someone I was interested in jerking around. The last thing I needed or wanted was to have him go all *Sons of Anarchy* on me, so I was going to make damn sure we did things his way. Or at least make him think it was his way.

"I like you. You sound like a man with a plan." Boulder kicked back with his beer.

His enthusiasm for my suggestion was just the invitation I'd been seeking from the head of the household. I grabbed the chair next to him—despite the overwhelming scent of Old Spice—and turned it around to straddle the seat and use the back for an armrest. "Damn straight. Now, Rocket, after last season, the sky's the limit on whatever you want, man. The fans love you, the sponsors are foaming at the mouth to put your face on their products, and—"

"Who could blame them? I'm freakin' gorgeous!"

"Hey, you're beautiful, babe. But did you know that Detroit is my home city?"

Denver shook his head, and I jumped right back in, not wanting to lose the momentum. "It is. You know what that means, don't you? That means I have a special kind of relationship with everyone who's anyone with that team. Most importantly, the deal makers. They trust me, and so should you. I've already talked to them on your behalf, in fact—hope that wasn't too presumptuous of me—and I know they're willing to pay big money to get you on their roster. And I'm going to make sure of it."

I was stiff-legging it into the end zone, ready to do my own touchdown dance. It was going to be damn sexy, too: a lip bite, some body rolls, and a couple of air spanks to a make-believe ass. I was getting a boner, because I got off on this stuff. Maybe it was a little kinky, but at least it wasn't as masochistic as the whole shower debacle this morning. The subject of said debacle chose that moment to throw a flag on my play and put an instant deflate on the celebratory chub in my slacks.

"That's true, but then so would every other NFL team. We might even be able to get you back in Colorado. How's that sound? You want your son back home, don't you, Mrs. Rockford?" Cassidy was still playing the mama bear card. No way was she going to win with that, but it was a nice try.

Mrs. Rockford laid her hands over her heart. "Do you really think that's possible?"

Boulder put a comforting arm around his wife, and a little piece of me died. "Of course it is, woman. Denver embodies all that is Colorado. That's what we named him, and that's where he belongs."

Dammit, she was good. Whalen had stolen the lead with that ambush. The Rockfords harbored an intense love for their home state. It was a genetic sort of loyalty—hence the names of all the male children in their family. Each was named after a city, and they all had the same middle name: Colorado.

Right. So I was called back to the line of scrimmage. No big deal. I still had a lot of plays on my cuff.

"You could absolutely do that. I thought you'd want to go with a team that you could take to the championship, but if you want to try to build up your home team, we can do that, too. Like I said, the sky's the limit."

It got really quiet then, but the smirk on Cassidy's face said a thousand words. "Aren't you going to brag about all the deal makers you know with Colorado, Shaw?"

Sometimes I really hated her.

I shrugged; her attempt to make me look stupid was going to come up short. She and I both knew it. "I don't have to. I know football."

Cassidy rolled her eyes. "For the span of his career, he was in Europe. He knows soccer."

"I know money." No matter how often she slammed me for being a superficial jerk born with a silver spoon in my mouth, she couldn't argue the point.

"So do I. I also know that money might build a house, but it won't build a home."

I glared at her. Mostly because she was a megabitch, but then I realized she'd just given me an opening. Turning to Denver, I said, "Would you rather make friends or money? The decision's up to you."

"Finally, we agree on something." Cassidy leaned forward. "The decision *is* completely up to you, Denver. You're lucky that you have a great foundation to support you in making it. And there's one more thing we agree on. Whether it's my vision for your future or Shaw's, ultimately, Striker Sports Entertainment is the agency for you."

Well, would you look at that? The little do-gooder was going for the "there is no 'I' in 'team'" approach as well. Only she was using a different angle: the suck-up.

Denver gave a thunderous clap as he kicked his chair back and stood. "That's enough business for today, man. My public awaits." Grabbing the longneck in front of him, he finished it off in three gulps and slammed it back down onto the table, earning a raucous roar from his personal cheerleading squad and a disapproving look from his mother. "Bartender, another round for all my friends!"

Cassidy and I took our cue and stood to say our goodbyes. One never wanted to overstay one's welcome when courting a major player in the game. Not only that, but spending too much time with one athlete made the others jealous. I had a lot of number ones, and each of them thought they were my most important, because that was what a good agent did. And it was true. Whoever I was negotiating for had my total focus until the deal was done and I needed to move on to the next client. But if the first guy ever needed me for anything, he'd have it back again. I liked my clients happy, so I gave them my all. I'd do the same for Denver Rockford, if he'd just give me the chance.

Denver and I clasped hands, and he pulled me in for a bro hug. I took the opportunity to throw out one more pitch. Hopefully, one that Cassidy wouldn't have a chance to shoot down. "Just pass me the ball, Rocket. I promise, you won't regret it."

Denver laughed as he pulled back. "I hear ya, man. We'll be in touch, okay?" He turned to my co-worker with a lascivious look in his eyes as he went in for a hug that was going to land his big paws on the cheeks of her ass.

Cassidy slapped his hands away and gave him a stern glare. Christ, it was the same look his mother had given him. "When I want you to touch me, Denver Rockford, I'll let you know."

She might as well have kicked the box out from under her own feet to dangle from a noose, because she'd just hung herself. I was a little disappointed, to tell the truth. I'd wanted that honor, but I'd settle for whipping up a quickie contract on a napkin to get the freshly scorned Rocket Man's retaliatory commitment.

Denver and his ginormous ego did not disappoint. "Do you know who I am?"

Oh, this was great! I reached inside my pocket to pull out my pen while looking around for that napkin.

Cassidy put her hands on her hips. "Yes, I do. You're a potential client with idle hands in the off-season. But that'll be easily fixed once we get you signed and into some OTA drills."

"Good God, woman! Sassy turns me on," Denver said with a fake swoon.

Mama Rocket might've had to hop up to do it, but she landed a swift smack to the back of his head. "I didn't raise you to be disrespectful to women, son. Apologize."

"Ouch, Mom! Not in front of the paparazzi!" He rubbed the back of his head and sulked away to lick his wounds.

So much for the quickie contract. I needed to do some serious regrouping after this disaster of a meeting.

Cassidy giggled. Fucking *giggled*. Then she turned to Delilah and beamed. "He's a cute one."

"He didn't get those manners from me."

Denver hopped onto the stage and grabbed the microphone, back in superstar mode with his embarrassing moment forgotten. The DJ already had Elton John's "Rocket Man" keyed up and waiting for him.

Delilah shook her head at the beginnings of her son's dramatic performance. "He's an idiot, but he's my idiot. I swear, he's a good kid."

"I believe you," Cassidy assured her. "And just so you know, he really can't go wrong with SSE. We'll take good care of him and always work toward what's best for him, even when it might not be something he particularly likes."

"I appreciate that." Delilah gave Cassidy a hug, and for the first time since we'd arrived, I got a Mama Rocket smile. "He'll go with SSE. We'll see to it. Which one of you he signs with will be up to him, though. Best of luck to the both of ya."

As she turned to walk away, Cassidy and I headed for the door. I supposed I should be happy we at least knew he would sign with the agency. Damn right Wade would be happy about that. But there was still the matter of the partnership. I felt a little worse for the wear, less confident than I had been when we'd first arrived.

I still had an ace up my sleeve, though. A surefire way to make her weak in the knees and bring her down a peg or two.

"Pass you the ball?" Cassidy said, interrupting my thoughts. Obviously, she'd heard my private comment to Denver. "For what? So you can drop it? You do know that fumbles are bad, don't you, Matthews?"

"Not if it's the other team who's doing the fumbling, Whalen."

"We're on the same team."

"Are we? Because the last time I checked, teammates don't face off against each other."

"They do if the coach is trying to get one player to up his game to the level of the first stringer's. I hope you took notes." She gave me that high-and-mighty smirk and then slipped into the back of the car.

It seemed I'd underestimated my opponent.

CHAPTER 5

Cassidy

I hit Monkey Business at exactly six minutes past the five o'clock hour, which wasn't like me at all. Mostly because I was so anal retentive about my work that I checked and rechecked my notes, made new ones, and rechecked those before I went anywhere, every day. Not today. Today's anal fixation leaned toward the expulsive side, and for the life of me, I couldn't figure out why I was fixating on the anal thing to begin with. Oh, wait. Shaw Matthews was the reason. After all, he was a giant ass.

The moment I crossed the threshold to the pub, Chaz slid a cold one down to the end of the bar, and it was waiting for me when I got to our table. I chugged the icy ale like a college frat boy doing a headstand on top of a keg at a toga party. That was five hours ago. I hadn't stopped drinking since, though I had slowed down.

For all intents and purposes, Quinn and Demi had believed me when I'd told them I was celebrating my mini victory over Shaw, but I knew that was a lie. The truth was, I'd tried everything else to get that damn dream out of my head and nothing had worked. Tying one on didn't seem to be working, either.

Shaw was perched atop his regular stool at the bar, of course, also drinking. I had a sneaking suspicion that his bun had nothing to do with a victory either, seeing as how I'd outmaneuvered what he'd thought would be a sure thing. Served him right. He knew that using one of his clients to get the upper hand with another was in fact underhanded, since it was a cheat. Plain and simple. I'd put the smackdown on what he'd thought was going to be a slam dunk.

Ignoring Shaw's presence had always been hard to do, though never impossible. Until now. For some reason, I couldn't stop stealing glances in his direction, even consciously admonishing and correcting myself. He was leaning over the bar in such a way that the slight angle of his back showcased his ass perfectly. I'd never thought of myself as an ass chick, but I knew for a fact I was a Gerard Butler chick. Which qualified me to say that Shaw's ass was very Gerard Butler–ish in that it was fleshy enough for a nice bite but still firm enough to be manly. The slope from his back rounded out to a nice double palm–sized cup and then dipped elegantly into his thighs. If I had to guess, I'd say it had the same golden tan the rest of him appeared to have. As he leaned farther across the bar to take a playful swat at Chaz for something he'd said, I unconsciously followed, hoping his tucked shirt would pull free to reveal whether or not he had back dimples to compliment the smile below.

The forward lean was a bad idea. Mine was, anyway. The room had started to tilt on its axis a bit, which was good. That meant the booze was working. Though I supposed my keen observation of Shaw's backside should've been clue number one that it was.

I wasn't quite drunk, but I definitely wasn't as wound up as I had been all day. In my current state, I'd convinced myself that it was perfectly reasonable that the dream had messed with my head. It was, in fact, in my head, after all. But I couldn't quite shake my curiosity about whether a romp with Shaw would be anywhere near the same outside of the dream. Or, better yet, whether his bedroom talk would be anywhere near as naughty. Yesterday he'd been nothing more than a self-important jackass in a suit who charmed the pants off anyone who could get him somewhere in the world. Today I saw him differently. He was still a self-important jackass in a suit, but damn, he looked good in it.

"Uh-uh. Why is she crying?" Quinn asked. Thank God. I needed the distraction.

I looked up to see that Sasha's normally glamorous face was tearstained and that a tall, fair-skinned man with the body of a soldier and a haircut to match was escorting her to our table. Though her escort was no stranger to Monkey Business or us, Landon Mercer's presence meant he'd ridden to the rescue once again, and that implied only one thing. Sasha had either been the dumper or the dumpee in her latest relationship. If you could call her dating fiascos relationships, that is.

Though Landon now worked as a security consultant for a local government agency, he was a proud marine at heart—loyal, honorable, and strong. He was everyone's hero, but for one woman, he was a superhero. And he was content to stay by her side, picking her up and dusting her off after every failed relationship, because that was the kind of man he was.

"Ah, jeez, Sash." Demi engulfed her roommate in a comforting hug the second Sasha took the seat next to her, with Landon still at her side. "What happened this time?"

Sasha's voice was thick with tears. "He said I'm selfish."

The woman's heart was entirely too big, and she had a thing for fixer-uppers. This time, it had been an unemployed pothead with kids he couldn't afford to take care of. But there was a long line of abusers, addicts, and cheaters in her past, all of whom had made her believe that she was to blame for her inability to fix them. Worst of all, she'd trusted them—she was so damn good-hearted she couldn't understand that loving a person unconditionally was only a bandaged solution to the wound beneath, and wounds that deep needed stitches only years of therapy could sew. Sasha wasn't a therapist. She was a beautiful woman with a pure soul who came from wealthy parents, and she would be better off once she learned to supplement her codependency with flipping houses instead of men. At least a house couldn't break her damn heart.

"How much, Sasha?" I simply asked what everyone else was already wondering.

She bowed her head and fiddled with the tissue in her hands. "I don't know. A little over eight grand, I guess."

Quinn threw his hands into the air. "You've gotta be freakin' kidding me! Really? And you've been dating this one for how long now?"

"Fifty-one days." She shrugged. "Give or take."

"Fifty-one days, she says." Quinn leaned across the table. "Eight thousand dollars in fifty-one days?"

"Don't start with me, Quinn. It's not like you don't take money from Daddy."

"Hold on a minute. Did you just compare—" Quinn began, but I shushed him. He growled a little but managed to rein in his outrage to say something semiproductive: "Sasha, honey, Daddy and I are in love, and we've been together for six years. Six years, not fifty-one days. He does things for me because he loves me, not because he wants *me* to love *him*. Do you understand the difference? You can't buy someone's affection."

"I know! I know!" Sasha slumped in her chair. "I screwed up. Again. There, I said it. Are you happy?"

Demi pulled at some of the flattened curls in Sasha's hair. "Sweetie, your broken heart could never make us happy. It makes us growly because we love you and you deserve so much better than these losers you've been dating. You need someone who will treasure you. Someone who could never fathom bringing mental, physical, or emotional harm to you. Someone who loves you because of who you are and not what you can do for him. Someone who rides a white stallion—"

"And is hung like a stallion," Quinn threw in.

"—and has a superhero complex. Metaphorically speaking, of course."

"Someone like Landon," I added. Instantly, panic jolted my insides. I heard the words; I swear I heard them. Unfortunately, it wasn't before they blasted their way past my lips. Demi and Quinn snapped their heads toward me and froze like deer in headlights, with their eyes wide open and their mouths clamped shut. If it hadn't been for the background noise, I would've sworn someone had pressed the pause button on the world. And then Landon cleared his throat and pulled at his collar while shifting in place.

Oops. Yep, I was definitely tipsy.

"Um, you know . . . because he's a marine and he drives a white Bronco."

"So did O. J. Simpson," Quinn pointed out.

"Good point. Look, what I meant to say," I backpedaled, "is if a guy's not lifting you up, then he's holding you down." It was true, and therefore a magnificent save. "Maybe you should take some time to be good to yourself instead of feeling like you have to take care of someone else."

For some odd reason, I felt like we should've joined hands to sing a chorus of "Kumbaya" or some Disney movie's theme song.

"Yeah, I know you're right. All of you are. I have the absolute best friends in the world. I don't know what I'd do without you."

Demi sighed and then stood, pulling Sasha out of her chair as well. "Come on, sugar lumps. Let's get you home with some Chunky Monkey."

Quinn clapped. "Oh, ice cream! I'm in," he said, jumping out of his seat to link one arm through Sasha's. "Are you coming?" he asked me.

I might have glanced toward the bar on that one. When my eyes locked with Shaw's right before he jerked away, something told me to stay. It was that stupid dream haunting me again, but I was damned if I could shut it down.

"Go on without me. I'm going to have another beer, and then I'm heading home."

"Oh, uh-uh. You're not walking home by yourself. Have you lost your mind?" The way Quinn was gaping at me, I'd not only lost my mind, I'd grown two heads as well.

"Don't worry. I'll make sure she gets there safely." Imagine my utter shock when Shaw pulled a Landon. He also pulled out the chair next to me and took a seat as if he'd been invited to do so.

Quinn's expression morphed into a devilish smirk. "That'll work," he said, aiming Sasha toward the door and leaving as if I had no say in the matter.

I would've thrown out a formal protest, but then Landon laid a hand on Demi's shoulder to keep her from leaving, and I was distracted again. "Do you know where he lives?"

"I certainly do," Demi said, already grabbing a pen from her purse. After scribbling an address on a paper napkin, she handed it to Landon. "You go make sure he loses her number, and I'll get started on cleaning up his mess."

"Roger that," he said, looking over the address.

I'd never seen Landon upset. He was a good guy through and through, and no one would ever be able to change my mind about that. Though he was a marine, he never came off as a Billy Badass, never strutted his stuff like he was the toughest man in the room or carried a chip on his shoulder. He was just Landon, but I'd often wondered what he'd said to the men of Sasha's past. All I knew was that they never came back around after one of his visits.

I tilted my head to regard him, and, oddly, the room didn't flip upside down. "You could put both of you out of your misery if you'd just tell her, you know."

"Tell her what?"

"That you're in love with her."

Landon smiled, and the sincerity of it would've brought me to my knees if I'd been standing. How could Sasha not be caught in his spell? "When she's ready for me, she'll see what she needs to know for herself." And that was the truth of the matter, wasn't it? He gave me a friendly wink, then nodded at Shaw. "Be careful going home."

"Will do, man," Shaw said as Landon walked away. Then he sighed. "Well, I guess it's just you and me now." He draped his arm across the back of my chair and slouched, with his long legs sprawled out in front of him. When his other hand rested naturally on his thigh, I was once again distracted. Only this time, it wasn't a saving grace. It was the forbidden appeal of the fruit on the tree. And a slithering trouser snake that wanted to be my new best friend.

Crap. No good could come of this.

Shaw

If the pattern of my luck had been any indication at all, succeeding at seducing Cassidy Whalen was going to be a Hail Mary at best. Or so I'd thought until the universe finally decided to smile upon me, all the planets aligned, and some cosmic miracle landed me on my bar stool at Monkey Business, watching the target of my plan get all loosey-goosey and, hopefully, uninhibited.

I would never take advantage of a drunken chick. Never. So I was glad to see that Cassidy knew how to handle her booze. She'd gotten to her buzz and then slowed to a pace that allowed her to keep it without crossing the line. Which meant I could feel good about knowing that if I were successful, I wouldn't be crossing the line, either. All I needed was for her to be uninhibited enough to let down her guard so she was more receptive to my charms.

When Quinn had asked her if she was leaving with the girls and him, I'd thought for sure my plan was in the shitter. But then she'd turned toward me, which was unexpected, and there was a bit of something sultry about the way she'd looked at me when she'd caught me staring. That was when I saw my opening and swooped in to take advantage of the situation, as was my specialty.

Of course, Cassidy had to be Cassidy. And though I didn't think it was anything I couldn't handle, she sure as hell wasn't going to make it easy. Nope. I was going to have to work for it.

"I don't need an escort home. I can take care of myself." It was only the fourth time she'd said it since I'd settled up both our bills—because I was a nice guy and all—and we'd left Chaz to his lockup.

"I have no doubt whatsoever that you possess the ability to rip the nuts off any man who dares to get near you, but I gave my word to Quinn, and I intend to keep it."

Cassidy pivoted with all the grace of a toddler to walk backward while still talking. In her slightly inebriated state, her coordination left a lot to be desired, but if I told her that, she'd only try to prove me wrong by performing a choreographed gymnastics floor routine on a sea of concrete. "Ha! You have no honor, Shaw Matthews. If you did, you wouldn't have pulled that move with Denver earlier."

Tucking my hands into my pockets, I grinned at her. "I'm sure I have no clue what you're talking about."

She scoffed. "You know exactly what I'm talking about. Don't play dumb." And then she turned her back to me again.

Of course I knew what she was talking about. My plan had backfired on me, though. Nate had assured me that Denver Rockford was in the bag, that he'd talked me up and the contract was as good as mine. He was wrong. So the second I was out of the car and out of earshot of Cassidy, I'd called my number one and given him a healthy dose of "You suck!" Of course, that wasn't the best idea I'd ever had. It just so happened that Nate was at the arena, about to take the plunge when I'd called. I deserved the "Dude, I'm about to dip into the megaramp! What the fuck?" as well as the hang-up that had followed before I'd had the chance to apologize. He'd had a point. What kind of agent called his client before he was about to compete to say some messed-up shit like that? I'd forgotten that he was qualifying for the Summer X Games, which was yet another epic fail on my part.

A rumble of thunder rolled in from the bay, and I looked up to see the dark clouds that had swept in to block the light of the moon. The air was thick with moisture and the promise of rain. California never saw much by way of precipitation, but when it did, it was usually a quick burst that dumped buckets before passing. Stuck trying to figure out my next tactic already, the last thing I needed was for the rain to make the entire attempt a wash. We needed to get a move on.

Cassidy was at least seven steps ahead; apparently, everything had to be a goddamn competition with her. I'd let her have her way this time, only because it afforded me an awesome view of her ass and those long legs—legs that were attached to wobbly ankles in, if I had to guess, four-inch heels.

I had two choices. I could either let her keep going and bask in her inevitable fall, or I could rescue her from herself and get us somewhere dry before we got drenched. If luck stayed on my side, we'd make it to her place just as the rain hit, and propriety would force her to reciprocate my good deed by asking me to come inside until the rain passed. Perfect.

"Hold up a minute." Cassidy kept walking even though I knew she'd heard me, which didn't exactly shock me. "Cassidy, stop!"

She came to an abrupt halt and hoisted her messenger bag higher on her shoulder before turning on me with a huff. "What?"

"You're going to break your neck in those things." I squatted when I reached her and lifted one of her feet, forcing her to grab my shoulders for support.

"What are you doing? Get off of me, jackass!"

The first heel slipped off without much of a hitch, only because I'd caught her by surprise. I had to wrestle the other one off. She had cute feet, with the nails painted a racy red that matched her attitude.

"You expect me to walk barefoot? On a public sidewalk? Have you any idea how unsanitary that is?"

"Don't be such a chick. You can wash your feet when you get home. Come on."

She didn't budge. "Give me back my shoes."

"No."

"I'm not moving from this spot."

Another rumble of thunder sounded overhead. The rain would be here soon, and she was standing still with her arms crossed over her chest like a petulant child. If she wanted to act like a child, I supposed I should treat her like one.

With a frustrated growl, I turned my back toward her and stooped low. "Get on."

"What?"

"I said get on. I'll piggyback you."

"I am *not* getting on your back. Have you lost your mind?"

"Apparently. I volunteered to see you home, didn't I? No idea what possessed me to do that." When she still didn't move, I straightened and faced her. "Look, it's about to pour down rain, you refuse to walk barefoot, and I refuse to let you injure yourself in these things you call shoes. So for once in your life, be a fucking girl and let a man help you."

"Didn't you just tell me to stop being a chick?"

The growl that accompanied my glare must have been intimidating, because she uncrossed her arms in an act of concession. Only it wasn't concession at all. It was to point out what she thought to be obvious. "Maybe you didn't notice I'm not dressed for a piggyback ride?"

Oh, I'd noticed. I'd been noticing all day and all night. The constant donning of those damn high heels had done a sexy number on her calves and ass, but that was entirely beside the point at the moment, since she was being a huge pain in *my* ass.

"Pull up your fucking skirt and get on my fucking back so I can get you home before I lose my patience and my temper."

"Okay, fine! You don't have to be such a jerk about it."

For the sake of my own sanity, I ignored the last bit and instead gave her the shoes, which she yanked out of my hands. To my surprise, she was able to shut her trap long enough to use my shoulders to catapult herself up and onto my back.

Holy shit, but the warmth of her core on my spine sent wicked signals to my cock.

"You weigh a freakin' ton," I lied as I hoisted her into a more comfortable position, which didn't in the least help the issue growing in my pants. Neither did the way she wrapped her legs around my waist so that those calves were rubbing my junk.

She smacked the side of my head. "I do not, but thanks for not smelling like the douche you are."

"You're welcome. Which way?"

She pointed forward and then put her hand back on my chest.

Maybe it was all in my mind, but I could've sworn she was feeling me up. There were piggyback rides, and then there were piggyback rides. And it was the piggybackee that determined the difference. For one thing, there was the way she draped her arms over my shoulders to press her fingertips into my pecs instead of leaving them around my neck. And speaking of my neck: most riders managed to keep their chin on a piggybacker's shoulder so they could look forward, instead of burying their face in his neck and inhaling deeply.

Christ, she was still smelling me, and those luscious lips were there—not puckered, but definitely touching skin. When she sighed, I groaned. My faux pas was covered when a fat drop of rain landed on the bridge of my nose, and then another fell on my cheek, and then the top of my head, and then on my shoulder.

Cassidy started giggling. "Now what are you going to do, Shaw?" Her voice was sensual, a breathy dare at my ear. A shiver ran down my spine, but it was warm and nice, nothing like the chill she normally caused. Jesus, did she just nuzzle my neck?

Of all the parts of my body, my neck and ears were the most sensitive. If a woman knew what she was doing, her manipulation of them could be every bit as effective as doing the same things to my cock. Well, maybe not *every* bit as effective, but damn close.

Closing my eyes, I swallowed the lump forming in my throat and got myself under control. The part of my plan I'd been counting on was lost. I couldn't even make a run for it, because what had started out as a few drops had quickly turned into the downpour I'd known would hit us. Before I could formulate a new plan, Cassidy shimmied down my back and bolted down the dark alley to our right.

"Shit!" I ran after her, finally catching up as she ducked under a balcony that only barely shielded us from the rain, and I had to press up against her for even that much. "You wouldn't walk down a public sidewalk with bare feet, but you'll run into a dark alley?"

Cassidy looked up at me, her loose hair wet and sticking to her face like slivers of peach peel. "Drastic situations call for drastic measures." It hadn't escaped my notice that her skirt was still pushed up her thighs.

"Oh, yeah?" I leaned down to her ear. "So did you nuzzling my neck fall under drastic measures as well?"

"I did not nuzzle your neck!" she said, shoving me out into the rain. I laughed and stepped back to her, holding my ground when she tried to do it again.

Growling out her frustration, she turned to look toward the street. "This is all your fault!"

"My fault? How the hell is this my fault?"

"I could've been home by now if you hadn't taken my shoes."

"You're delusional."

"*I'm* delusional? Let me tell you what you are. You're a pompous, superficial ass who thinks he's smarter than everyone around him. So much so that you won't even consider for one second that someone who's been doing her job longer than you might actually be able to do that job better. You think you have all the answers, that you can't possibly learn anything more about—"

I grabbed her jaw in one hand and fisted her hair in the other, pulling back to force her face to tilt up. And then I kissed her.

The second she registered what was happening, she clamped her mouth shut. Her lips were stiff and unresponsive, but she wasn't pushing me away, and I'd come too far to back down without giving it my all. Dipping low at the knees, I pressed closer, the bulge in my pants finding her warm spot and doing a bit of nuzzling of its own. Cassidy jerked and gave a surprised sound, then settled back against me instead of protesting. With that small victory, my lips and tongue went to work, softly coaxing her into submission. When the fleshy fullness of her mouth became more pliant, I knew I'd succeeded.

Slowly, I backed off, still holding her in place so I could look down at her. A bolt of lightning streaked across the sky, illuminating her face and those wild green eyes. "Shut up," I said, and then I kissed her again before she could think to stop me.

Kissing was an art form, and if done properly, it told a person so much more than "I sort of dig you." My kisses were soft yet firm, with long, probing strokes from my tongue, gentle nips from my teeth, and lips that worshipped the flesh they were granted a taste of. A kiss like that told a person, "I want to devour you, and you're really going to like it when I do."

Though I'd planned to seduce Cassidy, I was surprised by how much I was enjoying the kiss. More surprising was the way Cassidy was kissing me back. It seemed I'd sparked her competitive nature once again. The woman was so damn infuriating. I allowed her to push her fingers through the hair at the nape of my neck because I liked that kind of shit, but when she tried to break free of my hold to maneuver into one more favorable to her own agenda, I shut it down. There was a flurry of hands and arms the split second I released her to grab both her wrists to pin her to the wall behind her. Cassidy narrowed her eyes at me, but something told me she wasn't really all that pissed. Maybe it was the way she looked up at me when she took her bottom lip between her teeth and slowly let it pull free. Or maybe it was the way the muscles in her body were coiled tight and ready to spring into action at the first slip of my hold. Or maybe it was the way she eyed my mouth, practically begging for another shot at it.

Though it was cruel, I leaned in and hovered over her lips. When she tilted her head up for another taste, I eased out of reach. "I kiss like I eat pussy."

Cassidy closed her eyes and groaned, all that strain melting from her muscles. But I had no intention of letting up on her, so I kissed her again, knowing she wouldn't be able to think of anything other than how that kiss would feel between her thighs.

Another bolt of lightning lit up the sky, this one with a brightness I could register even behind closed eyes. And if I needed further proof that the storm was picking up intensity, the echoing clap of thunder overhead was it. Mother Nature was not happy. Perhaps I should've seen her fury as an ominous sign to stop what I was doing, but I found the darkness of the night, the ire of the storm, and the cozy recess in which we'd found ourselves to be seductive. For all intents and purposes, we were within public view, but the deluge of rain had emptied the streets and given us enough privacy to be discreet.

And the way Cassidy was moving against me was all the permission I needed to keep going. And I wanted to see what she'd do, so I freed her hands.

Pulling the neckline of her shirt to the side, my lips found the pulse of the artery there. I nipped at her because I couldn't help myself, and she responded just the way I wanted. Her head tilted farther to the side and she wrapped her arms around my shoulders, pushing her fingers into my hair and urging me on.

Oh, Cassidy was not going to be the soft and gentle sort; nor did she really want that from her lover. This pleased me as well. I didn't get off on causing harm to women, but I did like for them to know who was in charge.

"Yeah, you like that, don't you?"

"No." The heaving of her chest and the way she was biting her lip told a different story.

I reached up and pulled her lip free, my thumb sweeping over the fleshy peach morsel before my fingers trailed down her chin, her neck, and then her collarbones.

"No? Hmm . . . that's weird. Because I could've sworn you

did. Let's see if you like this." With expert ease, I found her nipple and pinched it, rolling it between my thumb and forefinger. Then I dipped even farther, using my teeth to tug at the hardened peak through her wet shirt. She groaned and arched her back, pushing me closer still.

Through her soaked shirt, I could see her green bra. Nice, but it was in the way. Creamy mounds of flesh dipped into a delicate valley on her chest. Something told me her breasts were going to be fucking beautiful. In my enthusiasm to see for myself, I ripped her blouse open, sending buttons flying through the air.

Cassidy froze and looked down at what I'd done. "Really? You're such an asshole!"

"Want me to stop?" Without waiting for her answer, I took the weight of her breasts in my palms, kneading them through the silky softness of her bra.

"Did I say I wanted you to stop?"

The pad of my thumbs teased her hardened peaks. "I'm just asking to be polite."

"Oh, that's rich. You took my shoes, got me soaking wet in the rain, half naked with bare feet in a dirty, dark alley, and now you want to be polite?"

She had a point. So fuck it: I kept the momentum going by giving the cups of her bra a rough tug to get them out of my way. Damn, but my hunch was spot-on.

Her breasts weren't huge, but they were a handful and more than I could fit into my mouth, so I'd call that perfect. Her skin was pale, the sort of creamy pale that was common among red-heads, and her nipples were the same color as her lips, pink with a hint of peach. I palmed one breast while I gave a soft kiss to the taut bud of its twin. Cassidy inhaled sharply when I followed that up with the scrape of my teeth. My tongue wanted in on the action, so I sucked her nipple fully into my mouth and teased its raised peak with a series of flicks and licks. Pulling back, I squeezed her breast and let the pert bud pop free.

Cassidy arched again, her hand moving between us to yank at my shirt.

"What are you doing?"

"You're taking liberties. Why shouldn't I?"

It was cute. It was also about to get both of us into some serious trouble. Trouble I'd been seeking, true enough, but the reality was that we could never come back from this, so it was a risk we both needed to be willing to take. My little buddy jerked in my pants, telling me to stop thinking too much and let the woman have what she wanted.

"If you go below the belt, you're giving me permission to do the same." It was a fair warning.

"I'm curious," she said.

"About?"

"I want to see if you're as big in person as—" She stopped abruptly.

"As what?"

"As all the women in the office say you are."

I drew my head back. "Really? How big do they say I am?"

"Big."

"Hmm, I hate to disappoint you, but the truth is, none of them would actually know." I never mixed business with pleasure, though it seemed I was hell-bent on breaking all the rules with Cassidy to make sure I won the partnership. But was it really just about the partnership? I shook the thought free because I couldn't afford to think like that.

Taking her hand, I maneuvered it between us until she was cupping the bulge in my pants that had grown to astronomical proportions. "That should give you a pretty good idea, but you won't know for sure until you see it up close and personal." With just the right amount of pressure, my hand moved back and forth over hers so that we were both stroking me through my pants while Cassidy watched. "And if you want to see it, you're going to have to take it out yourself."

There was a hint of something devious in the way she looked up at me from beneath thick lashes. "You don't think I will?"

I rolled her nipple under my other palm, but kept her locked in my stare. "No, I don't."

Cassidy slipped her hand out from under mine, and her fingers worked my belt loose. She was bluffing. No way did I believe she would follow through. That was, until she did. The button was the next to go, and then her cold hand dipped inside my pants to fondle my cock.

"Christ!" I bent and nipped her neck again, earning another moan of approval as I undulated against her palm. In her excitement, she squeezed my cock, but it was the kind of squeeze I really liked.

When I'd worked my way up her neck and to her ear, I whispered, "But you still can't see it."

The woman was so predictable. Issue a little challenge and she would rise to meet it.

Cassidy unzipped my wet pants before pushing them over my hips and halfway down my ass, which was plenty far enough to allow my cock to spring free. Oh, God. The release into the cold air was heavenly, and the only thing missing was the weight of her stare. I wanted her to see me.

I was in fuck-the-rain mode then, and stepped back so she could get a good look. Rain soaked every stitch of clothing I was wearing, but I didn't give a shit. It was worth it to relish the hungry look in her eyes when she took me in. The man-eater was starving for a taste, and I was going to offer up my cock as a willing sacrifice.

"Well?"

"Impressive," she said, taking it in her hands and stroking me. If she'd had any idea how much I liked that, she probably would've stopped, so I kept my composure, to the best of my ability. "Nice and veiny . . . smooth and thick."

I laughed. "Oh, so now you're a cock connoisseur?"

"I gave you a compliment, Shaw. Take it. I don't give them often."

She pulled me in closer, so that the head of my cock touched the exposed skin of her stomach with each down stroke of her hand. My bowed head gave me an excellent view of the expert way she worked me. Damn, I wanted her. And not even just to seduce her. I wanted to fuck her, because if she rode a cock anywhere close to the way she was jacking mine, I was in for quite the experience.

Still stroking me, she used her other hand to pull me down to kiss her again. Only I couldn't take credit for that kiss. It was all Cassidy, which made my balls ache and my cock even more rigid. Her tongue took over, stroking mine with the same intensity as her hand on my cock, until I thought I couldn't take the sensation anymore. I'd heard she was a multitasker extraordinaire, and this bit was proof positive of that.

And then my hand found its way under her skirt to her abdomen and inside her panties. The groan I gave when I felt how wet she was for me was unscripted, but my exploration of her tender flesh was not. I fucking loved the warm, wet glide of my fingers through the silky flesh of a woman's most intimate parts. I loved even more the way Cassidy clung to me and moaned when I teased her clit and then dipped my fingers inside her.

Damn, she was tight. So tight my cock nearly exploded. There would be no slow and gentle here. Nothing about the two of us would ever be slow and gentle. This was about exploitation, a means to an end—an opportunity for me to gain the upper hand and put Cassidy in her place. At least that was what I'd kept telling myself.

Pulling my fingers free, I stroked her again, massaging her clit until she was on the brink and then thrusting them back inside her. Cassidy's head fell back, her eyes and chin set in defiance even as her thighs parted wider. There still wasn't enough room to do the job adequately. She was already pissed over the blouse, so fuck it; I ripped her goddamn panties off, too.

Her mouth opened to say something, but I cut the bitching off when I stole her breath on the return to business. And I showed zero mercy on the fast and hard. The clench of her walls around my fingers and the choking squeeze of her hand around my cock were excruciating and glorious at the same time. Fuck, I'd known she'd like it rough.

"Oh, yeah. That's it right there, isn't it?" I growled.

She couldn't answer. Hell, it didn't even look like she was breathing. Maybe that was because she was on the verge of coming. I could feel her bearing down, practically smell her arousal in the air, and the charge arcing between us had nothing to do with the electricity from the storm.

My cock was forgotten when Cassidy opted for the hard grip on my shoulders instead. I bit her lip because I knew she liked it, and I pushed my fingers in to the knuckles, stroking the rough patch I found deep inside with a beckoning. And then the pulsing began.

Cassidy broke our kiss and buried her face against my neck, gifting me with the throaty sound of her orgasm. If she hadn't been at my ear, I never would've heard it, and damn, I would've been missing out. Never had any woman sounded so innocent and wicked at the same time. How the fuck could I have possibly gotten harder? Her moan was like an aphrodisiac, and I wasn't quite ready for it to stop. So, I switched back to the thrusting, harder and faster until I could feel the quake it sent through her body, and she kept coming. Over and over again.

The folds of her pussy would be swollen and tinged red from the ferocity of my finger fuck. Good. I hoped any discomfort she felt in the morning would serve as a reminder of who'd given her the pleasure that had accompanied it.

And then I stopped, allowing her to catch her breath. Normally, I'd want some reciprocation, but tonight, I was all about the giving. After all, if she got it good enough, she'd fall all over herself to get it again. Which meant she'd slip in other places as well.

"Are you afraid of heights?" She barely managed a shake of her head. "Good," I said and then squatted, taking her left leg and draping it over my shoulder. Looking up at her confused expression, I smirked. "Better hold on."

If she was confused before, I'd say she was stupefied when I braced for her weight and did the same with her right leg, forcing her skirt up and around her waist. She clutched my head when I stood, lifting her into the air for a reverse shoulder ride.

When I settled her back against the building, she suddenly found her voice. "Are you freakin' crazy? What are you doing? Put me—"

I loved stunning her to silence, and I did it once again when my face found its way to that juicy little pussy of hers to lavish it with my mouth. I would've stopped to check that her silence wasn't an indicator of distress if the way she fisted my hair at the roots and moved against my mouth hadn't clued me in that she was better than fine. In fact, I'd say she was fucking excellent. And I wasn't complaining, either. The taste of Cassidy was exquisite on my tongue. She was soft and wet, her clit eager for the attention I gave. And hell yeah, I gave it, coaxing the hardened pebble to another orgasm. When her thighs tightened around my head and her nails scraped my scalp as she straightened against the wall to push her lower half closer, I knew she was there.

I lapped at the silky cream of her release, and my eyes drifted shut at the surprising sweetness that exploded onto my tongue. I'd pegged her for sour. Or, at the very least, stale. But everything about her, from her plump lips to her pert breasts, her voluptuous ass, and her juicy pussy, was fresh as the rain that kissed the parched streets of Southern California.

It made my goddamn cock leak.

Careful not to scratch her on the brick, I stepped back from the building and let her legs slide down until they were snug in the crooks of my arms. Slowly lowering her, I stopped when all that hot and juicy was level with my groin. With a bit of adjustment, my cock was nestled in her folds and I was moving against her.

"Are you done?" I asked, teasing her clit and then her opening with pressure from the tip. "Or do you want more, Cassidy?"

"More." She used my shoulders and the wall behind her for leverage, angling her body to take the head inside herself. Jesus, even the heat of her on the tip of my cock was incredible, but dammit, she wasn't calling the shots, so I pulled out.

"That's not how this works, woman."

"I took sex ed. I'm pretty sure it is."

"That's not what I'm talking about."

"You don't want to fuck me?"

"Oh, I want to fuck you. I just want to hear you say you want to fuck me, first."

"Because that's not clear to you right now?"

God, there was that smart mouth again. I chuckled humorlessly and then spread my arms wider, forcing her legs to do the same. With an unapologetic thrust, I entered her.

We both moaned at the sensation of the stretch and fill

because, damn, she was tight and I was thick, so it felt fucking amazing. The instinctual need to feel all of her urged me to plow forward, but I was careful to go slow. I didn't want to hurt her. Not just because I wasn't the douche bag she thought me to be, but because then we'd have to stop and I really wanted to see if she could take all of me.

Cassidy's mouth fell open, that bottom lip of hers quivering, and I realized that she must be cold. Though it wasn't freezing outside, the rain had had a cooling effect on the temperature and we were wet, so the wind from the storm was having its way with that. I felt it, too, but it was a fair trade-off for the warm and moist I was receiving. Especially when the warm and moist was wrapped tight around my cock.

Body heat was all I had to offer, and though I hated Cassidy and shouldn't care about her comfort, my cock was buried deep inside her and I wanted to keep it that way. Using my whole body, I covered her, even taking that quivering lip into my mouth with a slow suckle. Friction was another generator of heat, so I increased my pace. She should have been acclimated to my size and able to take it by then. Still, I paid attention to any sign that would indicate she wasn't. When I found none, I fucked her.

I fucked her like she needed to be fucked.

I fucked her like she wanted to be fucked.

Cassidy clung to my shoulders as I widened my stance and bent at the knees. Deep thrusts worked her G-spot while my groin kissed her clit with each roll of my hips. And then she bit me. Fucking hard. It would leave a mark, but then again, I'd marked her pussy with the finger bang. Still, just to be sure, and because her perceived tit for tat couldn't go without answer, I spread her wider again and thrust into her with enough force to move her up the wall of the building. She'd be feeling that in the morning, too.

"Oh, God," she moaned. "You're a fucking dick."

"Potty mouth," I said, still thrusting hard. "Maybe I should take my cock out of your pussy and fuck your dirty mouth instead."

Cassidy moaned. Oh, hell yeah. Miss Prim and Proper liked the dirty talk.

The sound of a sliding door being opened on the balcony above preceded the voices. "It's really coming down. Come look at this, honey," a female voice said.

Cassidy went stiff, her eyes wide when she looked up and then back at me. I kept going, kept thrusting and rolling my hips until the fear in her eyes turned back to lust. My teeth were at her neck again, nipping with each thrust. This time, Cassidy's moan was loud because she fucking loved it.

"What was that sound?" the woman above us asked.

"Shh," I whispered in Cassidy's ear. "They'll hear you. Or is that what you want? Do you want them to see you getting fucked by the man you hate most in the world, Cassidy?"

Her nails dug into my back and she bit my shoulder again, stifling her moan. Oh, I think she did. She wanted them to see her getting fucked in a dirty alley in the pouring rain like the naughty girl she was.

"It's just the thunder, Marie. Come back inside before you get struck by lightning with all that foil in your hair."

"Do you want Marie to go?" I asked Cassidy. "I could call her name so that she looks over the railing."

"Oh, God," she whispered, and then the walls of her pussy gripped me, squeezing hard with a pressure that pulsated. Cassidy came hard on my cock, her face turning toward my neck once more to let out her cry.

"Christ, woman," I groaned, pounding into her and letting

the milking sensation bring me to orgasm as well. My arms were shaking, and my balls were drawing tight. Damn, I needed my release. So I took it, but I was smart about it.

I never came inside a woman. Not only because I didn't want to be in "baby daddy" territory but also because the act was too damn intimate. So when I felt the rocket fuel gearing up for blast-off, I pulled back and turned my hips, grunting out my ejaculation on her thigh instead.

Holy shit, but the creamy softness of that nook in her thigh was almost as pleasurable as her pussy. Almost. And I'd made a mess of it. Oh well. I'd given her multiple orgasms, even taking one into my mouth; the least she could do was clean up one of mine in return.

"Put me down," she ordered, back in full Cassidy form.

"Are you sure you can walk after that?" I asked, having earned the right to be conceited. And she damn well knew it.

"I think I can manage."

Once again, her mouth had to go and ruin a good thing. She didn't deserve my kindness, but I set her down easy anyway—getting off always put me in a good mood. The rain still poured down.

The first thing she did was tug her bra back into place, and then she took off her blouse to clean up my mess. Since I'd ruined her shirt, I took mine off and handed it to her; then I got busy putting myself back together again as well. I wasn't really concerned with how I looked—there was no hope for that—but public indecency was a punishable crime I didn't want to be charged with.

"If you ever speak of this," Cassidy said, pulling her skirt back into place, "I will deny it emphatically."

I bent over and picked up her shoes, handing them to her.

"Darlin', you're going to have to do better than a fuck in an alley to get me to defame my character like that."

Her head snapped up, the insult to her ego making her pale skin blotch with anger and maybe even a little embarrassment.

She was damn good. Probably the best fuck I'd had in years. But she was still the opposition, and I never gave the opposition the upper hand. Especially when the opposition was a bitch.

Snatching the shoes from me, she slipped them on with a huff. "Oh, it will never happen again." She took a step to leave, then braced her hand against the wall, finding her legs wobbly.

Yes, it would.

I smirked and simply said, "Okay."

Once she regained her balance, she walked out to the street and turned to the right. I followed her, lagging a bit behind. I wasn't sure how far we had to go to get to her place, but I was for damn sure going to see her to her door after what we'd just done. When she walked up to the entrance of the building I'd just fucked her against, I was confused.

"What are you doing?" I asked.

"I'm going home. You weren't expecting a good-night kiss, were you?"

And then it was clear. Cassidy could have run inside her building when it had started to rain, but she hadn't. Instead, she'd taken the soaking and run barefoot down a dirty alley. Why? Had she wanted what we'd done to happen?

"Not in the least."

"Good. Because I'm pretty sure what you just got back there was more than sufficient."

She didn't say anything else. She simply walked inside and left me half naked and soaking wet on the sidewalk, wondering who'd just played whom.

CHAPTER 6
Cassidy

I lived for weekends. Saturday nights, in particular. And not for the hippest clubs offered up by one of the trendiest cities in the country. No, I was sort of anti . . . well, all of that. For me, Friday evenings were spent recuperating from the long week, and Sundays were spent preparing for the next, but Saturday was my day to do nothing whatsoever. And I had the perfect place to do it; an escape, and I didn't even have to travel far to get it.

Living on the top floor of a twenty-story apartment building in the heart of San Diego had its advantages. Best of all was the view from the rooftop balcony Quinn and I shared. That was where I kept a crappy little garden, where I'd botched every bit of gardening advice given to me by Ma and, instead, only managed to torture Mother Nature's seedlings until they were wilted and in need of some serious herbal CPR. Within a couple of months of moving in, I'd switched to greenery that was nearly impossible to kill, and so far, the plants had been hanging in there, but the prognosis wasn't good.

My rooftop was also where I'd come to watch the sun play its magnificent tricks on the water of the bay. In the evenings, it morphed from a deep sea blue to liquid silver to hues of gold and

chocolate or pinks and oranges at sunset, until finally the reflection of the sun was replaced by those of the city lights dancing
across a canvas of pitch black. But neither the private garden nor
the view of the bay was what made my rooftop a sanctuary.

It was the sky. Always the sky for me. For as long as I could
remember.

Stonington, Maine, was a fishing village with a population of
just over a thousand. If you lived there, it was because you were
born there. You fished lobster or worked the docks, gave your
neighbor the shirt off your back, and loved your country with
a passion that ran soul-deep. It was small-town America, a place
where everybody knew your name and you couldn't get away
with jack squat without someone running to tell your da and ma.
So there were days when Casey and I would sneak away to our
secret spot on the roof of my house. It was this cute little alcove
between the pitches that gave us just enough room to hide out
and still have a spectacular view of the harbor. Every time Casey
and I disappeared, our parents would read us the riot act for wandering so far from home. We never told them we'd been right
above them the whole time.

Casey and I would sit for hours on that roof, just watching
the clouds and making up stories to go with the shapes we found
there. I was the best at that part. Most of my stories were funny
and some of them were even pretty epic, but then there were also
the romantic tales. Those were the ones when Casey would touch
my hand and look at me like nothing else in the world mattered.
Like there was only him and me and those clouds and nothing
else. I suppose at the time, there wasn't.

That small stretch of time when the sun disappeared and twilight turned to dusk was when we sat quiet, like we were both
holding our breath and waiting for the last sliver of sun to fade
from the sky. Then dusk turned to night and the stars took center

stage. That was where Casey had shined. I'd been in awe of his stories, and the reflection of the stars in Casey's baby blues as he'd told me about the hero Perseus sitting atop his flying Pegasus as he rescued Andromeda from the sea monster was a sight that would forever be burned into my memory. He'd known everything there was to know about stars. Though he'd never admit to it if I'd asked, he'd been skipping his homework so he could learn about them just to impress me. Because he knew I'd loved them. I still did.

The stars weren't the same in San Diego. They weren't as bright, and if they were twinkling, they lacked the luster and sparkle of the ones back home. The one constant, though, was the moon. I could always count on it to be there, to be the brightest thing anyone could see in the night sky, no matter where they were. The same moon I was seeing was the same moon Casey would be looking at as well. I'd talked to that moon like writing in a diary, pretending that somehow, Casey could hear me through it. Sometimes, all the comfort I'd needed was to believe that somewhere on the other side, 3,258 miles away, Casey might have been talking to me, too.

Casey Michaels knew me better than anyone else ever could. The epitome of a lobster fisherman, he was six foot one, 180 pounds, usually wearing a T-shirt and flannel button-up, with sandy blond hair, blue eyes, a scruffy face, and a slight bow to his blue-jean-clad legs. His steel-toed boots carried a mighty man who worked every bit as hard as his father and his father before him. Casey was nothing if not traditional, a legacy, and he was my hero. He'd also been my best friend and my constant partner in crime from the first day either of us could cognitively recognize the other.

Our mothers had been best friends before us. Those two had done everything together. They'd flirted with the boys down by the docks together, gotten married on the same day to the two lucky fellows that had fallen madly for them (also on the same day), and had even gotten pregnant at the same time. Their friendship had begun on the day they'd met and realized that both of their first names started with the same letter. So Abby had named her son Casey, and Anna had named her daughter Cassidy. They were like sisters in every way. And even though Casey and I had been raised like siblings, we'd never felt that way. Our connection was something else entirely, something foreign that no one else could touch. Which was a good thing, because that would've made things extremely awkward when we'd started dating, even more so when we'd lost our virginity to each other.

Casey was all I'd ever known, and I'd loved him for my entire life. He knew my secrets and my fears, and I trusted him more than anyone else on the face of the planet. He was an extension of myself, and although we'd never defined what we were to each other, there had never seemed to be a need to. Whatever we'd had, we'd always have it. But then I'd left him all alone.

Whether or not I'd go to college had never been a question in my mind. That was, until I'd started to receive acceptance letters from all over the country. I remembered the look on Casey's face when I'd gotten the first one. We'd both been excited. In fact, he'd picked me up and swung me around until I'd thought the resulting dizziness might get the best of me. And that kiss he'd laid on me. The memory of it still made my lips tingle to this day. But then reality was like the Jaws of Life prying us apart the moment Ma said, "My little girl is leaving home," and we realized . . . I was leaving home.

Casey's grades hadn't been spectacular, even though I'd tried to tutor him. But none of that had mattered because he'd always known, *we'd* always known, that he would follow in his father's footsteps. He'd be a fisherman, which meant he couldn't come with me. And I couldn't stay.

Boston College had been my choice because it was close enough to Stonington to allow me to go home for every break. Still, it had been an expensive education, and Da and Ma had sunk every dime they'd had into it and then some. Lobster fishermen earned an honest living, but it was the sort of check that only just got our family by from year to year. The extra expense of my education, including law school, had cost Ma the savings she'd been setting aside to open a bed-and-breakfast. She'd sacrificed her dream so that I could have mine. So when it came time to look for a job, I took the position at SSE. It was a gazillion miles away from Casey, but it was the only offer at the time that afforded me the ability to give back to Ma what she and my da had sacrificed. Now Ma had her bed-and-breakfast, but Stonington, Maine, didn't rank high on the tourism list, so she was spending more to keep the Whalen House running than she was bringing in. The regular checks I sent back home relieved the strain on Da's wallet and let Ma continue to live her dream.

When I'd left for college, I'd told Casey I'd be back, and he'd told me he'd always be waiting. We'd kept the promises we'd made, but after school, my trips home dwindled down to a week at Christmas and another during the summer. For the past couple of years, the summer trips had fallen off; I simply had too much work to do. I couldn't afford a vacation when my clients needed me.

But for those few days when I was home, Casey and I had picked right back up where we'd left off. Like the teenagers we'd once been, Casey would steal one of Abby's hand-sewn quilts, lace his fingers through mine, and practically drag me down to the docks. In the dark of night, we'd sneak aboard Thomas Michaels's boat and into the cabin for some quality naked time. Most of my trips home had been spent with Casey between my thighs, like we were trying to catch up on all the fucking we'd missed out on over the past year and squirrel away some for the next year to come. Inevitably, I had to say goodbye again.

And each time I had, my heart had broken a little more. Eventually, we had to be the grown-ups we'd become and admit that things were no longer working the way they were. We'd officially ended the relationship, giving each other the freedom we both ultimately wanted, to see where life would take us. But we knew we'd always be lifelong friends, and if fate ever brought us back together, maybe we could try it again.

Per his normal Saturday night routine, Quinn poked his head through the balcony door and paused the phone conversation he'd been having long enough to say, "Hey, Cass. I'm home," before proceeding on. Or so I thought. Until he suddenly stopped dead in his tracks, backed up two steps and angled the phone away from his mouth again, and said, "Hold on. Who have you been f'ing?"

"What?"

Quinn put the phone back to his mouth. "Yes, girl, she has been F'ed."

"What are you talking about?"

Tilting the phone down again, he turned back to me. "Demi wants to know who it was."

"Who was what?"

"Don't play with me, Cassidy Whalen. *Whose dick have you had inside you?*" he enunciated. "Did you understand that?"

Yeah, not going to answer that one, I thought. I put on my best "you're crazy" face and scoffed. "Me? Having sex? Pfft, I wish!"

Quinn looked me over suspiciously, and then his expression eased. "False alarm," he said, resuming his conversation. "Something must be wrong with my Spidey senses. I'm usually always right, but she's looking just as constipated as always. She *needs* to get laid. When's Christmas?"

I should've been insulted, but I was too busy being relieved that I'd managed to pull off the fake-out. Quinn really was good at detecting that sort of thing, but I didn't want anyone, even my best friends, to know what I'd done with Shaw. They could keep a secret, so that wasn't the issue. The problem was that I knew they'd be able to tell how much I'd liked it. And I'd been trying to lie to myself about that part.

Sex with Shaw wasn't like sex with Casey. I don't know that I'd say it was better, just that it was . . . different. Casey had always been loving and gentle, but Shaw was rough and dirty. He'd found my weakness with the savage way he'd scraped his teeth along my hypersensitive skin. And the things he'd said, that sound he'd made when he'd first felt how wet I was for him . . .

His moan had been the sort of sound that was just on the edge of a growl, a tortured groan of wonder and approval. He'd been pleased by my body's reaction, and the knowledge of that was quite satisfactory. The sudden warming of my skin now had nothing to do with the air around me. I squirmed in my chaise lounge from the memory that caressed my brain and sent pleasure signals down my spine, and was reminded of the soreness left in the wake of his sexual fury. Jesus, why had that turned me on?

I'd like to say that I'd made a bad decision while under the influence, but I'd be lying. I'd known exactly what I was doing. Though I wished like hell that drunken disorderly conduct had been the case. At least then I would've had a viable excuse as to why I'd made out like a streetwalker in a cootie-infested alley in the middle of the pouring rain. The fact that it had actually been raining in Southern California should've been enough reason for me to take cover, but no . . . I'd fucked in it. And worse, I'd fucked Shaw Matthews in it.

What was next on the seven plagues of the Apocalypse list? Locusts? Frogs? Blood on the moon?

Maybe it had been the best sex of my life, but hell would freeze over, pigs would fly, and frogs would grow hair before I would ever admit that to Shaw Matthews.

God, I hope none of those is a plague. I needed to find a church and a confessional. Fast.

That was the good little Catholic schoolgirl in me speaking.

The naughty little Catholic schoolgirl in me—oh, the irony—was still basking in her postcoital bliss while conspiring with my cooch on how we could make round two happen. I had a feeling liquid courage wouldn't be needed the second time around, but it had sure helped last night. Holy Mary, Mother of God. I'd nuzzled his neck! I'd pulled his freakin' cock out! The only bit of redemption I had was that at least I hadn't put it in my mouth.

But I'd wanted to. And I was pretty sure Shaw wouldn't have stopped me, either.

I might have instigated things, but he'd been right on board, issuing his dares and challenges. He must have thought I was stupid, that I didn't understand that he was throwing down the gauntlet just because he knew I couldn't resist picking it up. And the only reason he'd do that would be if he'd wanted me every bit as badly as I'd wanted him.

But why now, all of a sudden? That was another puzzler, wasn't it?

I cocked my head to the side and stared up into the vastness of space. "What's your angle, Matthews?" The neurons in my brain must have been putting on one heck of a light show as I scrambled to figure it out, but the answer to my question wasn't written in the stars.

"I'm out," Quinn said from the doorway.

I shook myself from my stupor and turned to him. "Where are you headed?"

"Daddy's back from his business trip, but his wifey thinks he won't be back until Monday morning," he said with a mischievous grin. "Demi and Sasha are already at Monkey Business. You going?"

"Nah. I think I'll just hang out here. I've got some work to do, anyway."

"On a Saturday night?" he asked, then rolled his eyes. "Typical. Okay, well you just stay here with your moon and stars and your laptop and your pie charts or your moonpie chart of the stars or whatever. But real life is happening down on Earth, Cass. Not up in space. It's dark, lonely, and cold up there. I recommend you snuggle up to a nice hot body. That's what I'm about to do."

"Stars are hot."

"They're also full of gas."

"And Daddy isn't?"

"Well, yeah, but I can snuggle him. You can't snuggle a star."

I could argue further on semantics alone, but I understood the point he was making. Nothing was keeping me from Monkey Business other than the fact that I wasn't ready to face Shaw, and I knew he'd be there. The weekend would be my buffer. Surely by the end of it, the shock of what we'd done would have worn off.

"Have fun with Daddy, and don't do anything I wouldn't do," I said, turning back around and relaxing in my chair.

"If that's not a contradictory statement, I don't know what is," he mumbled, and then I heard him walk away. The front door opened and closed with a click of the lock, and I was alone.

Alone was good. No distractions meant I could get more done, think a little more clearly. Though if recent memory served me correctly, my stupid brain weaving its wicked thoughts in my subconscious and then conscious mind was exactly the distraction that had gotten me into the mess in which I currently found myself in the first place.

I just needed the weekend. One full weekend of no Shaw and

then I'd be ready to face him on Monday. I rested my head against the chair and closed my eyes to enjoy the solitude, but I quickly opened them again when a deluge of images depicting Shaw's fuckface converged on my peaceful tranquillity.

Dammit. What had I done?

The past fifty-three hours had been torturous at best. Not that I was counting. And I'd been asleep for over half that time. The peaceful weekend I'd hoped for had been riddled with thoughts of Shaw, Shaw, and more Shaw. Oh, and Shaw's cock. And mouth. And fingers, too.

Quinn had spent the weekend in some luxurious location with Daddy, so I'd had nothing to take my mind off what I'd dubbed the worst mistake of my life. Left alone, I'd discovered that my crazy thoughts turned to crazy actions. So if all I'd been thinking about was frolicking naked in the rain with a man who liked to give reverse shoulder rides, some frustrations had been bound to build up. I'd felt forced to relieve some of those frustrations by any means necessary, and really, there'd only been one way. To my credit, I'd honestly thought masturbating would be like killing two birds with one stone. Not only would it get rid of the perpetual ache in my nether region but also, perhaps, I'd finally be able to stop the insanity and get off the Shaw Matthews loop-de-loop.

That line of thinking had led to something like a dozen orgasms over two days. See? Crazy begets crazy, and I was begetting it all over the place. I'd even tried to swap the image of Shaw for one of Casey, but that devious bastard had kept creeping back into my fantasies like a demonic horror movie that refused to let me get any peace.

If his haunting presence over the weekend had been any indication, he was going to be just as impossible to get rid of in the physical sense.

Rosary beads, holy water, and salt along the perimeter of my office were probably the only things that would work. If only I'd thought of that an hour before, I would've had time for the pit stop. Well, I had time, but not if I was going to avoid an egocentric with cause to be arrogant. He'd be insufferable, and I couldn't handle that so soon after. As it was, I'd already forgone my coveted morning coffee stop so I wouldn't accidentally bump into him, the stalker. I mean, what would I say? Worse, what would *he* say?

Stepping off the elevator and then into my office suite, I saw my hopes of avoiding him go straight out the window. Shaw was perched on the corner of Ally's empty desk with a cup of coffee in each hand and an arrogant smile on his face. Really, I wanted to punch him in the throat. I'd made it a point to get there before everyone else, including Ally, and he'd still beat me. Again.

Shaw Matthews was Beelzebub himself.

"Good morning, Whalen. I'm glad to see you're walking okay." He smirked. "I can hardly tell you were royally fucked a mere three days ago. What's your secret?"

Dammit. My heart became animated, its arteries morphing into arms with hands that rattled its cage. Before, his presence had irked me and made me want to slam his face into the wall. Now it made me feel exposed. Not the kind of exposed that might make one feel naked in a roomful of strangers but the kind of exposed where a girl was glad to be rid of her clothes because that meant being one step closer to going at it like gorillas in the wild.

It took a great deal of effort, but I managed to get it together, determined not to let him see me sweat. Or breathe hard. Or mount him like a Catholic schoolgirl on spring break.

"It really is inhumane to be tortured so early in the morning" was my witty retort. And it had come in the nick of time, within the allotted space for such a remark without it looking suspiciously like I'd been affected by his presence. So, feeling the high from that small victory, I rolled with it. For all Shaw knew, the last time we'd seen each other was a very distant memory, one that had meant nothing at all to me. He'd been mediocre at best. I could pull that off, couldn't I?

"Tortured. Funny. Here," he said, handing one of the cups in my direction.

I scoffed. "Good idea. Poison should put me out of my misery."

"It's a grande three-Splenda white chocolate mocha," he said, as if I should know what that meant. I did. It was my normal drink order. Entirely too specific for him to have guessed it. Maybe I hadn't been far off the mark on my original stalker theory.

"When you took off like a bat out of hell from the coffee shop the other morning, Tiff said you were a regular. So I asked her what you normally ordered and decided to be a human and bring it to you." He pushed it toward me again. I wasn't going to accept it, but then I smelled the white chocolate and my pride was damned.

"Thank you," I said, taking the cup. "Have a good day." That was all the nicety he was going to get from me.

Opening my office door, I walked inside and set the cup and my messenger bag down, then started going through the mail left on my desk from Friday afternoon. Free coffee or not, I was in no mood for his bullshit.

Undeterred by my intended rudeness, Shaw and his smart mouth followed me. "So did you happen to talk to Rockford over the weekend?"

Right. Apparently, he felt like our little tryst qualified as something more. That definitely needed to be nipped in the bud. "First coffee, now small talk? I'm sorry, but did I miss the memo where we're pals now? It was a one-night stand. Get over it."

"I'd rather you were under me."

Lame. I laughed at his failed attempt. "You're such a guy."

Shaw sighed. "Must we always be at war?" His voice was fraudulently sincere, but then again, I'm sure he meant it to be.

I didn't want to play anymore, and he certainly wasn't taking the hint, so I had to hit him where it hurt. "Yes, needle dick, we must."

Shaw chuckled. It sort of made me want to laugh at my own joke, too, but I didn't. "Needle dick? I believe the word you used Friday night was *impressive*."

"I was drunk. Everything looks bigger through beer goggles."

He set his coffee cup down and stuck his hands in his pockets. "Oh, so that's how you want to play this?"

"Play what? I'm not playing anything." I was acutely aware of the fact that I'd been cycling the same pieces of mail through my hands in an attempt to keep up the façade of boredom.

"Right. You want to act like what we did only happened because you were drunk, but you and I both know that's not true. You weren't drunk. It happened because you wanted it to happen. I wanted it to happen. And no one but you and I will ever know about it, so you don't have to pretend you didn't like it."

"Whatever you need to tell yourself to feel good about your less than stellar performance," I said without even looking at him. A move that was sure to piss him off. Good.

"Wow. I certainly would've thought the massive orgasms I so generously bestowed upon you would have at least melted three inches off that glacier of an ass attached to your backside. Guess I was wrong. It happens. Not often, but still . . ."

"Are you saying I have a big ass, Matthews?" I quipped back. "Because I'm pretty sure you weren't complaining when you had two handfuls of it, trying to get your rocks off inside me."

"Not inside you. On you. There's a difference."

From the corner of my eye, I saw him stand. I was relieved that he'd decided to leave, because I didn't know how much faster my heart could beat without exploding in my chest or whatever. But that saying about what happens when you assume hadn't come about for no reason. Shaw hadn't stood to leave at all. Instead, he walked across the room to the door and shut it, locking it as well.

"What do you think you're doing?" The accelerated heart rate took a backseat to the blood boiling in my veins. He was taking liberties in *my* office, the jackass.

Shaw didn't say anything. He just stalked toward me with a shit-eating grin and a spark of something naughty in his eyes. Oh, bloody hell. I was so going to lose this game.

"Did you think about me over the weekend?" He was still coming at me; I hadn't even realized that for every step he took forward, I was taking one back in retreat.

I did my best to keep my voice from shaking, though I was pretty sure I failed miserably. "Pfft! You wish. I hate to break it to you, Matthews, but you weren't that good." I was a liar, liar, pants on fire. Though in truth, my pants—or skirt, rather—only felt like it was on fire because of the blazing hot juices that were pooling in my panties.

In the meantime, my archnemesis/best lay of my life was still advancing, and my back was to the floor-to-ceiling window with nowhere left to go. I liked it.

Shaw cocked his head and looked me over, his eyes sweeping down the length of my body and then stopping to stare right at my crotch. God, could he sense it? When his tongue ran along the inside of his bottom lip and then his teeth scraped across the tender flesh, I started to think maybe he could.

"Mm-hmm. See, I think I was. I think you thought about how my thick cock stretched and filled you, how I expertly worked your pussy with my mouth, and how good your orgasm felt as it pulsed around my cock."

His strong arms caged me, the window at my back cutting off any possible escape route, and then we were flush. The heat of his body was a delicious contrast to the chill of the glass, and God, he smelled good, but I was determined to stand my ground in hopes that his little play would backfire and force him to wave the white flag. Instead, I could feel the rigid lines of the muscles on his chest, and my traitorous nipples hardened at the sensation of the warm skin beneath his shirt and the smooth length of his neck, which begged for my tongue.

He leaned in and spoke against my ear. "Are you wet for me now?"

Holy Jesus . . .

I set my chin indignantly, an attempt to fake him out. It might have worked if actual words of denial had accompanied the action.

His hand drifted down to my hip, and he pulled me closer. "You want to do it again. You want to fuck me and be fucked by me. I know because I've seen the erotic woman you really are. You can't fake that, Cassidy. I can smell it from a mile away. I can smell you." And then he nipped at my lobe.

Goose bumps broke out all over my body. Oh, my God . . . the things that man said and did. Bedroom talk aside, there was something carnal about the whole nipping and teeth-scraping thing. I wasn't the sort that got off on pain, and I had no desire to be bitten so hard that the skin broke. No, for me, it was the act itself. A show of dominance, and though I was a woman who was well in control of her life and every aspect of it, for the first time, I wanted to let go. Not to be tied up and used strictly for his pleasure but to, for once, not have to be the one in control.

I was sure he knew it. Which meant he was up to something.

"You're a cheating bastard." I have no idea how I managed to eke out the words, but I did.

Shaw chuckled. "Rule number one: Know your opponent's

weaknesses and never hesitate to exploit them to gain the upper hand."

He had me there. It was so textbook. "And what's your weakness?"

Another chuckle. His breath carried the aroma of creamy coffee mixed with a hint of mint. It was divine. "Getting lazy on me? I thought you had a thing for the intense research of your subject."

"You say that like I want to study you. I don't."

"One of the many differences between you and me is that I can at least be honest with myself. And you, too, for that matter. For example, I can admit that I jacked my dick raw thinking about you this weekend. Want to know why?"

My knees nearly buckled at the imagery, but I didn't falter. "I couldn't care less."

"I call that bullshit." Shaw bent at the knees and then rubbed his length against me. He was hard. Dammit. "I couldn't stop thinking about how unbelievably tight your pussy was. I squeezed my dick and squeezed it"—he rolled his hips with each "squeezed"—"and I still couldn't simulate that same tightness."

My hands were now fists at my sides, straining with the effort not to let them unfurl. I wanted to grab his ass and help him get closer. Hell, I wanted to pull up my skirt, release his cock, and use his shoulders to hoist myself up and onto it. But that would've been a gross betrayal of my sensibilities. I was losing control, and that simply wasn't acceptable.

The picture frame on the corner of my desk caught my attention, and guilt sucker-punched me in the gut. Again. But something was different about it. I realized it wasn't that I felt like I was betraying Casey. It was just that I didn't want him to see the good girl he'd grown up with being so naughty with someone like Shaw.

I mustered what little bit of restraint I had remaining and

shoved Shaw away. Because I hated him. Because I hated that I wanted him. Because I could tell from the look in his eyes that he hated it, too. And that just turned me on even more.

"Remember all those times you snickered behind my back and said I walked around with a stick up my ass?"

Shaw grinned like a twelve-year-old boy. If we'd been on a playground, no doubt there would've been some nana-nana-boo-boos right along with someone sticking someone else's head in doo-doo.

He needed to be reminded that we were grown-ups at play, so I reversed the roles and leaned in close enough that he could feel my body heat without the pleasure of my touch. "You can't hold the stick in place without some serious muscle contractions. Kegels don't have shit on me. Hope the memory of it was enough to last you, because you'll never feel it again."

"Is that so?" Shaw reached for me a second time, but I put my hand out to keep him at arm's length.

He looked down at my hand on his chest and then back up at me, the childish grin he'd been sporting replaced by something that looked a lot like carnal sexuality. That was probably the first time any woman had ever smacked Shaw's hand away from the cookie jar.

I hid my victorious smile as I pushed off and walked over to my desk, putting Casey's photo facedown.

Opening my messenger bag, I spotted the scrap of fabric I'd intentionally packed there. "You thought you were going to come in here and do what? Remind me of something that I couldn't possibly forget happened?" I shrugged. "I haven't forgotten. But what I'm really curious about is what you thought would happen after that. Did you think I'd fall to my knees and beg you to do it all over again? Because I won't. I've been there, done that, and now I'm moving on. No big deal. But for the record, I did think about you this weekend. Only not the same way you thought about me. While you were playing spank the monkey and wishing you could be inside me again, I was retching over the toilet." That wasn't true, but I had my best game face on, so he bought it. "Now get out of my office, Shaw. I have work to do."

"This isn't over," he said, with a grin that was confident and devastating enough to make me nervous.

"I just said it was, didn't I?"

"We'll see." Shaw turned to walk toward the door.

And because I simply couldn't resist, I followed. "Hey, Matthews!"

He spun around, not expecting me to be right behind him. His eyes went wide when I held up my hand to reveal that the pair of panties he'd ripped off me were tucked in my fist. Before he had a chance to process my intent, I sent the undergarment sailing through the air and into his face. He caught it as it slid down his chest.

"You owe me a new pair of panties." With a satisfied smirk, I turned my back on him and began what I was sure was a very sexy saunter back toward my desk.

I heard him chuckle, and then my office door closed. It wasn't until then that I plopped down in my chair and breathed a sigh of relief. If I was going to keep up with Shaw, it was going to take some work. Hopefully, he'd bail before I needed to wave a white flag of my own.

I really hated to lose.

The rest of the day was business as usual. I did what I did best, while Ally continued her research on Denver Rockford and then passed the intel to me so I could burn up the phone lines, making promises I knew I could deliver on. Guess what? It got me a private meeting.

Booyah! In your face, Matthews!

CHAPTER 7

Shaw

It was Tuesday afternoon and Denver Rockford wasn't answering my phone calls. And he wasn't returning any of the messages I'd left for him, either. Boulder was sending me the crickets as well. Needless to say, I was feeling properly ignored.

I loathed being ignored. It was a condition that stemmed from my childhood, but I didn't need to pay a shrink gobs of money to tell me that. My parents were well skilled at forgetting about me, and that was fine, because I'd learned how to take care of myself at an early age. I was just glad I hadn't had the baggage of a little brother or sister to take care of as well.

Jerry and Clarice Matthews were self-absorbed pricks who didn't care about anyone but themselves. Maybe I even inherited a little bit of that. Made sense. How a person evolved in life was part genetic makeup, part influence from their surroundings, part learned behavior, and part sheer force of will. Thankfully, the universe had been on my side and had given me the determination and balls to break the mold and fashion one that allowed me to become my own man. Though watching Jerry and Clarice still left a hideous aftertaste in my mouth for relationships. I might even have a phobia of commitment courtesy of those two dysfunctional dipshits. The only reason they'd beaten the statistics and remained married for close to three decades was that neither one of them wanted to put in the time, effort, or money to get a divorce. Seemed to me that dealing with each other on a daily basis was more like sucking the life out of their own lungs, but some habits were hard to break, I supposed.

Maybe it had been the ugly image I'd been forced to endure as a kid that had led to my narcissistic tendencies, but I refused to play the victim.

Nothing had been handed to me on a silver platter. Not even the internship abroad, courtesy of Monty Prather. I'd busted my ass and earned that, right along with my stripes. I wasn't gifted a prime position at the San Diego office. I'd had to prove myself with the foreign leagues before he'd handed me the key to Striker. And under his guidance, I'd thrived at my chosen profession. *Without* a college education to boost my chances.

People had me pegged all wrong. Cassidy had me pegged all wrong. But the misconception was still better than the truth, so I let them believe it. I'd given them the misconception with the mirage I'd constructed for their viewing pleasure, after all.

Cassidy was right about one thing, though. Every move I made was calculated. And each calculated move benefited me in some shape or form. I was skilled at reading people and picking out the parts of them that I could manipulate to further my cause. And I did it seamlessly. Detecting a person's most viable course of action was an art form, but finessing it to my advantage was a gift. Once I had someone in my sights, they didn't stand a chance of denying me what I wanted. I made sure of it because I didn't like to be told no.

Cassidy had told me no. She was the first woman to ever have done so. To say it put a spike in my determination would be an understatement. But, stunned, I'd had to retreat and regroup.

My frustration at being ignored by Denver had been fueled by my frustration at being denied by Cassidy. The balance was off. Way off. And I needed to buckle down and find my vantage point.

Being forced to work late wasn't helping matters. The weekly staff meeting had been rescheduled for today, earlier in the week than usual. Most likely because Wade was anxious to hear how close Striker was to nabbing Denver. You'd think the least he could've done was be on time for it, but apparently, the round of golf he'd decided to have with his old pal and my mentor, Monty Prather, after lunch had run longer than expected. It was a selfish move, but what choice did we have when the man calling the shots was also the man who signed our paychecks? More specifically, I wanted to sample a little bit of that puppeteer power, and the only way that was going to happen was by winning the partnership. Kissing Wade's ass was part of it. So there we were in the conference room at seven o'clock, a little over a dozen agents doing their best to look sharp and happy to be there, when in reality, we were tired, hungry, and just wanted to go home.

The wall of floor-to-ceiling windows only emphasized the fact that it was now dark outside, making the interior lighting seem harsher. But Cassidy looked fresh as the morning dew. In fact, there was a bit of pink on the bridge of her nose, like she'd spent the day lounging by the pool on vacation. How the hell the woman managed it was beyond me. I was going to have to find a way to up my A game and fuck her into exhaustion if I stood a chance of keeping up.

"Status report on Rockford . . . Matthews, go."

God, why did he have to start with me? My going first meant Cassidy could do a one-up, but I didn't have a choice. "It looks really good. I've actually been spending quite a bit of time with him lately," I lied.

Cassidy swiveled to face me, one brow lifted. "Really? Wow . . . What have the two of you been up to?"

I shifted in my chair, caught off guard. I was never caught off guard. Though I'd rarely ever had to use it, I'd found a joke and a smile was always a good cover. "You know what they say: what happens in Vegas stays in Vegas."

"So you went to Vegas? Is that why you look so tired?"

Bitch.

She left me no choice; I had to make her look dumb. "Uh, no. It was just a figure of speech." I glanced around at the rest of the room, laughing as I shook my head and pointed at her.

I dropped the smile when she said, "Oh. I see. Then what did you do?"

The ever-present challenge was there in her eyes. Jesus, I didn't know if I wanted to throw her down on the table and choke the living daylights out of her or fuck her to death. Either way, I was seeing a tombstone with her name on it.

Sitting forward, I got serious. "The last time I checked, we were in competition with each other. It would be stupid for me to show you my hand."

She slid her glasses to the tip of her nose and leaned over, making a huge show of examining my hands. "They look pretty empty to me."

"That's because all of my tricks are up my sleeves." I winked, and then the room erupted into laughter.

Cassidy laughed as well, but I didn't think her chuckle was sincere. "I'd think you'd want to brag if that were the case."

"Bragging wouldn't be very sportsmanlike."

"Oh, don't mind me. I insist." She crossed her arms and leaned back in her chair. It was the most relaxed I'd seen her at a staff meeting.

"So do I," Wade said.

Dammit. "Well, I can't tell you everything, but I can say we had lunch today."

Cassidy perked up again. "*Today* today?"

I nodded, suddenly wary of my answer, but having said it out loud, I couldn't go back on it.

"Huh. He must have really been hungry, seeing as how he had lunch with me today, too." She sat forward and looked directly at me, her brow cocked in challenge. "The Hole, La Jolla. Denver had two lobsters and a steak cooked medium well. Hard to imagine he'd still be hungry after that. Unless he has a tapeworm, in which case we should seriously urge him to seek medical attention. What do you think, Shaw? Should we send an ambulance over to his house?"

She picked up her cellphone from the table, prepared to do just that. Christ, talk about dramatic.

Suddenly feeling the weight of every pair of eyes in the room, I pulled at my collar. "No. I misspoke. We didn't actually eat. I guess it was more like drinks. I just didn't want Wade to know I'd had a drink while on the clock."

Wade chuckled. "Don't worry about me, Matthews. Whatever it takes to get the job done, son."

Bam! Points for me. I smirked at Cassidy.

She smirked back and then reclined in the chair again, with a finger tapping her chin and her eyes on the ceiling. "Hmm . . . See, Denver and I spent a good part of the day together down by the beach, discussing a strategy for his future, and then we had a late lunch, so I'm confused about the timing."

Well, that explained the touch of sun on her nose. I tensed, wishing like hell I could take back everything I'd just said. But the problem with lies was that it took more lies to cover the first one. "Oh, yeah. He told me. It was after that."

"Ah. I see. Well, isn't that convenient?"

Our eyes locked and stayed that way, even while Wade congratulated both of us and insisted that we continue to push until we had the golden goose. After that, he said whatever it was he said and concluded the meeting. Everyone else must have been eager to leave, since they cleared out of the office like cockroaches scattering for cover when the lights were turned on, but Cassidy and I still had unfinished business, and we both knew it. The energy arcing between us was palpable, different from our encounter in her office yesterday morning and every bit the same as in that alley the other night. A pattern was emerging, muddy but becoming clearer. I'd never thought of competition as an aphrodisiac, but I couldn't deny the raw, carnal urge to topple this woman and show her who the dominant being between us was.

In more ways than one, she'd been a naughty girl. And I was about to make her be even more naughty.

Standing, I walked over to the door to close and lock it. "You went behind my back and got a private meeting with Rockford." The light switch was the next to go.

If it hadn't been for the city lights streaming in through the window behind her, I wouldn't have been able to see her silhouette, half-shrouded in darkness, as she stood and set that damn chin of hers. "And you lied about having a private meeting with Rockford."

Funny that she made no comment about or questioned what I was doing, though I knew damn well she'd heard the lock click.

"I didn't want Wade to think we weren't coming through for him." I stalked toward her, keeping to the shadows and using the lack of light to my advantage.

"No, you wanted him to think *you* were coming through for him." Her voice was shaky, however much she tried to cover it. Not knowing where I was must have sucked for her. Cassidy Whalen operated best with information at her fingertips. She was fly-ing blind now.

"Maybe, but you didn't have to call me out like that in front of the whole damn room."

Her head snapped in the direction of my voice, sound the only sense she could cling to. I watched as she swallowed, the lump slowly pushing up and then down her elegant throat. "Of course I did. You didn't really expect me to play nice, did you? All those other women might roll over so you can mount and fuck them, but not me."

"Oh, yeah? I can't fuck you?" I was close, and she knew it. Really close.

"No."

Bullshit. She gasped when I lowered the zipper of her skirt and pushed it over her hips to pool at her feet. And then my arms were around her waist and her back was at my chest. She didn't even try to fight; I knew she wouldn't. Not even when I slipped my hand inside her panties.

Christ, she was so wet for me. A sound that I wasn't even con-scious of making found its way out of my chest, like a predator's warning to any others that might be lurking in the shadows. She was claimed. My prey. My meal.

Cassidy purred in response, and my fingers were positively soaked.

"Are you sure? Because it certainly feels like I can."

Her muscles tensed, prepared to spring into action if only to prove me wrong.

"Don't move."

She could've at any time. I wasn't holding her prisoner, and I would never take a woman against her will.

Hesitation caused her muscles to tense and relax. Even further still when my hand started a slow rocking motion inside her panties. My palm massaged her clit while my fingers teased her opening. Slowly. Oh, so slowly. Tense and relax.

I understood Cassidy better than she thought. Logically, she knew she should stop me, but she wanted this. She needed it. It was a part of her natural instinct I ventured to guess she'd never explored.

Instinct was a curious thing. A person could disguise it, but they could never really escape it. Everything always swung back around to instinct.

And logic was overrated.

Cassidy shifted, her stance widening and her hips moving to work in tandem with my manipulations. And then her hands were on mine. But they were eager. Too eager. Slow and steady was the pace I preferred at the moment, and she would have her release only when I was ready for her to. It seemed Miss Whalen needed a distraction.

"Unbutton your blouse."

She hesitated, so I did as well. "Do it or I'll stop."

The dim light of the world outside the windows allowed me to see her shaking hands as they rose to do as I said. There was that instinct again. Cassidy had to follow directions. It was ingrained in the very fiber of her being.

And because she was being a good little girl, my stroking resumed. Only this time, the excruciatingly torturous hard-on in my pants got in on the action as I dipped at the knee and ground against her ass. God, that ridiculously sexy ass.

Silence. There was nothing but silence as we both worked on our tasks. No, not silence. Our breaths were audible. The rustling of our clothes was audible. My grunt, her barely decipherable moan was audible. But the rest of the world stood still.

Cassidy was done with her blouse. "Open it," I said. She did, but then she attempted to lean forward to push it off her shoulders, making an assumption I hadn't given her permission to make. Tightening my hold around her waist, I stopped her. "I didn't say to take it off."

I could sense her frustration, but I didn't give a damn. The lesson I was teaching was all about what it felt like when the tables were turned and her opponent wasn't playing fair. She'd made me feel exposed at the meeting, and I was doing the same thing to her now. Cassidy needed to be broken, to flounder and know what it was like to be at the mercy of an adversary. Only I was lenient enough not to do it in front of a room full of her co-workers. So regardless of how much I wanted to cup her breasts or swing her around to take their hardened peaks into my mouth, I wouldn't.

Presented with no other choice, Cassidy leaned into me, her head lolling to the side on my shoulder and her arms falling to cling to my hips. Her neck was exposed, and I was granted a fantastic view of her silk-covered breasts, the creamy flesh beckoning me to sample. She was beautiful. Every inch of her body was pristine, as if her skin had been airbrushed to hide flaws that simply did not exist.

Through the valley of her chest, I was given another view: my hand moving beneath the silky sheath of her dainty panties. Forward and back, synchronized to perfection with the rise and fall of her chest. She moved against my hand, giving up her quest to take control and simply riding it out. Her head rolled on my shoulder, her back arching to push her hips toward my hand on the down stroke and then toward my crotch on the up. Closer and closer she brought the tips of my fingers to her opening. She wanted them inside her, but she wasn't calling the shots.

The grip on my hips tightened and she became bolder, moving against me and positioning her neck at my lips, as if begging me to do what we both knew I wanted to do. Not yet.

Cassidy threw caution aside, her mouth turning toward mine

and one hand abandoning its post on my hip to find purchase at the nape of my neck. She pulled me to her, taking the kiss I had not offered, and I granted her that one reprieve. Her lips were plump and pliant, parting to accept my tongue, but I gave her only a brief taste before pulling back to suckle the meaty morsel on the bottom. Jesus, she had fantastic lips.

I couldn't allow myself to get carried away. I had a point to prove, after all. So I denied her further access and stayed just out of reach. Her breaths were hot but sweet on my lips as she struggled to climb the apex of the pleasure I was bringing her. Again and again she lifted her mouth to mine, disappointed when each attempt was met with failure. I couldn't help my internal smirk at her plight, but again, at least it wasn't in front of a room full of her co-workers.

Finally, she gave up and turned her head to the side again, offering the graceful slope of her neck for my viewing pleasure. An agonizing groan trickled from her lips and the juicy little nugget beneath my palm became engorged even as her soft folds grew impossibly slicker. Oh, that was exactly what I'd been waiting for.

Her rocking became short bursts that quickened and intensified the sensation she was receiving courtesy of my hand. The grip on my hip tightened as she struggled to find purchase, and a desperate whimper turned into a throaty moan that was building in passion.

Right there.

My mouth latched onto her skin, teeth scraping the sweet spot between her neck and shoulder. And then I pinched her nipple through her bra and plunged two fingers inside her at the same time.

Cassidy went stiff, paralyzed by the orgasm rocketing through her body as I massaged the rough patch of flesh inside her and coaxed it further. Clamped lips muffled that throaty moan, and the arch of her back pushed her ass so close to my crotch that I thought my cock might actually punch through the zipper to enter her.

She was lucky. My intention had been to bring her to the edge of the cliff and then to leave her dangling there without letting her come. But damned if I could help myself. Knowing I'd done that for her was like a surge of power shooting straight to my ego and my cock, and I couldn't deny myself the resulting high.

But there was still the issue of the kraken inside my pants, which was hyperanxious for release.

Pulling my hand from her panties, I turned her to face me. A feat that wasn't difficult in the least, thanks to the natural muscle relaxer I'd just bestowed upon her. "Let's see if you can give as good as you get," I said.

Cassidy's eyes widened in surprise when I pushed down on her shoulders and sent her to her knees. Working my belt loose and then my pants, I pulled my cock free and gave her a wink.

"You don't expect me to—" she started, but I cut off her blah, blah, blah when I brazenly put the head of my dick to her lips and pushed forward to effectively shut her up.

God, it was just like my shower. The relief at the silence, the visual of her lips wrapped around my cock, the warm and wet suction—it was perfection. And towering over her like that with my cock shoved in her mouth was every bit as empowering as making her succumb to the pleasure she'd received only by my generosity.

The corners of her mouth stretched to accommodate my presence, and damn right that was an added ego boost. It wasn't that I was unusually long, but I knew my girth was impressive. Which is exactly why Cassidy slapped at my abdomen when I slowly pushed all the way in to test her limits. If she could have, I knew she would've bitten me. Luckily for me, my cock filled her mouth and then some, nixing any freedom of movement.

She wasn't happy about my forcefulness, or so I gathered from the digging of her nails into the backs of my thighs. And that was through my slacks. But then again, I hadn't been happy about her smart mouth making me look stupid at the meeting either, so we were even.

I did grant her some freedom of movement, though. Mostly because as much as I wanted to fuck her mouth, I wanted her to suck my cock even more. And boy, did she ever. To my surprise, Cassidy didn't fight me there. If I had to venture a guess, I'd say she was even determined to do a good job. Like she thought she'd somehow have me eating out of the palm of her hand if she did. Maybe, but that remained to be seen. Judging by the wicked glint in her eyes when she assumed control, I'd say she'd found herself another challenge. I could see nothing but reward in my future, so I let her have at it.

Only there was something I had to do first. The glasses were history. And then reaching behind her, I popped the contraption that had been holding her hair atop her head and watched as it spilled free. A now untamed mane of thick, ginger waves cascaded down her back and over her shoulders, and I was well pleased. Looking down at Cassidy on her knees before me with her suffocating blouse hanging open, her perfectly ironed pencil skirt crumpled on the floor, her every-strand-in-place hairdo now a mess, and my cock making a dirty girl of her prim and proper mouth, I felt like the king of the world.

And the blow job was pretty awesome, too. It was hard to believe that someone who worked so damn hard at being a stuffy bitch could suddenly morph into a sultry vixen, but this was the second time I'd seen it from Cassidy Whalen. There was definitely more to her than met the eye; however, I wasn't about to let myself fall into that trap.

With my hand at the back of her head, I guided her until she found the pace and stroke of her mouth that felt damn good to me. And then she was on her own, needing no further guidance. Quick learner, that one, and I was happy about it. Just like every woman's body had to be learned for personalized pleasure, so did a man's. Cassidy was good to go, even under the pressure of impending lockjaw.

Cupping my balls, she stroked them with the perfect amount of pressure, though I was acutely aware that if she wanted to be a bitch, nothing good could come of my current position. I let that thought go, though, because her hands were soft and her mouth was wet, and her tongue was doing this unbelievable thing to the head of my cock.

My head fell back and I closed my eyes, fighting the urge to thrust and grind. When the pressure began to build, for a split second, I considered coming in her mouth. But I stopped myself; I wasn't done teaching her a lesson yet. A lesson that wasn't going to be taught if she kept sucking me like she was, so I pulled out of her mouth.

Cassidy looked up at me, those big, green orbs confused and screaming her need for direction.

"Stand up," I told her.

As she did so, I pulled out the chair she normally sat in during meetings and sat my naked ass in it. And then I angled it toward her.

"Unless you want to lose another pair of panties, I suggest you get them off your body. Get rid of the rest of it, too. Except for the shoes. Leave those on."

It was another power play. If she wanted me, she'd have to prove it by undressing herself. And she did, quickly hooking her thumbs under the band at her hips and pushing them down her legs. The blouse and bra were the next to go, while I stroked my cock and watched. She stood there in those goddamn shoes, naked and self-aware, with her arms crossed over her abdomen, waiting for me to make my next move. I stalled, letting the weight of self-consciousness take its toll as I studied her. So fucking sexy.

Cassidy's figure wasn't perfect, but it came damn close. She could've been a mermaid out of water and shed of fin. It was amazing what could be found when layers of ice and stone were chiseled away. Harsh city lights played across her flesh, the casts of shadows overcoming the peachy hues and making her skin look porcelain. Her breasts were full, her waist slender, her hips generous, and her legs long. And at the most southern point of her body, a thin strip of soft, orange curls parted the V and led my eyes to the hidden cove of promise.

"Shaw—"

"Shh," I said, cutting her off. "Come here."

My plans had changed once again. I was going to have her against the window. I was going to have her bare and on display to the world as I fucked her from behind. But then I realized . . . I didn't want anyone else to see her.

Cassidy stopped in front of me, and I cupped a thigh with one hand, urging her closer still, until she was forced to use my shoulders as leverage to climb the chair and slip her legs inside the openings under the arms on either side. And then, finally, she was straddling my lap.

Slowly, I eased her onto me, feeling the tight sheath of her insides as her walls stretched to accommodate my girth. Good God, I wanted to explode when she rocked her hips back and forth, sinking farther and farther with each stroke until she had taken all of me.

Cassidy's lips were parted, her breaths shaky as she clung to my shoulders and found a rhythm that was favorable. There was no hurried frenzy, and there was no bouncing up and down porno shit going on, but it had absolutely nothing to do with emotions, either. This was fucking. Slow, purposeful, feel-every-fucking-centimeter-of-it fucking. Whatever I thought of Cassidy's attention to detail before didn't matter now. They said the devil was in the details, and I believed it, because this was sin manifested into something tangible, something mere mortals were never meant to experience.

She reached between our bodies, and I watched as she pulled back the hood of skin to reveal her clit and then rolled her hips forward again to put the friction where it was most beneficial. Have mercy, but a woman who knew what she wanted and how to get it was the one thing that would make me lose my goddamn mind.

Fisting her hair in both hands, I pulled her down to me and ravaged her mouth. How the hell she tasted so sweet when she was so fucking mean, I'd never know. And I didn't much care to figure it out, because she was rocking back and forth, rolling her hips and arching her back to brush her breasts against my clothed chest. Instantly, I regretted not getting rid of all of my clothes, too, just so I could get down with the skin-to-skin.

Cassidy's movements slowed, her strokes going deeper and becoming heavier as she ground against my pelvis with more purpose. The kiss was broken and her head fell forward, her eyes closed and lips parted. The rhythmic pulsing began, her walls contracting around my cock and pulling me under with her.

The semi-silence was broken with the "Fuck!" that I could no longer hold back.

Not wanting to lose the momentum of her orgasm, I filled my hands with the cheeks of her ass. Cassidy grasped the arms of the chair and used them to hold on as I picked her up and pushed her back down. Over and over and over again until my balls were tight and my cock was ramrod straight and prepared to . . .

Jesus fucking Christ! I yanked her off me just in time to come all over both of us, though I'd intended something much neater. Semen shot out in spurt after spurt, my hand working to make up for the strokes I'd missed by pulling out. In truth, it had been a close call. I almost hadn't made it in time.

I never came inside a woman, and I nearly always used a condom. No idea why I hadn't with Cassidy, but I wasn't concerned about diseases. Someone as compulsive as she was would be sure to keep herself clear of STDs. And she was too damn moral not to tell a man if she wasn't.

It was the threat of impregnation that I was most worried about. A man with a background like mine had no business knocking up a woman. I sure as hell didn't have the time for a kid, and I had no desire to play daddy.

"Sorry about the mess," I joked.

Cassidy was already scrambling off my lap and grabbing her messenger bag. Rummaging through it, she finally pulled out some tissues and handed me a couple.

"Thanks," I said, taking them.

"It's not the first time I've cleaned up one of your messes, and I'm sure it won't be the last," she said, wiping at her own abdomen.

There was that smart mouth again. How was it that I'd silenced her before? Oh, yeah, with my cock shoved down her throat.

"Then the next time, I suggest you let me get off in your mouth," I quipped back.

Cassidy picked up her panties and stepped into them. "Coming in my mouth will never be an option, Matthews. So don't get any bright ideas." Her bra was next.

I stood to tuck my dick and my shirt back into my pants.

"You're acknowledging the likelihood that there will be a next time?"

"No," she said, slipping the bra straps over her shoulders and looking around for the next piece of clothing.

I was done—the advantage of not stripping down completely. So I picked up her blouse and walked it over to her. She made a move to snatch it out of my hand, but I yanked it back before she could while also pulling her against me with an arm around her waist. None too gently, I kissed her, only releasing her when she shoved against my chest and took the shirt anyway.

Hot and cold. And that was fine by me. It gave me a chuckle.

Fucking Cassidy was fun, but there was no cuddling afterward, and I had no desire to stick around while she lashed out at me because of her lack of self-control. So I was out, but not before issuing a warning.

"For the record, telling me no only makes me want to prove you wrong."

CHAPTER 8

Cassidy

God, I'd done it again!

Only this time, I hadn't let Shaw fuck me. I'd fucked him. Or ridden him. Damn good, too.

I was a slut.

Not just any normal slut, either. I had turned into a pathological slut. Streetwalkers demanded more respect. At least they got paid for dishing up the goodies as easily as I had.

Shaw would be at Monkey Business, of course. But he wasn't the one I dreaded seeing. If Quinn's f'dar had been ringing before, it was going to be screaming now.

The second I crossed over the threshold, it began.

"Cass! Oh my God!" Every eye in the place turned to stare at me when my roommate shouted my name across the pub with dramatic flair.

Crap. It was just as I'd thought. I turned to make a run for it, but then I came face-to-face with Shaw striding through the door, so I screeched to a halt and swung around, only to stop halfway when I spotted Denver Rockford sitting at the bar. *What the what?*

I did a quick scan of the scheduler in my head to see if we had an appointment I'd forgotten about, which was highly unlikely. Though Shaw *had* been fucking my brains out lately, so maybe something had been jarred loose up there. But then I realized that I would never invite a potential client to my personal hangout spot, so I was thoroughly confused.

"He's here for me." Shaw's warm breath at my neck gave me a start. I almost turned on him to ask what the hell he thought he was doing—we were in a public place, for Pete's sake—but then I realized he was just edging past me. I was pretty sure he didn't really need to cup my ass as he did so.

Wait. Exactly when had it become okay with me for Shaw to get frisky as long as it wasn't in a public place?

"Will you get over here, please?" Sasha put her arm around my shoulders and guided me toward my judge and executioner, laughing all the way. Which was either really disturbing or meant she'd gotten over her heartbreak and was in better spirits. She'd probably even moved on to her next disaster.

When we got to our table, I pulled out my regular chair and scooted it as far away as I could without raising suspicion. If by some miracle I managed to escape Quinn's f'dar and the girls couldn't see it written all over my face, I certainly didn't want to take the chance of them smelling the sex on me. I'd stopped at the bathroom at the office and had taken a quick whore's bath in the sink, but I'd swear I could still smell Shaw's cologne.

Demi rolled her eyes. "Quinn has good news—"

"Outstanding news, jealous," my roommate corrected her.

"—but he wouldn't tell us until you got here," Demi finished, never once looking up from her nail filing.

"Oh, yeah?" I asked, relieved. Quinn was practically jumping out of his skin with excitement. Whatever it was, it was big. It was also probably enough to squelch the f'dar. "So what's up?"

"Daddy bought a penthouse for us!"

"What? But, Quinn, I like the apartment we have now. I don't need or want a penthouse."

"Not *us* us," he said, pointing between him and me. "Me and Daddy us. I'm moving out. Onward and upward."

I was stunned. It wasn't that I'd thought Quinn and I would live together forever, but I certainly hadn't thought Daddy would ever come out of the closet, either.

"Oh. So he left his wife?"

"Of course not."

"But you said he got a penthouse for the two of you."

"Right. Daddy thinks it's too risky to keep staying in hotel suites, even under fake names. So he bought the penthouse so that I could live in a nice place."

"You already live in a nice place." Sasha looked every bit as concerned as the rest of us, though we knew to tread lightly.

"Nicer."

"And living in this nicer place also means you're available to him whenever he has the time for you." Demi was toeing the line that had been drawn in the sand. If she tripped over it, Quinn would do some tripping of his own.

He tilted his head, eyes narrowed with a challenging stare. "Say what you really want to say, fuzzmouth?"

Demi stopped filing her nails and sat forward. "Okay, fine, I will. This dude is using you, Quinn. And you're letting him. Why? Because it's better than being alone?"

Quinn crossed his arms and legs and sat back, comfy as you please. "At least I'm not pussyfooting around with what I really want instead of reaching out and taking it."

"What's that supposed to mean?"

He nodded toward the bar, and Demi's attention followed. I could see the pain in her eyes the second she spotted a voluptuous blonde who looked remarkably similar to her leaning over the bar and giving Chaz's bald head a flirtatious polish. What was worse was that Chaz was flirting back, leaning into her hand like a purring kitten. The chick didn't look very classy at all. In fact, the ample tits practically spilling out onto the glossy wood made her look easy. Not that being well endowed was a crime, but jeez, she was really putting it to work.

"You're going to mess around and someone is going to snatch that man up. And then you'll be all alone."

"So? I'd rather be alone than made to feel second-best." Demi peeled her eyes away from Chaz and found Quinn's. "He's never going to leave her, you know. You deserve better."

"Better than a posh penthouse, an unlimited spending account, and Jennifer Aniston's personal decorator?"

Demi thought about that for a moment. "Touché," she said, sitting back and resuming her manicure.

"You bet your sweet candied ass, touché." Quinn looked down at his watch. "Now, if you'll excuse me—and even if you won't, I don't care," he said, standing to leave. "The very expensive timepiece my lover used to decorate my wrist says it's time for me to scurry off to meet him. Don't want to keep Daddy waiting."

"Oh, no. We wouldn't want that," Sasha mumbled.

"Shush, woman." Quinn leaned down and whispered conspiratorially into her ear: "Watch this."

He walked over to the bar where the Demi look-alike was still flirting it up with our bartender friend. Quinn was never overly effeminate, but that didn't mean he couldn't turn it on when he wanted to. It was very apparent that he wanted to right then. Before he even reached the bar, he called out Chaz's name with a giggle and an exaggerated sway of his hips. Only he didn't stop at the bar. Quinn put a knee on the stool to hoist himself higher, used his hips to nudge the girl out of the way, leaned over the bar, took Chaz's face in his hands, and then kissed him on the mouth. Not a tongue-in-the-mouth kiss but not a quick peck, either.

There was a collective gasp at our table, followed by a wicked giggle when the blonde reared back in shock.

Most straight guys wouldn't be okay with another man laying one on them like that. But Chaz wasn't most guys. He loved Quinn every bit as much as we did and knew this had nothing at all to do with his homosexual friend wanting to get frisky with him. Plus, he was comfortable enough with his own heterosexuality not to think that a kiss from another man would suddenly turn him gay. So there were no fists swung or disgusted shove-aways. He took it. He took it because he knew why it was happening. And it wasn't the first time. A first for the Quinn kiss, but not the first time one of us had cock-blocked him.

Quinn pulled back and swept his thumb over Chaz's lips as if he were removing lipstick, which wasn't there, since he didn't wear any. "Gotta go, babe. I'll see you at home when you get off, and then I'll get you off again." Quinn turned to look at the blonde and gave her a wink. "Nice try, honey, but you're wasting your time."

The blonde grabbed her purse with an insulted huff and made a beeline for the door.

Chaz's shoulders sagged in defeat. "Ah, man, why'd you have to do that?"

"You know why" was the only explanation Quinn gave. He looked back at Demi, so that Chaz couldn't see his face, and mouthed, "You're welcome," followed by an air kiss.

Demi and Chaz had been doing this really weird mating dance for as long as I'd known them. Only neither of them had gone in for the lift or the dip. They were the real-life Baby and Johnny, sans the bump and grind. Chaz was from the wrong side of the tracks, and Demi didn't care. He did, though. In his mind, he wasn't good enough for her and probably never would be. Add to that the insult to his machismo because she made a lot more money than him, and the resulting stalemate looked less like a bump and grind and more like two uncoordinated and slightly inebriated barflies trying their best to learn the steps to a country line dance.

A burst of raucous laughter caught my attention—and that of everyone else in the room—and I turned to see Denver and Shaw yukking it up, complete with fists pounding on the bar top.

I could've gone over and inserted myself into the fun, but I decided to let Shaw have this one. The soreness between my thighs was a stark reminder that I'd been letting him have a lot of things lately that I shouldn't, but *qué será será, c'est la vie,* and all that jazz.

With an exhausted sigh that was every bit as much mental as it was physical, I stood and gathered my things. "I'm out, too. Do me a favor and keep an eye on those two?"

"Why? Who is he?" Sasha was getting her ogle on while mentally calculating how to get Denver into her bed.

That wasn't the shocking part for me. I drew my head back and looked at her, genuinely bewildered by how clueless she'd just sounded. "Are you serious right now? That man's face is plastered all over every magazine cover and billboard imaginable. He's the most exciting thing to hit football in, like, forever, and he happens to be the target of my latest obsession, and you don't know who he is?"

I could practically hear the click of the lightbulb. "Ohhhh . . . that's Denver?"

It took everything in me not to smack her on the forehead. "Yes, that's Denver."

"Can you introduce me?" She had that look in her eyes, and I could see the whole disastrous relationship playing out from beginning to end.

"That's so not going to happen."

Demi smirked. "Besides, he only has eyes for our dear Cass." She gave a wave with her fingers while looking toward the bar. Denver was looking back. At me.

"He's so big and sexy and *beefy*." Sasha actually licked her lips as if she were a cartoon character envisioning a nice juicy steak.

"Beefy?"

"Oh, yeah."

I tilted my head to regard him, and the appeal began to take shape. It wasn't like I was incapable of recognizing a fine specimen when I saw one. Denver was definitely a manly man, tall and thick, with skin and hair made golden by time spent in the California sun. The crinkles at the corners of his Sinatra blues came to life with the lift of his cheeks, a smile that was infectious even if you didn't feel like you had anything to smile about. Under different circumstances, I probably would've been attracted to him, but he was my client. Or at least I wanted him to be. And there were rules, ethics.

As if I were a star in a sitcom, a little thought bubble formed in my mind with Wade Price's face and prodding reminder. *Bring home that win. By* any *means necessary.* I think bubble Wade was trying to tell me that a slightly inappropriate friendship with Denver would fall under the "by *any* means necessary" category. It seemed I already had his attention; would it be so bad if I played it to my advantage? I mean, there was a partnership on the line. And Shaw was having drinks left and right with the man like they were best buds, so it wasn't like he was exactly playing fair. I wasn't sure my moral compass would allow me to follow through on it, but there was one thing I did know for sure: it was never going to happen if Sasha got there first.

"Sasha, seriously. It's creepy. And he's got, like, two feet on you." Hopefully, that would be enough of a deterrent.

"Whatever. I'd climb him."

Or not.

"A man like that can have any woman he wants and usually does. Pass." At least Demi was sane. Or maybe her immunity was due to the expedition we all knew she wanted to make to the peak of Mount St. Chaz. And mount him she would, if given the chance.

"Right. So, I'm going to go home and get some sleep. No mounting of my client while I'm away," I told Sasha before kissing her on the cheek.

As I made my way toward the door, I simply couldn't resist giving Shaw a little perspective. Honestly, it was his own fault. He shouldn't have been looking so smug when he glanced over Denver's shoulder at me. So I made a little pit stop and gave Denver a playful hip check. "Are we still on for tomorrow?"

Wow, it sure hadn't taken me long to make the leap. I'd gone from "Hmm, that's an angle I might be able to work" to "Yup, grabbing that bull by the horns and riding it all the way home" in less than five minutes. That had to have been a record.

Denver gave me a wide, flirtatious grin and put his arm around my waist. "You know it, babe."

"Good. Don't stay out too late. You're going to need your rest."

I didn't linger any longer, not even to rub the salt into Shaw's newly inflicted wound. I'd done it. I'd crossed the line, and there would be no turning back from it now. I didn't know how well I'd sleep that night after that, but I knew it would drive Shaw crazy trying to figure out what had just happened. Somehow, it made it all worth it. At least for now.

My week just kept getting worse from there. On Wednesday morning, I avoided him well enough—face-to-face, that is—but there was still the pesky matter of my wandering thoughts and my body's involuntary reaction to those thoughts. On more than one occasion I had to stop what I was doing and start all over again; I simply wasn't processing the words I was reading.

"Hello? Earth to Cass . . ."

I'd zoned again and hadn't even realized it. Shaking myself from the stupor, I looked at Ally. "Did you say something?"

"Is everything okay with you? You seem a little off today."

"Oh, yeah, I'm fine. Just . . . you know, keeping late hours studying the Denver Rockford file. You know how anal I can be."

"Do I ever. I also know how anal you are about not being on time," she said, tapping her watch.

Checking the clock on the top right corner of my screen, I felt a jolt of giddy-up-and-go zip through me. I was late. Well, not late but not early, either. I might have closed my laptop a little harder than was necessary, and I was probably leaving something important behind as I shoved things into my messenger bag, but in less than ten minutes, I'd changed into attire that was appropriate for the outing with Denver and was out of my office and sprinting toward the elevator as the doors were closing.

"Hold the door, please!" Hopefully, whoever was aboard wouldn't be a jerk and pretend not to hear me.

A masculine hand with a Rolex draped around the wrist reached out and stopped the door. I groaned to myself because I'd know that hand anywhere. More to the point, I'd know those long, thick fingers anywhere. Blindfolded and with a single touch from them. They were well skilled, and if the man attached to them ever decided to pick up playing guitar, I was sure he'd be a freak genius at it. But it was those delicious protruding veins that stole the show.

Maybe it was weird, but I had a thing for veins. They showed virility, proof that the blood that pumped through them was strong and resilient. Since I'd come from an Irish family, it was in my DNA to search out those two traits in a man.

The door pulled fully back to reveal Shaw standing there in all his arrogant glory, a wide grin plastered over his face. "This is a new look for you, Whalen. Is the world coming to an end?"

He might have held the door, but he was still a jerk. It was a tank top and shorts, for Christ's sake. No reason to be so dramatic.

I gave him a sarcastic smile in lieu of words, since the only ones that sprang to mind were "bite" and "me," and he might take them as an invitation. Not that he'd ever waited for one before. I should've walked away and opted for the next lift, but doing so would be like an admission of defeat. So I gave him a wide berth and moved to the farmost corner. Away from him. And then the doors closed, leaving us all alone. Great. Things always seemed to happen when we were left all alone.

Closing my eyes to focus on what might be the most important task of my career, I managed to bring everything back into perspective. Denver Rockford was the only man I needed to have on my brain, and he wasn't so much a man as the golden key to what had once been Monty Prather's office suite. Eyes on the prize.

"What are you and Denver doing today?" Shaw had his eyes on the prize, too.

I knew the curiosity would kill him. But I wasn't about to give.

"I'll share if you will," I offered, only because I knew he wouldn't. No doubt, he'd liquored up Denver at the pub last night in hopes of getting him to sign on the dotted line.

Shaw's smile was a nonverbal *touché*. He wasn't stupid, and he knew I wasn't, either. No matter how much he'd like for me to be.

"You're taking advantage of the man's weaknesses. Low blow. I thought you were more of a goody-goody than that."

Well, that came out of left field. "Excuse me?"

Shaw shrugged, his eyes doing a sweep of my body to take in my attire. "He thinks you have a banging body, and you're capitalizing on it."

"He said that?" I realized a little late that I sounded hopeful and had to change it up. "Because if he did, I'll have to set him straight and let him know that unlike you, I do not use my body to get ahead. I earned my position the old-fashioned way. Through hard work and perseverance."

Shaw stuffed his hands into his pockets and rolled his eyes. "Blah, blah, blah, blah, blah."

I was stunned silent by his rudeness.

He cocked his head, his eyes lingering on the exposed flesh of my legs and warming it. "Though I found his words to be less than poetic, I knew the point he was making. Of course he finds you irresistible. Like a siren, so much about you calls to a man, seducing him closer to imminent danger. But there's a problem, a contradiction that causes a push and pull in the attraction."

I shifted, hoping the movement would divert his attention away from my hips. It worked, though the crossing of my arms only drew him to my breasts. "Not that I care about your opinion in the slightest, but it's always good for a laugh. So what's the contradiction?"

Finally, he found my eyes, and the corner of his mouth lifted into that cocky grin. "The seduction only works as long as your mouth stays shut. Though I can think of at least one way you can and have put it to better use. But then maybe you were just using me as practice for the big game?"

Smacking him across his stupid face for that comment would only give him the upper hand. Literally and figuratively. Thankfully, I kept my head about myself and saw the goad for what it was. Shaw wanted me to be upset. He wanted me to rant and rave and scream like a lunatic. But I wasn't going to let him strip me of control.

"You're absolutely right. If I'd sleep with you, that must mean I'd sleep with anyone for any reason."

He shrugged. "Hey, who am I to judge? But just so we're clear, seducing Denver is a cheat."

"Is that what you think I'm doing?"

"I'm beginning to think it's your specialty. I've experienced it firsthand, so I know how potent your charms can be."

"Ha! I *seduced* you?"

"Absolutely."

"And what purpose would that serve?"

"To distract me."

"You're distracted? That's your excuse for falling short? Are you really that weak?"

Before I could so much as blink, I found myself hoisted from the floor and pinned to the wall in an over-the-top show of strength.

"I wasn't talking about physical weakness, you brute."

Shaw grinned, proud of himself. His hands were like branding irons on the cheeks of my ass, the skin-to-skin contact made possible by the leg openings of my shorts. And then we both had a major realization at the same time. Only I was a little better about disguising mine, though probably not by much.

Crap. I knew I'd forgotten something.

Shaw's jaw ticked with the grinding of his molars. "You aren't wearing panties." Another tick of his jaw. Did his nostrils just flare? "You're going to meet Denver without panties on?"

To be precise, I wasn't wearing the bottoms to my bathing suit. In my hurry, I'd forgotten to put them on. But I was in a unique position to screw with Shaw's head a little bit more, so I took it.

I threw his grin back at him. "Jealous?"

He set me back on my feet as if that one word had scorched him. "No." But he'd taken too long to answer.

The elevator came to a somewhat jerky stop with the ding of a bell that seemed entirely too loud in the awkward space we'd created. I may never know why at that exact moment I was suddenly glad I wasn't wearing any panties, but I was. Maybe it was because there was a sense of freedom about going commando. Something that put a little sultry pep in my step and gave me cause to wave the upper hand I'd been given. And so with no more than a confident smile, I said, "You should be."

Shaw

As soon as the doors parted, Cassidy swept past me as if I weren't even there.

I guffawed at her rudeness before I realized the race she'd set in motion. Everything was still a competition, of course, and sometimes it was the small victories that really helped put things into perspective. So, naturally, my pace quickened and the race to the front doors was on. *Damn her and her ability to make me act like a lunatic.*

Cassidy must have heard me approaching because she picked up the pace, doing that thing where you're not sure if the person is walking really fast or jogging really slow. The stupidest part was that I did it, too. When we hit the revolving door at the same time, we came to a standstill. I was on one side and Cassidy was on the other, both of us unwilling to give in our effort with the door. Her to push through, and me to obstruct its movement and keep her from beating me. Either way, neither of us cared that we were drawing attention from a lobby full of people.

"Let. *Go!*" Cassidy growled between clenched teeth. She shoved her full weight against the plane of glass.

I'd barely been pushing against the gliding door, but when I saw how much effort Cassidy was putting into beating me, a wicked idea sprang to mind. San Diego's sidewalks were crawling with hundreds of people going about their merry way, and it was only human nature for one to stop and take in another person's humiliation if it happened right in front of their face. I was what one might call an opportunist, so there was no chance in hell I was going to let that go without capitalizing on it.

"Fine," I conceded with a polite smile.

Then I stepped back quickly to clear the door and let it swing forward, sending an unprepared Cassidy stumbling onto the sidewalk, tripping over her own feet. To my dismay, a passerby caught her before she was sent careening to the hard cement. Okay, so I hadn't really been out to cause her physical harm, but her utter embarrassment had certainly made my day.

"You okay, lady?" I heard her human safety net ask just as I strutted out. With a chuckle, I might add, because damn right it was funny.

Cassidy stood straight and glared daggers at me as I walked by. "I'm okay, thank you very much," she said, and then she stalked off in the opposite direction while adjusting her ruffled clothes.

Turning to head down a side street, I stopped when I knew I'd be out of sight but still have a vantage point to watch her without being seen. As soon as she was in her awaiting cab, I made a dash for the one on the corner and slipped into the backseat.

"Follow that taxi," I said, pointing in her direction. Whatever Cassidy Whalen was doing to schmooze Rocket Man, I was going to find out. And then I was going to top her.

CHAPTER 9

Shaw

Topping Cassidy was going to prove harder than I'd thought. How the hell was I supposed to compete with a romantic picnic for two at the beach? Talk about unethical. Miss I-Do-Not-Use-My-Body-to-Get-Ahead was a liar, liar, bikini bottoms on fire. At least she'd managed to get those on before her seductive strip-tease from her shorts and tank top, during which Denver had been drooling like a cartoon wolf with tongue wagging and eyes popping out. I half-expected him to make it rain on her as if she were a dancer onstage at a seedy little club east of I-5.

Denver had somehow sequestered a cozy, less touristy spot in a little alcove somewhere north of La Jolla. I knew because I'd followed them. And then I'd hidden behind a vine-covered oak tree amid some purple-and-yellow flowers that smelled decent but were also ground zero for a swarm of honeybees. They were pesky, but I was willing to leave them to their business of gathering pollen as long as they left me to my business of gathering intel. If only I could hear what was being said. From this distance, it was like watching the television on mute: I got the gist of what was going on, but some volume would've been nice. There was nothing I could do about it, though, unless I wanted to get caught. Which would defeat the purpose of my spying.

For a couple of hours, I just sat and watched as the lovebirds ate fruit and cheese and drank wine while cozying up on a blanket for two under an oversized umbrella. It was hot, but the breeze from the ocean and the shade from the tree made it somewhat bearable. I'd taken my jacket off and rolled up my sleeves half an hour in, getting as comfortable as I could for who knew how long. Somehow, I was going to have to find a way to woo Denver back over to the Shaw side. As long as Cassidy kept throwing those tits around, it wasn't going to be easy.

I excelled at observation. It was the primary skill that had gotten me as far as I'd come in my profession. All those days and nights when I'd slipped into locker rooms or onto the sidelines, seat-hopping in the stands, working my way into parties in the clubhouse and sometimes even in the luxury suites had been made possible only by my ability to not draw attention to myself. Ford Field, the Palace, Joe Louis Arena, and Comerica Park: I knew the layouts of all of them like the back of my hand. They were my first, second, third, and fourth homes. And each one of them was better than the hellhole that should've been first on that list.

A punk kid from Detroit sitting in a forgotten corner of a crowded stadium VIP box could learn a whole lot if he simply kept his mouth shut and paid attention to the way the big players worked the room. Owners, investors, agents, elbow rubbers, celebrities, athletes, potential recruits, and coaches . . . they all liked to talk. Mostly because they liked to show off. Whether it was their knowledge, physical skills, or wealth, it didn't matter. I picked up on everything that counted until I'd learned enough to outtalk any one of them. I was good, and it paid off big-time.

I caught my first break when Denarius Williams, a Pro Bowl

cornerback with a wild streak, had let the time run down to seconds on the clock right before his deadline to choose a new agent.
Smothered by the overwhelming attention he was receiving, he'd
been unable to make a decision. So, on a whim, he'd consulted
the nineteen-year-old with nothing to gain.

"If you were me, who would you go with, kid?" he'd asked.

"I'm not a ballplayer, so I don't think I can answer that, Mr.
Williams," I'd told him.

"Okay, fair enough. If you were one of them," he said, pointing to the crowd of suits, "what do you think would be the best
plan of action for me?"

It was the first time anyone had ever asked my opinion, and
I'd known exactly what to say. So I'd hunkered down into my
own skin, shrugged off the intimidation I should've felt, and laid
it all out on the line. At first, he was amused by my enthusiasm—
clearly, nothing about that conversation had ever been meant to
be taken seriously—but when I gave him a rundown of all his
stats, specified the gaps in Detroit's roster where he would be
most beneficial, and spelled out the leverage that would be his for
the taking while he was negotiating his contract, he got quiet. So
did everyone else in the room.

Denarius's smile was back in place, only this time, it was because he was impressed. "What's your name, kid?"

"Shaw Matthews." And that was the first time my name had
meant something. Better yet, all those big deal makers now
knew it.

"Well, you might not play ball, Shaw Matthews, but you certainly know how to play the game. It's too bad you're not with
any of these agencies, because you've got real promise."

"Who says he's not with any of us?" One of the suits stepped
in next to me and put an arm around my shoulders, extending

the other toward Denarius, who took it warily. "Monty Prather of Striker Sports Entertainment. Shaw here is my personal protégé, a real gem I recently stumbled upon and took under my wing. He's quite the prodigy, isn't he? Makes me damn proud."

Denarius's attention was back on me, his well-groomed hairline practically peeling away to reveal the wheels turning in his head. "Is that right?"

I looked at the self-assured man at my side, prepared to out him at the slightest hint that he was working an angle he had no intention of following through on. I don't know what it was about the nod and wink he'd given me, but I understood that Monty Prather was the future, my foot in the door that would've never been opened to me otherwise. So I took it.

In that moment, the scared boy who'd come from nothing had morphed into a man determined to have it all. "Yes, sir, it is," I'd said, beaming with confidence. "And we'd be honored to play the game for you."

Denarius had given a small chuckle and nodded. "Okay, then. Let's play."

Monty had squeezed my shoulder with pride, and two weeks later, the tagline "Striker Sports Entertainment . . . Let us play the game for you" had been scrawled across the sign on the front of the building that served as ground zero for SSE. The following day, I'd been sent to Europe to learn the contract negotiating game with the foreign leagues, and Monty had stayed in constant contact with me, taking a personal interest like the father I'd never really had.

Cassidy's piercing squeal ripped me from my memories, and I looked up to see her running toward the water, with Denver hot on her heels. Well now, wasn't that a page ripped straight out of a romance novel? Too busy frolicking to pay attention, Cassidy was caught unaware by the surf and knocked to her giggling ass on the sand, where she was pummeled by a wave. Served her right. But Rocket Man—oh, he was such the hero, swooping in and lifting her out of the water bridal-style, to save her from what? Getting sand in the crack of her ass?

Pfft! I didn't need to see any more. And I especially didn't need to see the way Denver was leaning in for the kiss that would thank him for his bravery. It was so clear what was going on. Those two were a thing or were about to become one. Cassidy had Denver in the bag, and probably in the sack as well.

Grabbing my jacket, I stood and stalked back toward the open road where the cab had dropped me. I didn't even care if they could see me. Besides, they were too busy with each other to pay attention anyway.

It didn't take long to wave down a cab, and then I was on my way back to sulk in a tall ale at Monkey Business. I needed to think. I wasn't a quitter, and I'd worked too hard to get where I was to walk away without anything to show for it. There had to be something I could do, and I was sure it would come to me if I could just block the visual of Denver Rockford and Cassidy Whalen out of my stupid head. My imagination was getting the best of me and conjuring up all kinds of scenarios whereby Denver had her bent over in front of him while fucking her from behind. Shit.

She wouldn't actually do that, would she?

The stunt Cassidy had pulled was unethical at best. And even though I'd wooed more than my fair share of women to land an athlete, I'd never slept with the athletes themselves. It made things too messy. Surely Cassidy was smarter than that. Maybe all she'd done was flirt a little. Maybe she hadn't let him touch her like that at all.

Why the fuck did I care?

Cassidy

I learned something new about myself yesterday. Apparently, there were gobs of "Do me!" seeping from my pores. That was the only explanation I could come up with for why my mortal enemy, Shaw Matthews, was fucking me like crazy while my potential client, Denver Rockford, was trying to woo the panties right off me. If only he'd opted to meet me at the office instead of the beach, he could've saved himself the time and the effort. Thanks in large part to my cluttered and now forgetful mind. Yes, I'd lost my mind and forgotten who I was. Obviously.

I should have known better. I really should have. Denver had never made it a secret that he was crushing on me, and there I was, parading around in my bathing suit while he was indulging in an alternate universe where he and I were a couple. I knew it was wrong, but I didn't stop the delusion. I had let him run with it, even partook in the fantasy. All the while, I'd talked myself out of acknowledging the very real fact that this was a date, not a routine luncheon with a client. I'd done the thing that had disgusted me most about Shaw: I'd taken advantage of a situation that I shouldn't have.

Bring home that win. By any *means necessary.* Wade's voice had been the constant stage direction during my stellar performance. Shame on me.

Most of the conversation Denver had, he had with my breasts. But did I attempt to cover them up in the least? Oh, no. I lathered the girls up with sunblock instead. How could I stoop so low? My real assets couldn't be stuffed into a bikini top; they were in my head, for crying out loud.

And now Denver had the wrong idea.

But then so did Shaw. Okay, so that might have been a slight advantage, but how far was I willing to go to get the partnership? I'd thought sleeping with Shaw was the lowest of the low, but as it turned out, I could limbo my way on down to leading on a client. My da would be so disappointed. His little girl was nothing more than a common slut profiting from a case of quid pro quo.

My office door burst open, and Shaw marched in without so much as a courtesy knock. "There she is. Little Miss By-the-Book."

Well, this conversation was off to a good start. It could only go downhill from here, so I saw no point in continuing it. "I am in no mood for your crap today, Matthews. Get out."

Naturally, he ignored me and kept right on rambling. "Though it looks like you're reading from *Fifty Shades of Grey* instead of the employee code of ethics."

I looked up from my laptop and took my glasses off like that was going to help me better understand what he was going on about. "What?"

"I thought we both agreed that doing the client was a no-no."

Sitting back in my chair, I sighed. "Yeah, well, I just couldn't help myself. Something about cold cuts and cheese turns me into a wanton hussy," I said with a far-off stare that was every bit as facetious as the words. "We just had lunch, idiot."

"Chains and whips, chips and dips . . ." Shaw shrugged and took a seat on the corner of my desk as if he owned the spot. "It's all the same, right?"

"Oh . . . my God. You're ridiculous!" He was also loud and hadn't bothered to close the door behind him, so I got up to do it myself. As I passed by him, I caught a whiff of his cologne and almost stopped to bury my face in his neck, but I didn't. Luckily, his mouth and his outrageous accusation had kept my brain sharp and my inner slut at bay.

"So am I right? Did you and Denver hit up a little red room of pain?"

Wow. This was a side of Shaw I'd never seen before. He'd always been an ass, but something was different about his assiness at the moment.

"Will you keep your voice down?" I hissed.

"Why? Are you worried your assistant is going to find out just how kinky her boss really is, how unscrupulous her morals are, that she'd go to any length to get what she wants?"

Ally knew better. I wasn't like that. Maybe I was screwing Shaw, but he made me crazy enough to do stupid things. I could plead temporary insanity on that one and no court in the world would argue. But a client? No way. For a moment I considered the very real possibility that Shaw must have used the tactic often. It would explain why he was so quick to assume the same about Denver and me.

Shaw took my arm as I passed again and prevented me from going back to my chair. "Did you do it? *Him*," he corrected himself. "Denver, that is."

Yanking my wrist out of his grasp, I crossed my arms over my chest and glared at him. "I can't even believe we're having this conversation right now. Look at you. You're not just being a jerk; you're serious. And really pissed."

He stood then, towering like a sentinel in the face of a pressing threat. Shaw wasn't overly muscular, but he was physically fit, and at the moment, all that toned mass was taut and at the ready. Slowly, he moved his hands to his hips, as if any sudden movement might spook me. He was probably right to do so. Admittedly, I was on edge, wary of the forehead vein that was zigzagging down from his hairline like a lightning bolt that might arc out and strike me down at any moment. Plus the ticking-jaw thing was back. But his eyes. His eyes were eerily calm, fixated on my every move.

"Just answer the goddamn question, Cassidy. Did you or did you not fuck Denver Rockford?" At least he'd lowered his voice, but I wasn't sure I liked the unnatural quiet of it. It was like talking to a criminal who might or might not be a serial killer.

"Did *you*?" I knew the answer before I even asked the question, but I was trying to prove how silly the whole topic was. I'd no sooner screw Denver than Shaw would, and he knew it. Or at least he should have.

"No. But then I wasn't half naked on a beach, frolicking in the ocean until I was so exhausted I couldn't help but fall into his arms."

I gasped, which was such a chick thing to do, but it couldn't be helped. I was shocked. "You were *spying* on us?"

Shaw smirked. "I prefer to think of it as intense research."

My hands found my hips and sat there judgmentally. "Which some might call stalking."

"And some might call what I saw exhibitionism. It's illegal in every state, you know."

"Oh, whatever! I wasn't frolicking in the ocean, and there was no exhibitionism. The fruit Denver brought for lunch attracted some bees, and I'm terrified of them. So I took off running and headed for the water because it was the only safe place I could think of to get away from them. That's what you saw. Not that I owe you any sort of explanation."

"My eyes weren't playing tricks on me. He was cradling you bridal-style, and that look the two of you exchanged was quite intense."

"Denver is a mountain of a man, with arms as big around as my head. When he wants to pick you up, you don't know about it until you're already in the air. He was trying to be a hero. It wasn't my idea. And before you go there, neither was the kiss."

Shaw just stared at me. For what seemed like an eternity. "You kissed him?"

Crap. He apparently hadn't seen that part.

"No . . . *he* kissed *me*."

He threw his hands into the air. "Ah! I see now."

"Hard to believe, since you can't see past the end of your own nose, but entertain me. What is it that you see, Shaw?"

He started pacing then. "This isn't a tactic for you at all, is it? You're not trying to put yourself into a position to coerce Denver into signing with you so you can win the partnership."

I sighed, exhausted by the conversation. "You're not making any sense. Stop beating around the bush and get to your point, please."

"You really do want him. Not just as your client, but in your bed."

That cinched it for me. He'd lost his ever-loving mind.

"Wow. You are really grasping at straws. You have to hear how silly you sound right now. Plus, you're being contradictory. I thought you just said I was trying to put myself into a position to—"

Shaw interrupted before I could finish: "You're trying to put yourself into position, all right, but which is it? Flat on your back or down on your knees?"

I narrowed my eyes at him. He had gone too far and he knew it, though it seemed he'd passed the point of no return and was just going to keep running.

"Are you wet? Just thinking about all that . . . what did you call him? Oh, now I remember: *mountain of a man*. You're just gushing between the thighs, soaking those panties. *If* you're even wearing any, that is. All this time, I thought you were a do-gooder. Little did I know, you were just doing it good. Real good. Good enough to get ahead, right? How many others have there been?"

That was it. I'd had enough. I slapped him. Hard. And then I pushed him away so I could lift my skirt and prove that I was indeed wearing panties, but I wouldn't be for long. "Here, you can have them. Put them on, parade around, and see what it's like to spend a day in them. You can even stick your hand inside to stroke your own cock, for all I care, because that's the only way you'll be getting into my panties ever again." The silky red fabric went sailing from my fist and hit him in the chest before dropping to the floor at his feet. "And for the record, I can fuck whomever I want. I don't require your permission to do so. *Get out!*"

Turning my back to him was somewhat dramatic, but then I was feeling quite proud of myself. I owned the saunter over to my desk, though it was a move I'd soon regret.

I never heard him approach from behind. Then again, there was no time to. One strong arm wrapped around my waist, and his hard chest was pressed to my back. I was about to rip him a new one when he forcefully bent me over the desk while grabbing a handful of hair and pulling until I had no choice but to arch my body.

Oh, God. I really *liked that.*

His warm breath was at my ear, too fast for anyone in complete control. "You think you have the upper hand?" His free hand was rough as it pushed and pulled at my skirt until cool air kissed the naked skin of my bare ass. "You don't." The swift smack of a palm landed on one cheek, and the resulting sting made me jump. "*That* was the upper hand."

I recovered quickly, and instinct was my guide as I backed into his crotch. Or at least I attempted to.

"Ah, ah, ah . . ." Shaw's grasp on my hip denied that bit of friction.

It was crappy timing that I should choose the moment of his admonishment to look up and lock eyes with Casey's photo on my desk. But it wasn't enough to shame me into stopping this impromptu encounter that promised a healthy release by the time Shaw was done. If he didn't deny me the way he was threatening to. Regardless, it was enough to make me reach out and turn the frame facedown. Casey didn't need to see what was about to happen, and I didn't need to see Casey while it was going down.

"Tell me what you want, Cassidy. Is it Denver?"

God, what a tangled web I'd been weaving. Denver, the best chance of making my career; Casey, the best friend I'd ever had; and Shaw, the best sex I ever would . . . Such a shame I couldn't mash them all together to make the perfect man.

Shaw cupped my ass and slid his hand down to slip his fingers between my dripping folds. He made a sound that was half growl, half groan when he felt how wet I was. "That better not be for Denver."

I shook my head as much as I could in his tight grip.

"No?" He pushed two fingers inside me, and I inhaled sharply at the delicious presence, gushing even more. "Is it for me?"

I nodded. It wasn't an admission I'd wanted to make. Not to Shaw.

Shaw bent and put his lips to my ear. "Do you want me to fuck you?" He pulled his fingers almost all the way out and then pushed back inside, deeper this time.

Once again, I nodded.

"Say it."

"I want you to fuck me. *Hard*."

"Good girl," he whispered.

Dammit, he was right. My good girl was so naughty, and my naughty girl was becoming so good at it. It was high time I embraced them both and sliced out a bit of sinful heaven. Or was that heavenly sin?

But Shaw didn't give me what I wanted. Instead, he dropped to his knees to watch as he got his finger fuck on, and get his finger fuck on he did. Holy Jesus! Having freedom to move my head again, I looked back over my shoulder, my mouth gaping as I watched how enraptured he was by the sight before him. He bit his lip, one strong hand on the small of my back to hold me down and the other working purposefully—not too slow, not too fast—to bring me to orgasm. I could feel it pending, knew it was boiling and ready to give him the reward he was working toward. And then Shaw nipped at the cheek of my ass, quickly replacing his fingers with his tongue.

I came, gripping the edge of my desk and slamming my eyes shut. Somehow, I'd kept enough presence of mind to bury my face in my arm to stifle the accompanying moan, but I wasn't sure how long I'd be able to keep quiet. Shaw kept lapping at me, catching my orgasm on his tongue and swallowing it down until, finally, it abated and I could breathe again.

Then, without warning, he stood and fisted my hair once again so he could maneuver my head into an uncomfortable position and kiss me hard on the mouth. The taste of my orgasm on his lips and tongue was exquisitely addictive. It was Shaw and it was me—two things that should never be combined. Yet I couldn't get enough. I attempted to twist around for a better angle, but his hold and the unrelenting set of his body sent a message that was loud and clear. I would not get anything Shaw was not willing to give. And he wasn't taking requests. It thrilled me, and I was completely on board.

Abruptly, he pulled away, and with one swift thrust, he entered me. I was unprepared, and this time, my moan would not be denied. I wasn't even aware that he'd unleashed his cock in the first place, but I didn't really care about the details. He was inside me, and the sensation of the stretch and fill was like sweet, sweet relief. I hadn't realized how badly I'd been craving him, but I had. God help me . . . I had.

Shaw

Cassidy moaned when I pushed inside her, and I couldn't have that. She was never loud, but in the silence of her office, every sound seemed amplified. I couldn't and wouldn't stop, but I also wouldn't risk us getting caught, either. So I grabbed the buckle of my belt and pulled it through the loops. "Here," I said, handing it to her. "Bite down."

I expected her to argue or look at me like I was crazy, but she didn't. She understood damn well what I wanted, and she took the belt without question. Some part of me reveled in the knowledge that I'd not only have a notch in my belt from fucking her but I'd have her teeth marks etched into the leather as well. Christ, that was a powerful thought.

Even more powerful was the sight before me. Cassidy's ass bare and bent over her own desk—the place where she worked tirelessly to thwart my every attempt to catapult past her—and submissive to my will. Damn sexy. But I wanted more. I wanted to watch the shift of power, bask in my own dominance over her. Straightening, I palmed the cheeks of her round ass, none too gently. My thumbs swept her crevice and spread her wide. All of her intimate parts were on display, and she was at her most vulnerable. Her pussy stretched tight around my cock, the slick walls gripping and milking me with each retreating stroke. Goddamn, it was beautiful.

Shifting my weight to my left leg, I switched the angle and got my grind on. Slow and purposeful, so she could feel every detail of my cock. A dip at the knees gave me an even better angle from which to see all her juicy pink bits. So soft, so feminine, so harmless. But there was nothing harmless about Cassidy, was there?

I pulled almost all the way out before slamming back inside.

Cassidy jumped, because damn right her insides were at my mercy, and I had none to give. Just like she showed none to me.

"Don't move," I warned, pinning her in place. I did it again. And again. And again. Picking up my pace and driving deep, driving hard. The clinking of the metal buckle on my belt was like an applause for my performance and it drove me even further. So far that the momentum of my thrusts shoved her forward on the desk, and I had to grab her hips to pull her back toward my crotch. There would be no running from my cock. I would have my way. I would make her submit . . . one way or another. Digging my fingertips into her flesh, I pushed that goddamn skirt up; it was riding down and threatening to rob me of my view.

I almost wished it had.

My brain got all sideways on me with the new detail that had emerged. Cassidy had been hiding a secret, it seemed. There, perched on her left hip, was a tattoo of a single shooting star in blue with the name *Casey* etched beneath it in elegant script. A twinge of jealousy spiked from my insides, but only for a moment, before I remembered that I didn't do jealousy. This was only about leveling the playing field, asserting dominance over my competitor, and reminding her of her place. And if I was lucky, maybe the constant maddening craving that had been growing for her would finally go away. I *needed* it to go away.

So I covered up the goddamn tattoo with my thumb, and I fucked her. I fucked her hard and without mercy. Not a sound other than the slap of skin on skin and my own muted grunts. Cassidy took it. She took it and she didn't say a word or try to stop me. She liked it. Hell, I'd bet she even loved it.

But that goddamn tattoo was burning under my thumb, eating through my skin like liquid acid. And no matter how powerful I felt with each punishing thrust into Cassidy, satisfaction eluded me. My grip tightened and my pace quickened as I chased after it, but my control was quickly slipping. *What the fuck?*

I was very much aware of each milking orgasm she'd had. Three, to be exact, but there would be none for me. Out of breath, frustrated, and confused, I pulled free of her tight cunt and quickly tucked my deflating cock back into my pants before she could tell I was half limp.

Cassidy dropped the leather from her mouth and straightened. "What's wrong?"

When I took my belt back and started feeding it through the loops on my slacks, Cassidy put her hand on my arm. "Shaw?"

Her recoil as I looked up at her was unexpected. I wasn't sure what she saw on my face, though if it was anything like the chaos banging around in my head, it must have been scary. But again, I didn't give a shit. So I yanked free of her hold and made like a speeding bullet toward the door.

In truth, I didn't know what was wrong with me. But even if I had known, I sure as hell wasn't going to share with her.

CHAPTER 10
Cassidy

I had absolutely no clue what was going on. Everything was in chaos. Or so it seemed. And time to think about it over the weekend had made matters even more confusing.

I was fully aware of what the episode in my office on Thursday was all about. Shaw had felt emasculated, like he needed to prove something. Though I wasn't quite sure what that something was. What I did know was that I'd been nothing more than a tool in his quest to do so, an obstacle he needed to overcome. The fucking had been a spillover of the disagreement, an argument turned physical—only sexual instead of violent. We hadn't been two people engaging in the act of sex for mutual gratification. No, it had all been very one-sided. Shaw's comeback to my panty-throwing tantrum wasn't a witty retort but, rather, a show of dominance. Clearly, *he* had been fucking *me*. And then he stormed out of there without release and without giving me the chance for a rebuttal. I'd had no say in the matter, and even though I shouldn't have, I'd liked it. He'd taken the alpha title, and I'd surrendered it without putting up much of a fight. I was a little disappointed in myself, because I'd never been one who easily admitted defeat. But, somehow, I didn't feel defeated. All those orgasms felt like mini victories to me, even if they were made possible only by his generosity.

Nevertheless, Shaw's abrupt departure in the middle of our—let's call it "confrontation"—was still playing havoc with my head. The fact that he'd left without a word was like putting an exclamation point on the upper hand he'd already claimed. Dammit. My being okay with it wasn't sitting well with me. Though I knew it was impossible, I was afraid my submissive stance over my desk might lead to a submissive stance where Denver was concerned. Not that I'd literally bend over a desk for him like I did for Shaw, but that I might slip and let Shaw take the lead there as well.

Then there was the matter of Casey. Well, Casey wasn't really a "matter" per se, since he wasn't physically here, but I still felt his presence in my thoughts and heart. He'd been the only man I'd ever cared about, so why was I thinking about him in the same circle as Shaw? Much like I'd done to his picture on my desk, I pushed the thought of Casey aside once again to focus on the two more pressing issues: Shaw and Denver.

Both had gone MIA. Denver hadn't returned my phone calls over the weekend, and Shaw hadn't bothered to show up for work today. Shaw also hadn't been occupying his regular bar stool at Monkey Business. That was a huge miss. Chaz hadn't a clue what was up. Or so he'd said. And he'd stuck to his story even after Demi had put the whammy on him with that way she flirted to get anything she wanted. I had a sneaking suspicion something was happening on the QT. That or Shaw and Denver had gotten together and swapped stories like two chicks who'd just realized they'd been seeing the same guy. Technically, I hadn't been seeing Denver, but I hadn't done anything to make sure he was clear on that point, either.

Feeling the lateness of the hour from the long day, I unlocked the door to my apartment and stepped inside, closing it behind myself only to sink against it. A sense of abandonment punched at my chest for a moment. Not because Denver and Shaw had pulled a disappearing act on me but because my closest friend wasn't there. Quinn had moved in with Daddy over the weekend, and although none of the furniture in our apartment was missing—it all belonged to me—I still felt the emptiness.

With a heavy sigh, I pushed off the door and went over to the kitchen bar to put my messenger bag down. From there, it was on to the bedroom to change my clothes. I'd no sooner kicked off my shoes and shed my skirt than my cellphone rang. No way was I going to miss a call from Denver, so I ran out to the kitchen and dug through my bag to retrieve it before he could hang up.

The second I saw the caller ID, my heart leapt into my throat. My hands were shaking as I slid my finger across the bottom of the screen to answer the call. "Casey?"

"Hey, Cass. How's my favorite girl?" That deep, raspy voice with its heavy New England accent almost brought me to my knees.

A tear fell down my cheek as I sank to the floor and cradled the phone to my ear. The sound of his voice . . . Oh, God, the sound of his voice was like a hug from his arms. I hadn't realized how much I'd needed to hear it. Maybe that was the reason I'd been thinking about him so much.

"I'm good," I lied. "Working hard, trying to land a new client."

"Oh, yeah? Who's your victim this time?" I could hear the chuckle in his voice and imagined the crinkles at the corners of his eyes and his dazzling smile.

I couldn't help but smile as well. Casey had a knack for making me feel all warm and fuzzy on the inside. "Denver Rockford."

"No kidding? Tell me something: is he as much of a show-off in person as he is on the field?"

"Worse," I laughed.

"Bet he's got a thing for you."

That was Casey: he always thought everyone else was out to get his girl, because to him, I was the biggest catch in the ocean. And every time he asked the question, I could confidently tell him he was wrong. This time, it would be a lie. Seemed I was doing a lot of lying to him during this call. So instead, I opted for "Stop being silly." It wasn't a yes or a no, but it was still misleading.

"I'm not being silly. Whether we're together or not, you'll always be my beautiful girl."

"Casey . . ."

"All right. I'll stop embarrassing you." There was a pause and then: "I'm really proud of you, Cass. I know you don't hear it often enough, but I am. And for what it's worth, you did the right thing. Even if you are a million miles away from home . . . away from me."

"Casey?"

"Yeah?"

"I've really missed you."

"I know, Cass. I miss you, too. Every single day." He went quiet on the other end, but it didn't matter. He was there and I was here, yet we were still in the same place together. "Look out your window. You see it?"

The moon was only partially full, and wisps of clouds were floating by, but it didn't matter. My heart swelled all the same, because I knew exactly what he was getting at. "Yeah, I see it."

"So do I," he said. "Whatever . . . whenever."

Whatever was wrong or right, whenever I needed him most, he'd be right there. Just like the moon. That was what he meant. He'd made that promise the last night we'd spent on my rooftop before I'd left home for good, the night we'd broken up. And he'd always been true to his word.

"Same goes for you."

"Yeah, yeah . . . I'm fine. I've got a strong back and an even stronger mind, with the will to survive. You don't have to worry about me."

"What about our folks? How are they?"

"They're alive and kicking. You should probably call your ma, though. You know how she gets about not hearing from you."

"I just talked to her last week." Or at least I thought it had been last week. Doing the count in my head, maybe it had been the week before. I blamed Shaw and all his nonsense for getting me so sidetracked.

"Hey, don't shoot the messenger," he laughed. "Other than that, you know I'm holding down the fort here."

"I do. You're sort of my hero."

"Aw, that's sweet. Just sort of, huh?"

"You know what I mean." I cradled the phone to my smiling cheek. "Thank you."

"You don't have to thank me, Cass. We're family. That's what we do." There was another pause and then: "So how's the super-jerk?"

I was stunned for a moment at the question. The superjerk was Shaw, and I'd always talked about him with Casey, since the day he'd arrived at Striker and waltzed into that boardroom like a hotshot who was going to blow everyone else out of the water. I'd proven him wrong time and time again since then, and shown him that a woman could dominate in our world. I wasn't sure who was dominating whom now.

"That bad, huh?"

"You have no idea," I said.

"Then tell me."

But I couldn't talk about Shaw with Casey. Not anymore. Not when I wasn't sure where the truth began and the lie ended.

"It isn't worth the breath. Tell me about what's been going on with you."

"There isn't much to tell. It's Stonington, Cass. Nothing happens here." He laughed again.

"Then tell me what you did today. From the time you woke up until the time you called me. And go slow. I just want to hear your voice."

"Aw, darlin' . . . you're the sweetest part of me." He liked to say stuff like that to make me feel girly, and it worked every time. "Okay, so once upon a time . . ."

Though it was a normal day, Casey had this way of making the mundane seem spectacular by adding a wee bit of pizzazz and a lot of embellishment. This time, he told the tale as if he'd been a newcomer. He walked me through Stonington and his day on the boat like a virtual tour of the imagination. Every detail he provided was as if he'd seen the village where we'd grown up and met its locals for the very first time. It was a brilliant idea, one that reminded me about all the comforts of home and made me long to be there with him on our rooftop, under a sea of stars. To add insult to injury, Ma had apparently cooked up a batch of her famous chili and shovel-fed it to Casey—not that it had ever taken much effort on her part in reality.

Our laughter finally died down sometime later, when Casey reminded me that he was three hours ahead on the East Coast and needed his beauty sleep. A fisherman's alarm had him up and at 'em before most people switched to the cool side of the pillow. And Casey was no slacker. In addition to being the most adorable man I knew, he was also hardworking, with a blue-collar sex appeal.

I thought I'd be sad to hang up the phone, but I wasn't. I felt better than I had in a very long time, assured and more confident. Casey's "Show 'em no mercy, beautiful girl" was just the kick in the pants I needed. First thing in the morning, I was going to track down Denver, set him straight on what an appropriate relationship between a client and an agent was supposed to be like, and then I was going to do what I did best: bring home the win.

But tonight I needed food. Or at least that was what the rumbling in my tummy was telling me. Eating at home was something I rarely ever did, since I was usually out with my friends; luckily, Quinn always made sure we had the necessities, just in case. Chicken noodle soup sounded pretty good, so I dumped it into a bowl and popped it into the microwave and headed off to change into my jammies. Jammies, for me, consisted of a simple T-shirt and a pair of cotton shorts. By the time I was done, so was the soup. The crackers were a tad on the stale side, but they'd do. Soup, spoon, and water in hand, I decided to park it on the couch and do something else I rarely ever did: watch television.

Grabbing the remote, I clicked the TV on and settled in. Naturally, the channel had been set to whatever station would be broadcasting entertainment news, because Quinn liked to keep up on which celebrity was doing what and with whom. I was going to change it, but then breaking news hit, and I choked on a stupid noodle when Denver's face was plastered to the screen.

"San Diego quarterback Denver 'Rocket Man' Rockford was in the center of a scene that led to the arrest of sports agent Shaw Matthews earlier this evening. Matthews was reportedly arrested for assaulting a member of the paparazzi outside a Las Vegas strip club after this video was shot."

The screen cut to a shaky video clip showing Denver climbing onstage to get his bump and grind on with a barely legal blonde with a blackout bar across her obviously naked chest. She bent over for a Miley Cyrus twerk on his crotch, which was disgusting enough, but then all hell broke loose. While Denver was in the middle of "making it rain" on her, a plump woman in her forties stormed the place shouting, "That's my daughter! She isn't even eighteen, you pervert!" Sidekick Shaw went pasty white and scrambled to get Denver off the stage at right about the time the cameraman made his presence known, which sent Shaw into a frenzy of trying to get Denver to safety while blocking the camera's view and pushing the paparazzo off.

The film kept on rolling as they made it out to the sidewalk, where the cameraman pushed up against Shaw while the underage stripper's mother was dragging her out by the arm and yelling threats of legal action at Denver; on TV, Denver's every other word was bleeped out. Once Shaw had him inside the car, another cameraman muscled his way inside in an attempt to get even more footage. That's when it happened. Shaw grabbed the cameraman and yanked him out, shoving him to the sidewalk, and then took the camera from his hands and smashed it to the ground. A police officer charged Shaw there and then, pinning him to the car and twisting his arms behind his back.

It made me cringe. "Ouch! That's gotta hurt," I said out loud, even though no one else was there to hear me.

"Rockford's camp hasn't issued a public statement as of yet. In other news . . ."

Yeah, I really wasn't interested in any other news. This was exactly why I never watched television. Nothing good ever came of it. Hitting the power button on the remote, I sighed. "Well, at least I know where they've been hiding out."

And then my cell phone rang again. Only this time, it wasn't Casey. "Cassidy Whalen," I answered.

A prerecorded voice greeted me from the other end. "This is a collect call from . . ."

"Shaw," the automated system provided in his voice.

" . . . an inmate at the Clark County Detention Center." There was a lot of legal mumbo jumbo after that, but I was too busy rolling my eyes to pay attention. I did, however, accept the call.

"Hey, buddy! How's Vegas?" I asked when the connection was finally made.

"Cute." I didn't think he meant it. "How much do you know?"

"Not much. Just what's plastered all over *TMZ*. I've got to hand it to you, though: it made for some pretty great entertainment. I suppose you're going to want to tell me your side of things now?"

"Not particularly. Besides, I don't have time. I need you to do something for me."

"I'm not bailing you out. You can rot in there for all I care."

"I'm desperate, but not that desperate."

"The fact that you're on the other end of my line, calling from a Las Vegas jail to ask me a favor, would indicate the opposite."

"Look, I just need you to check on Denver and be sure he made it back okay."

"You lost Denver?" I shrieked. "Nice. Real nice, Matthews. You know he's impulsive, and you've got him in the city of sin on top of that." I felt like a baby mama lecturing the father on his bad parenting skills.

"He's not impulsive. He just likes to show off a bit. Will you check on him or not?"

"I tried calling him all weekend. I highly doubt he's going to suddenly answer now." And then I had an even better idea. "I'm calling his mother."

"No! Cassidy, don't call the man's mom on him. That's not cool."

None of this was cool.

"Bye, Shaw. Be sure to keep your back to the wall in there. Your ass is much too pretty for your own good." Before he could say anything else, I hung up the phone.

Shaw

Cassidy had disconnected before I could ask her to call Chaz for me. Which meant I'd likely be sitting in a jail cell until a court hearing, where the judge would, hopefully, let me go on my own recognizance. In hindsight, maybe I should've used my one phone call to ring up my only friend instead, then had him make the embarrassing plea to my competitor. I'd had hours to bang my hungover head against the wall because of that bad decision. Well, all of the bad decisions I'd been making as of late, really.

Christ, what a weekend. In the wake of my loss of composure with Cassidy on Thursday, I'd had a little pep talk with myself. Whatever malfunctioning my brain was suffering from had to be righted. I was Shaw fucking Matthews, and Shaw Matthews never lost control. Least of all to a chick. Looking back at the whole painful ordeal, I could at least be honest enough with myself to admit that in an effort to assert my dominance, I'd become weak. Not anymore.

All of this debauchery had started with the partnership, and the partnership was where it would end. I couldn't lose sight of that. No matter how good the pussy, Denver was the finish line. The problem was that Denver also had pussy on the brain. So I'd decided to give the man what he wanted and, thank God, I knew where to get it for him. What started out as a party with Yvonne and one of her very good friends ended up with us ditching the girls and skipping town on a last-minute Vegas getaway instead. Denver's idea, of course. Denver's idea, but my tab. Fuck it. It would be worth it in the end when he signed on the dotted line and made me a very happy man with the secured future I'd been busting my ass for.

Thanks to Cassidy, my little buddy wasn't working quite right anymore. Though for some odd reason, he wanted to come to life at the thought of her. Traitor. Otherwise, I would've stayed in town and fucked Yvonne all night. That was what I should've done. At least then I wouldn't have been escorted to the pokey by the oh so polite boys in tan. I also wouldn't have been booked and charged with one count of misdemeanor assault and one count of malicious property damage, also a misdemeanor. My fingers wouldn't be stained with ink, and my reputation wouldn't be just as tarnished. I'd partied with my clients plenty, but never had it resulted in scandal and arrest. And Denver wasn't even my client. Yet.

The click of the lock on my cell door sounded intimidating, courtesy of the acoustics caused by cement walls, a high ceiling, and a stainless steel toilet. A decent-looking Hispanic woman was on the other side, short and mannish in build, with her dark hair in a bun, but she had a cute face all the same.

"Matthews . . . you've been sprung, and I need this cell for the next fuckup, so let's move."

I was pretty sure she wasn't supposed to talk to me like that, and I didn't appreciate her tone; nor did I have a clue as to how I'd been *sprung*, but I wasn't going to argue the point. The officers took their sweet time about getting my personal effects and the paperwork for my release, which was funny because it sure hadn't taken them anywhere near as long to process my ass into the system in the first place. Okay, maybe it wasn't so much funny as it was annoying as hell. But I was out the door with my manila envelope and without a clue about who'd made it possible or where I should even begin to start looking for Denver.

Fishing my phone out of the envelope, I scrolled through the long list of missed calls—all from my current clients, most likely wanting to voice their concerns—but found none from Denver. I was about to call him when I noticed that my battery had zero life, and, of course, I had no charger with me.

"Great," I said aloud.

It was then that a rare breeze came at me, carrying the overpowering scent of Old Spice. When I heard the thud of boots on pavement and the jingling of what I could only assume was a wallet chain, I knew who'd bailed me out of jail.

"Mr. Matthews," came the burly voice of Denver's father.

I turned to face him with a smile, though I wasn't sure if I'd be met with a fist to the face for letting Denver get so out of hand in the public eye. "Mr. Rockford, please tell me Denver is okay."

"Oh, yeah. He's just fine, son. And you gotta stop being so formal with me. Gives me the heebie-jeebies. I'm just regular folk, no better than any other Joe on the street, so call me by my name."

"Can I assume you paid my bail?"

"Nope. That was all Denver, though we thought it best if I came here to do the deed. That boy probably needs to stay out of the limelight for the time being."

I cringed. "Yeah, I'm sorry about that."

"Don't be. You took one for the home team, and we won't soon forget that. In addition to the bail, Denver will also be covering any attorney expenses and fines that come out of this mess. It's the least he can do for all the trouble he caused."

"Wait. You're not mad at me?"

Boulder gave a hearty laugh and slapped his meaty paw on my shoulder, but thankfully I had the balance not to stumble forward from the blow of it. "Hell no! Boys will be boys. Besides, once Denver gets something set in his head, he does it. The best thing you could've done was tag along with him to keep him out of trouble. Otherwise, I guarantee things would've been worse."

Well, damn. Looked like I'd actually managed to score some points after all. Whether it was enough to one-up Cassidy or not remained to be seen.

"Where is he now?"

Boulder kept his arm around my shoulders as we walked toward the parking lot. "Numbnuts is back at the hotel with his mama. She hasn't shown him a bit of mercy since we landed, either. We managed to get hotel security to open the door for us and then found him passed out, hugging the toilet in his suite." He laughed in that way fathers do when their sons have learned a lesson the hard way. "If Cassidy hadn't tracked him down, we probably never would've known which hotel he was staying at. She's pretty amazing, that one. Smart."

In the parking lot, he pointed to the passenger door of a silver subcompact car.

When I raised a brow in question, Boulder said, "Don't laugh. It was all they had available on short notice, and I'm not one for having somebody else drive me around like I'm some bougie pansy."

" 'Bougie'?" I laughed, caught off guard.

"Hey, I can keep up with you young ones. I'm hip, cool, amaze-nuts."

"You mean 'amazeballs'?"

"Whatever. Just get in the car, smart-ass." Nothing about Boulder's demeanor said he was insulted. At least not until he climbed into the driver's side, his large frame folding up like an accordion. "God, I wish I had my bike," he said before starting the wind-up toy.

I remembered my first impression of him and couldn't help

asking, "Your bike wouldn't happen to have a chrome skull, would it?"

He looked at me, surprised. "With an opened jaw for the headlight. Now, how'd you know that?"

I smiled, pretty damn proud of myself that I'd nailed it. "Just a hunch."

"You're pretty smart, too, you know. Either way my boy decides to go, I'm glad to know he'll be in good hands."

"Does that mean he's definitely decided to go with Striker?"

"Yep" was all he offered, and that was okay by me.

I used the short drive to the hotel to get on a friendlier basis with Denver's father. Motorcycles turned out to be a topic that enthused Boulder, so I was quite pleased to ask him as many questions as I could about them. Older men love to "school" the young on that sort of thing, and I was eager to learn. Once we made it to the hotel, we went straight up to Denver's suite, planned his great escape out the back entrance, stuffed his big ass into the back of the car like a sardine in a can, and Fred Flintstoned our way to the airport, where a private jet was waiting for takeoff. Again, my treat.

Jesus, I was glad this horrible nightmare was coming to an end. But I still wasn't looking forward to facing Cassidy the next day. Seeing the smug look on her face might actually be a fate worse than the one I'd already endured.

CHAPTER 11
Cassidy

Having a super-famous son couldn't be easy. It was bad enough to find out that your child had been onstage with (what turned out to be) an underage, half-naked girl, making a fool of himself and generally acting like a lascivious idiot. But to also find out that he'd pretty much abandoned the one person who'd at least tried to protect him was like a slap in the face to the people who had raised him to be a good person. That slap was going to earn Denver one of his own . . . to the back of the head.

Delilah hadn't been a happy camper when I called to rat out her son, but she and Boulder had hopped a flight to McCarran International all the same. Which had left me with the task of—within the span of their one-hour flight—tracking down whatever hotel Denver might have checked into. I'd gotten lucky in that he actually had retreated out of the public eye instead of catching his own flight back and leaving Shaw stranded in jail. Though Shaw had made some really stupid decisions and shown some gross negligence in the handling of Denver, for Denver to then desert him was a deed worse than Shaw's.

A phone call from Delilah was the only insight I had as to what was going on, but she'd assured me her son was safe and sound and had been sleeping it off when they'd arrived. She'd nurse him back to a condition that would enable him to fly without causing even more of a ruckus, and then she was going to have a stern talk with him. Boulder had bailed out Denver's accomplice, though Shaw would need to return for a court date in the not so distant future.

I'd done my research on Shaw's misdemeanor charges as well—that was just the sort of thing I did—and I'd learned that he'd likely be out only around three thousand dollars or so. Assuming this was a first-time offense. It was. I knew because I'd, of course, also conducted a lot of research on the likes of Mr. Matthews when I'd heard he'd been hired and rumors of his big-shot ways spread like wildfire through the office. Maybe I'd felt threatened, but I'd rather think of it as sizing up the competition. After all, you have to know the enemy before you can defeat him.

Shaw skipped work again on Tuesday, but I knew he was back in town—I'd finally talked to Denver, who had apologized profusely for nothing in particular. He didn't owe me any sort of apology, though I supposed his sending my calls to voice mail had been rude. It wasn't that I'd felt particularly slighted by it—busy clients did that sort of thing all the time—but he still needed to squirm for a bit to learn a valuable lesson: Thou shalt not ignore thy potential agent. Or something like that.

There was another person I was interested in watching squirm, as well. I felt like I was due a front-row seat to whatever humiliation Shaw would be feeling once he saw me again, and Monkey Business was just that. If he was going to show his face at all, it would be there. So I left work early and got real good and comfortable, with an icy brew from the tap in hand. There I sat, catching up with my friends and minding my own business (read: stalking the bar for Shaw's arrival and walk of shame), when an audible gasp drew my attention toward Quinn. Who looked as pale as the living dead. He was staring toward a man and woman who'd just come through the door, and he wasn't making a sound, though he definitely seemed to be trying to.

Naturally, I was concerned for my friend, so I put down the cellphone I'd only been pretending to read messages on. "What is it, Quinn? What's wrong?"

He closed his mouth and then opened it again, but still nothing came out. I couldn't be sure, but there might have been tiny beads of sweat forming on his brow. Obviously, he was in some sort of distress.

"Amazing. It's like a ventriloquist stuck his hand up his butt to move the mouth but forgot to throw the voice." Demi snapped her fingers in front of Quinn's face. "Hey, Queer Eye, stop making fishy faces and spit it out. Who is that?"

"Daddy . . ." came his dramatically whispered voice. "And his *wife*."

So the three of us girls did a double take, which made it what? Like six takes? Okay, so we gawked and didn't even bother to cover it up. It was the first time any one of us had ever laid eyes on Daddy, and his wife was with him, too? Well, that was a twofer we'd be crazy to miss.

Daddy was a hunk. I wasn't sure why that surprised me, but it did. I'd expected some burly old guy with too much around his center and not enough on top of his head who had a thing for young men that were way out of his league. That wasn't the case at all. Daddy was tall with a medium build and had obviously spent some time at the gym. Every part of his being was well groomed, from his dark and dapper haircut to his clean-shaven face to the tailor-made suit and handmade custom Italian alligator shoes. He looked like a million bucks, and I'd bet he smelled like it, too.

"Good God, he's gorgeous," Sasha said, swooning.

"Pierce Brosnan," I blurted out, not realizing I'd been squeezing Quinn's hand. "He looks like freakin' *Pierce Brosnan.*"

"You're tapping that?" Demi asked.

Quinn pulled his hand free of my grasp. "Uh, you don't need to know the specifics of who's tapping whom. But I do need to know what *he* is doing *here*, of all places, with *her*?"

"Her" was beautiful, a match suitable for such a spectacular specimen of a man. It was all for show, I was sure: a superficial need of someone in his position to be seen with someone who was every bit as glamorous as his lifestyle. Her platinum-blond hair was perfectly coiffed, her makeup was flawless, and her diamonds sparkled so bright she needed sunglasses just to wear them. And, wow, she had the best figure money could buy. It didn't stop there, but jeez Louise, I wished it had because I was on the verge of a very embarrassing shoegasm.

On her delicate feet were red-and-black couture d'Orsay T-straps with a smitten heel befitting a pinup girl the likes of Marilyn Monroe, and they matched her red Monica dress perfectly. Quinn was right. Why in the world would someone who was dressed for a night out with the social elite be at a workingmen's watering hole?

With a synchronized turn of our heads, we watched as the pair practically glided across the room like they owned the place and took a seat at a table against the far wall. When Daddy glanced in our direction, we averted our eyes, but not Quinn. Quinn looked like his heart had been shattered to smithereens.

"Hey, are you okay?" I asked, taking his hand—much more gently this time.

He was still glaring across the room. "Look at her. She's a hateful bitch. Do you know she threatens to turn his kids against him every time he tells her she can't have something she wants?"

"That body has had kids?" Demi asked. Sasha elbowed her. "Ow! What? She looks good."

Through clenched teeth, Sasha mumbled something at Demi that sounded an awful lot like "Shut your piehole," though I could've been mistaken. Her face softened when she turned toward Quinn and said, without clenched teeth, "I don't get it. Why are they here?"

"I'm about to find out," Quinn said, standing. "Daddy's on the move."

Sure enough, Daddy was headed toward the bathrooms, giving a slight nod in that direction for Quinn to follow.

I felt bad for Quinn, I really did, but until he learned to value himself enough to demand the very best, he'd always get shorted in the end. This situation seemed like a ticking time bomb ready to go off in his face at any moment.

I still had time to kill since Shaw hadn't shown up yet, so I turned to the next subject on the board. "Who's the new flavor of the week, Sash?" I asked before taking a drink of my beer, which was quickly warming to room temperature. Since her last dating debacle, I hadn't heard a thing on the man scene, which was unusual. She usually rebounded pretty quick.

Sasha wasn't paying attention. In fact, she hadn't even heard my question. Instead, she was staring toward the bar. At Landon, which was an interesting turn of events. But the way she was looking at him was somehow different than she ever had before. "Have you guys ever noticed how hot Landon is?"

Demi and I looked at each other and burst out laughing at the same time.

"Finally!" I said, slamming my hand down on the table.

That got Sasha's attention. "What's so funny? You don't think he's hot?" And then the pouty lip came out. It truly was adorable.

I could see how it got her out of parking tickets and other sticky situations.

Demi cuddled her close and kissed her cheek. "D'awww. What's funny is that you're just now realizing it. I swear, Sasha, sometimes I worry about you, but I knew you'd find your way in the end."

"What way?"

Demi took Sasha's face in her hands and turned her in the direction of the bar where Landon was standing. He looked over his shoulder at her, as if he could feel her eyes on him, and winked. My heart grew three sizes in that moment. It was the single most swoony thing I'd ever seen, because I knew. I knew how he felt about her.

"Oh" was all Sasha said, with those doe eyes blinking. I could almost see the light coming on behind those big baby browns. She'd finally gotten it.

"Bartender!" I yelled toward Chaz. "Another round for me and my pals. We've cause to celebrate."

Shaw was a no-show. Again. Curse him for making me wait to rub his nose in the colossal screwup that would forever define his career. If the universe bestowed any favors on me, anyway.

Quinn had emerged from the bathroom, quite the happy camper, to say that Daddy and "the old ball and chain" had come to Monkey Business at her request. Daddy thought she must have been suspicious of his extracurricular activities, but it turned out she'd simply had a hankering for pub food. I said I thought it was rude for Quinn to be referred to as an extracurricular activity, which earned me the evil-eye warning from my closest friend, so I shut up about it.

We were granted a never-before-seen performance by Sasha when she morphed into Flirty Sasha and aimed her sights at Landon. She asked him out. Boldly and quite loudly, I might add. He looked surprised and maybe even a little disbelieving, but in the end, he went with it, not making a big deal out of the situation—mostly because Landon never made a big deal out of anything. He just took things as they came. And so they left with their arms linked, their courtship officially under way.

On Wednesday morning, while I was curious to know how Lansha's (the new blended name the rest of us had debated over and settled on) date had gone, I was on a mission. A mission that found me charging toward Shaw's office to see if he'd finally decided to bring his slacker butt to work. If he had, I was going to get my two cents in before he could make any kind of excuse about having some meeting to attend or a phone call to make.

His suite was dark when I popped in, but I could see that the light in his office was on from the crack under the door. So Ben hadn't yet arrived, but maybe Shaw had. Without knocking—because Shaw rarely ever did—I barged inside. Sure enough, there he sat behind his desk with a pile of pending contracts before him, acting all "early bird gets the worm" when in reality he was playing catch-up from his extended weekend getaway. When he looked up and saw me, he sighed and took off his glasses, which I had no clue he wore.

"I wondered how long it would take you to pounce," he said, slumping in his chair. "Come on in and shut the door. We don't want to give the gossip hounds something to howl about."

He was right. The office staff kept a keen eye on our every move, just waiting for something juicy. It was our own fault; we'd rarely ever paid attention to the audience of our showdowns.

Once I'd closed the door, Shaw cut to the chase: "Go ahead. Get it out of your system. I have a lot of fires to put out today."

That was when I realized I didn't know what to say. I'd been waiting for so long to go off on him, and when I finally had the chance, I had no idea what to go off on him about.

"Well?"

"You made me mad." Not very witty, but true. "How dare you—?"

"How dare I what?" Shaw sat forward. "How dare I play dirty? Or is it, How dare I steal Denver away so I can have him to myself for a while? Or is it maybe, How dare I try to butter him up by catering to his needs? Or, most likely, How dare I do *exactly* what you've been doing, too?"

Obviously, he had been better prepared for this face-off.

"Oh, yeah?" Really? I didn't have anything else to say to that?

"Yeah."

We sounded like children.

And right on cue, my hand found my hip. "Well, at least I didn't create a scandal for him."

"There is no scandal. No charges were pressed against him because he didn't do anything wrong. The club was at fault for hiring someone underage. Denver had no way of knowing. No charges pending. Happy?"

No. "It's still bad publicity."

He sighed and pinched the bridge of his nose. "You obviously didn't watch the news this morning. It's all over the place. Denver has been cleared of any wrongdoing. He's issued a public statement, apologizing for his behavior and speaking out against the unlawful exploitation of women, underage or not."

Oh. But . . . "The feminist activists of the world will eat him alive."

"I'm sorry. Did I forget to mention he's donated an insane amount of money to the National Organization for Women? Because yeah, he did that, too. Under my advisement."

I had to admit that Shaw's swift and effective handling of the situation made me nervous. "So he signed with you?"

"Not yet. But it's looking good." The smug smile for which Shaw was famous crept onto his face. "Scared?"

Yes. "No."

"You should be."

My thoughts flashed to the elevator ride before my beach date with Denver. I couldn't believe Shaw was throwing my own words back at me. "Get your own material."

Shaw's laugh was too confident. So was the way he relaxed into his chair like he was sitting on a throne. "Aww, are you pouting, Whalen? It sucks when you know someone has pulled ahead of you in the race, doesn't it?"

"You're not ahead."

"It would appear that I am."

"A little friendly advice?" I was desperate.

"Just because we fuck on occasion, it doesn't mean we're friends. Get over yourself."

I ignored another attempt to cut me with my own words. "You should be more careful. While you're trying to score the golden goose, your other hens might fly the coop. Not showing up for work and ignoring your existing clients will only lose you the partnership. Wade won't put up with it."

Shaw tossed his pen onto the desk. "I appreciate your concern about my clients, but you can rest assured they're well tended. None of them have been slighted in the least. And my time away from the office was approved by Wade, not that it's any of your business."

Speak of the devil. Wade's muffled voice was just outside Shaw's door, bidding a good morning to Ben, who had apparently arrived while Shaw and I were going at it.

"Is he in?" Wade asked Ben.

"I'm pretty sure he is, sir. His light is on, and I thought I heard voices coming from inside."

If I could hear every word as clearly as I just had, how clearly had Ben heard us?

My eyes went wide as saucers. "Do you think he heard the part about fucking?" I whispered.

"Shh! I don't know, but we're not going to take any chances." Shaw rolled his chair back. "Here. Hide under my desk."

"What?" I was *not* going to crawl under his desk.

"If there's no one in here, the conversation couldn't have happened, right?"

I supposed that made sense.

"So get down there and keep your trap shut. When Wade's gone, I'll send Ben to make some copies or something, and then you can leave."

There was a courtesy knock at his door then, the kind people only make to alert you to the fact that they're coming in, whether you invited them to or not. Having no time to think it through, I panicked and made a mad dash for the cubby under Shaw's desk. It was roomy, but not so much when Shaw scooted forward to take his natural place. Which meant his crotch was right in front of my face. Fantastic.

"Morning, Matthews! Still cleaning up the mess?" Ha! Shaw was about to get reamed, and I was going to get to see it all go down. Well, since I was trapped under a desk, I guess I was going to hear it go down.

"Good morning, sir. The mess is gone, and we're back in business."

The seat on the opposite side of the desk creaked with what I assumed was Wade's weight. "Wonderful! You really saved the day, son. I won't soon forget it. Things could've gotten really ugly on this."

Son? I couldn't believe it. He was actually getting away with the colossal fumble. No flag on the play. If this were an actual game and I were the coach on the opposing team, I'd demand a review.

"I know. But it was my fault to begin with. I never should've let it get as far as it did."

Damn right, he shouldn't have. I nudged the inside of Shaw's thigh, tempted to give him a horse bite. He kicked back and missed.

"Be that as it may, you kept it together and showed strength under pressure. Commendable."

Oh, he did, did he? Maybe he just didn't have the right kind of pressure on him. Though I knew my asinine idea could backfire in my face and get us both caught, I couldn't resist the urge to make Shaw look stupid. Wade was still going on and on about what an asset Shaw was to Striker, how the company he'd helped build from the ground up was a better place because Shaw graced it with his presence, how the accounts he'd wrangled were among the most coveted. I was sick to my stomach. Shaw had screwed up, and he was being showered with praise. So since I knew he couldn't do a damn thing about it, I unfastened his pants and pulled his cock out.

No idea why I'd done that, but the ball was in the air on a Hail Mary and there was no turning back now. Oh, Shaw tried to stop me, but without throwing a monkey wrench into all the admiration that was coming his way, he couldn't.

How was it possible that the man was hard? I supposed I shouldn't have been surprised that compliments gave him a boner, but Jesus. I'd always thought the extent of his egomania had been an overexaggeration of my own imagination. Apparently not.

Shaw shifted in his chair, desperately trying to get me to release his cock.

"You look surprised, Matthews."

I bet he did. It was all I could do to contain my snickering.

"This isn't the first time I've ever given you a compliment, is it?"

"Um, no." Shaw cleared his throat when I licked the tip of his cock. "No, sir." I could've sworn his voice had raised an octave. "It's just that I didn't expect one after what had happened. But, um, thank you."

I took him fully into my mouth, and as I did so, my head hit the bottom of the drawer above me, which forced Shaw to shift again in his seat to account for the sound. But I didn't let go. Not even when he slipped a hand under the desk to try to push me off. Hooking the insides of his thighs, I held my place.

Wade hadn't a clue that his Boy Scout was getting a blow job right in front of him. Though Shaw's cock was quite large, I was sure Wade had bigger things to worry about. "So, how much damage to our chances?"

Shaw leaned his upper torso all the way forward so that his hips scooted back in an attempt to pull his cock out of my mouth. It didn't work. I was locked on tight. Though it was comical to watch him try to disengage while still maintaining a coherent conversation. "Actually, I think you'll be happy to hear there was none. I got it straight from Rocket's father that he will definitely be signing with Striker. Congratulations, sir, you got your prize."

That certainly called for retaliation. I sucked hard, pulling back and then taking him deep again. Shaw's grip on my shoulder tightened, but he was no longer trying to shove me off.

"Holy shit, Matthews! You did it? You got the contract? Well,

hell . . . we need to call a staff meeting and make the official announcement."

My teeth scraped the skin, and Shaw's voice found that octave again. "No, sir." He paused for a moment before continuing,
which gave me the green light to get to work. "I'm sorry, but I
didn't get the contract."

Wade got quiet, and I stopped, afraid he might have heard me.
"Whalen got it?"

"Not yet. But I did get the guarantee from Mr. Rockford that
his son will sign with our agency. Denver has yet to decide which
agent he will go with. Though I feel confident about my chances.
In spite of my error in judgment."

Over my dead body. I was done playing with him. I wanted
him to squirm, to look like an idiot in front of Wade. So I pressed
my tongue along the length of his cock as I pulled back, swirling
it around the head before taking him in again. Over and over, I
repeated the same movement, Shaw's hidden hand now finding
the back of my neck.

"Yes, well, that's good news all the same. But I wouldn't count
your chickens before they hatch. Whalen is a formidable opponent. She knows how to suck 'em in."

"Oh, she definitely knows how to suck, all right," Shaw mumbled.

"I'm sorry, what was that?"

"Nothing, sir."

I took him all the way to the back of my throat and then swallowed. Shaw moaned, and it was all I could do to keep from
laughing around the cock in my mouth.

"Are you okay, Matthews?"

"Hmm? Yeah, yeah. I've just been having this pain in my leg
since Vegas. I think I might've strained a muscle or something."
And there was the squirm I'd been searching for.

"You should have that checked out." Crap! It hadn't worked. Wade was oblivious.

"You're right. I'll do that as soon as possible."

I heard the creak of the chair again as Wade stood. "Okay, well, congratulations on saving the day. I'll leave you to your work now."

He was leaving? No! I'd done all of that for nothing?

"Thank you. I'd walk you out, but you know, the leg and all." I hated Shaw Matthews.

"No need. I know my way around here. Take care of that, you hear?"

"Will do. Have a good day." I'd begun to release Shaw, defeated, but he put a stop to that when he fisted my hair. "And, I'm sorry, but could you please ask Ben to come in on your way out? Thanks."

The door opened, and I could hear Wade doing just that. Within seconds, Ben was at the threshold. "Yeah, boss?"

"Lock and close my door, please. I have a very important call to make, and I don't want to be disturbed for any reason. Understood?" Shaw's voice was direct and left no room for questioning.

"You got it," Ben said, and then I heard two clicks. One for the lock and the other for the door.

And then Shaw finally looked down at me. His cock was as far in my mouth as it could go without choking me, and he wouldn't turn me loose. The expression on his face confused me. I wasn't sure if he was pleased with what he saw or angry. Though I knew he was angry, didn't I? Of course he was. I'd just tried to sabotage him in front of our boss.

That might not have been the smartest idea I'd ever had. If that look had been any indication, I'd say I was in for it.

So I tried to pull away again, stopped once more by Shaw's hold.

"Where do you think you're going, Cassidy?" The smirk he wore resembled that of a cat toying with its meal. "You haven't finished. Well begun is still only half done, and we both know how strict you are about the follow-through."

Pressing his shoulder blades to the back of the chair, Shaw kept control of my head as he backed himself out of my mouth only to roll his hips forward again. "Nice and slow now," he said.

As if I had any say in the matter. For a moment, I allowed myself to play with the idea of biting down, but in the end, I decided against it. My last harebrained idea hadn't exactly worked out in my favor. I was getting lockjaw to prove it.

"Deeper."

I gagged when he pushed too far.

"Yeah, I like that."

He liked that? I sure as hell didn't. So I put my hand around the base of his cock, keeping him from doing it again. Throwing up all over a man's crotch while giving him a blow job wouldn't be sexy in the least, no matter what he thought. He was delusional.

"Aww, that's no fun," he said with a fake pout. "But have it your way." The grin that followed worried me more than the smirk from before.

And with good reason.

Shaw's hold tightened and he lifted his hips, beginning a series of short but quick thrusts in and out of my mouth. He groaned, watching the whole thing play out like we were two porn stars hamming it up for the camera.

"Look at me." His order was a half growl. When I did as directed, he followed up with "Oh, yeah . . . that's my good girl."

I didn't know what it was about his words, but the pooling moisture between my legs was no illusion. I loved that I'd pleased him. And it made no sense at all. Suddenly, I felt like that porn star and slipped into the role, clawing at his thigh with one hand and stroking his cock with the other. Meeting the thrust of his hips with the bob of my head, I took him on, hollowing out my cheeks and sucking him hard.

With a steady rhythm established, Shaw stopped fucking my mouth and let me have my way. And have my way, I did.

His cock became even more rigid and his body strained as he settled into the chair and braced for what was undoubtedly one hell of a massive orgasm building. Shaw was silent, but I could hear his breaths and a stray grunt here and there. It was taking a lot for him not to make a sound, and the knowledge of that was like a big pat on the back. I was doing that to him. I was making him feel damn good. And I could take his pleasure away at my whim. Power. It was sheer power. But rather than abuse it, I drew confidence from it. Though I'd never wanted to give Shaw any sort of satisfaction, I wanted to give him this.

So I sucked, and I licked, and I coaxed his orgasm from the pit of its origin. When Shaw's fingers tightened on the armrests and he went white-knuckled, I knew it was coming. Or, rather, he was. There was no time to figure out whether I was a spitter, a swallower, or none of the above because the release was already there and filling up my mouth. Squeezing my eyes shut, I took it in big gulps and swallowed it down.

Shaw's cock went flaccid in my mouth and I finally pulled away, giving the head one last, sweet kiss. And then the jackass attached to it ruined the whole moment when he handed me a tissue from his desk and said, "You missed a spot." I narrowed my eyes and snatched it from his hand. "Just right there," he said, pointing at the corner of his own mouth.

I wiped at the spot and gave him a flippant smile. "Better?"

"Yep." He scooted his chair back to give me room to crawl out from under his desk, which I did quickly. "Thanks for cleaning up after yourself. That was pretty cool of you."

"You're not welcome."

He laughed, pulling me down into his lap. "I was just joking. Don't be so mean."

"I'm mean?" I jumped out of his lap, prepared to lay into him.

Shaw put his finger to his lips to stop my rant, then pushed a line on his phone to dial an extension. "Ben?"

"Yeah, boss?"

"I need you to print the Kershawn file and make six copies of each contract. And I need it right away for a meeting. Understood?"

"Roger that. I'm on it."

When the line went dead, Shaw walked over to the door and listened. After a moment, he cracked it, then opened it all the way. "You're free to go," he said, extending an arm in invitation. Checking myself over to be sure my suit was in fair condition, I stalked past. But not before tucking the used, semen-soiled tissue into his jacket pocket.

"I'll get even," I assured him as I walked away.

"I'm sure you will."

CHAPTER 12
Shaw

Cassidy Whalen had just given me every white-collar working man's ideal fantasy. A blow job from under the desk. The real thing had been a bit more risqué than was safe, and she was damn lucky her stunt hadn't gotten us caught. In truth, the danger factor had been a serious turn-on, but that was besides the fact.

Just having her under my desk and knowing she was that close to my cock was enough to give me a hard-on, but when she brazenly pulled it out and then put her mouth on it, I nearly lost all composure. That woman was going to be the death of me. Wade couldn't leave soon enough. I knew it had all been a game to her, some sick and twisted idea to throw me off. But messing with a man's cock like that was no game. And I was hell-bent on having her finish what she'd started. To my delight, she hadn't put up a fight.

Cassidy could bitch and moan all she wanted, but when it came right down to it, she wanted me every bit as much as I wanted her. Every single second of every single day. So when she'd said she'd get even, some very disturbed part of me had cheered. I was looking forward to it, even if I was a little paranoid.

"Dude, you got a hit out on you?" Chaz asked.

"Huh?"

He laughed, finishing up with drying one freshly washed mug and moving to the next. "You keep looking over your shoulder. Let me guess: you have another psycho stalker."

There might have been an incident a few months back with this one chick who'd started writing our marital vows before the stain on the sheets had even dried. I'd tried to let her down easy, but the "I'm not looking for a committed relationship right now" that came out of my mouth went into her ears sounding more like "I wasn't looking for a committed relationship . . . until I found you."

"Man, I don't know what it is about you that makes these women so crazy."

I shrugged. "What can I say? I'm cursed with a big dick." All men brag even when it's a lie. But it isn't bragging if you can back it up. I could.

The door opened and Landon walked in with Sasha, which was no surprise; neither was the fact that they were holding hands. But what was a surprise was the kiss on the lips he leaned in to give her, followed by a charming little peck to the tip of her nose, before he reluctantly turned her loose to join Cassidy and the others at their table. I was aware that I was staring, but then again, so was about half the room, all the women swooning even as Sasha gave a girly giggle I hadn't heard from her before. The color to her cheeks and the way her eyes lit up with the smile she was sporting—also different—left no room for question. She was smitten.

And so was my friend. Landon's few steps to his normal place beside me at the corner of the bar was full of confidence and—what were the kids calling it now?—swag. Landon had swag.

"Holy fuck! When did that happen?" I asked him, sounding a lot like a chick waiting for him to dish the deets. Yes, men talk, too. As much as women love to think they have the market on gossip cornered, they don't. Bro talk is just a little more sacred because we infuse the bro code into it. Which means we aren't likely to go blabbing what we know, for fear that our shit will get leaked as well.

"Last night, man," Chaz answered for him. "Sasha looked at him and it was just bam, on."

Landon laughed. "Shut up and give me a beer."

Landon was a very private person. He never talked about his personal life or boasted about the hottie he'd been seeing. Mostly because we all knew he'd been saving himself for Sasha. Not that he'd ever said it out loud. We just knew. The only time a man was ever that protective of a woman was when he cared about her to the core. And Landon was one hell of a badass when it came to Sasha: silent but deadly.

Chaz reached into the refrigerated locker below the bar and popped the top off a longneck before sliding it across the glossy surface of the bar to Landon. "So how did it go?"

Landon took a drink, considering the question. "You saw the smile on her face, didn't you?"

"Hard to miss," I answered.

He gave a self-assured nod that wasn't ego-driven in the least. "That's all the answer you need. And her happiness is all I need."

Chaz gave Landon's arm a playful punch. "Yeah, and at least I know I won't have to kick your ass for hurting her."

"Nah, she's had enough hurt, man. I'm going to show her what it's like to be with a real man now."

"Well, I say it's about time you two got together. It took her long enough to get there, but all that matters is that she did." I gave him a congratulatory clap on the back that he damn well deserved. And he wasn't the only one. "What about you, Chaz?"

But Chaz hadn't heard a word I'd said; he was watching Demi

as she came through the door and walked across the room to join her friends at their regular table. The smile she gave him was beyond flirtatious. So was the demure "Hey, Chaz" and the finger wave.

"Are you ever going to get off your ass and do anything about that?" I asked. No idea why I suddenly thought I was the king of relationship advice, but it was pouring out of me without a filter.

"Dude, she walks in and my dick gets hard." He adjusted himself to prove it. "I'm just glad I work behind the bar, so no one can see it. I can't even hook up with anyone else to try to fuck her out of my mind, because every time I try"—he nodded toward the table where the object of his affection sat giggling, no doubt over Sasha's retelling of her date with Landon—"the cock-block brigade squashes it. I'm surprised they haven't cut off my hands so I can't jack off. Don't think Quinn hasn't threatened it, either."

Oh, I was sure of it.

Landon lifted his beer to his lips. "I think you should just get over yourself and ask her out already."

"Says the man who sat back quietly and waited for the chick to do all the dirty work," Chaz countered.

The bottle cap Chaz had left sitting on the glossy wood went sailing through the air, and he ducked, narrowly escaping it. The three of us laughed as he retaliated by whipping the towel across the bar, just missing Landon.

"At least I didn't let something as silly as a paycheck keep me from being with the one I wanted."

"Hey, I'm a man. And as a man, I need to be the man. And a man is a man is a man."

Landon and I looked at each other and burst out laughing.

"And a paycheck is going to prove you're a man?"

"Easy enough for you to say. You and Cassidy make about the same."

I choked on my beer. "Whoa! What?" There were a thousand and one words I wanted to say in that moment, and not one of them would come out, but I did manage three: "What the fuck?"

"Nice," Landon said. "You're just going to throw it out there like that, Chaz? No finesse, no easing into it, just . . . bam!" He shook his head in disbelief. "You're right, you are a man."

Chaz shrugged. "What?" Then he looked at me. "Ah, shit, man. Are you okay? You look like you're going to be sick."

That was because I *was* going to be sick. "Why . . . why would you say something like that?"

Landon cut off the words Chaz had been about to say. "I'll handle this, if you don't mind." Landon faced me then, not looking entirely comfortable about the situation. "We could be way off base here, and you may not even want to talk about it, which would be fine, but we've noticed that you seem to be really distracted by Cassidy—"

I shushed him before he could continue; hearing him say her name out loud made me paranoid as hell. The chick table was far enough away, but these particular chicks had ears like parabolic microphones.

Landon gave me an apologetic look and made the necessary alteration: "You seem to be distracted by a certain young lady we all know and love."

Know? Yes. Love? Not in a million years. "Speak for yourself," I said, taking a poetic gulp of my beer. "You're confusing love with hate. It's a common mistake."

"Well, you know what they say, thin line and all, man." Chaz wasn't helping matters.

"Yes, and denial isn't just a river in Egypt," Landon threw in for good measure. "When two people compete so heavily against each other, it's usually out of a mutual respect. I'm guessing you choose to go up against her because you know she's the only person who can keep up with you. Imagine how that might play over into the bedroom." He laughed.

I didn't have to; I already knew the answer. Well, not so much the bedroom as my office, her office, the boardroom, and a dark alley. My little buddy perked up at the memories.

"In fact," Landon continued, though I wished he'd stop, "this thing between you and her is textbook playground behavior. A little boy tugging on a little girl's pigtails isn't any different from you kidnapping the account up for grabs and playing keep-away with her. Negative attention is better than no attention at all."

"Awww," Chaz cooed. "Shaw's got a crush."

There was nothing more disturbing than seeing a tatted-up, muscle-bound bald guy get all mushy with a dreamy gleam in his eyes. The guy wore a leather cuff, blue jeans, a tight T-shirt, and combat shitkickers, for Christ's sake. It just wasn't right.

I felt cornered, like they were ganging up on me. "Don't you have some work to do, beer wench? Those customers at the other end look like they're about to climb over the bar and get their own drinks." It wasn't only a distraction; it was the truth.

Chaz glanced over to see for himself, flipped me off, and then headed in that direction.

I turned my attention back to Landon. "Where did all this come from, anyway?"

He got comfortable against the bar. "Extensive training in ob-servation is part of my military background. I've a keen eye for human behavior. It's how I knew it would be better to sit back and wait for Sasha to come to me, rather than to approach her.

"See, each and every time she dated someone who asked her out, it ended almost as soon as it began. Sasha has this innate need to fix people, so the guys she dated were always charity cases. She'd do her thing, and maybe things were okay for a little while, but their presence in her life was conditional, based on whether she continued to give without taking anything for herself. And it always ended the same. They selfishly used her up, and then when she needed them the most, they were never there to rescue her. A thing like that will take a toll on a person. There was never any balance, so those relationships were doomed to failure. She needed to see who would be there for her in the very same capacity that she was there for him."

"And that has what to do with me, Dr. Phil?"

"Balance," he said simply. "All the constant back-and-forth between you two means that, like with a seesaw, one of you is always up and the other is always down. The rapid and extreme highs and lows make everything else appear distorted. Your mind needs more than a moment with both your feet on the ground to regain clarity. Otherwise, bad decisions are made. Like, say, a trip to Vegas that ends with you behind bars and in the company of some interesting characters." He laughed again when I rolled my eyes. "All I'm saying is, an unstable mind is a clinically insane mind, my friend."

It sounded really insightful, but it just wasn't me. "Landon, I love you, man, but you're wrong about this one."

"Okay," he conceded and then looked away. The discussion was over. That was one of the things I liked so much about Landon. He was uncomfortable about getting in my business, but on the very rare occasion when he did, he was never pushy about it.

Damn . . . was he right, though? Giving him the once-over, I took in all the calm and confidence that oozed from his pores. His eyes had seen a lot, even if his youth made that seem impossible. If there were such a thing as past lives, I would swear he had lived a thousand.

I glanced over my shoulder at Cassidy, watching as she gathered her things to leave. For a split second, she looked up at me and our eyes met. I could see her on the other end of that seesaw, a wicked grin in place as she prepared to catapult into the air and send me crashing back down to the ground. As if she were reading my mind, a smile tugged at the corner of her mouth when she walked past me and toward the door. She was up at bat, and I had no clue what she had in store for me. It was in that moment that everything Landon had said became clear.

I swallowed what was left of my beer and took a couple tens out of my wallet, putting them on the bar as I stood. "Catch you guys later."

Chaz nodded. "Later, man."

Landon gave me a quiet salute, but the knowing in his eyes congratulated me on finally getting it. And then I was out the door, hot on the trail of Cassidy Whalen.

Landon was right. My problem as of late was that everything had been off-kilter and it mucked with my brain *and* my cock. It was time for me to regain some balance. And the only way I knew how to do that was for Cassidy and me to be even.

Cassidy

Outside my apartment door, I dug in my bag for my keys, wishing Quinn were on the other side waiting for me with a large glass of wine. I missed my old roomie. He could always make the end of a really crappy day better, with some Chunky Monkey or much needed dose of alcohol. I was mentally and physically exhausted, my body bordering on a complete shutdown. My movements were purely instinctive at this point—unlocking the door, flicking on the light, shutting the door, stepping into the empty room, yadda, yadda, yadda.

Going directly to my bedroom, I ignored my growling stomach's demand for food. The shower was calling my name, and the promise of its pelting spray against my aching muscles was difficult to ignore. Shedding my clothes, I examined the cause of my current debilitation. The answer came readily and was really no surprise: Shaw Matthews.

My mental fatigue lay on Shaw's broad shoulders. I'd racked my brains all day trying to devise some way to outsmart him and had fallen short. Everything I had come up with could backfire right in my face. I had to be careful with how I handled things and not give Denver the wrong idea.

The physical exhaustion was a result of the constant stress of waiting for the other shoe to fall. Again, Shaw's fault. I was walking the razor's edge, my entire body wound so tight, I was surprised I didn't explode and fly across the room like a deflated balloon.

The steam and heat from the shower helped alleviate some of the stiffness from my neck and shoulders, but I could use some more downtime before I turned in for the night. I slipped my plush cotton robe on, eliminating the need for pajamas, and headed for the terrace.

Settling into my favorite spot—which I'd aptly dubbed "the nook"—on the padded chaise lounge, I knew this was my haven. The spot where I could gaze up at the stars and unwind from whatever crap life handed me. It rejuvenated me, mind, body, and soul. I closed my eyes, feeling the breeze play across my face. The steady buzz of the city below was better than any white-noise machine. I could feel myself sinking deeper and deeper into the cushions, my muscles growing heavy with fatigue. And with every passing second, the tension left my body, until I resembled nothing more than a wet sponge.

A faint clicking disrupted my silent reverie, but my heavy lids refused to budge. Quinn hadn't told me he had planned to show up tonight, but he rarely called ahead.

"Quinn? Is that you?"

"You know, you shouldn't leave your door unlocked," came a deep, rich voice that left goose bumps along my flesh and penetrated my chest to explode and disperse a thousand microbeads of warmth to all of my body parts.

That definitely wasn't Quinn's voice. I jumped up and turned around in my seat, coming face-to-face with none other than Shaw Matthews.

"What are you doing here? How did you get in?" I looked back through the windows toward the door as if the answer were somehow going to be there.

"I just told you. You left your door unlocked."

Searching my memory, I mentally went back in time to find the information that would prove him wrong, but I came up short. I'd been so exhausted when I'd come in that I probably hadn't bothered with the lock, which was weird because it had seemed like everything else had been on autopilot and that was definitely part of my normal routine.

"No worries; it's locked now." The sound of his voice brought me back to the present, and I snapped to, finding Shaw ogling my chest. I looked down. It seemed that in my hasty clamoring to get a visual of my intruder, the top of my robe had come loose, and loads of nakedness was now on display.

"Hey, my eyes are up here, Matthews," I said, shutting down the free peep show.

"Well, if your cleavage would stop staring at me . . ."

God, what was it about that snarky grin that made my vagina so damn happy to see it?

"Aren't you on probation or something? Can't you get in trouble for breaking and entering?"

Shaw cocked his head to the side and regarded me with something mischievous lurking behind those not-so-innocent blue eyes. "Didn't you go to law school? I'm not on probation, and again, the door was unlocked, so I didn't break anything."

"Fine. You entered without permission, though."

Shaw leaned over and whispered, "There's no law against entering."

"Yes, there is. It's called unlawful trespassing." When he sat on the end of the chaise, right between my legs, I got flustered. "What are you doing?"

He ignored me. "So call the police." His hand was now stroking the inside of my leg, and my first thought wasn't to kick him off but that I was thankful I'd just shaved. Clearly, I was an idiot whose priorities were way out of whack.

"I should." Yep, that was all I could muster.

And Shaw's hand was sliding higher. "Do it."

"I will."

But I sat there, unmoving and barely breathing.

Shaw, on the other hand, was pushing back the flaps of my robe to get a better view of my naked thighs. And that wasn't the only thing under there that was naked. "Well?" he finally said.

Distraction. I needed a distraction. "What are you doing here?"

The snarky grin was back, and before I knew it, Shaw had gripped my hips and pulled me toward him. Not only that, but at the same time, his head forced my thighs apart and his hot, wet mouth descended upon my exuberant vagina.

Well, that was one way to answer the question, I supposed.

His tongue made a long sweep of my pussy from back to front, and then his lips closed around my clit with a lingering suck that nearly drove me mad.

"Oh, God. I . . . I w-want you t-to . . ." Closing my eyes, I growled in my frustration at not being able to get the words out. "I want you to leave."

"No, you don't. You *should* want me to leave, and that's what your brain is ordering you to say, but your mouth had an awfully hard time telling the lie, didn't it?"

His mouth wasn't having a hard time with anything. Not even while words were coming out of it. Jesus, he was good.

"You think you're so smart? Tell me, Shaw . . . how many licks does it take to get to the juicy center of a Cassidy Pop?" Where in the world had that come from?

Shaw stopped and quirked an eyebrow, wondering the same thing, I was sure. "One . . . *if* you start there. Of course we could always test that theory, but I can't guarantee I won't take a bite before the test is complete."

His warm breath mixed with the cool night air with each word he spoke, a concoction that elicited a sensation I'd never felt before. I craved more of it. And Shaw gave it when he hovered over my pussy and simply moaned. And then he descended again, his lips working in the same way there as they did on my mouth when he kissed me.

I was powerless to stop him. I wanted what he was giving so generously. And his head moving between my thighs was an incredible sight to behold. Slowly and methodically, he devoured me. A nice drawn-out tease, followed by the intention to please, was the source of my undoing.

His tongue lapped at my clit, becoming faster and more urgent. Christ, I needed something to hold on to, and the chaise wasn't doing the job, so I fisted his hair. Shaw must have liked that because he moaned against my hypersensitive flesh and brought his mouth even closer, burying his face in my pussy.

The silky warmth of his tongue mixed with the textured scruff of his face drove me mad, aching for release. And just when I thought it might be mine, Shaw backed off, but not fully away.

"Uh-uh-uh," he said, kissing the inside of my thigh. "Not yet."

He used his hand then, the tips of his fingers massaging my clit, slowly and fully, in maddening circles. I heard myself moan, a sound that was more like a pathetic pout. Or had it been a plea? Either way, Shaw found it amusing. His quiet chuckle and subsequent groan of approval made me want to please him even more so I could hear it again.

Long fingers stroked me, and his mouth returned to shower my wanton flesh with delicate kisses. Spreading my folds, Shaw watched as he toyed with my clit some more, blowing his breath across the engorged bud and enjoying the way it made me squirm. I arched my back, trying to draw his mouth closer, but I was again chastised. "Behave," he warned, and then he slapped at my clit.

However sick it might make me, I liked it. And I wanted him to do it again. So I grabbed his hair and tried to force him closer. "Please?"

I was rewarded with another punishing slap. Only this time, I moaned out loud, giving away my secret pleasure. His exhalation was audible; so was the growl. Shaw was again well pleased. And insatiable.

As his mouth tasted me again, it had nothing to do with my pleasure; rather, it was for his. He licked and sucked at my clit, his tongue exploring every hidden nuance of my folds. For every drop of my juices he tried desperately to claim as his own, my body was more than willing to supply even more.

Something otherworldly was building inside me, expanding until I thought it would burst forth from my body, causing me to spontaneously combust into nothingness. But Shaw wasn't oblivious to it. Despite his submergence, he read my body and took note of every telltale sign. I was there, just on the cusp. Any microsecond, I was going to . . .

Shaw pulled back again, thwarting my orgasm.

I growled. Loudly. The sound echoed through the white noise of the city below. And then I grabbed his face, forcing him to my mouth. Jesus, I tasted so good on his lips. Licking and suckling them, I became something I'd never been before. My tongue pushed inside, dominantly taking over and having my fill. Shaw indulged me for only a moment before he pushed away and held my shoulders to the back of the chaise.

"Stop."

Of course, I ignored him and lunged forward to stroke the bulge in his pants, which I could only barely see by the light of the stars and moon. Oh, my God. He was so big, so hard. My eyes closed, and I bit my lip as I massaged him through his clothes. I wanted him. Inside me. Deep and hard. But I was again denied when Shaw grabbed my hands and pinned my wrists together while wrapping them in his tie, which I hadn't even seen him remove. Yet that didn't seem to be satisfactory for him, because he lifted my arms, pushing them back and around the top of the chaise, tightening the restraint until I could feel the pull in my muscles. There would be no escaping until Shaw decided to free me.

"There. That's much better," he said. His fingers ghosted over my cheek to my jaw and neck, my collarbones, and then just under the lapel of my robe. "Your skin is so soft." His voice was a whisper of his touch. And then he yanked the lapels open, revealing my naked breasts fully.

I gasped. Both in surprise and excitement. A cool breeze drifted in from the bay and kissed my nipples, hardening the raised buds to a pucker. Shaw took my body's reaction as an invitation and covered one with his hot mouth, the other with a kneading squeeze of his hand. I squirmed, trying to find some much needed friction to my pussy, but I was denied even the relief of rubbing my thighs together, because Shaw's presence there made it impossible.

He sucked my nipple into his mouth, his tongue teasing it even as he pulled back to scrape it with his teeth. Lapping at it again and again before gifting me with the hard pull, he was the master of control. And I had none at all.

My back arched with the same degree of my surprised gasp when Shaw plunged two thick fingers deep inside me. I'd been so distracted, I hadn't expected the move—not that I was complaining in the least. He didn't even give me the chance to recuperate before his fingering became exact, fast and hard. Thrusting in and out at a maddening pace, he looked right into my eyes. The expression on his face was sure and confident, arrogant. He knew, without a doubt, that he'd hit the mark.

Pushing all the way in to the knuckles, his fingers worked back and forth, manipulating my G-spot. "Do you want to come, Cassidy?"

I couldn't talk. I could only barely breathe. But my head was surprisingly capable of a nod.

"When?" he asked, pulling out and then pushing back in to toy with the spot again. "Now?"

My hips pushed into his hand as much as he would allow and I closed my eyes, feeling the sensation build from somewhere down low. I moaned, quietly, biting down on my lip and letting my head lull to the side.

Shaw leaned in, his lips at my neck. "Oh, yeah. You're so close," he whispered against my skin.

I wanted to feel his skin against mine, but he was still fully dressed—with the exception of his tie, that was. Even still, I'd take the warmth of his body through his clothes if he would just come closer. I arched into him, and he pulled back again. It didn't matter; I was there. I was going to come. I bore down hard, the muscles in my body clenching in preparation.

And then he stopped again.

My body sagged in defeat. As the torturous sensation once again ebbed, I wanted to cry.

And then he started back at the beginning. Over and over again, Shaw brought me to the brink of release and then denied it, proving that my pleasure was only his to give. I enjoyed every painstaking second of the build and hated every abrupt departure. I tried to hide my tells, but Shaw couldn't be fooled.

His lips brushed mine, tenderly. An act that contradicted the cocky gleam in his eye. He was enjoying the power he held. And I wasn't even angry with him because of it. This was what Shaw did. He challenged me, made me want the win more than I'd wanted anything else in my entire life. Whether it was a client, the partnership, or simply an orgasm. He pushed me. And I rallied in response to it.

I was acutely aware that he could choose to torture me all night and into the morning, never giving me release. He could walk away right then, leaving me bound and exposed to the world. He could even whip out his phone and take pictures or record a video with which to blackmail me.

But he wouldn't.

He wouldn't because he and I had an understanding of each other. He wouldn't because he and I both knew that he'd want the chance to do this again.

So when he buried his face between my thighs, I relished the feeling for as long as he would allow it. Spreading myself wide for him, I watched his head move back and forth, and I committed the sight to memory. But no sight was better than the expression in his eyes when he looked up at me and gifted me with the view of his tongue working my plump clit.

And then those magical fingers joined in on the party, working me from the inside while his lips, teeth, and tongue handled the business on the outside. Even though I knew he'd probably only deny me again, I couldn't ignore the mounting surge in my abdomen. I didn't even bother to try to hide it from him—his will would win out in the end either way.

I moaned and rolled my hips against his face, meeting the pace of his fingers thrust for thrust. Shaw's head moved back and forth, up and down, missing nothing. And then his teeth bit into the flesh just above my clit, and I gasped, not expecting the pain. But it was a different sort of pain, a sting that was every bit as welcome as the sweep of his tongue over the same place to ease it. He'd marked me. And I was okay with it.

Hardly missing a beat, his attention went back to my clit, the tip of his tongue flicking back and forth, coaxing it to do its part even as his long fingers did the same with that glorious bit inside me. The dual sensations of his mouth and fingers, the sounds of the night, my exposure to anyone who might be watching through the windows of the buildings surrounding us, and the cool breeze from the bay, which battled the rising heat of my body . . . they were all too much. My head fell back and I looked up at the stars in the sky, silently begging the universe to have mercy.

And then it happened. I closed my eyes, and the orgasm I'd been waiting for took flight like a shooting star. It soared higher and higher, leaving a trail of fire in its wake, until it exploded into a million smaller bodies of light that littered the metaphorical sky.

Shaw gripped my hips, keeping me close to his mouth as he continued to lick and suck and work my pussy. I'd never come so hard. The anticipation had nearly killed me, but when the moment finally came, it was indescribable. The sweet, sweet torture had been worth the reward, and I wanted to thank the man responsible for it—but, of course, I wouldn't.

Shaw looked up at me, his tongue making a languid sweep of his lips. "Now we're even."

I couldn't talk. I wasn't able to form coherent words yet, though it appeared there was no need. Shaw stood, loosened the binding at my wrists to reclaim his tie, and then walked away without another word. My arms were sore, but I managed to sit up and turn to see him move through my apartment and out my door.

Pulling my robe closed, I sank back into my chair with an unexpected smile on my face. "Indeed we are," I said to the night.

For the first time, I started to see Shaw in a different light, and I realized that the things about him that irked me so much were also the things that drew me to him. He was abrasive and cocky, but he was the only person who could exhibit any kind of control over me. I wasn't sure how I felt about that. Although I knew I should be superpissed at myself, some girly part inside of me got all warm and fuzzy over the idea. Maybe it was then that I realized I wasn't the typical woman. Romance and niceties didn't do it for me. I wanted a gentleman with a firm hand who could make me feel like a woman needing to be tamed. It was almost therapeutic to relinquish the carefully orchestrated, obsessive control over every detail in my life. If even for a moment. I supposed I should thank Shaw for that. Sinking even deeper into my postcoital bliss, I knew I wouldn't.

CHAPTER 13
Shaw

Today was going to be a very good day.

Everything was set and in place: the luxury private jet I'd chartered was primed and running, the weather was clear, the pilot was on board and through all his checks, the attendant was tending to the hors d'oeuvres, and the bar was fully stocked. All that was missing was the guest of honor and the key to my future prosperity, Denver "Rocket Man" Rockford.

Yes, we were going on another adventure together, but this time, we'd both be on our very best behavior. The intended destination this time around was for business, not pleasure. All the key decision makers for Detroit were on standby and waiting for our arrival. I was going to walk Denver through the whole process and show him exactly what I could do for him as his agent. Nothing was going to stop me from bringing home the win; I was more determined than ever to nab it for my own.

Admittedly, I'd been pacing back and forth and checking my watch every few minutes, afraid he wouldn't show or that he'd cause our takeoff to be delayed. When the car I'd sent for him pulled onto the tarmac, I'd never been more relieved. A quick bolt to the latrine to check myself over in the mirror found everything in place. I was more nervous than a kid going on his first date, mostly because I'd set up this meeting more than two weeks ago, when the announcement that Denver was on the hunt for a new agent first broke. It was a huge risk, but I'd been so confident that I'd have him signed by now. I didn't. Much to my dismay. Cassidy's game had been a whole hell of a lot stronger than I'd originally anticipated, and I was lucky that Denver had even agreed to the trip after our last debacle. Otherwise, I wouldn't just look like an idiot to myself; the whole Detroit football staff would write me off.

But this . . . this was my big chance, and everything was lining up perfectly.

"Good afternoon, Mr. Rockford. Welcome aboard," the flight attendant said. "I'll take your luggage, sir."

With my winning smile in place, I emerged from the bathroom to greet him. "Rocket! Hey, man! You're just in time."

But my excitement got caught in my throat in much the same way it would have if someone had grabbed me by the balls and given them a twist. Denver turned to offer his hand and assistance to an uninvited guest. Well, uninvited by me, anyway.

"Look who decided to join us!" he said with way more enthusiasm than I could have mustered.

"Miss me, Matthews?" Cassidy stood there, dressed in a little black number that clung to every curve she had. Some I'd known about, others I hadn't. Wasn't sure how that could be possible when I'd seen the woman naked more than once, but the truth was the truth. And her hair was down, cascading over her bare shoulders like liquid fire that wanted to get in on the clinging action. It was safe to say she definitely was not there on business.

"You gotta be fucking kidding me," I mumbled under my breath. Forget how sexy she looked. She was on my goddamn jet, on my dime, with my client. Just raining all over my parade like a monsoon.

But I couldn't lose my shit in front of Denver.

"Cassidy," I greeted her with a false smile. "How is it that you came to join us?"

She didn't have to answer because Denver jumped all over the question before she could. It was quite heroic. "Oh, I asked her, man. Hope that was okay?"

My smile stayed plastered in place, though it was hard to swallow around the lie that coated my tongue. "Absolutely okay. The more the merrier."

"Mr. Matthews, the captain is ready for takeoff. If you'll all take your seats and fasten your seat belts, we'll be on our way." Our stewardess was quite the looker. I'd handpicked her specifically, not for my benefit but as one more way to make a good impression on Denver.

"Thank you, . . . Annette," I said, reading her name tag. If the smile she gave was any indication, I'd say she was flirting with me. Though I supposed she might have just been doing her job. Then again, I was Shaw Matthews.

Someone cleared her throat—no surprise who that might have been—and the exchange came to an abrupt end. Turning my attention and my smile back to my guests, I gestured toward the ivory leather couches that lined either side of the passenger cabin. Denver motioned for Cassidy to go ahead of him, like any gentleman would do, and then he followed, sitting next to her and fastening his own belt. Beads of sweat took up residence on his forehead, and his face was pallid, ghostly.

"You good, man?" I asked as I took my seat across from them. The culprit behind the sudden onset of his discomfort wasn't anything new to me.

Denver rested his head against the seat. "Yeah. Got it taken care of already."

Cassidy looked between us, confused. "Got what taken care of?"

"No alcohol this time, okay, buddy?"

He chuckled. "Not to worry. Vegas was a very hard lesson to learn, but learn I did."

"Is someone going to fill me in?" Cassidy sat forward and pegged Denver with a stare he couldn't easily avoid.

A nonchalant shrug was the precursor to his explanation. "I have this thing about flying, in that it scares the shit out of me." He gave a nervous laugh. "So my doc prescribed this sedative that technically shouldn't be mixed with alcohol."

"Oh." The aha moment registered in her eyes first and then dinged through all the checkpoints in her body like a pinball, until she relaxed back into her seat again.

"Yep. So, sorry, but I'll be knocked out in no time."

It was my turn to shine again. "Hey, the bed in the private cabin is really comfortable. As soon as the captain says we're good on the seat belts, you should crash. It's a four-and-a-half-hour flight, so that's more than enough time for a nap."

"Right on. Good looking out, man."

"Wait. This thing has a bedroom?"

I kept my laugh in check, but it pulled at the corner of my mouth all the same. "Of course it does."

"That had to cost Striker a pretty penny. How did you get Wade to agree to it?"

I did laugh this time. "Wade didn't need to agree to it, because Striker isn't paying for this trip. I am."

Cassidy's brows lifted in surprise, then furrowed. She certainly hadn't expected that twist. And now she knew exactly the lengths to which I was willing to go for the win. Would she meet me tit for tat? I doubted it.

The plane began taxiing down the runway, picking up speed as it went. I held on to my armrests, not saying or thinking about anything more than a safe takeoff. Unlike Denver, I didn't get freaked out about flying, though I had to admit that takeoffs and landings made me a little nervous.

Denver's eyes were clamped shut, and he was holding on for dear life, but Cassidy sat unaffected. In that dress. With her legs crossed at the knee and her gorgeous calves on display, like a pin-up model posing for a calendar shoot. The four-and-a-half-hour flight was going to seem twice as long if I had to look at her for the duration.

In no time at all, we were off the ground and in the air. Denver was sweating bullets and looked like he might want his mommy. It was almost poetic to see a hulking mountain of a man show such vulnerability. Fear of flying wasn't his only weakness, though. During our trip to Vegas, he'd also told me about his fears of clowns and miniature dogs. If anyone ever wanted to scare the shit out of the man, all they'd have to do would be to dress a Chihuahua in a clown suit and sit it next to him on a plane. He'd likely never survive the takeoff.

The captain came over the intercom and went into his spiel about our altitude and anticipated time of arrival. After he gave us the all clear to move about the cabin, a nearly knocked out Denver got to his unsteady feet.

"Oh, let me help you," Cassidy said, shedding her seat belt and standing so quickly that the two of them almost butted heads.

Denver put his hands out to gain some semblance of balance. "It's okay. I've got it."

"Here, let me." Standing as well, I hooked his arm over my shoulder and took some of his weight, which felt like all of my own.

Annette, our very lovely stewardess, led the way to the back cabin. Once inside, Denver fell, face-first, onto the bed. Out like a light. Without being asked, my beautiful assistant carefully removed his shoes and placed a pillow under his head; he immediately grabbed it and hugged it tight.

"Thank you," I whispered.

"It's my pleasure, Mr. Matthews. Is there anything I can get for you and your other guest at this time?"

I looked toward the main cabin. All the preparation I'd put into the flight alone had cost me a fortune, yet I had a feeling most of the refreshments would go untouched. "We can handle the drinks. Why don't you make yourself and the captain a plate and take it easy?"

The smile she wore was one of the most beautiful and sincere I'd ever seen. Under different circumstances—though I wasn't sure anymore what those circumstances would be and why they weren't the case now—I probably would've ended up fucking her in the galley.

"Are you sure?" she asked.

With a sigh, I nodded. I had no clue how Cassidy had come to be on my jet, or why she was dressed like a night out on the town was part of the agenda, but I intended to find out.

"Very well, then. I'll excuse myself to the service cabin. If you change your mind, you need only pick up the telephone." With another breathtaking smile, she took her leave. I watched as she did so, admiring the gentle sway of her hips. But the sight didn't have the same effect on me as it might have once upon a time. Maybe the culprit behind my indifference was the near-obsessive thought that kept rumbling around in my head like Jack's giant in search of his golden egg–laying goose.

Only my golden goose wasn't Denver, like I had originally thought. It was Cassidy. Dammit. When had that happened?

Closing the ultrathin door to the private cabin where Denver was now sawing some serious logs, I made my way into the main sitting area. Cassidy was thumbing through a magazine—*Sports Illustrated,* not *Cosmo*—like she hadn't a care in the world, while I was trying desperately to come to grips with my mounting jealousy.

Jealousy wasn't an emotion I was used to feeling. Hell, I'd cut myself off from feeling most emotions, in fact; it was just better for business. Some of the biggest mistakes made in the industry happened because agents got their feelings hurt. I had no intention of being one of those agents, but something had to be done about all this "what the fuck is she doing here with him" that had attached itself to the left side of my brain and was sucking the life out of my ability to think rationally.

I didn't know what Cassidy saw when she looked up to find me coming at her, but it was clear by the expression in her eyes that it was both unexpected and welcome. There was no warning even to myself—then again, I wasn't thinking rationally—before I'd snatched her up, crushed the devastating curves of her body against me, and claimed her mouth.

Mine.

Cassidy

Holy something wicked this way comes, Batman!

Shaw marched toward me with purpose in his long stride, anger in the hard lines of his face, and pure lust in his eyes. Jesus, what a sight.

But it was nothing compared to the way he hoisted me up as if I didn't weigh a thing and fit my form perfectly to his. The warmth of his body, the scent of his skin, the control of his kiss . . .

a kiss that made every passionate exchange in chick flicks look like a peck on the cheek by comparison. Shaw's lips were soft yet firm, slow in the way they moved against mine with expert control. His fingers pressed into my skin, drawing me impossibly closer, while his tongue made an appearance to coax an invitation to mingle with my own. The invitation was accepted, and I didn't even bother to fake opposition.

Oh, God . . . his mouth. His glorious, glorious mouth. I was instantly reminded of everything Shaw could and had done with it. His lips, teeth, and tongue made promises that didn't need to be spoken aloud because I was very much aware that he could deliver.

I was a goner. Done for. Crippled by his physical presence and drunk on the taste of him.

And then he moved to my neck, showing no mercy to the spot that joined my shoulder. It was my weakness, the place where the direct path to my pleasure began, and he knew it. "Why are you with him?" he asked without slowing his assault.

I could've told him I was there to keep an eye on Denver, since he had been so careless with the quarterback of late. I could've said I wanted to use the vantage point to track his movements in order to outmaneuver him. I could've told him I simply wanted to be a thorn in his side. But I didn't. I didn't because I knew that any one of those truths would have given him too much satisfaction. And there was only one way in which I was interested in satisfying him.

I took control then, forcing him to trade places. There was little resistance. Nuzzling his neck, I inhaled deeply, intoxicated by his scent. With a nip to his skin that made his hardened cock flinch against my stomach, I grinned victoriously to myself while moving along the taut tendon there to his ear. "Why do you care?"

My response was dubious, not at all what he'd wanted to hear. And he made damn sure I knew it.

Fisting the hair at my nape, he drew my head back and forced me to look at him. His eyes darkened to the color of storm clouds. "Answer the goddamn question, Cassidy."

"Because I want to be." It was the partial truth.

His jaw ticked. "I'm not okay with that."

"I don't recall asking your permission."

"Why do you insist on making me crazy?" Palming my breast, he squeezed hard, as if he were punishing me for the response. Little did he realize, I liked it. A lot.

Wicked intent was in the driver's seat of my next words: "Because I can."

He growled, roughly shoving his big hands under my dress to grab my ass. But he didn't stop there. With a grip that made me wince with the sort of pain I found to be quite pleasurable, he lifted me from the floor, forcing me to hold on or fall. Though I had a feeling falling would not have been an option, as it would have also provided an escape. Shaw wasn't going to let me go anywhere until he decided I could.

I linked my fingers behind his neck, looking down at him with a smirk I knew would taunt him further. "Now what? Are we going to put on a show for the cockpit crew?"

His brow furrowed.

"FAA regulations require cameras in the main passenger areas."

Shaw looked around the cabin, his eyes finding the proof. Then his frustrated frown got turned upside down. Obviously, he'd come up with a solution. "You're not getting off that easily," he warned, and I prayed he didn't mean it literally. Especially after the torture he'd put me through during our little experiment the other night when he'd brought me to the edge over and over again only to deny my release.

When he turned and headed toward the back of the plane, I laughed. "What are you going to do, put me in the bed and fuck me right next to Denver?"

Shaw wasn't laughing when he said, "I should." I believed he would have if that was the only option.

With careful precision, he managed to open the door to the bathroom and walk both of us through before closing it again. The interior of the room was quite impressive, much larger than in a regular passenger plane and decked out, though I shouldn't have been surprised, given the extravagance of the rest of the jet. But when Shaw put me on the sink counter and got busy with his mouth on my bare shoulder and his hands on pulling down the bodice of my dress to expose my breasts, it was the floor-to-ceiling mirror behind him that seized my attention. Not that what he was doing didn't feel good, because holy crap did it ever, but I could see it all in that mirror, afforded a view I hadn't ever been granted before, and it excited me to no end.

My dress was now pushed up around my waist, and Shaw was making fast work of pulling my arms out of the sleeves to let the top bunch there, too. I was mentally thanking the dress's designer for the stretchy material while silently hoping it didn't get stretched out of shape too badly before all was said and done. That wouldn't look suspicious at all.

The heat of Shaw's mouth found the hardened peak of my breast for long, pulling sucks, and I closed my eyes to relish the feeling, though not for long. I didn't want to miss a thing, and with this new position, I didn't have to. But the mirror wouldn't give me a better angle to see what he was doing than simply looking down, so that was what I did. Shaw's cool blues met my stare with approval. He liked that I wanted to watch, and he gave me a show for it, exaggerating the movement of his tongue and making sure I could see each manipulative flick of my nipple. When he took the whole peak into his mouth and sucked slowly and purposefully, that was the part I liked the best.

And then his hand was inside my panties, and the seductive groan that always accompanied his first feel of my wetness was my reward. "Shh . . . you'll wake Denver," I warned him.

"I don't care" was his jealous response. And that was when it hit me. All of this had been about his little green-eyed monster. Shaw was jealous of Denver. He wasn't mad that I'd crashed his party—he was peeved that I'd shown up with another man. Some part of me rallied, owned the knowledge, and soared with a hefty boost of confidence.

So I grabbed his face and forced his mouth to mine to cover a moan of my own. Damn, but his fingers were so very talented and Shaw was in the mood to show off. I spread my legs even wider, arching my back to give him a better angle. The way the man massaged my clit should've been an Olympic event, because you better believe that took crazy skills. Biting his lip, I held still, waiting for the orgasm I knew would come at any moment. Yes, he was that good.

And it did come. I buried my face against his neck and held back my moan as Shaw continued to work me. Hearing his heavy exhalation was all the proof I needed that my release had driven him crazy. At least he was behaving and no longer trying to make sure Denver knew about the naughtiness we were up to.

When my orgasm subsided, Shaw stripped me of my soaked panties while I released his cock. I wanted him inside me. Even more so when I pushed his pants over his hips and saw how hard and thick he was. It was enough to make a grown woman cry, but instead, I admired the appendage as if it were sculpted art. Except I could touch this sculpture.

Shaw's cock was beautiful, with a nice, robust head that sloped into a prominent ridge. Soft skin stretched taut over his rigidity, and the shaft was as tan as the rest of his body. But Jesus, the veins . . . the veins were plump with the lustful blood that raged through them in that moment.

"I need to be inside you," he whispered.

Yeah, I needed him there, too.

Taking his cock out of my hands, he bent at the knees and positioned himself at my entrance while scooting me forward until I was only halfway on the edge. And then he pushed the tip inside. Another one of those long, audible exhalations came from him; I looked at his face and nearly came again when I saw his eyes close in ecstasy. There was just something about knowing you could make a man feel that good.

He pulled back again, opening his eyes and gazing directly into mine as he pushed in once more, going a little deeper.

"You feel so incredible," he said, and then his attention went to the place where we were joined. Mine followed, and we both watched as he repeated the retreat and advance, over and over again until he'd worked himself inside.

The stretch and fill of Shaw's penetration was unlike any sensation on earth. And the vision of all that masculinity coated in my juices was one I would never forget. Neither would Shaw, if the way he was still watching in rapt fascination was any indication.

And then, finally, his head fell back and he leaned in, grabbing two handfuls of my ass as his pace quickened. I hugged him to me, holding on and trying desperately to draw him closer, though the feat was impossible. Oh, my God, he felt so good moving inside me, but when he pressed his forehead to my shoulder, that was when the show really began.

Shaw's warm breath washed over my bare skin, his fingers dug into the cheeks of my ass, and the muted grunt of each thrust struck right to my core. And right behind him was my new friend, the mirror.

The tail of his dress shirt was in my way, and I couldn't have that. I spread my thighs wider, slipping my arms under his and grappling with his shirt, bunching it up in my hands and revealing the treasure it had attempted to hide. The two dimples at the bottom of Shaw's back congratulated me on my find, while the muscles of his ass clenched and relaxed in time with his thrusts.

"Holy shit," I half-whispered, half-moaned, but it didn't distract Shaw in the least. Neither was he distracted when I bit into his shoulder, though the deeper thrusts were sort of a clue that he'd liked it.

I should've been disgruntled when he pulled back and took my view away, but when it became clear he'd done so to get his grind on—a grind that I got to watch—I was quite all right with it. And hello? Shaw manscaped, so it was soft, hot skin on my engorged clit while a fat, juicy cock was stroking my insides into a knotted-up frenzy of sensation after sensation.

"You like that?" he asked, and then he nipped at my lip. "Watch me, Cassidy. Watch me fuck you and know that it's my dick inside you."

Shaw pulled almost all the way out then and pushed back in, grinding his groin against my clit again and again. When I made a desperate sound, he put his mouth to my ear. "You want to come on my cock?"

I bit my lip and clutched him to me, trying like hell to find some sort of purchase with my fingers in his back. The angle granted me the view of his clenching ass again, and I held on tight, letting it feed the need inside me. He smelled so good, and felt so perfect, and looked so sexy. And I swear I could hear my own heartbeat thumping in my chest, the pressure of all that blood taking aim at one spot in the very core of my being and feeding it, and feeding it, and feeding it until it spilled over and flooded my extremities with the unbelievable sensation of my orgasm.

I bore down, the walls of my pussy pulsing with each wave, squeezing the thick cock still moving inside me. Shaw felt it, too, and he rode it out, taking full advantage.

The plane started to shake, and I panicked, but Shaw looked at me and shook his head. "I'm not stopping," he said so fast I barely heard him.

Leaning back, he watched again as he fucked me, harder and faster, his thrusts becoming shallower. The plane could be falling out of the air for all we knew, and Shaw was still fucking me. The expression on his face was so concentrated, so driven to chase the euphoria that must have been right at his fingertips. We could die before he ever captured it, but he'd use his last breath to make sure he did. What was it about his devil-may-care attitude, his putting his pleasure before our safety that turned me on so much?

Shaw pulled out, stroking his cock with the same pace and intensity until he gave a grunt and his release spilled onto my pussy in spurting streams. I almost wanted to cheer for his success, but I didn't have the energy. With a heavy sigh, I rested my head against the mirror behind me, trying to get my heart under control. The turbulence had stopped, the threat to our lives now at bay, but my concern was whether the angry jarring had been enough to wake Denver.

Shaw must have been concerned, too, because he was grabbing washcloths from the cabinet and getting them wet in the sink beside me. The first he handed off to me, and then he used the other to clean himself up. Once he'd done a thorough job, he went to work on straightening his clothes.

I had to admit, Shaw had always been meticulous about his appearance. I could tell he took great pride in how he looked, which said a lot. Luckily for him, he was naturally flawless to begin with.

"Oh," I said, spotting something on his shoulder. "Sorry. Some of my makeup must have rubbed off."

"It's okay," he said with a shrug. "I've got a jacket."

A groggy Denver stirred in the room next to us, and I went stiff.

Shaw laughed, though quietly. "I'll slip out and go check on him. You get yourself together and come out when you're done."

"Wait. Why are you being so nice?" I asked warily.

He fastened his belt and looked in the mirror, running his fingers through his hair. "Because now that I've fucked you, I know there's no chance you'll be fucking *him* tonight."

My mouth must have dropped open in shock, because Shaw pushed my chin up and then gave a chaste kiss to my lips. "Don't take too long," he said, opening the door and leaving before I could get my vocal cords to form any of the profanity I was mentally screaming at him.

Oh, my God. I was having an illicit affair with Beelzebub.

CHAPTER 14

Shaw

Detroit had pulled out all the stops for Denver's arrival. Of course, I'd known they would. After all, that was where I'd learned to do the same. It wasn't every day a superstar quarterback who could have his pick of teams offered his undivided attention, so when he did, you'd better damn well appeal to the things that were most important to him. For Denver, that was money and notoriety.

A chauffeured Escalade picked us up from the airport and drove us to the stadium, where every major decision maker imaginable was on standby, waiting to greet us. They were all smiles, prepared to say yes to anything Denver might ask for, even if it was their current number one's head on a silver platter. The owner's box was loaded down with a buffet fit for a king, while talks of every perk imaginable were flung at Denver from every direction. Dollar signs, dollar signs, dollar signs, and lots of ego stroking. I was surprised there weren't women stationed under the table to suck off the man of the hour on top of all that, though having a few of the team's most glamorous cheerleaders arrayed around the room made up for the oversight.

Denver wasn't the only man in the spotlight. A lot of claps landed on my back, as well. It felt good, the respect I'd been given. Some of those men had been like fathers to me, but they knew how all of this would go down. Denver hadn't yet chosen me, but if he did—*when* he did—they damn sure wanted my support to persuade him to sign with Detroit.

Cassidy just hovered somewhere in the background, not really a part of the conversations taking place. It wasn't that they didn't know who she was, but the fact that she really had no part of this deal meant she represented nothing more than the woman on Denver's arm. And I was okay with that . . . this time.

The tour of Ford Field brought back a whole lot of memories of my time spent there as a teenager. This was where my career as an agent had all begun, where Monty Prather had taken an un-educated kid and turned him into a lean, mean signing machine. Ford Field had been my salvation even before then, keeping me off the streets and out of harm's way when no one else was there to protect me. Some life-changing moments that I would never forget had happened right there.

Like the time I witnessed a player having a scene with his wife in front of the whole team after a practice. She'd apparently got-ten a call from some chick claiming to have been sleeping with him and had gotten a little psychotic over it. One thing had led to another, and before I knew what was happening, that douche bag had stormed off and left his very hysterical, very hot wife in a crumpled mess in the middle of the field. She'd embarrassed herself for the sake of love, and he'd abandoned her there like she hadn't mattered in the least. I'd seen it one too many times with my own mother and father, and I'd offered her some comfort. There had been no way for me to predict what would result from my kind deed. I'd been a seventeen-year-old kid at the time, and she was twice my age, but she'd made me a man when she'd taken my virginity. Damn, had she ever. Eventually, I'd gotten revenge for her when my very first client took her cheating husband's spot on the roster and with double the pay.

I was soaring by late in the evening when we finally wrapped things up at the stadium to head over to the MGM Grand, where I'd booked our rooms. Denver's arm was over my shoulder when we walked out, making us look every bit like a team. Cassidy was on his other arm, pouting, from what I could tell. No deals had been made yet, but I saw no reason why they wouldn't be in the very near future. Life was fucking good.

And then I hit a brick wall.

It wasn't until I got us checked in at the hotel and the front desk agent handed me the keys to the rooms I'd reserved that I realized there were only two. Two keys for two rooms. One for me, one for Denver. Which left Cassidy where? She damn sure wasn't going to be shacking up with her boy toy. Not on my watch, and certainly not on my dime.

Tucking the keys into my pocket, I turned to face them with a smile. "Ready?"

Cassidy looked more than ready, as did Denver. "Hell yeah, man. I'm jet-lagged and half hungover from all the excitement today."

Well, that had me beaming. Denver was feeling properly worshipped, which made me start mentally arranging the furniture in my new office at Striker with the word "PARTNER" in gold on the door. Things were definitely going my way, and all the shit I'd done, all the ladders I'd climbed, all the asses I'd kissed would be worth it in the end. Finally, I'd be able to settle down and know that I'd done it. I'd accomplished something with my life.

Not bad for a kid from Detroit who'd started out with nothing more than a sliver of hope and a silver tongue.

Getting through the lobby to the elevators took longer than

expected, thanks to a group of people shouting Denver's name and asking him to pose for selfies or sign autographs. It wasn't a bad thing. As long as the fans loved him, we were guaranteed a fat payday. I might have even enjoyed the dirty looks some of the women were shooting Cassidy, but eventually I managed to get the object of their affection into the elevator and behind closed doors.

"Damn, I'll never get used to that," he said, and then he brushed a stray lock of hair back from Cassidy's face. "You okay?"

She nodded with a weak smile. "Just tired."

The exchange seemed a little too sweet for my liking, though it solidified the sacrifice I was willing to make to ensure that whatever was going on between them didn't cross the line.

Once we'd gotten to the eighth floor, I steered them down the hall, then stopped before the side-by-side rooms. I handed one key to Denver and the other to Cassidy.

"What about you?" Cassidy asked.

"I'm, um . . . I have other plans," I told her.

The way her brow furrowed in confusion was sort of cute. "You're not staying here?"

It was then that I saw an opportunity to flip the table and maybe make her little green-eyed monster come out to play. "It's not often that I get to come back to Detroit, so when I do, there's someone I like to visit." I gave her a wink, really selling the line I wanted her to buy.

"Oh. That sounds nice," she said, and then: "I should probably get a shower. I feel so nasty from that flight."

Bam! There it was. Green-eyed monster was in the house. But then mine also decided to make an appearance when I started to question the tone in her voice. Did she mean she wanted to clean up so she could be with Denver after all? Or was she saying she was disgusted by what we'd done earlier? Either way, it was a well-executed stab.

"You know, that's an excellent idea," I said and then turned to Denver. "Hey, buddy? Do you mind if I use your shower real quick?"

His chuckle was mischievous, and his knowing look right on time with the bro code. "Of course, man," he said, opening his door. *"Mi casa es su casa."*

The shower was sublime, but finding Cassidy in the hallway when I stepped out was not. She'd changed clothes, makeup and hair in place. Though she looked more relaxed in her jeans and oversized shirt, the deer-in-headlights expression was a dead giveaway that she was up to something. So was the fast pace with which she walked toward the elevator.

"Where are you going?" I asked, following her.

"Nowhere. I just, um . . ." She shrugged, attempting to act nonchalant and failing miserably. "You know, thought I'd go for a walk. Maybe check out the casino. What about you?" She pushed the down button to call the lift.

"I told you . . . I have someone I need to see."

"Oh. Yeah. That's right." She shifted from foot to foot. "Well, have fun!" With a quick wave, she stepped onto the elevator like she didn't expect me to as well. I rather enjoyed bursting her bubble.

"Detroit really isn't a safe place for a woman to wander around by herself at night," I warned her when the doors closed. "You shouldn't leave the hotel, and if you do, please make sure you stay in a crowd of people."

She nodded with an "Mm-hmm, sure" that wasn't convincing. Turning her to face me, I finally got her attention. "I'm serious, Cassidy. We may have our differences, but I wouldn't want to see anything happen to you, either."

She looked at my hand on her shoulder, and I removed it. "I'm a big girl, Shaw. I'll be fine. You just go do whatever or *whoever* it is you're going to do."

When she turned toward the doors with her arms crossed over her chest, I smiled victoriously. She was jealous. And I liked it.

The doors opened, and she walked out without another word. I watched as she did so, admiring the view from behind. Damn, but she had a fantastic ass. Shaking myself from the stupor, I went in the opposite direction, toward the main exit, and stepped outside.

"How can I help you, sir?" the doorman asked.

"A cab, please."

He blew his whistle and one of the waiting cars pulled up in front, stopping to let the doorman open my door. Slipping a twenty into his hand, I nodded my thanks.

Before I'd even gotten situated in the backseat, the driver was on it. "Where to?"

"Seven Mile," I answered, closing the door.

"East or west?"

"East."

He turned in the seat and gave me the once-over. "Dressed like that? Are you sure?"

I didn't need to look at myself. I knew what he was talking about. Someone dressed like me in that neighborhood was a walking target. But I had to do what I had to do. "Yes."

He laughed and shook his head. "It's your funeral. The fare is going to be twenty-seven dollars, payable before I leave this curb."

Some things never change. This was one of those things. Cabbies got their money up front for two reasons. The first was to make sure they didn't get stiffed. I pulled two more twenties from my wallet and stuck them through the plastic barrier that separated us. "Keep the change," I said, knowing he deserved the hefty tip. And then he put the car into gear.

I would've called an old friend if I'd had one. But I didn't. Having friends in Detroit meant having someone to lose. It hadn't always been that way. I'd just been forced to learn a hard lesson very early on in my life.

One day when I was a young boy, I'd been at my only friend's house. We'd been doing what any other kids our age would've been doing: playing with cars in the middle of the living room floor while his mom cooked dinner and her boyfriend watched the sports channel from the couch. There'd been no warning before the front door was kicked in and a man wearing a ski mask charged the space to use the boyfriend's forehead for target practice. He blew the guy's brains out right in front of us, soaking my favorite Superman T-shirt in blood and God only knew what else, and then he walked out like he hadn't a care in the world. Chaos erupted after that. My friend's mother wailed so loud it pierced my ears, and neighbors were soon crowding the room to gawk at the scene. No one noticed the kid who walked out like an emotionless zombie. I made it home sometime later, though I couldn't recall the journey. And then I cleaned myself up and crawled under my bed to huddle in the corner, shaking and in shock. It wasn't right for a child to be exposed to so much horror, and even then I knew that for as long as I lived, I'd never be able to erase the events of that day from my mind.

I didn't make any friends after that. It was safer that way.

Now I was a successful man with a white-collar job, living in an upper-class neighborhood. It was easy for someone on the outside to assume that they knew what I was all about. But how could one person pass judgment on another without ever bothering to find out where they'd come from? Seven Mile Road was a place that stayed with you, no matter where you went or how long you were away, though I didn't have to let it define me.

The car came to a stop at the edge of hell, and the cabbie told me to get out. Even though I'd lived here for the majority of my life, I still wasn't prepared for the sudden rush. This was the second reason cabbies were paid up front: so they didn't have to put themselves in even more jeopardy by waiting for their money, which stood a good chance of being stripped away before it ever reached their hand. Cabdrivers never ventured beyond a certain point. If they did, they weren't guaranteed safe passage. In fact, they were almost assured of robbery and very probably faced homicide.

The instant I was out of the vehicle, the driver took off like a bat out of hell. Instinct kicked in then as if I'd never left this place, and I headed for the shadows.

Cassidy

No sooner had Shaw hopped a cab than I was hot on his trail. For whatever reason, I had to see where he was going. Or maybe it was that I had to see whom he was paying a special visit to. It was probably an old girlfriend, which sort of made me nauseated.

If I'd been nauseated before, I had the fear of God put in me when the driver of my taxi came to an abrupt stop and ordered me out of the car, then practically burned rubber in his haste to bust a U-turn. Talk about rude! He definitely wasn't a people person, but I couldn't waste time contemplating the mental issues of a total stranger when I had to play catch-up with Shaw, who had a good lead, thanks to my insistence that my driver hang back a bit.

It didn't take me long to find him, though it was weird that he, too, was keeping to the darkness instead of walking down the middle of the sidewalk. For a second, I wondered if he was trying to sneak up on someone, but it didn't take me long to figure out the situation.

Holy shit, I was in the middle of a war zone. A very, *very* scary war zone. Only there were no heroes sporting the red, white, and blue, ready to save the day. We were on our own.

Abandoned buildings lined both sides of the street, interspersed between gas stations and car parts stores that were in such a state of disrepair that I couldn't tell if they were still in operation or not. The streets were virtually empty except for the occasional vehicle that either crept by at an eerie pace or sped down the street like there was an emergency. The luxury SUVs with twenty-four-inch wheels, chrome grilles, and thumping stereo systems stood out like a sore thumb in an area ravished by poverty. What would someone who could afford something like that be doing in a neighborhood such as this?

Shaw was ducking in and out of the shadows, half-sprinting from one to the next, and I followed his lead, undetected. Though I nearly mucked that up when I tripped over a random door that had been thrown out onto an overgrown lawn. What did it say for an area when a person was safer in the shadows than in the light?

My heart was racing, and it had nothing to do with the pace I'd been keeping. No, it was frantically trying to break out of my chest and make a run for safety, the cowardly traitor. This was the stupidest idea I'd ever had. Even if Shaw did eventually end up somewhere safe, what about me? He couldn't know that I was following him, which meant I'd be left in this postapocalyptic universe, and maybe even end up fighting for my life in some underground thunderdome where survival was a blood sport the residents of Seven Mile saw as nothing more than entertainment.

Black smoke and the sound of crackling wood drew my attention as we passed yet another charred home, though this one was freshly ablaze. There were no firefighters on the scene, no police officers to block off the area, and no concerned citizens standing out front wringing their hands and praying for the safety of the house's occupants. No one cared. Not one person. By morning, it would simply add to the skeletal landscape of this part of urban America.

I considered for a moment that perhaps we'd wandered onto the set of a horror flick, but the chances of that weren't all that high. Though how cool would that have been? It certainly would explain the heebie-jeebies that had been dancing along my spine since the moment I'd been practically shoved out of the cab.

A gunshot rang out in the distance and I ducked, terrified that a stray bullet might inadvertently find its way through my unprotected chest. Shaw didn't flinch. He just kept going. Probably because it was harder to hit a moving target. Kevlar would've been nice, but not standing in one place to invite violence upon my personage sounded good, too. So I got with the program, picking up the pace. And I thought real hard about attracting Shaw's attention so he could hold my hand.

Without a doubt, my life was in danger. I'd never been more relieved than when Shaw stepped inside an apartment building. Though I seriously rethought that when I peeked through the window in the door and saw the inside. This building could have been marked for demolition. The walls and floor were filthy, the hall littered with trash and broken glass, and the piping could be seen through holes in the drywall. Only one ceiling light was actually working, and my imagination ran wild with the possibility that nefarious rapists might be lurking in the dark, waiting for the chance to get their hands on a woman like me.

"I am so *not* going in there." Another shot rang out, closer this time, and I changed my tune. "Bring it on, perverts," I said, throwing open the door and putting my back to the wall the second I was inside.

I barely caught sight of Shaw as he turned the corner at the top of the stairs, and I crept up, trying to stay low while also testing each step for squeaks. I'd come too far to get caught now; plus, I didn't want to alert anyone else to my presence. At the top of the stairs, I managed to slip into an obscure corner, where I waited and watched. Shaw was standing three doors down, his hand prepared to knock but seemingly suspended in air. And then, finally, he did it.

"Who is it?" came the rough bark of a lady's voice.

"Shaw" was his simple response.

The clanking of a chain lock and the loud click of a dead bolt sounded before the door was wrenched open. Light from inside the apartment spilled into the hallway, though, thankfully, not enough to expose me. The woman on the other side propped herself against the doorjamb with a cigarette in one hand. She was petite, the clothes hanging from her frame seeming to swallow her whole, and her bleached-blond hair looked dirty in its messy ponytail. Makeup was smeared under her eyes, but the rest of her face was bare, giving away the many wrinkles that pulled at her gaunt cheeks. This woman had seen a very hard life, and it didn't look like it was ever going to get any better. I couldn't imagine Shaw being with someone like that.

The woman took a drag off her cigarette and blew the smoke out, not even bothering to aim it away from Shaw. She also didn't bother to look for an ashtray before flicking the ashes onto the hallway floor. Then again, it wouldn't have made much of a difference.

She took another drag, her exhalation sending bursts of smoke out with each of her words. "I'd convinced myself I'd never lay eyes on your face again."

Shaw's sigh was loaded with guilt and maybe even a little resentment. "It's nice to see you, too, Ma."

Whoa! If this had been a soap opera, there would've been a dramatic *dun-dun-duuun* right before a loud gasp. Which I apparently made. Loudly. Not the *dun-dun-duuun*, but the gasp. And the gasp was loud enough to cause Shaw's head to whip around with narrowed eyes. I was convinced he had superhuman powers that could penetrate the dark with that look, and I was right.

The second he spotted me, his eyes went wide and his jaw started ticking. "What the hell are you doing here?"

Stepping forward, I started inspecting the walls and ceilings. "I was thinking about investing in some real estate. I heard that this building is for sale."

Shaw wasn't buying it. He came at me, grabbing my elbow and pulled me close. "Do you have any idea how stupid it was for you to follow me? How dangerous this place is?"

"I'm vaguely aware, yes."

He gave me an incredulous look. "You're vaguely aware? That's all you're going to say?"

"Well, no. You didn't let me finish." Letting my eyes travel anywhere other than to him, I continued: "What I was going to say was, I'm vaguely aware, yes . . . *now*."

For a long, uncomfortable moment, he just stared at me. Not knowing whether or not he expected something more, I added, "Can I meet your mom?"

"No" was his quick response. "You're going back to the hotel."

I pointed over my shoulder toward the door. "You want me to go out there? By myself? I mean, I survived the duck and tuck on the way here, but I don't really think it's wise to tempt fate."

"Are you coming in or not?" his mother asked from the relative safety of her apartment.

It was a good question. "Yeah, why don't we go inside?"

Shaw kept his eyes on me when he answered. "I'm sorry, Ma, but I have to head back to the hotel."

Ma blew out a puff of smoke. "Whatever" was all she said before she stepped back inside and closed the door. Just like that. As if she'd been inconvenienced by the interruption. Which didn't seem very motherly at all.

I looked from the closed door to Shaw and back, confused and waiting for an explanation. None was forthcoming.

"Not a word," he said. "Let's go."

Yea, though I walk through the valley of the shadow of death . . . I wished I had a rod and a staff to comfort me. Or a Buffy the Gangsta Slayer. Yeah, that would've been cool.

CHAPTER 15

Shaw

Apparently, my "Not a word" had been too vague. Cassidy hadn't said a word; she'd uttered what seemed like a million. In fact, she nearly got us caught by a truckload of bangers on our way back to the hotel because she wouldn't shut the hell up.

I was aggravated and pissed off, but most of all, I was embarrassed. Not by the woman who both infuriated me and made my dick hard enough to shatter bulletproof glass. No, I was ashamed that the dark secret, which I'd thought I'd kept so carefully hidden, had been brought to light. Somewhat, at least.

I hadn't answered any of Cassidy's questions. They'd started out nice enough, mostly about my mother and my childhood, but when I went mute on her, she started to sound more like the attorney she'd trained to be, and those questions amped up to accusations. A judge to intervene and call for order in the court while issuing warnings about badgering the witness would've been nice. The woman didn't know when to leave well enough alone. And by the time we'd gotten to the hotel, and I'd only barely shoved her inside her room to keep from disturbing Denver, she'd crossed over into tearing me down on a very personal level.

"You're a real piece of work, Shaw Matthews! I knew you

could be malicious when it came to business, but it's an entirely different level of ruthlessness to have the sort of money you do and still allow your own mother, the woman who gave you life, to live in such deplorable conditions. You're no superhero. You're the villain."

Cassidy's verbal assaults were like knives launched with wicked precision, and the last barb was a direct hit. She had no clue the hell I'd gone through and the guilt that still lurked underneath my skin. I might have done some shitty things to dig myself out of the gutter, but even I had a moral compass. "You don't know the first thing about me, Whalen. You know what they say about assuming things, hmm?" I had made it a priority to hide my past for a reason, and Cassidy had the tenacity of a pit bull. She could easily peel back the layers and expose my dirty little secret with tonight's Nancy Drew routine.

"What do you expect, Matthews? If it walks like a duck . . ." She let the words trickle off, shrugging her shoulders. "You're a selfish bastard and an egotistical prick who doesn't give a damn about anyone but yourself." Something akin to disappointment flashed in her kelly green eyes. Surely Cassidy wasn't upset by her ruminations. There were no touchy-feely emotions involved in what we had. It was purely a physical release.

"Oh, so all those orgasms I've been giving you lately were doing what for me?"

"Quit trying to change the subject. This isn't about sex, it's about how you can allow your mother to live in squalor."

I needed to shut her up. She was poking at my sore spot, making me want to confess the truth. I had tried to get my mother out of the hellhole we called home sweet home. She refused to budge. Mostly, because she wouldn't leave my lousy-ass father. There's only so many times you can get kicked in the teeth before you walk away. And I had.

"But isn't that what we do, Cassidy? There's nothing personal between us. We fight, we fuck. Why change things now when we've gotten so good at it?" I took a step closer, shrinking the distance between us. Caging her in. The pupils in her eyes dilated, and a beautiful flush bloomed across her cheeks. Then she lifted her chin and rolled her shoulders as she prepared to go toe-to-toe with me. And when she refused to back down, displaying that sexy as hell backbone I'd come to love, my dick grew impressively harder. "I'll even let you throw a few things, if it'll get you hot and bothered."

"You're an asshole." The whispered accusation had no bite. She was as turned on as I was and probably wet as hell. I wanted to dip my fingers inside her panties to test my speculation.

"That's what you like about me." Finally. We were back on familiar ground. I took another step, until we were inches apart. So close I could see the thrumming of her pulse at the base of her neck. So close I felt the warm caress of her breath as it washed over my face. Her lips parted and I watched, mesmerized, when her pretty pink tongue came out to lick the plump mouth I envisioned wrapped around my cock.

"My personal life is none of your business. So let's just stick to what we do best." I bent my head with every intention of kissing the sass right out of her. Of making her forget everything she'd witnessed tonight. Of keeping what was between us strictly sex. Nothing more.

Cassidy closed her eyes, and her submissive posture had me doing a silent "Hell, yeah" and a fist pump. I had her right where I wanted.

Then a slash of pain made me rear back; she'd bitten my lip.

"Jesus Christ, woman!" I wiped the back of my hand across my mouth; I wanted to wipe the smug expression off her face.

Despite the fact that I was harder than concrete and could drill a hole with the divining rod in my pants.

"You're not going to win this one, Matthews. I'm not one of your groupie whores who readily spreads her legs when you crook your little finger. You're not that good. I have standards, and I refuse to sleep with a man who'd stoop so low as to leave his own mother in such deplorable conditions."

I saw red. My sore spot was throbbing like a bitch, and her constant pestering had breached my limits. "Standards? Hah—I beg to differ. Let's discuss how cozy you and Denver have gotten over the last few days, shall we? Just how far have you fallen off your high horse to get the contract signed, sealed, and delivered? I may be an asshole, but at least I don't try to play myself off as something I'm not."

"I don't like what you're insinuating."

I shrugged, exhibiting a casualness that, surprisingly, I didn't feel. But we had been playing the same cutthroat game, and it was difficult to switch things up in the last inning. "If it walks like a duck—isn't that what you said?" Guilt caused an uneasy feeling to settle in my stomach. I might have taken a step too far in our sick little tête-à-tête, basically calling her a whore—condemning her actions by my own assumptions that she would use her body to get Denver to sign with her instead of me. *Who's the ass now, Matthews?*

And why the hell did the thought of Cassidy getting horizontal with someone else make me almost lose my shit?

As I was lost in my inner ramblings, a blinding pain erupted from my right temple. Apparently, Whalen was trying to knock some sense into me, because she'd tossed the room service menu at my head. Judging by its thickness, I'd say they had quite an extensive selection.

"Son of a bitch!" I yelled, rubbing my brow.

"You are a complete jerk. How dare you stand there and call me a . . ."

I glanced up; why couldn't she finish her deserved rampage? That previous sick feeling in my gut congealed and sat like a two-ton weight at the sight of her unshed tears. I couldn't tell if she was hurt or pissed. All I knew was that I didn't like to be the one responsible for making her cry.

Cassidy flew at me like a defensive tackle, hell-bent on taking me out at the knees.

Guess we're going with pissed.

I let her expel her rage, her tiny fists hammering hard at my chest, until I realized that the woman packed a mean punch. Damn, but I would be sporting a few well-earned bruises tomorrow.

I slipped one arm around her waist, pulling her in tighter, and used my other hand to cease her maddening blows. Her lithe frame wriggled against mine, causing my already aching cock to jerk with the need to be free. We had been in this position before—anger fueled with lust—but something seemed a little off. Different. Somehow we had crossed an invisible line. It was one thing to provoke Cassidy with empty taunts, but I had a problem with letting her believe I thought less of her. She was an admirable advisory. Hell, we were both guilty of playing dirty when it came to getting Denver to sign on the dotted line.

"Let go of me," she ordered, as she tried to break my hold. When I pressed harder and the outline of my erection pulsed between us, she stopped moving. But the small whimper that passed her lips was unmistakable.

I decided it wasn't time for voicing things better left unsaid. Whatever the fuck we had, whatever name you wanted to put on it, it was good—damn good. And it was mutual. "You want this just as much as I do, Whalen. Your body can't lie. Right now, nothing outside this room exists."

"I hate you." She spat the words like they were too vile to remain in her mouth.

And, really, there was only one appropriate response to that. "Good," I growled against her lips before I took possession of her mouth in a bruising kiss that left no room for further discussion. We were done talking.

If she had given me any clue that she wasn't on the same page, I would have stopped. A hesitant look, a backward step, anything. But she didn't. She met me with just as much vehemence, just as much lust. The heat of her mouth, the way she sucked hard on my tongue, and the sting as she tugged at the ends of my hair were proof of how fine the line was between love and hate.

We stumbled toward the bed, with Cassidy tumbling onto the mattress first, her hair spilling over the pillow. I wanted to bury my face in the silky strands as I made her mine. Standing above her, I unfastened my pants, letting my dick have a temporary reprieve as I enjoyed the view.

"Get rid of the jeans," I ordered, unbuttoning my shirt.

Instead of complying, she tossed her head and gave me a scathing look. But I didn't miss the way her knees parted slightly or how her fingers had a death-grip on the duvet. Her silent "Make me" was a challenge I couldn't refuse, and I was struck with an inspiring vision. One that, once seen, could not be ignored. I flashed her my most confident smile, grabbed both her ankles, and pulled her to the edge of the bed. With a careful, yet skillful maneuver, I spun her around until she was bent over the bed and her butt was in the air. She had on a pair of skinny jeans that did amazing things to her ass. They could also make for pretty good constraints in a pinch. I wasted no time stripping her jeans down to her knees.

Cassidy's muffled moan was like gasoline to a flame. Dropping to my knees, I spread her cheeks wide and licked her from front to back with one long stoke of my tongue. She was wet, aroused, and her creamy goodness coated the insides of her thighs. She arched off the bed, granting me better access. I accepted the unspoken invitation and buried my face, delving as far as I could before coming back to the forbidden opening that was like a bull's-eye for many of my very dirty, very carnal fantasies. It was taboo, the most intimate gift a woman could give a man. Eventually, it would be mine. But right now, I wanted inside her tight little cunt.

The fact that Cassidy wasn't protesting had my balls drawn tight and pre-come leaking from the head of my cock. She was completely still, only the quivering of her thighs giving her away. She wanted it, too.

I bent to taste her again, already addicted to the sweet tang of her juices, needing more. I held her open with one hand while roughly removing my pants with the other. And it wasn't lost on me how badly my hands shook. In an effort to pull myself together, I focused on a thousand different football stats as I tried not to blow my load before I entered the Holy Land.

Keeping her legs pinned together, I slipped my cock between her thighs, loving the dual sensation of her hot juices and the confines of the snug space. Cassidy squirmed, moving against me like a cat in search of attention. Our little bout had turned her on, and though she'd never admit it, the proof was saturating my dick. Nice and lubed, I ignored her huff of protest when I pulled free and spread the cheeks of her ass to fit my cock to the cleft. My shirt was in the way, and I couldn't have that, so I got rid of it real quick, never missing a stroke. Back and forth I moved, and every time the head passed over her rear entrance, she moaned.

I did it again, applying more pressure. On cue, a sound that went straight to my dick accompanied the lift of her hips. Fuck me . . . if I didn't get inside her soon, I was going to come all over her ass like a pubescent boy.

Because of my girth, I wouldn't attempt to breach her ass tonight. But that didn't mean I couldn't give her a hint of what to expect in the future. A little finger play at the back door went a long way toward making a woman lose her damn mind, if done properly. And I was all about fucking Cassidy Whalen all sorts of proper. With a quick thrust, I pushed inside her, using short, quick bursts until I was sheathed. "Goddamn!" The curse burst from my lips without warning.

Cassidy rose up on one arm in an attempt to take more of me, but I needed to regain some sense of control. With a firm but gentle grip, I lowered her back down until she was almost flush with the mattress. My hand remained cupped around her neck, a dominant hold meant to convey power. As the walls of her pussy clamped tight around me, I almost snorted at the thought. With every pulse of her pussy, I felt my influence slip further away.

Grabbing her hips, I dipped low at the knees and braced for the fucking I was about to bestow. One hard, deep thrust was followed by another and another, sending her body rocking forward on the bed. The rhythmic sound of skin slapping skin was amplified in the room, and the smell of sex permeated the air. My gaze stayed riveted to where my cock jutted in and out of her body. With each frantic thrust, her shirt rode up, exposing more of her skin, and that fucking tattoo stared at me with a silent taunt. Sweat dripped in my eyes and off my nose, but I refused to blink. It was like I had to fuck the ink right off her delectable backside.

"Who the fuck is Casey?" Even I could hear the grunting strain of my voice. I hadn't meant to ask, but my ire would not be denied, and she was going to answer my goddamn question.

When she tried to look over her shoulder at me, my hand to

her head kept her in place, refusing to let her see how the sight of that tattoo affected me.

"My personal life is none of your business. We fight, we fuck—isn't that what you said?"

I should've known she'd throw my own words back at me. I just didn't get why they were so damn difficult to accept.

I pounded into her pussy quick, hard, and deep. Cassidy mewled and stretched across the bed, gripping the sheets as if her life depended on it. "Did he ever fuck you like this?" I growled, increasing the pace until my eyes nearly rolled back inside my head. She might have Casey's mark on her body, but I was determined to make sure she'd never forget what it was like to be fucked by me.

Spreading the cheeks of her ass, I swept my thumb over the puckered skin there. Cassidy moaned, and I nearly lost my load. "Oh, yeah. You'd love having your ass fucked," I told her.

And then I eased my thumb inside, giving her a small taste of what she could experience if I took her ass like I wanted to. But I wasn't the selfish bastard she'd called me out to be, and I was hell-bent on proving it.

Cassidy's body arched off the bed, and she cried out with an orgasm I hadn't even seen coming. The walls of her pussy constricted so tight around my cock, I thought it might actually do some real damage. But I didn't stop. Nor did I remove my thumb. Grinding into her sweet pussy, I closed my eyes and let the pulsing constriction pull at my cock. Damn, I wanted her to taste herself on me.

I grabbed Cassidy and flipped her over while spinning her around on the bed. Clearly, she was shocked by the sudden movement, but when I pulled her forward so that her head was hanging off the side and pushed my cock down and into her mouth, she got with the program. With no hesitation, she hooked her arms around my thighs and greedily licked at my cock, taking me deep.

"Good girl," I groaned, clenching my ass cheeks.

There wasn't much room for her to move, so I decided to help her, pumping in and out with shallow strokes, while taking care not to gag her.

"Christ, that's good." I let myself become consumed with the mind-boggling sensations riding my body until it was almost too much. Then her thighs fell open, exposing the blood-red lips of her pussy, practically begging for more attention.

I recognized a golden opportunity when I saw one, so I leaned forward and slid two fingers inside. I curled my hand, hitting the spot I knew would make her gush. When her knees drew up, I knew she was close. Wanting to help her along, I added a third finger and buried my face between her thighs. Cassidy's moan as she came a second time was lessened by the presence of my cock, buried at the back of her throat. But I felt the vibration all the way to my toes. Her release was unrestrained as she rode my face, and I was completely surrounded by her musky scent.

Wrapping my arms around Cassidy's tiny waist, I carefully stood, bringing her with me while still eating her pussy like it was the last time I'd ever eat anything. Cassidy locked onto my thighs as if she were afraid I would drop her. *Not gonna happen.* I told myself it was because I didn't want to lose the fantastic blow job I was getting, but something hinted to me it was more than that.

I turned and reclined back onto the bed, switching our positions, and Cassidy never once stopped sucking my dick. She needed to be properly rewarded for her accomplishment.

Apparently, she had other ideas.

With a stealthy move I didn't see coming, Cassidy reversed course and cowgirl-straddled my crotch.

"That's not how this is going down," I told her with a smirk as I grabbed hold of her hips.

"Shut up." Her words were clipped, no-nonsense, and she was

already positioning the head of my cock at her entrance. Her eyes closed and her head fell back as she sank down onto it with a slow but steady descent.

I didn't think I could possibly get any harder, but I'd be damned if I hadn't done just that. All those long, ginger locks spilled down her back and over her shoulders as she lifted her arms and pulled her shirt over her head. Cassidy's hips never missed a beat while she took her time removing her bra as well. Back and forth she rocked, with an exaggerated roll of her body. The rosy peaks of her full breasts were pebbled and begging for a warm mouth, so I pulled her toward me, granting one its wish.

Cassidy wasn't having any of that, though. With her hands on my chest, she shoved me away and held me there, using my body as extra support for her ride. "You made your point. Now let me make mine."

Jesus Christ, but the woman was too damn sexy for her own good.

And then Cassidy did something I'd never expected of her. She used me. Plain and simple. I might as well have not even been in the room. With a slow and steady grind, she moved against me, taking her own pleasure without any concern for my own. I was nothing more than her tool as she leaned forward, putting the palms of her hands and all of her weight on my chest, and then she quickened her pace. She didn't even look at me. I wanted her to fucking look at me. But behind those shuttered eyes, she was lost to a world of fantasy, and I was hell-bent on making sure I was in there with her.

"What are you thinking about?"

"Shh" was her only response.

"Look at me."

Cassidy continued to ignore me, her fingernails digging into my chest as her ride became more aggressive. Her teeth pulled at her bottom lip, and her brows furrowed in concentration. When her lips parted and euphoria smoothed her expression, I knew where she was. Her hot sheath became even slicker with each advance and retreat, and she leaned forward and centered the grind on her clit. I cupped her ass, spreading her cheeks, knowing she'd love the feel of the pull on her rear entrance. She did not disappoint.

"Look at me, dammit!" I ordered, with an urgency I shouldn't have felt.

"No." She shook her head and continued to ride me.

But what was with the furrowed brow?

"Why the hell not?"

"Because if I do . . ." Her voice trailed off, and she stopped moving. Slowly, she opened her eyes, the truth reflecting there clear as fuck.

"Shaw—"

"Don't." I didn't want to hear it, didn't need to. I knew what she was getting at, and I wouldn't even let my own mind finish the thought. It for damn sure wasn't going to be said aloud. That shit was not happening. There was nothing touchy-feely about what was going on, and maybe we both needed a reminder of that.

Raw anger, potent lust, and steely determination made for a deadly combination. One that had me flipping her onto her back and gripping her hips to finish what we'd started. I fucked her. Hard and fast. Just as she was fucking me. Only maybe this time, I meant it in the metaphorical sense.

Cassidy held on for dear life, gripping my shoulders and breathing hard. I saw her through yet another orgasm, which brought the unselfish Shaw count to three. And then my balls drew up and I finally pulled my cock out to come all over her stomach.

Releasing her legs, I fought to catch my breath as I rolled away and onto the side of the bed. For the first time in my life, the sex had felt like more than just a release. I had no clue what she'd been about to say, but it scared me to death all the same. And fuck all if I knew what to do with that information.

Standing, I felt like a newborn fawn on unsteady legs, but I managed to cross the room to the bathroom without making a fool of myself. My little buddy was out for the count, lying against my thigh as if begging for mercy. He'd more than earned his reprieve.

Since I was a decent human being, contrary to anything Cassidy said, I soaked a washcloth in hot water and then returned to the bed. Carefully, I wiped the gooey mess from her softly rounded abdomen. She lay there, limp as a noodle, with her eyes closed and her breaths steady as my hand dipped lower and I gently cleaned her most intimate parts. It seemed almost impossible to me that a woman as tough as I knew she could be could also look so angelic.

Back in the bathroom, I washed myself before returning once more and slipping under the covers beside Cassidy. It had been a very long day, filled with emotional highs and lows, physical threats, mental assaults, and sexual acrobatics. Much like my little buddy, I'd also earned some downtime. My sleep-deprived brain didn't have the wherewithal to realize that I had subconsciously made the decision to stay the night. My last thought as I drifted off was how lying next to Cassidy felt more like home than if I had spent the night on my mother's couch.

Cassidy

Mornings were never an issue for me. Normally, I'd pop right up, ready to get the day started: another sunrise was another opportunity to meet a goal that would ultimately score the win. But this morning, my body was having a hard time getting to that enthusiastic point. So was my brain.

Snuggling into the cocoon of warmth that sheltered me from the frigid room beyond the covers, I let the steady rhythm beneath my ear seduce me back to the dark refuge of sleep. I couldn't remember the last time I'd been so comfortable, so carefree. My body was heavy, almost paralyzed in its refusal to budge, and I was content to let it have its way.

Lub-dub, lub-dub, lub-dub . . . I released a contented sigh, barely moving my head to settle in deeper to the sound. Until my sleep-addled mind got cognitive and realized that the sound was a heartbeat. My fingertips joined in, sending signals to upper management to clue it in that the warmth their nerve endings were sensing was coming from skin. Skin stretched over a taut muscle, and that heartbeat wasn't far beneath that.

I frantically searched my memory bank, trying desperately to put together the pieces of the puzzle, until they formed one giant-ass picture that made me gasp. My eyes shot open and my head sprang up, though the rest of me was still in ain't-gonna-happen mode.

Shaw Matthews's naked body was wrapped around my naked body. And oh, my God . . . I'd drooled all over his naked chest. The first order of business was to get rid of that, which I accomplished quite well with the use of the sheet. The second was to get him out of my bed.

So, I gave him a shake, only because I thought it was rude to punch someone in his sleep. "Shaw?"

"Hmm?" he answered, still very much asleep and snuggling in closer. The arm over my side tightened to pull me toward his chest, and his crotch played kissy-kissy with mine. Jumping Jehoshaphat, he was rock-hard.

"Oh, my God, get up!" I screeched while giving him a heftier jarring and doing my best to free myself from his clutches. I succeeded well enough and sat up, jerking the comforter away from him and wrapping it around myself for some semblance of decorum.

Shaw's brow furrowed in irritation, and he rolled over onto his back. "What . . . is the *problem?*" he asked, finally opening his eyes.

"You in my bed . . . is the *problem,*" I mocked him. "Why are you still here?"

He looked every bit as confused as I was sure I had when I'd first woken. I gave him a moment to think it over, and I could practically see the wheels turning in his head.

"I think maybe you've forgotten who's paying for this room. Technically, *you* are in *my* room. You don't hear me bitching about it." He started to sit up, but then grabbed his head and lay back down. "Ow! Shit!"

Oh. That headache would be my fault. Before I could apologize, while still yelling at him that he could've at least slept on the floor, a knock sounded.

"Cassidy?" came Denver's voice through the door. "Are you awake?"

I froze. So did Shaw. Our eyes went round as saucers.

"Get out!" I snarled, giving him a shove toward the edge of the bed.

He whisper-yelled right back at me: "And go where, out the window? He's standing right outside the door, woman!"

"Cassidy? Is everything okay in there?"

"Uh, yeah," I called back, getting out of the bed as well— still managing to keep the comforter around me, thank you very much. "Just a moment."

Looking around for a hiding spot, I started gesturing toward the bathroom to get Shaw going in that direction. I so could've been one of those marshaling guys with the lighted tubes on the ground at the airport.

Shaw took his sweet, still naked time getting in there, and I was left to do all the thinking for both of us, since he'd neglected to pick up his stupid clothes in the process. With a disgruntled huff, I quickly gathered them together and tossed them into the bathroom, lobbing his shoes one at a time. Shaw gave me the evil eye when one of them almost hit him.

"What? Oh, it wasn't on purpose!" I said with a dismissive wave before he finally closed himself in.

Securing the comforter a little tighter, I went to the door and cracked it open. "Good morning," I said, greeting Denver with as much of a smile as I could muster.

"Morning, sunshine! Can I come in?" He started forward, but I blocked his way.

"Um, I'm not dressed yet." I looked down at myself and then back at him with a demure smile.

And then I heard the incredibly loud, echoing sound of what I could only assume was Shaw handling his morning bladder relief in the bathroom.

Denver heard it, too. "What's that?"

"I, uh, I left the water running in the tub. I was just about to get in and wanted it to be good and warm." Sounded plausible to me.

"Oh. Well, do you know where Shaw is?"

Giving my head a slow shake, I said, "Nope. But you know . . . I think he said something last night about going to visit someone, didn't he?"

"Right. I forgot about that." Then Denver got a mischievous look about him. "Hope he got lucky last night. That dude needs to release some tension. Whew!"

I blushed. I knew it because I could feel the heat pool in my cheeks. Oh, he'd definitely gotten lucky.

Denver was trying to look over the top of my head, which wasn't hard for him to do, given his height. I casually popped up on my tiptoes to thwart the effort as much as possible. With my luck, he'd get a peek inside to find I'd forgotten Shaw's underwear hanging over a lamp or something. Oh God, I hoped my room didn't smell like sex.

Concern etched his brow as he gave me a once-over. "Are you okay? You look tired."

Leaning into the frame, I laid on the nonchalance pretty thick. "Oh, yeah. I'm fine. Just really want that bath and some breakfast, you know?"

"Definitely." He nodded his understanding. "Hey, how about if I go on down and get us a table at the restaurant to save some time?"

"That would be awesome! You are so my hero!"

"Want me to order for you?"

"Yes, please."

"Sausage or bacon?"

And then the toilet flushed. Oh, for the love of . . .

I did some fast talking, hoping to distract Denver. I also might have been a little louder than necessary to cover the sound. "Ham and eggs, over medium. And some breakfast potatoes, if they have them. And, um, thanks!" I said, closing the door before dumbass Shaw decided to strut his dumbass self out to give Denver a fist bump and a "Whassup, bro?"

Men were so stupid.

CHAPTER 16
Cassidy

The trip to Detroit had been one I wouldn't soon forget, for many reasons. For one, there was the sex with Shaw. It was hot, dirty, everything it had always been between us. With one exception.

It had also been completely different.

Shaw had refused to open up after I'd badgered him with a million questions, and for reasons I couldn't begin to understand, his aloofness bothered me.

And then there'd been his commanding voice: *"Look at me, dammit!"*

I couldn't. Behind my closed eyes, I had concocted the perfect fantasy. Shaw had probably thought I had been thinking of another man. Maybe even Casey. But the truth was more dangerous than that. I had been picturing a different Shaw. One who could be tender and caring. One I could easily fall for. One who didn't exist.

If I'd opened my eyes, I would have come face-to-face with the harsh reality: Shaw would never be the man I wanted him to be.

The second reason I wouldn't forget Detroit was that it was

where I'd realized that I had probably lost Denver to Shaw. And surprisingly, I couldn't muster up a good reason to warn Denver off from the deal that was in the making. Shaw had come through in a major way, and I had to respect that. Detroit had put up dollar signs in flashing neon lights and had thrown around extra perks like parade candy. It had been a huge risk on Shaw's part, as there were no guarantees that Denver would actually sign with him, and the offers from Detroit would still stand through any other agent. But I had a feeling Shaw knew the risks and wasn't worried about them. His confidence made me nervous.

So did the request from Denver, as we'd parted ways after our return to San Diego, to meet with me first thing Monday morning. I'd spent the remainder of the weekend pacing, poring over all my research, and scouring the net in search of any new information I might have overlooked, in an effort to come up with a possible counter to Shaw's game-changing play.

Reaching out to Colorado's deal makers might have helped, but acting prematurely could cause more harm than good. Delilah Rockford had been another option, since playing the mommy card had worked twice before, but I didn't want to come off like a one-trick pony. And there was only so much leverage even the woman who gave birth to a man could hold. I did manage a call to San Diego to feel out the front-office's agenda where Denver was concerned, but because I lacked a connection on the inside, no one would to talk to me about a client who hadn't yet contracted with me. It was business, so I tried not to take it personally, though those rat bastards wouldn't be getting any special favors from me anytime soon.

I was stuck. And Denver was sitting across from me in my office, exchanging pleasantries like he wasn't about to drop the proverbial ax, which I could practically see suspended in midair above my head.

"Did you have a good weekend?" he asked, shifting forward and then back again in his chair. It was the fifth time he'd done so since he'd sat down.

"Um, yeah," I lied. "Just sort of hung out at home, unwinding from the trip. Traveling, even short trips, always makes me tense."

Denver nodded, but I could tell his thoughts were a thousand miles away.

I leaned forward, giving him my full attention. Whatever the matter was, it was big. Though I was sure I knew why he was here, it was clear the guilt was eating away at his conscience. "What's going on, Denver? Is something wrong?"

He looked right at me then. "Something is very wrong," he answered, and the need for me to understand practically jumped out at me from his eyes.

Holy crap, if this Hercules of a man started crying right in front of me, I'd be the blubbering idiot holding him. The mama bear in me wanted to let him off the hook and tell him it was okay if he'd decided to go with Shaw, that we could still be friends and hang out and all that jazz. I could do that for him. I could make everything better, because I was a fixer by nature.

"Denver, look, it's fine. If you want to—"

Before I could finish, the door to my office burst open, causing me to jump out of my skin. A very excited Demi and Sasha were panting, with panic-stricken expressions on their faces.

"Cassidy . . . it's Quinn," Sasha said, wringing her hands.

"What about him?" I asked, unable to ignore the way my heart free-fell into my stomach. If anything had happened to him . . . if he'd been hurt . . . "Oh, God, is he okay?"

Demi did this thing where she shook her head and nodded at the same time. "All we know is, he's in crisis mode."

I understood exactly what that meant. Quinn had a flair for the dramatic. Usually, he was riding an extreme high, but when he crashed, he crashed hard, and we never really knew how that might end.

"What happened?"

Sasha threw her hands into the air and let them fall back down. "We hadn't seen him all weekend, and then finally, he returned my call this morning. He was a blubbering mess, and I couldn't really make out everything he was saying, but it was definitely something about Daddy being a bastard. He also mentioned something about pills and wanting to be numb so he doesn't have to feel the pain anymore."

"What?" Now I was panicking.

Like I'd said, Quinn had a flair for drama, and though he had threatened self-harm before, he'd never followed through on it. Regardless, we couldn't and wouldn't ignore it. "Why didn't you go over there?"

"We did!" Demi said. "We went over to his place to check on him, but the door is locked and he won't open it. He's also not answering his phone anymore. We thought you might have a key."

"Shit, I don't." Quinn and I had discussed it, but we'd never done the exchange. "We have to get over there."

Sasha pulled her cellphone out of her purse. "I'm calling Landon now so he can pick us up."

"Good idea," I told her, and then I realized I was forgetting about one very important person in the room. "Um, I'm so sorry, Denver. Can we finish this later?"

He stood, genuine concern written all over his face. "For fuck's sake, don't apologize, Cassidy. Your friend needs you. In fact, I'll go with you, if that's okay?"

"Sure, sure." I grabbed my purse and hurried to the door, hot on the heels of Demi, who already had Chaz on the phone as well. Ally looked up from her desk when we passed, worried. "I've got to leave," I told her. "Cancel the rest of my appointments for the day, and if Wade asks, tell him something urgent came up."

"I'll take care of everything," she said with an encouraging smile, and I knew she would.

I was still looking back at her when I stepped out into the hall-way, which caused me to almost rearrange my own face during a near collision with Shaw's chest. My knees threatened to buckle under the weight of seeing him again, but thankfully, he'd been paying attention and caught me by the shoulders before I fell on my ass.

"Whoa, whoa, whoa! Where's the emergency, gang?" he asked, taking note of the brigade.

There were things Shaw and I needed to discuss, but right now my thoughts were solely on Quinn. I had to leave.

"I can't do this right now," I said, pushing him aside as I started toward the elevator.

"Ouch! What'd I do?" The ouch was nothing more than the blow to his stupid ego.

Demi repeated the situation since—surprise, surprise—we had to wait for the elevator anyway. I guess maybe we did have the time, but I certainly didn't have the patience.

"I'm going with you," Shaw said, stepping into the lift with us.

Thank God for Landon and his testosterone-driven need to own a big truck. His Armada was a party bus capable of holding our whole crew. By the time we'd reached the building that held the penthouse suite Quinn shared with Daddy, Chaz was pulling up next to us on his motorcycle. We didn't waste any time with pleas-antries because only one concern was on all of our minds. Quinn.

The elevator rode up at a snail's pace, or so it seemed, though I was sure it was faster than taking the eighteen flights of stairs.

Quinn's number had been on constant redial on my phone, but he hadn't answered for me, either. The last time, I could tell he'd sent me directly to voice mail, so I'd left a message for him.

"Quinn, I swear to God, if you've done something incredibly stupid like die, I'm going to kill you." No, what I'd said hadn't made any sense, unless you counted that I'd jump in front of a train so I could track his ghostly butt down and commit spectral homicide, thereby sending him to purgatory. That would teach him to ignore me.

Finally at his door, I knocked once, twice, three times. A chorus of his name being called by almost everyone present echoed through the corridor, but he didn't answer. So I started pounding. "Quinn! Open this door right now!"

Sasha put her hand on my shoulder, silently asking me to back up and give her a shot. "Quinn, sweetheart," she said, using the sugary approach, "we love you and we're here for you. Open the door, sweetie. Please?"

Still nothing.

Demi shoved her way through the crowd and got down to it: "Stop being dramatic and open this door before I call the fire department to break it down!"

"You don't have to call them," Shaw said, shocking the hell out of me. "Step aside."

And because I'd been struck stupid, I did. There was a door standing between my best friend and me, and I had no idea what condition I might find him in. My emotions were in the driver's seat, and everything else could be dealt with later.

Shaw centered himself before hurling his full weight toward the barrier at an angle that turned him into a human battering ram, with his shoulder in the lead. It took him a couple of runs, but finally, the wood on the frame splintered and gave way.

I'd been to Quinn's lavish digs right after he'd moved in. We all had. This didn't look anything like the same place. The plush alpine-white carpet was there, and so were the crimson walls, but the furniture and decor that had given the space its European hoity-toity appeal were gone. It was bare, empty. Nothing on the walls, no drapes at the windows. All that was left were remnants of packing tape, boxes, and bubble wrap, scattered about the floors and counters like someone had moved in a hurry.

"Quinn?" I called out. Damn the rest of the place. My best friend was the most valuable asset those walls had ever or would ever see, anyway.

"I'm in here," came his tearful voice from the bedroom.

I'd never been so relieved. Nor, in an effort to get to him, had I ever moved so quickly. I didn't know if it was to ensure that he was okay or to kick his ass for making me worry. Definitely to ensure that he was okay, and *then* I'd kick his ass. If Demi didn't beat me to it. Or any of the rest of our friends, since they'd all managed to push their way past me to get at him.

"Oh, my God! You scared us to death!"

"Why didn't you answer the door?"

"Why didn't you answer your phone?"

"Are you okay?"

"Did you take anything? Quinn! Did you take anything?"

Wow, so I wasn't going to have to say anything at all. Quinn was sitting against the far wall, with his clothes and shoes scattered about the room. No way had he done that. Quinn was much too meticulous about his attire to do such a thing, even in a fit of rage.

Overcome by all the questions flying at him, Quinn put the heels of his palms to his temples as he closed his eyes and rested his head against the wall with a huff. "I'm sorry I scared you. I didn't answer the door because I didn't want to *see* anyone, and I didn't answer the phone because I didn't want to *talk* to anyone. No, I am *not* okay, but no, I didn't take anything. Though if any of you have a magic pill that will just make it all go away, I'd sure appreciate it."

I got down on the floor with him—awkwardly, thanks to the stupid pencil skirt I'd put on for the office this morning—and snuggled into my distraught friend's side. "Make what go away, Quinn? What's wrong?"

"What's wrong? *What's wrong?*" He threw up his hands. "All you have to do is look around you to see what's wrong."

"Let me guess," Demi said, flanking his other side, and Sasha took the seat before him. "Jennifer Aniston's decorator didn't get paid, so she came and repo'ed everything?"

Chaz snickered, but I did my best not to smile, while giving our inappropriate friend a disapproving scowl.

Sasha had done a better job of it than I. "Seriously. What happened?" She opened her purse and took out a pack of tissues, handing them across the way.

Quinn took one and wiped at his nose. "Turns out . . . Daddy doesn't like ultimatums. And neither do I."

"What ultimatum?" The level of concern I heard in Shaw's voice, along with his recent display of heroism, had me questioning everything I thought I knew about him. Was this a new development or something that had been there all along and I had refused to see?

"I did it, okay? I told him I was tired of being kept hidden, that it had taken me too long to come out of the closet only to be shoved back into it. I tried to make him see how much happier we could be if we didn't have to keep our love from the rest of the world." Quinn's diatribe interrupted my silent musings, and I placed my attention back where it should be, on my best friend.

"And what did he say?" The cracking sound of Chaz's knuckles was every bit as intimidating as his voice.

Quinn rolled his eyes, his annoyance at the answer preceding the actual words. "He kept going on and on about his children, about his wife, saying he wasn't ready and probably never would be. And then he said if I couldn't be happy with him the way things are without ever expecting more, there was no need for us to stay together." Quinn shook his head. "I should've just kept my mouth shut."

Demi put her arm around him. "But, sweetie, you weren't happy like that."

"Does it look like I'm happy now? Take a look around. I lost everything. And now I'm homeless," he said as he leaned his head on Demi's shoulder and sobbed into her hair.

"Good God," Demi said, holding her nose and edging away. "When was the last time you showered?"

Quinn pulled back to look at her. "Seriously? My life is over and you're insulting me?"

"Oh, stop being so dramatic. Your life is far from over. He was just a man, and there are plenty more where he came from."

"But I love him, and he doesn't want me."

Demi shrugged, matter-of-factly. "Rejection sucks. But it doesn't mean you give up. If the one you want doesn't want you back, it's not a big deal. Someone who does will come along. I promise you that."

I couldn't help but notice the way Chaz's body flared up, his energy sending waves of "over my dead body" through the air. Good. Maybe that was the incentive he needed to finally get off his ass and do something about it.

"Maybe, but until then, I'm all alone."

"All alone?" Denver said, stepping forward. He looked at each of us and then at Quinn. "How can you possibly be all alone when you have six friends who dropped everything to be here for you? *Six!* Do you have any idea what I'd do to have just one?"

Quinn must not have noticed him before, though I wasn't

sure how a behemoth like Denver could ever be missed, crowded room or not. "Holy shit . . . what is Denver Rockford doing here?" He turned away and wiped at his cheeks and eyes. "Oh, God, I'm a mess. Don't look at me."

Denver copped a squat right along with us. "No, you're not. Your head's a mess, and maybe even your heart, but none of that translates to your outward appearance."

"Liar," Demi coughed. Honestly, I didn't know what we were going to do with her, but we really wouldn't have her any other way.

Denver, however, really surprised me. I'd seen so much machismo from him that I never would've guessed he had it in him to be this person standing before me now. He was handling Quinn so well, saying just the right thing at just the right time.

What a lousy friend I'd turned out to be. I'd been so consumed with my own crap that I hadn't been there for Quinn the way I should have. I hadn't even known he was considering broaching the topic with Daddy in the first place. Of course I wouldn't have tried to talk him out of it, so we'd still be in the same situation, but that sort of thing was something a best friend should have known was about to go down.

"Quinn, I'm so sorry you're hurting," I told him. "I know this really sucks, and there's really nothing anyone can tell you that will make you feel better, but everything happens for a reason."

"Everything happens for a reason, he was never good enough for you anyway, you deserve so much better, and the sun will come out tomorrow, betcha bottom dollar, blah, blah, blaaaahhh," he said. "Logically, I know all those things. The problem is that I'm not feeling very logical right now, because my heart has been blown to smithereens. And I just feel like . . . like ripping his fucking head off!"

"Then do it," Denver told him. "Not literally, of course. Figuratively."

"I vote we don't take the literally part off the table just yet," Demi said. When everyone looked at her, she shrugged. "I'm just saying . . . I'd like to get my hands on him."

Chaz groaned. "Dammit, woman! You are always trying to make me go to prison."

Demi drew her head back. "How is that making you go to prison?"

"Because if you touch him, he's going to want to touch you back, and then I'm going to have to stop him from breathing."

"Awww," Demi cooed. "You'd kill someone for me?"

Chaz shifted, looking around at his boys to see if they thought he was less of a man somehow. Then he puffed up his chest and set his shoulders high. "Yeah. Of course I would."

The pink hearts floating in the air around Demi were something magical only women had the power to see. Except in Demi's case, they looked more like tattooed hearts with Cupid's arrows piercing their centers.

"You know what? You're right, Denver," Quinn said, getting to his feet and ignoring the slightly disturbing version of the "I like you, do you like me? Check yes or no" game Demi and Chaz had had going on for as long as I'd known them. He marched out of the bedroom and toward the front room, leaving the rest of us to scramble after him.

Quinn stopped when he saw the door and turned to look at us, pointing in that direction with an expression that said, *"What the fuck?"*

Shaw read him loud and clear. "Oh, yeah, about that . . . I, um . . . I sort of broke your door."

Quinn straightened and seemed almost pleased. "Good," he said with conviction. "You can tear it off the hinges for all I care.

"Just look at this place. This was supposed to be mine, and he took it all away . . . to give to *her*." He turned, surveying every corner. "Well, she can have him. But she's not getting this god-damn penthouse without having to do as much cosmetic surgery to it as she's done to her own silicone-and-plastic self."

Quinn went over to the fireplace and picked up the decorative poker, everything about his walk screaming revenge.

"Quinn, what are you going to do?" I asked warily. Sensing that he wasn't going to answer my question, I made to follow so I could see for myself, but Shaw held out his arm to bring me to a gentle stop.

"Let him go," he said. "He needs this."

"Needs what?"

Seconds after Quinn disappeared into the master suite, I found out. Quinn's growl was infused with true anger and resolve, a battle cry one might have heard from a soldier who'd been over-run yet determined to take as many of the enemy as he could with him to the grave. The crunch of fracturing glass followed, and for a second, I got that feeling of unease superstitious people must get when they realize that seven years of bad luck is on the horizon. But all of that went away, released with each tinkling of the bathroom mirror's shards as they hit the sink and floor.

I understood then. Quinn did need this. In a way, I was jealous that I didn't have an outlet of my own. Though the responsible thing for me to do would have been to stop him, for once in my life, I didn't feel like being the sensible one. I wanted my friend to have this. I wanted him to have it for the happiness he'd been denied and for all the times he'd been taken advantage of and hurt without the satisfaction of retaliation.

Moments later, Quinn stepped out of the bedroom with his head held high, even though his cheeks were streaked with tears.

"Are you okay?" Sasha asked.

"Nope, but I'm getting there," he said. "You might want to stand back, sweetie."

Landon put his hands on Sasha's shoulders and pulled her against his chest protectively just as Quinn drew the poker back like a bat and took a mighty swing. I flinched when he hit the crimson wall, leaving a gaping hole in the aftermath of his fury. The chalky plaster hanging by threads of paper from its mouth reminded me of fleshy organs spilling from a traumatic wound. If the disturbing sigh of satisfaction from Quinn as he admired his work was any indication, I'd say that was just the effect he'd been going for.

But he wasn't done yet.

Moving to another spot on the same wall, he inflicted wound after wound. I stopped flinching after the third and smiled victoriously along with him. When he was done, Quinn stepped back to admire the work with a tilt of his head. The misfortune of the one who broke Quinn's heart was equal to obliteration on a level that was every bit as personal as the misdeed itself. Daddy's request that Quinn keep his secret had been denied.

The truth would not be as easily erased as the relationship, because it was written on the wall. Well, carved into it. Giant letters spelled out, "HE'S GAY!"

Quinn dropped the poker in dramatic fashion before dusting off his hands. "What's done in the dark will always come to light, bitch," he said, then turned his back on it to face us. "I'm ready to go home now."

Home was exactly where he belonged. I was his family. *We* were his family. And if being a child of Stonington, Maine, had taught me anything, it was that a family took care of its own.

I linked arms with my best friend, and we headed for the door. "Don't worry, Quinn . . . you'll always be welcomed home, because family is the one thing you can count on." I looked over my shoulder, shooting laser beams of guilt at Shaw with my eyes. "Or at least that's the way it *should* be."

CHAPTER 17

Shaw

Cassidy Whalen was a persistent little brat. I'd lucked out well enough over the weekend when she hadn't made an appearance at Monkey Business, though I'd planned a speedy escape if she had. But when the entire hubbub with Quinn had gone down and she'd made the comment about family, I'd known she hadn't let go of what she'd seen in Detroit. That woman was going to be the death of me.

I'd played nice enough in order to get Quinn's things moved back into their place, but even then she'd kept taking jabs at me. So much so that the rest of our friends had stopped and asked what was going on between the two of us. Cassidy had laughed it off, feigning innocence, and I'd looked at her like she was crazy—because she fucking was—and even though I knew they hadn't believed either one of us, they'd let it go.

So yeah, the second Landon had dropped us off at Monkey Business, I'd headed in the opposite direction. I'd rather be home alone than surrounded by my friends while being ridiculed by the woman I'd been fucking on a regular basis.

Climbing three flights of stairs—the elevator in my building was out and had been since the day I'd moved in—I was relieved to finally make it to my door with key in hand.

"Wow, so this is where you live, huh?"

I should've been startled, but I would've known that voice anywhere. Closing my eyes to the annoyance, I struggled to get my blood pressure under control. Cassidy had a really bad habit of turning up where she wasn't wanted or invited. She must have been a cat in a past life, because I had no clue how she'd made it up all those stairs behind me without making a sound.

Reluctantly, I turned to face her. "What the hell are you doing here? Did you follow me again? Christ, woman!"

"I'm a sports agent, which makes me a professional stalker. It's what I do. And I'm damn good at it." She leaned against the wall with her shoes in one hand and not a care in the world.

"Yeah? Well, I'm not one of your clients, so why are you stalking me?"

"Because you need to explain yourself to me."

I cupped my balls in a smart-ass sort of way. "Yep, still there. Which means I'm a man and don't have to explain myself to anyone."

"I just want to know how you can come home to your posh apartment and lay your head down on what I'm sure is the most comfortable pillow money can buy and sleep at night, knowing your mother is all alone in a condemned building in the middle of a gang-infested neighborhood. You tell me the answer to that, and I'll leave." Cassidy's voice got louder with each word she spoke, which I was sure the landlord's mother, who lived across the way, really appreciated. "And in case you get any grand ideas, you're not going to be able to fuck your way out of it this time, Shaw Matthews."

I felt like banging my head against the wall. "Jesus Christ . . . Go home, Cassidy. I have neighbors. I'm not going to stand out in the hallway arguing with you all night."

She shrugged and crossed her arms. "Well, then I guess you better invite me in, because I'm not going anywhere."

Like that was a threat I couldn't handle. She for damn sure wasn't stepping a foot into my place. "Not a problem. I'll just go inside and leave you out here alone."

"Suit yourself. I'll make a quick phone call and beat and bang on your door until Denver shows up to break it down like you did with Quinn's. Whatever works for you." She pulled her phone out of her purse.

Damn it! Denver would probably do it for her, too.

With a heavy sigh, I conceded. "Fine. Let's just go somewhere else so you can get this out of your system."

Cassidy blocked the door to the stairs. "Why can't we just go inside your apartment?"

"I'd think you'd want someplace more public so I can't fuck my way out of whatever it is you keep going on about." I gave her the grin I pulled out only when I wanted a woman to be at my mercy. "And if I have you that close to my bed, damn right I'm going to fuck you in it."

She leaned in, her intimate proximity drawing me closer to her body's warmth. "I think I can handle myself," she said, and then she snatched the key to my apartment out of my hand and bolted for the door, leaving me to catch myself on the wall.

Before I'd righted my balance, Cassidy had my door unlocked and swung wide open.

"Fuck." A life that I'd tried so damn hard to keep private had just extended an open invitation to the last person on earth I'd ever want to let in on the secret.

Cassidy

To say I was confused would've been an understatement. When I'd thought of Shaw's decorating tastes in the past, I'd imagined something modern and chic, maybe even a bit futuristic. But the reality proved I'd been way off the mark. His taste was nonexistent. And I didn't mean nonexistent as in he didn't have any taste; I meant nonexistent in the literal sense.

"Where's all your stuff?"

Shaw's apartment didn't look much different from the penthouse suite we'd left a mere couple of hours before. There was no plush carpet or crimson paint, just plain hardwood floors and whitewashed walls. To Shaw's credit, there was a recliner and a table in what I assumed was the living room, but no other furniture that I could see. Not even a television.

"What you see is what you get." Shaw nudged past me and inside, gesturing for me to do the same with a swing of his arm.

"I don't understand," I said, stepping over the threshold so he could close the door behind me.

"What's the matter?" Shaw walked into the middle of the room with his arms spread wide. "Not posh enough for you?"

Tearing my eyes away from the nothingness, I saw a side of Shaw I wouldn't have ever dreamed could exist. He looked ashamed, and it punched at my gut, but his underlying air of cockiness refused to go away.

"You know, I'm really disappointed in you, Ms. Whalen. For someone who's such an ace in research, you really dropped the ball on this one."

"What are you talking about?"

"Do you seriously not know why there's no furniture in my

apartment?" He paused, tilting his head with his brows lifted expectantly. "Think about it. I'm sure it'll come to you."

Crossing his arms and leaning against the bar that separated the kitchen from the main living space, he waited. And I was more confused than ever.

"I'm in no mood to play guessing games with you."

"All right, then I'll give you a hint." He uncrossed his arms and stood straight. "I can't afford any furniture right now."

I guffawed. "Right. Funny."

"It's no laughing matter, I assure you. And I'm not real happy about it, either."

He was serious, which made no sense. Maybe I would've believed him if he'd said he'd sent all of his money home, but I'd seen how his mother lived, so that obviously wouldn't have been true.

"You make more than enough money to furnish an apartment. Plus, there's the corporate allowance."

"I make enough money to *pay* for the apartment," he said. "The rest of it goes to supplement the corporate allowance, which I use to fund things like private jets to Vegas. And Detroit. And the most expensive hotel suites. And limousines with drivers, meals at upscale restaurants, a tailor-made wardrobe, concert tickets, yacht parties, and strippers. Et cetera, et cetera."

I felt so dumb. I still didn't get what he was trying to tell me, and I'd always considered myself to be pretty smart.

"You've gotta spend money to make money," he clarified.

"You're not rich?"

"I'm guessing we have about the same yearly income. Are you rich?"

I shook my head. "But you're always flaunting all that money?"

"So you *assumed* I had lots of it." Shaw put his hands on his hips and started pacing. "See, that's the problem here, isn't it? From day one, you made all kinds of assumptions about me, based on rumors, without ever bothering to find out the truth for yourself. You thought you had me all figured out, so you didn't need to get to know me, right? I never stood a chance, because you fucking hated me before I showed up for my first day."

It was true, and I suddenly felt like a gigantic ass about it, but he wasn't exactly innocent, either. "Well, maybe if you weren't such a jerk who kept himself so closed off, people wouldn't have to make assumptions about you. And besides, it's not like you tried to give anyone a different opinion."

"Oh, so the attorney thinks I'm guilty until proven innocent. Is that it? A little backward, if you ask me. Where did you say you went to law school?"

"Don't give me that. People saw exactly what *you* wanted them to see," I said, stabbing an accusing finger in the air. "But the truth? The truth is that you're a liar."

"Excuse me?"

"You heard me. You're a liar. Your whole life is one big, fat lie. It's sad."

"No, the truth about my life is sad. The lie is much more preferable. To me, anyway. And it certainly hasn't hurt my career." He walked into the kitchen and opened the refrigerator, pulling out a beer. "Want one?"

"What I *want* is to know what you've been hiding." Though part of me wished I hadn't stumbled upon the lie, I still couldn't walk away from the truth.

"Why? Will it really make a difference in the way you think about me? Haven't you already made up your mind?" He cracked open the bottle and threw the top on the counter.

"Change my mind, Shaw. Who are you really? What was so bad about your life that you needed to live a lie?"

"Everything," he said with a humorless chuckle. "But if you want specifics, fine, I'll cut myself open so you can watch all the ugly bleed out onto the floor. My old man is a fucking con artist who couldn't hold down a job to save his life, but hey, at least some of that artistry got passed down to me. And my mom? My mom is an alcoholic who cared more about where she was going to get her next bottle than feeding her own kid. I was an inconvenience to both of them, a mistake that was never supposed to happen, and most of the time, they acted like it hadn't."

"I don't believe that."

"And I can tell you exactly why you don't" was his arrogant response.

I rolled my eyes, preparing to listen to his nonsense.

Shaw walked toward me, beer in hand. "I'm willing to bet you were an only child. Am I right?" He circled me as if I were on display for his scrutiny. "Mommy and Daddy gave their little princess everything she'd ever wanted in her whole life. They told you that you could be anything you wanted if you put your mind to it. Because that's what good parents are supposed to say. And you believed them, because they loved you, and took care of you, and kissed all your boo-boos. So you wanted to make them proud."

Shaw came full circle to face me again. I met his gaze, standing strong against the inquisition. "Are they?" he asked. "Are they proud of the way you sit up there on your pedestal, gazing down at the rest of the worker bees, playing the same old record over and over again? *I worked so hard to get to where I am,*" he mocked me.

His mask of condescension was replaced with one that was as hard and unforgiving. "Until you've walked a mile in my shoes, sister, you don't know what hard work is."

"This isn't about me. It's about you."

"Oh, you don't like to be put under a microscope and judged, but it's okay for you to do it to someone else? I see. Well, by all means, let's get back to the topic of me, since we both know what an egotistical asshole I am."

He put a sarcastic finger to his chin while looking up at the ceiling and resuming pacing before me, like a prosecutor looking to make a plaintiff nervous. But I wasn't the one on trial, so the intimidation tactic wasn't going to work.

"Where were we? Ah, I remember. Unlike you, I didn't have the privilege of a college education and a postgraduate degree. No one paid for me to study at some highbrow university. You talk about how you started from the bottom and worked your way up the ladder. Well, if you started at the bottom, I guess I should say I started twenty feet underground.

"Everything I know was self-taught. Nothing was handed to me. Here's the thing people don't understand about coming up in Detroit: a man can work a full-time job, backbreaking labor, and it still isn't enough. That's why there's so much crime there. To support a family, you're pretty much forced to turn to dealing drugs, killing thugs, and posing for mugs." Stopping again, he plastered on a fake smile that, under different circumstances, would've been breathtaking. Oh, he was well practiced.

"But I wanted to be better than that," he continued. "I wanted the white-collar dream so bad I could taste it, and I wasn't afraid to get a few calluses on my hands in the process. You see, I knew that if I wanted any kind of a life, something better than what my folks had, I was going to have to make it for myself. So yeah, I cut some corners, but I only did what I had to do to break the cycle."

"And what about your family? You just left them there to fend for themselves?"

"Ah, my family. It always comes back around to that for you, doesn't it?"

I couldn't quite understand why it didn't for him. Your blood was where your roots began, and roots were what made a person strong. "Where I come from, your family is the most valuable asset in life. I won't apologize for that."

"Let me tell you something about *my* family," he started. "Most every single night of my young life, I slept at the stadiums. Just hid from security, because I knew the guards' schedules like the back of my hand. And I did that because at least I was safe there. And my parents . . . never bothered to look for me. Hell, I don't think they cared—or even knew, for that matter—that I was gone."

The sadness I felt for the little boy in Shaw reached deep into my chest and gave my heart a squeeze. Ma and Da always knew every move I made, and if they didn't, someone else in our little village did, and you better believe they'd find out soon enough. When you came from a place where everyone cared, could you ever really know what it was like for someone who had no one?

"They didn't give a shit about me, so why should I give a shit about them?"

I softened. "I'm sorry you had to go through that. It's not the way it's supposed to be."

I suddenly realized how wrong I'd been about Shaw. He hadn't had everything handed to him on a silver platter. He hadn't had anything handed to him at all. In fact, he'd had to work a thousand times as hard as I had to get to the same place.

"Hey, no worries. I came out okay. Look at me now. I eat at fancy restaurants, sleep with any woman I want—including you— rub elbows with the rich and famous, carry a certain amount of influence, and people know my goddamn name."

"In an empty apartment," I tacked on.

"It won't be empty once I sign Denver," he said, taking a swig of his beer. "That partnership is the game changer for me. I'll finally be able to settle down in one place and feel like I've accomplished something. It's the beginning of a new life, everything *I've* worked so hard for."

"You think that's going to make you happy?"

Shaw shrugged. "How could it not?"

"Because it'll be tainted by all the lies you told to get it. Nothing good can come from a lie."

"I didn't tell any lies." The wink he gave was full of confidence, like he'd won on a technicality, but I still had him.

"Pretending to be someone you're not is still a lie."

Shaw started laughing. It was the sort of laugh that came at the expense of another rather than from a genuine tickle of the funny bone.

"What's so funny?" I asked, unnerved.

"You." The sigh that followed was every bit as fake as his laughter. "You're actually standing there with a straight face, judging me—again, I might add—when you're doing the exact same thing."

He'd clearly lost his mind, and I was definitely insulted. "I am *not* pretending to be anyone other than who I am."

"No?" Shaw's penetrating gaze went straight through me, like he could see into my soul. "Are you sure about that, Cassidy?"

I wasn't, but until I knew what he was getting at, I wasn't going to make any profound confessions. "You're projecting."

"Ooh, fancy word, counselor."

"Oh, just make the point I know you're dying to make, Matthews."

"Okay." He straightened and put his beer on the counter. "For someone who's so by the book, you sure are blurring the lines, aren't you?"

"What do you mean?"

"Denver, for one," he said, holding up a finger like he was keeping score. But of course he would; everything was a competition to Shaw. "What is it that you're doing with him, exactly? Are you fucking him or trying to be his agent? Because if you don't genuinely want to be with the guy, then you're leading him on in order to get the contract. And that's pretty fucking unethical."

God, he was right. I'd been chastising myself over the very same thing from the moment I'd known Denver had a thing for me and I'd capitalized on it. My shame had been weighing heavy on my shoulders ever since. But I had every intention of righting my wrong the next time he and I saw each other. "Denver and I never—"

Shaw cut off my explanation: "Wait. I'm not done." Another finger went up. "You have a tattoo of some guy named Casey on your ass that you don't care to talk about. I mean, I could be wrong, but most women wouldn't tattoo a man's name on their ass unless he meant something to them."

Guilt sat in my stomach like an iron anchor that had crashed to the sea floor. Casey was one subject that was off-limits. "I'm not going to talk about Casey with—"

"Still not done," he said. "And then there's me. The man you claim to hate, yet fuck on a regular basis." His intention was to cut me with the statement, but the words dripped with seduction. To prove the point, he crossed the space that separated us, backing me against the wall with a slow, methodical advance, until the heat of his body teased my skin. I didn't dare look up at him; I knew if I did, I'd want to kiss his lips. "No way can a woman hate a man that much and still fuck him the way you fuck me."

I could hear both of us breathing as the heaviness of his statement settled in. "Denver . . . Casey . . . me . . . You're living three different lives. So which is the real *you*, Cassidy?"

The mirror Shaw had forced me to take a long, hard look into was more than I'd bargained for when I'd decided to follow him home. This was supposed to be about making him come clean, not exposing the skeletons in my own closet. But damn, what a cluttered closet it had become, and I hadn't even realized it. Maybe I had some cleaning of my own to do. And the truth of the matter was, I didn't even know the answer to his question.

I looked up at him then, taking a page out of his own book when I said, "Now who's making assumptions?"

The cocky laugh was back again. "At least I can own my truth. Your lies run so deep, you don't even realize they're there."

With my chin set confidently, I met his challenge. "I know my worth, and that's what matters."

"Yeah? So what's the going price? A partnership?" Shaw leaned in so close I could taste the intoxicating aroma of his cologne with each breath I took. His lips grazed the shell of my ear, causing my flesh to pebble. "Just how far are you willing to go to win, Cassidy? Is Wade next on your list?"

I snapped at the insinuation, shoving him hard with two palms to the chest and giving myself just enough room for the windup and release of a right jab to Shaw's eye. The searing pain that shot through my wrist was crippling, but I didn't show it; I was too pissed. My da would've been proud of his little girl, and Casey would've followed up with a left and a right and another left to finish him off for the insult. That was the way we did things back home. It was hard as hell to take the girl out of Stonington, but you for damn sure wouldn't ever be able to take Stonington out of the girl.

"Don't you *ever* again insinuate that I'm sleeping my way to the top!"

Shaw held his eye, momentarily stunned, but it wouldn't keep his fat trap shut. "People in glass houses shouldn't throw stones."

"Yeah, well, I didn't throw a stone. That was a right jab, asshole. Own *that*."

I'd had enough. Enough of being criticized for having a normal, supportive family, enough of being lied to, and enough of being called a slut. And I didn't care if I ever saw Shaw Matthews again.

A dramatic exit hadn't been my intention, but I was acutely aware that I was a walking cliché in that moment. I wasn't the only cliché, though. Shaw grabbed my arm to stop me, one eye clamped shut and the other doing its best to focus.

"Unless you want two matching black eyes, I suggest you let me go," I warned.

"Tell me the truth now, and I'll let you leave."

God, he just didn't know when to stop.

"What?" I asked with a huff.

"Why did you come here? Am I supposed to think you actually care?"

I rolled my eyes with an incredulous shake of my head. He wouldn't believe the truth. After all the hurtful things he'd said to me, I wasn't even sure I believed it myself. I certainly wasn't ready to make any grand admissions out loud.

"No, Shaw. I genuinely feel sorry for you." With that, I pulled my arm free. "I hope you finally get everything you've ever wanted. But you should know that it's going to be a lonely and miserable existence without anyone to love or to love you."

For the first time since I'd met him, Shaw Matthews didn't have a witty retort. He just stood there, saying nothing. Dumbfounded. I honestly didn't know if what I'd said had made a bit of difference. The topic of love was sincerely a foreign concept to him. How could he know the difference between something fake and something real when he'd never even known the love of a parent? A person like that was dangerous, capable of breaking many hearts. And not just those of his lovers. Anyone who ever gave a damn about him would fall prey. Well, I wasn't going to be one of his casualties, and I wasn't going to stick around to watch him crash and burn, either. So I left him staring after me as I turned my back and walked out of an apartment that was every bit as empty as its occupant's heart.

CHAPTER 18

Cassidy

I was still feeling raw from my conversation with Shaw the night before as the town car carried me to La Jolla for my makeup meeting with Denver at his place. Not having slept much, I was exhausted, and the sting of rejection from the conversation I knew was to come had already been playing havoc with my psyche. An emotional overload was imminent. Feeling like screaming one second and crying the next was the telltale sign. Or maybe I was about to start my period. Same difference.

Denver was going to dump me. As his agent, not his girlfriend. Even though I wasn't actually his agent . . . or his girlfriend. And I was going to have to dump him, as my not really boyfriend. Crap. Why did life have to be so confusing?

Guilt seemed to be a running theme in my life lately. Not only did I feel guilty about having to let Denver down and making a rash judgment about Shaw, but all the tossing and turning and thinking during the night had led me down another road. I'd started to see the similarities between Shaw and me. I'd called him out for not being there for his parents, but how had I been any different? I couldn't even remember the last time I'd been home to see my own.

And then there was Casey. I didn't know how I was supposed to feel about him. Worse, I'd never stopped to consider how he must feel about our situation. I'd been so selfish. If I were honest with myself, I'd have to admit I hadn't been any better than Shaw. So who was I to pass judgment on him and act so self-righteous? What he did in his life was none of my stupid business anyway.

That old Stonington mentality was ever present, ingrained in the very fiber of my being, and it would not be denied. Where I came from, everyone knew everyone's business and they all had an opinion about it that got crammed down your throat, whether you liked it or not. That was what I had done to Shaw.

Resting my head against the cool glass of the window, I tried to let the scenic beauty of La Jolla's hillsides distract me from my thoughts. Truthfully, I was glad Denver had sent a car to bring me to the privacy of his home so he could drop the atomic bomb all over my aspirations to represent him. It would have been embarrassing for me to be seen crying at the office.

Was that where I was in my life? Had I worked so hard to become a no-nonsense, nothing-personal-about-it, get-the-job-done businesswoman, only to be reduced to a sappy puddle of emo girl?

As we crested the hill, the car came to a gradual stop in front of a three-story Tuscan oceanfront estate that was absolutely breathtaking. Denver was standing in front of a mahogany wood door that dwarfed his frame, and the smile on his face rivaled the panoramic view surrounding him.

"Here we are, miss," the driver said. "If you'll wait right there, I'll get your door."

Screw that. I knew how to work a handle. As soon as Denver realized I was opening the door myself, he bolted forward. I had no idea why. It wasn't as if he'd reach me before I could get out, no matter how impressive his forty-yard-dash time was.

"Um, hey. So, uh . . . thanks for coming over," he said with a nervous edge.

I smiled to put him at ease, even though I knew he was about to demolish my hopes, because that was the sort of woman I was. Generous to a fault, mama bear by nature. Though for some reason, I simply couldn't bring myself to be any of those things for Shaw. "Of course, Denver. Don't be silly."

He beamed, but his delight never quite reached his eyes. "Come on. I'll give you a tour."

And what a tour it was. The lifestyles of the rich and famous always involved a waste of money I couldn't understand. Denver was a single man with no children, yet his home boasted six bedrooms with six bathrooms and two half baths, for a total of over eight thousand square feet. It was ridiculously big, with a state-of-the-art architectural design that had been carried out using the world's finest materials. He was living in the middle of a work of art. Who could relax and unwind from their day when they had to be concerned about breaking something?

Shaw wanted that. The status associated with the price tag was exactly his sort of thing. I shut down that line of thinking quickly; nothing good could come of it. My teeth had already begun to get their grind on, jaws locked tight to keep the insults from flying.

Denver was clearly proud of his home. Who was I to take that from him? Besides, it really was beautiful. Maybe I was just jealous.

The little she-devil on my shoulder kept whispering in my ear: *But all of this could be yours for the low, low price of . . . your soul.*

Not today, little she-devil. This was one wrong I knew I could make right, to free up my conscience for the other mishaps desperately in need of my attention.

When we reached the master suite, on the top floor, I began

to get nervous. Despite the early afternoon hour, Denver had this whole romantic setup out on a rather large deck, complete with a fire pit, twinkling white lights, and a bottle of champagne on ice. Crap. I needed to put the brakes on this, and fast.

"Denver, look. I think maybe we need to have a talk," I started.

"Well, yeah. That's why I brought you here in the first place, silly." He laughed nervously, then gestured toward the wrought-iron chairs with overstuffed cushions. "I think it'll be best if you have a seat."

I did as he asked, not bothering to get comfortable in case things got to be a little too cozy and I'd need to bolt to my feet. To my surprise, Denver remained standing.

"Aren't you going to join me?"

He ran his fingers through his sun-kissed hair. "I can't. I'm too nervous to sit."

Great. This was going to be worse than I'd thought.

"Listen, before we do this," he said, gesturing between the two of us, "there's something I need to let you know."

When he loosened the first two buttons of his shirt, I panicked and jumped up. "Oh God . . . Denver, I'm sorry, but I can't."

He looked wounded and confused. "Why? You don't want me anymore?"

"What? No!" I paused and took a deep breath, rethinking my approach; I certainly didn't want to hurt his feelings. "I mean, try not to take it personally, but I just don't think it's the best move for my career. You understand?"

"No, I don't understand. So all the time we've been spending together lately was about what?"

I took my seat again, burying my head in my hands. "Crap! I know, I'm sorry. It was so wrong of me. I let things get entirely too personal because I really like you. I guess I thought we were having a good time, building a connection that would help solidify our working relationship."

Denver sat next to me. "But it did. That's what I'm trying to tell you. All that time we spent together made me realize how much I really want you, but I don't want you to agree to take the next step until you know the whole truth about me."

I looked up at him then, exasperated. He obviously had something very important to say. "What truth?" I asked, even though it wouldn't matter. Before I left there, his feelings were going to be hurt.

Denver took a deep breath. "The truth is, I hired that cameraman to film me with those strippers."

"What?" I shrieked. Could he actually envision a scenario in which telling me something like that was going to make me want to sleep with him? "That's revolting!"

"It's not what you think," he said, getting to his feet.

I rolled my eyes. "Oh, good. Because I think you're a twisted pervert who wants to chronicle himself behaving disgustingly with young, innocent women."

"Cassidy, it's not like that at all. And, believe me, they weren't innocent. I paid them, too." The way he said it was like it was no big deal.

I was appalled and nauseous. "Oh, my God! That girl was underage!"

"But I didn't know. She lied. I swear!"

By that point I wasn't really hearing anything he was saying—I was too busy being flabbergasted. How was it possible that the man who was so kind to my best *gay* friend could be the same man who acted like such a pig with women? I just didn't get it.

"And Shaw went to jail for you!" I gasped, the realization suddenly hitting me. "Was he *in* on it?"

"No! No, no, no!" Denver said, his eyes wide. "He had no idea. I swear."

I shot to my feet. "Well, that makes it even worse! You left him in jail! *Left* him there! What kind of person does that?"

Denver paced, his face tinged red with frustration or embarrassment, maybe both—then again, I didn't care. He was an asshole, and whether he deserved it or not, he'd caught me on a very bad day.

"I was so drunk, not in my right mind," he said. "Then that fight broke out, and I knew it wouldn't be good for my career."

What a selfish bastard he was for thinking only about himself, and that was exactly what I told him. Or, rather, yelled at him. "What about Shaw's career? Have you any idea how damaging that could have been for him?"

"I know. I'm a piece of shit for it." Denver hung his head, but I didn't care how bad he might have felt.

"What were you planning on doing here today? Did you want me to see your little tapes? Is that it? Or did you think we were going to make one? Because that definitely is *not* going to happen, mister."

Denver stopped pacing, his head snapping up. "Huh?"

I was on a roll. "I can't believe you actually believe I'd want to be with someone who could do something like that. I mean, I have nothing against someone wanting to get their freak on, and I'm not exactly vanilla myself, but I just can't be okay with all of this."

In the middle of my rant, Denver shouted something I couldn't quite make out. Though maybe it had been loud and clear, because I fell silent as it resonated. I couldn't have heard what I thought I'd just heard.

"What?" I asked.

He looked directly at me. "I said I don't want to be with

you . . . because I'm gay. There. It's out." His expression was a mix of relief and terror.

"Oh. You're . . . gay," I repeated, still shell-shocked.

Denver took a seat just in the nick of time, his resemblance to a newborn foal making it obvious his legs were about to give out. His hands were shaking as he ran them over his suddenly pale face, covering his mouth like he wished he could take the words back. "I've never told anyone that before. Hell, I've never even said it out loud to myself before."

He turned to peer over his shoulder as if he expected someone to be there, listening in on his confession. It was paranoia, of course. We were on the side of a cliff, with nothing but jagged rocks and churning water below.

"I won't tell anyone," I promised him; it looked like he needed that reassurance.

"Good. Because you know as well as I do that it would hurt my career."

As much as I would've liked to be able to argue the point, I couldn't. Mankind had made some serious leaps and bounds toward tolerance, but it was nowhere near where it should be. Equality for all sounded noble in theory, but society was still having trouble making it legal on paper. Homosexuals in the military and on the playing fields were at an even greater disadvantage.

That was when everything started to click into place. "Wait—but you've been hitting on me and even kissed me."

Denver nodded, his lips pressed together. "Yeah, that's true. I guess I hoped we'd be seen, you know? I needed to be seen with a woman."

Thinking back on the events leading up to his big confession, I saw the puzzle pieces start to come together. "So you hired the cameraman to film you with the strippers because . . ."

Denver finished my thought: "I hired the cameraman and the

strippers and tipped off the paparazzi so that my *antics*," he said, forming air quotes, "would be leaked to the press. That way, no one would ever question my sexual preference. They'd just see me as a playboy."

"And things got out of hand?"

"You could say that. I'd had my anxiety medication, and then, knowing I was going to have to touch women," he said with a slight shiver, "I needed to be drunk to do it. I swear, I had no idea what would happen."

"Shaw was collateral damage," I said, understanding.

"God, yes," he sighed, letting his head fall back to rest against the chair. "I never meant for anyone to get hurt."

"I believe you," I said, giving his hand a squeeze. And then I laughed, feeling quite a bit of tension release into the air with the sound. "I have to tell you, I thought I was going to have to break your heart today. I feel so silly about it now."

He smiled. "Yeah, you were going off. *What were you planning on doing here today? Did you want me to see your little tapes? Or did you think we were going to make one?*" he mocked me. "Damn, woman. I thought you were going to castrate me there for a second."

"Well, what was I supposed to think?" I said defensively. "You've been coming on to me since the day we met, and then you bring me here with this romantic setup."

Denver laughed then. "The champagne, the lights . . . they were about celebrating, not making out, goofy."

My cellphone chose that moment to start vibrating from the breast pocket of my blazer, giving me a start.

"Celebrating what?" I reached inside my pocket and pressed the button on the side of the phone to send the call to voice mail. Whoever it was, they could wait.

"I want you to be my agent, Cassidy. I just wanted to do the whole full-disclosure thing first to be sure you'd want to take me on as a client. I mean, because if it ever gets out, I'll be a hard sell."

My heart nearly punched out of my chest with excitement over the victory that was propelling it. "You want me to be your agent? Even after I yelled at you?"

My stupid phone started buzzing again, really trying my patience. With another shove of my hand into my pocket, I silenced it.

He laughed again—amused by my childlike behavior, I was sure. "Yeah, even after you yelled at me. I need someone in my corner who's not afraid to put me in my place. You sort of remind me of my mother, and no one takes care of you like a mother."

"Thanks, Rocket, but I'm not really that old."

"Aww, don't be so sensitive. You know what I mean," he said with a playful shove. "Besides, you've had my folks sold with all that Colorado talk. They really want me home, and I know you can do that for me. So what do you say?"

"But Detroit offered you so much money." Even though I knew it was a point for Shaw, I wanted Denver to be sure he was making the right decision.

Apparently, he'd already given it a lot of thought. "I know, but money can't replace family. And if I have any hope at all of making it through this with everything I have going on, I'm going to need them more than ever."

Again, my cell went off. Whoever was on the other end of the line was going to get an earful from me.

"I'm so sorry, Denver, but can you excuse me for just one second?" I said as I begrudgingly yanked my phone out.

"Oh, yeah, sure. Go ahead."

"Thanks. It'll just be a second. I promise," I reassured him with a polite smile that disappeared the second I turned my face away. I answered the phone without even bothering to look at the caller ID. "What?" I said through gritted teeth, annoyed by the relentless interruptions.

"Cass, it's Abby," came the gentle voice of Casey's mom on the other end of the line.

Though she was Ma's very best friend, the fact she was calling could mean only one thing. Something very bad had happened to someone I loved dearly. The question was, who? Casey? Ma? Da?

I stood, afraid that if I didn't then, I'd never be able to again. Swallowing the dread lodged in my throat, I finally managed to push my voice out: "What's wrong? Is everyone okay?"

She was quiet. Too quiet. And my entire world was in free fall.

"Your ma took a tumble from the roof. She's hurt pretty bad."

"What? Is she going to be okay?"

There was a pause that I didn't like in the least, and then: "You should probably come home, sweetheart."

I went numb except for that tingling feeling you might expect to have when in a hypnotic state. Dazed and confused, on auto-pilot. "Right. Okay. I'm on my way." That was all that needed to be said for the time being, so I hung up.

If someone from home called to tell you that you needed to get back there, you went. They wouldn't call me unless something catastrophic had happened. So I didn't ask any more questions. I'd get more details on the way, but for now, any remaining functioning part of my brain needed to be focused on rearranging my life so I could get there as fast as humanly possible.

"I've gotta go," I said, picking up my bag before heading toward the exit. "Is the car still waiting?"

Denver stood and took my arm, bending at the knee to look me in the eye. "Wait a minute, Cassidy—did you hear me?"

I was sure I had, but I couldn't remember a damn word of it.

"I said I want to sign you as my agent." Oh, yeah. He was

smiling, excited, eager . . . all the things I should've been, while my mind was three thousand miles away.

My next words were painful but, since I was faced with no other option, necessary: "I'm sorry, Denver. I can't accept the position."

He looked like he'd been expecting the words. "Because I'm gay and it would be too hard. I understand." Denver bowed his head in shame, and I couldn't have that, because not a word of it was true.

"God, no, Denver. I don't give a shit what people think about your sexuality. It has nothing at all to do with that. I have a personal matter to attend to, and I don't know how long it's going to take. Please, you have to believe me."

He nodded, clearly trying to. The responsible thing would've been to stay right where I was until he knew I meant what I'd said, but time simply wasn't on my side. I was needed elsewhere, and I had no idea what horror was awaiting me.

"You should give the job to Shaw. You owe him at least that much, and he's going to make you a lot of money."

I believed every word of what I'd said; if Denver made money, it meant Shaw would make money. And that was his one and only true love. Not that I gave a shit. Some things were more important, and I'd be on my way to those very things within twenty-four hours. Less, if I had anything to say about it.

CHAPTER 19
Shaw

Touchdown!

I'd won. The most coveted quarterback in the nation, Denver "Rocket Man" Rockford, was mine. Though the actual signing hadn't happened yet, his call telling me to hurry over to discuss his future was all I'd needed to hear.

Suck on that, Cassidy Whalen!

I winced, the perma-grin crinkling the corner of my left eye sending a painful reminder that the battle had been hard fought. Damn woman had given me a shiner almost two days ago, and I still hadn't come up with a story that didn't make me look like a pussy. I supposed I'd deserved the mean right jab she'd dished out. Her personal shit was none of my business, though if she hadn't backed me into a corner and peeled the flesh from my bones like a premed student working over a cadaver maybe I wouldn't have felt the need to launch a counterattack in order to make my escape. No one had ever made me feel so raw. And I didn't like it. Not one bit.

When the car pulled up to Denver's house, I shook that shit off. Every carefully calculated move I'd made and every emotional barrier I'd thrown up had helped me become the business-savvy man I was today. And that man was looking at a very lucrative future, a future that was close enough to reach out and touch.

My new client was living large, indeed. It wasn't really that I hadn't already known that, but seeing was believing. And I was taking it all in. Stepping out of the car, I inhaled deeply, smelling the success saturating the air surrounding the expensive homes that enhanced the golden coast's landscape. Someone else just like me, someone who set goals and never quit until they saw them morph into realities, occupied each one of these homes. These were my people, and I felt like a king.

Turning toward the door, I pushed my shoulders back and started up the walkway as if I owned it. This was the sort of place I wanted. It was what I deserved. And I couldn't help the sense of accomplishment I had in that moment, knowing that with each advancing step, I was closer to getting it. If I kept on the road I was headed down, signed the superstar athletes, made all the right plays, scored the game-winning points, the name my good-for-nothing parents had given me at birth would finally mean something. Maybe then, I'd finally be good enough for . . .

I stopped the thought dead in its tracks. My own steps followed suit, and I turned around in a circle as if something in my surroundings would present an answer as to what in the hell could've possibly made my brain go there in the first place. Holy shit, but that line of thinking was ten kinds of fucked up.

Before I could examine the whys of it any further, Denver opened the front door to the house, his head drawing back as he examined my face. "Damn, man. What happened to you?"

I was sure he meant the swollen eye. "Sometimes it's not easy being Shaw Matthews," I said with a nonchalant laugh. "Don't worry, it looks worse than it feels," I lied.

"Still, better you than me." Denver's big meaty paw landed hard on my back. "Come on in, amigo, and thanks for getting here so soon."

"Hey, you're the man, and what the man wants, the man gets," I said with a dazzling smile.

"Gotta admit, I like the sound of that," he said, leading me into the main living area. He offered me a seat on the leather sofa. "Can I get you a beer or something?"

"I'm good, but thank you." I sat my briefcase down and adjusted my tie, anxious to get down to it. "So what's this all about?"

The beefy football star sat on the arm of the chair to my right, steepling his fingers as he looked for the words to start. "Right to the point, huh?" he laughed. "That's cool. Short and sweet works for me." The carefree expression he'd worn was replaced with one less preferable, one that made me nervous. "I know you put in a lot of work on the Detroit deal, and I really appreciate it."

I heard the hanging "but" echo before he even said it.

"*But* I've decided I'm going to sign with Colorado."

There it was. I'd been overly confident, thinking the summons here was about his decision to sign with me. That was wrong. Colorado was the angle Cassidy had been working. Shit. The biggest player in the game had chosen a girl to represent him.

I nodded, feeling hard-pressed to throw in the towel. "Colorado is a great franchise, with some of the most loyal fans around, but Detroit will pay a whole hell of a lot more money," I said, hoping it wasn't too late to change his mind. "I can do that for you, Denver."

"Oh, I know you can," he said reassuringly. And then he shifted uncomfortably. "You see, the thing is, there's a reason I want to go to Colorado. Money wasn't the deciding factor."

I had a feeling a certain redhead with a banging body had been key in his decision. Damn it. How was I supposed to compete with tits and ass? Though it might have been a little underhanded, we were at war, and I wasn't ready to wave the white flag without using every weapon in my arsenal. So it was time I pointed out the horrors associated with working so closely with a significant other. Most of all, the questionable intent. It was business, not personal. Okay, so maybe it was a little personal.

"Before you go any further, let me just point out the ethical repercussions of this situation." I stopped my rant when he tilted his head to regard me with disbelief.

"You already know?"

He'd brought Cassidy along as a date to my big show, and he didn't think I'd noticed? "Well, yeah. It was sort of obvious."

Denver looked down at the floor. "Wow. And you still went to jail for me?" He perked up then, scooting to the edge of his seat so fast it made me back up. "Hey, man, I'm so sorry about that, by the way. It was a shit move on my part. I never should've let it get out of control. And, dude, Cassidy went *off* on me about it."

Fuck me. Cassidy had come clean to Denver about our affair, and now he was feeling bad because he thought he'd stolen my girl after all I'd done for him. And worse, she'd gotten in his face about it?

"But you understand I had to set all that up to maintain my image, right?"

Things had officially taken a turn toward Weirdville. I wasn't sure we were even having the same conversation anymore. "As a playboy?" It was the only thing that made sense.

"Well, yeah." He gave a humorless laugh. "Can you imagine what it would do to my career if it got out that I'm gay?"

What? I needed a moment to recapture the tiny three-letter word I was sure I'd just caught. "Hold on."

Denver must not have heard me, because he went full steam ahead with his explanation: "I mean, I know there are supposed to be equal rights and all, but you and I both know they'd find some other way to push me out. And then the shit I'd have to go through with the other players and maybe even the fans . . ." He ran his hands over his short hair. "Man, I'm not planning any press conferences for the big reveal anytime soon. Truthfully, I'm still trying to come to grips with all this myself, but at least it seems to get a little easier to say each time I do."

The pause he took to contemplate his last statement was an opportunity I had to grab if I was ever going to get a word in edgewise. "Let me make sure I have all of this straight." I squirmed in my seat, searching for the right words. Though there really were only two to sum it up. "You're gay?"

Denver looked at me then, the realization that I hadn't known that all along settling in his features. "Yeah. Is that gonna be a problem? I mean, because if you think it would make your job as my agent too hard, I understand. But I'm going to have to ask you not to tell anyone else, because I need to handle that in my own way and on my own time."

I could absolutely respect that, but Denver being gay didn't matter to me. And though his concern about the impact it would have on his career was important, I wasn't scared. We could finesse that. It was the other little nugget of information hidden among all those words that was the tidbit my brain had focused on. "Are you saying you want me to be your agent, Denver?"

"Yes, I'd like to offer you the position of my agent." Each word was carved out as if by an X-Acto knife. Denver was leaving no room for further confusion. "What do you say? Interested?"

Even though it was ass-backwards, I felt like Renée Zellweger to Denver's Jerry Maguire. "Interested? Denver, man, you had me at hello."

I don't think he got the reference, at least if his "So is that a yes?" was any indication.

"No. That's a hell yes!" I laughed at his silly question. Not so much because it was funny but because I was giddy with joy at the words finally, *finally* being said.

"Whew! Good, man," Denver said, falling off the arm of the chair and into its seat. "You have no idea how stressful this has been on me. Maybe I can relax a little now."

Stressful on him? I chuckled to myself. Holy shit, the constant ups and downs I'd endured during this entire process had really done a number on my emotions. And I wasn't even an emotional guy. I needed a fucking drink. And a vacation. Someplace sunny and warm and full of half-naked, exotic beauties at my beck and call. But not yet. No way was either one of us able to relax. We had things to do, deals to sign, and money to make. I was in high gear, primed and ready to do the best work of my life.

Putting my briefcase on the coffee table, I opened it and started pulling out the contract I'd already prepared. Maybe it had been presumptuous of me, but damned if it hadn't been right on time. I couldn't wait to rub Miss Goody Two-shoes' face in this. My rabbit had snuffed her turtle and left it choking on my dust.

"Rocket, you won't regret this. I'm telling you, you made the right decision, man. Cassidy's good at her job and all, but the bottom line is, I'm the man for you. I'm going to make you so much more money than—"

Denver cut me off with a hearty laugh. "You're good, man, but I feel like I need to keep it real with you, just like you would with me."

"I absolutely would." My smile stayed in place even though my stomach was churning.

"You came in second place, bro."

"What?" My face was frozen, cheeks lifted high and skin pulled tight with the mask I was trying desperately to keep in place. Surely I'd misheard him. "But I thought you said you were going with me?"

"I am. But you weren't my first choice. I offered it to Cassidy yesterday, but she shot me down and broke my fucking heart. She was the only person, other than my mama, who ever put me in my place. I've got mad respect for that. So I would've signed with her . . . if she hadn't sidelined herself."

"She sidelined herself?" The words were forced through my clenched teeth and ticking jaw.

"Yeah. She pulled out, man. Said she was no longer interested. I thought it was because I'm gay and she couldn't get on board with that, but when I asked her, she said it wasn't. She wouldn't tell me the real reason. Just said it was personal and I should give you the job because I owed you at least that much. My mama told me to do whatever that little woman says to do. So"—he stuck out his hand—"congratulations, man. It's you and me against the world . . . just like you said."

Being the runner-up in a contest was almost worse than coming in last place: it meant you were good enough but someone else was just a little bit better. Ask any Miss America second placer and I'd bet they'd say it was an honor, but I wasn't a fucking chick and I didn't give a damn if Cassidy was prettier than me or had a better body. My biggest concern wasn't world peace or feeding all the starving children, because once upon a time, I had been one of those starving children, smack-dab in the middle of a war zone right here in the good ol' U.S. of A., and I'd survived. On my own. This was supposed to be my story about how I'd overcome the odds stacked against me to go on to be the most unlikely yet successful agent of all time.

Worse than coming in second was that the sense of accomplishment and hope for the future I'd been soaring high on seconds before had just been plucked out of the sky by a do-gooder looking to make herself feel better. Goddammit, I was a man. I wasn't Cassidy Whalen's charity case, and I didn't need her fucking handouts. But that was exactly what this was. She'd given me the contract because she pitied me.

No, Shaw. I genuinely feel sorry for you. Her words had carried the sting of a thousand killer bees when she'd said them before. But now? Now they crept across my skin like an army of flesh-eating fire ants looking to strip me clean down to the bone. Well, I wouldn't go gently. I was a scrappy motherfucker, with skin as thick as leather. The last thing a person wanted to do was attempt to get under it. Cassidy had. And I didn't like that one bit.

"You gonna leave me hanging?" Denver asked, his arm still outstretched and waiting. The unease of his body likely meant he thought I had a problem with his sexual orientation, and that simply wasn't cool.

"Nope," I said, taking his hand with a firm grip. "No worries. I've got you." And I meant it.

Whatever the issue with the she-devil who'd managed to derail my life from the track I'd been chugging down, it could wait. In the meantime, I wasn't going to take a chance on Denver changing his mind to go with someone else, even if it was like taking another dude's—or woman's—sloppy leftovers. So I got my shit together long enough to get the contract signed and wrapped things up here.

My next order of business was to make a stop at Striker to show Cassidy Whalen that Detroit side of me she'd never seen before. My Justin Timberlake was about to shed the suit and tie to get his Marshall Mathers on. As much as I'd tried to bury those instincts and pretend I'd been tamed, there was only so much poking and prodding a person could take before the beast got loose. She wanted to play God with my life? Well, I was going to show her the devil.

Stepping off the elevator at the office, I found the place looking more like a ghost town than the thriving hub of activity it normally was. A quick glance at my watch told me why. I'd been so distracted by my thirst for revenge that I hadn't even noticed the time. Everyone was gone for the day, but if I knew Cassidy Whalen, she was probably still here. Stalking her next victim, I was sure. So I made a hard right and headed in that direction, only to find her suite dark and just as empty as the rest of the place.

"Shit," I mumbled to myself as I turned to leave.

Wade Price was walking toward me with his briefcase in hand and a jacket hanging from his arm. I could be wrong, but I thought he even had a little extra pep in his step. "Well, you don't sound as happy as I'd thought you'd be."

"Um, sorry, sir. I needed to speak to Cassidy. Looks like I missed her, though."

"Let me guess: to gloat? Boy, you two are competitive to the very end," he said with a chuckle. "I hope you'll go easy on the poor girl. She's taking it pretty hard."

"I'm sorry? Taking what hard?"

"Don't be modest now, Matthews! You deserve the congratulations. It was a hard-fought contest, but to the victor go the spoils, eh?" he said with a hearty clap on my back.

"You already know I got the Rockford contract?"

"Whalen told me," he said. "And don't you be mad at her for spilling the good news before you could—she was pretty much forced to tell me in order to explain why the hell she was leaving."

"Leaving? As in she quit?" Oh, it would be just like her to do something that drastic, even if for no other reason than to rub salt in my eye.

"No, no, no. She didn't quit." He stared off in contemplation. "Or at least I hope that wasn't what all of that was about."

"All of what?"

He shrugged. "She asked for an indefinite leave of absence. Said there was something she had to take care of and she'd let me know more details later."

Son of a bitch. Just when I'd thought I couldn't be any madder at the woman, she'd gone and proved me wrong.

"Truth be told, I think she was feeling a little embarrassed by the loss and didn't want to show her face. Although she really doesn't have anything to be ashamed of. She's still my number one. Now that you have the partnership, anyway." He winked and threw his arm around my shoulders as we walked toward the elevator.

"When did this happen?"

"First thing this morning." The elevator door opened, and we stepped inside the car. "She spent some time coordinating things with her clients, and then she left."

Run, little girl, run. Run to your heart's content. Run until you can't run anymore. I'll still find you.

To my disappointment, Quinn was the one who answered the door, and he didn't look much happier than me with that scowl on his face.

"Where is she?" I asked, getting right to it.

Quinn slapped a slip of paper to my chest. "Was this your doing?"

I took it from him, reading the hurried yet elegant script.

Had to go home. Will be gone for a while. I'll call later to explain. Don't worry.

—Cass

I felt like roaring at yet another fucking wall being thrown up in what was turning out to be a goddamn maze designed with the express purpose of blocking me from having the final word.

"Why would you think I had anything to do with this?"

Quinn put one hand on his hip. "Oh, I don't know. Maybe because you just so happen to show up here, all in a huff, moments after I find the note?"

It wasn't my intention to be hateful with Quinn, I knew he'd been through it lately, but I really couldn't afford to waste time with an explanation I didn't want to give in the first place. "When is she going to be back?"

"You read the note. She doesn't say, but something tells me she's not planning on coming back at all. And the woman isn't answering her phone, either."

"Why don't you think she's coming back?"

Quinn leaned against the doorjamb. "You're just full of questions today, aren't you? My guess is you're the one holding all the answers."

I stared blankly at him, trying my best not to ask another question, though I supposed my expression must have done that for me.

Crossing his arms, he continued: "Look, I know I've been dealing with my own shit, but that doesn't mean I haven't noticed that my best girl has something going on. Y'all been fucking."

Whoa! "She told you that?"

The grin he wore was full of sass and pride. "No, but you just did."

I closed my eyes, trying desperately to rein it in. "Quinn, I'm sorry, but I need to talk to Cassidy. Where can I find her?"

"I'd say the airport, but you better hurry."

"Why?"

"Because I found her flight information written on the page

under this one on the notepad." He went over to the counter and ripped the sheet off the pad, handing it to me. "Here. Go get her, Romeo."

Christ, he had it all wrong, but if I told him that, he'd probably try to stop me from going after her. And Cassidy's flight was scheduled to take off in no more than an hour. Without saying goodbye, I pivoted on my heel and headed for the exit.

"You're welcome!" he shouted after me.

San Diego International Airport was just as much of a madhouse as the bumper-to-bumper traffic to get there. Then I had to go and make a scene when I tried to get to the gates without a ticket in hand, which meant I had to spend money on a ticket to Philadelphia that I had no intention of using. And to make matters worse, I was in so much of a hurry to catch Cassidy before her flight took off that I wasn't paying attention when I went through the metal detectors, prompting an intrusive pat-down that fell just short of my body cavities being searched. Normally, I liked to at least be on a first-name basis with someone getting that fresh with me. Two tits and a vagina would've also been preferable.

After that, I nearly collided with four different people who were also running to their gates, and I considered plowing through a group of elderly people with no place to be other than the middle of the major flow of traffic while they carried on their mundane conversation. Naturally, Cassidy's gate was at the far end of the terminal, directly opposite the front of the building, which meant no one else in the building had farther to go than me to get there. My calves were cramping and my pulse was at cardio-workout level by the time I reached my destination, but that didn't stop me from trying to break the handle off the closed door to the Jetway when I found I was too late.

"Whoa, whoa, whoa! What do you think you're doing?" A brunette put herself between the door and me to stop my assault. I almost hadn't seen her: she was less than five feet tall, and that was counting the bun on the top of her head. But when I looked down, she was mean-mugging me like she was a monkey's breath away from climbing me like a tree and giving my branches a shake.

"But they haven't left yet. They're right there!" I could appreciate the importance of international security as much as the next person, but if I'd already spent fucking forever being x-rayed and patted down to get to this point, what did they think I was going to do now?

Even if she was petite, my friend the gate agent meant all business. "Sir, if you don't back up, I'm going to have to call security." She put her hand on the phone, prepared to do just that.

"Ah, come on. You don't have to do that," I said, turning on the old Shaw Matthews charm.

Under thick, bright blue makeup, her eyes softened, though it didn't make a difference. "The flight has been boarded and the door shut. I'm sorry. You'll have to go to the ticket counter to see about catching another flight to Bangor."

"No, you don't understand. This isn't my flight. I just need to talk to someone on board before she leaves."

The gate agent's face took on a dreamy look I'd seen far too often when a woman got swoony on me. Clutching her chest, she sighed. "Aww, how romantic!"

"What? No, it's not like that." For a second, I thought about going with her assumption just to see if appealing to the woman's obvious need to believe in the chick-flick cliché would get me what I wanted.

"I'd love to help, but only ticket-carrying passengers are allowed on board."

Great. Finally, we were getting somewhere. "I'll go get a ticket then. Just don't let that plane take off."

"The flight is full. Besides, the door is already closed."

"Please?" I'd never begged for anything in my life.

She stuck out her bottom lip and gave me the puppy-dog eyes. "I'm so sorry. It's out of my control."

Surely there had to be another option. "When does the next flight leave?"

"You'll have to check with the ticket counter, sir," she said, then leaned in conspiratorially. "I'm not supposed to do this, but how about if I check on it for you?"

"Yes! Thank you so much!" I said, feeling a little relief now that she was willing to help.

"I see you have a ticket to Philadelphia in your hand."

Lifting the ticket I'd all but forgotten about, I shrugged. "Yeah, there was no other way to get to the gates."

"It's actually a good thing," she said, scanning the monitor before her. Then she looked up at me and smiled. "There's a flight to Bangor leaving Philadelphia at six forty-five in the morning. It's not completely full. You'll need to run to catch your first flight on time, and you'll have a long layover, but that's the best you're going to do."

"Where's my gate?"

"Gate forty. But you might want to go get that ticket to Maine first."

Looking up at the gate information, I groaned when I saw that we were on the opposite side of the airport.

"Thank you." The wink and smile I gave her was about my being grateful for the information she'd volunteered, even though I'd been acting like a dick. It wasn't like it was her fault, and I was sure she'd dealt with enough shit from every other person and didn't need mine.

I wasn't quite sure how far I was willing to go to say my piece to Cassidy, but as I watched her plane back out of its spot and taxi down the runway, I figured out the answer.

Moments later, I stepped up to the ticket counter and slapped my credit card down in front of the agent. "One ticket from Philadelphia to Bangor, Maine, please."

Apparently, I was willing to go another three thousand miles.

ACKNOWLEDGMENTS

Playing Dirty started slinging mud at me somewhere around the fourth chapter, and it didn't let up on its assault until the cavalry arrived. They pulled me out of the trenches, and together we launched a counterassault that ended with me owning its ass. Obviously, this page is dedicated to acknowledging those people who gave a little bit of their blood, sweat, and tears to help me make that happen. So let's get on with it, shall we?

I still can't believe how lucky I am to have scored my very remarkable agent, Alexandra Machinist, and my extraordinary editor, Shauna Summers. Though "agent" and "editor" seem like such blasé words to describe what you two do, because you truly make dreams come true. Thank you for taking a chance on me.

To my bestie, Patricia Dechant. You know what I want to say, even when I haven't done a very good job of saying it. So then you just rewrite it completely and make it all pretty and mushy. Much like you do to my life. You are my morning cup of joe, the emergency lifeline that yanks me back to shore when I drift too far, and the constant I depend on the most. If you ever try to quit me, I'll have to hunt you down and kill you, because you know entirely too much.

Huge thanks to Bobbie Butler (my ma), Maureen Morgan (my muse), Melanie Edwards (my dear diary), Janell Ramos (my sentry), Carrie St. Julien (admin extraordinaire), Whittney Sherman (my sister), Kimberly Rackley (my guru), Jowanna Kestner (my friend/beta/assistant), and Lance Grebe (my real-life Landon, a true hero). Each of you has a special role in my life. You are my anchors, my sounding boards, and my biggest cheerleaders. Love you. Mean it.

Big, puffy heart thanks to Casey Salsman. Your presence in my life has been vital to the completion of this book. Thank you for making me smile, for helping me find my words again, and for being my partner as we tag-team the world. You truly get me like I've never been gotten before. Please don't ever disappear.

Last but not least, I must thank my readers. You amaze me with your support, loyalty, and encouragement. Plus, you're super naughty and never judge me for being the same. The absolutely most important request that I could ever make is that you show your favorite authors some love. Leave those reviews and talk them up to all of your friends. We truly could not do what we do without you. I fucking love you and shit!

Shaw and Cassidy's rivalry heats up in the irresistible sequel to
USA Today bestselling author C. L. Parker's
Monkey Business Trio:

Getting Rough

Coming soon from Bantam Books.

Read on for a sneak peek . . .

CHAPTER 1

Shaw

"Simi, where the fuck am I?" I growled into my cellphone.

"I don't know, asshole" would've been an acceptable comeback, given my level of rudeness, but my ever-professional virtual assistant kept her cool. "You're traveling south on Upper Falls Road."

You're, a contraction from a voice recognition program. Wasn't technology nifty? Nifty, but not a whole lot of help. Left to figure it out on my own, I had to draw only slightly conceivable conclusions. The best I could tell, the flight I'd taken to Bangor, Maine, had somehow veered off course and into the Bermuda Triangle, which I was now convinced was a wormhole to an alternate universe where interstates hadn't yet been invented. That, or all of this had been an elaborate scheme my arch nemesis/part-time lover, Cassidy Whalen, had come up with in order to lure me away to a place where she could continue her torture routine and then eat my liver before dumping my body where no one could find it.

Truthfully, I'd be okay with the slightly creepy murder because being forced to endure that look of pity on her face every day for the foreseeable future was a fate worse than death.

I dropped my phone in the nook next to the gearshift, none

too gently, thanks to my mounting frustration. I was exhausted, running on fumes after a ten-and-a-half-hour flight and nearing a two-hour drive. The little monster inside my stomach was gnawing at me from the inside out, which I suspected was simply for the sole purpose of going in search of food on its own since I'd only placated it with airplane peanuts.

Simi dinged, either to warn me to take it easier on her delicate structure or to issue a reminder to bust a right onto yet another state route on my journey through God's country. Thirty-six more miles on winding roads to the island that laid claim to a small fishing village called Stonington. Cassidy's stomping ground. What in the world was I thinking when I'd decided to hop that flight? Oh, right . . . I'd wanted to give her a piece of my mind. But right now, I wanted a piece of chicken to put in my belly.

Making a left into the parking lot of a gas station, I parked the compact rental car I'd been forced into when no other option had been available and got out. The cartoon chicken on the sign in the window shouldn't have made me salivate, but it did. Maybe I was on the verge of delirium because gas station chicken couldn't have been a smart decision. I'd pay for it later.

The kid behind the counter was patient as I decided between chicken chicken, chicken tenders, or chicken nuggets. As he gathered my tenders and potato wedges, I thought I'd double-check that Simi knew what she was talking about, though I might have used a hushed voice to make sure she couldn't hear me doing so. The last thing I needed was for her to get an attitude about my not trusting her. Women could be so testy. Even virtual women.

"Hey . . . Dale," I started, reading his nametag. "Is it normal for there to be a lot of back roads around here instead of interstates?"

Chicken Dale half laughed. I guess he got that question a lot. "Yep. Where are you going?"

"Uh, Stonington," I said, taking my boxed meal.

He drew his head back like what I'd said was unusual. "Stonington?"

"Yeah. Why, am I going in the wrong direction? I knew it," I said, adding a curse under my breath.

"No, you're going in the right direction. It's just that no one goes to Stonington unless they're a local."

"Is that a bad thing?"

He laughed again. "Depends on who you ask."

"Great," I said with a sarcastic smile. "Thanks, man." I took my box, noticing the grease stains already soaking through. "I'm not going to die from eating this, am I?"

His shrug and expression that said it could go either way was answer enough. I'd either make it, or I wouldn't. Oh, well. We all had to go sometime.

After paying for my heart attack in a box and bottled water, I got back on the road. At least what was supposed to pass for a road, anyway. The winding, unpainted pavement was bad enough, but the bumps along the way reminded me of being a kid in a shopping cart passing over a grooved sidewalk, the vibration from each notch making my "ahhh" sound like a symphony of vocal acrobats. I might have even tried it out to prove a point since there was no one else around to see me making an ass of myself. Until my phone rang, that is.

"Hello?" I cleared my throat, trying not to sound so much like a bullfrog was lodged in it. "Ben?"

"Yo, boss man!" came his far too exuberant response. "How's Maine?"

"So far, so shitty. What'd you find for me?"

"Well, there are only two places to choose from and one is booked, if you can believe that, but I did score you a nice room at the Whalen House."

For some reason a massive migraine decided to strike like a lightning bolt from out of nowhere. "Wait. Did you just say Whalen?"

"Yep. And it's exactly what you think." I could hear the smile in his voice. "Lair of the Ice Queen, herself. Cassidy's parents own the joint. Per the four-and-a-half-star review, it's a quaint little bed-and-breakfast with a family atmosphere and all the amenities of home. You should fit right in."

I would've growled at him if I'd had the energy. "You're enjoying this, aren't you?"

"A little bit." At least *he* was honest with me. Unlike Cassidy.

"There's no other choice?"

"Nope."

"I'm firing you when I get back."

"Sure thing, boss. In the meantime, I'm pushing Denver's contract through to make everything real nice and legal."

Denver "Rocket Man" Rockford was where all of this had started. Cassidy Whalen and I had been in competition to represent the most coveted quarterback in the league and earn a slice of his pie, along with the partnership at Striker Sports Entertainment. I'd won. On a technicality. Denver had offered the contract to Cassidy first, but she'd turned it down and insisted he give it to me. All after she'd found out I wasn't the rich playboy I'd let everyone believe I was. If she hadn't been so goddamn nosy, so judgmental, so determined to pick me apart like a toad lying spread-eagle on a metal tray, I wouldn't be in a stupid tin can that only barely stayed on a fucked-up road on the way to a place no one else has ever even heard of.

I shoved my hand inside the greasy box, regretting it instantly when I found the scalding wedges, which must have been pulled from the vat of oil right as I'd walked into the gas station. "Son of a bitch!"

"Okay . . . I can hold it, if you want me to. But I've gotta ask.

Are you actually changing your mind about scoring the biggest deal of your life?" I'd almost forgotten Ben was on the phone. Maybe I hadn't been far off the mark with the delirium thing.

"Is that even a real question? Of course not. I just burned myself," I said, sucking on the wounded finger.

"Funny, I didn't feel a thing. Ba-dum-bum-ching!" He was a hair's breath away from being replaced by Simi.

"Grow up, Ben," I said, taking charge and acting like a real boss. "Book the room, get the contract on Wade's desk, and get me on a flight out of here first thing tomorrow morning."

"You got it. But, uh," he hedged.

"Spit it out." I was quickly losing what little patience I had left.

"Just a heads-up, there's a nasty bit of weather forecasted for Maine over the next few days. Best be prepared for a longer stay, mate."

"Then you better make sure you get me out of here before it does because I have zero intention of sticking around any longer than I have to. Call me with the details once you've got them." With that, I hung up and tried to get my greasy grub on again.

Having zero intention of sticking around any longer than I had to was exactly right, but it wasn't like I had a reason to be there in the first place. Christ, what the fuck was I doing in friggin' Maine? See, Cassidy Whalen had this way about her that got into my head and made me act like a stark raving mad lunatic. Because of that woman, I'd done things I'd never do. Like seduce a co-worker in order to win a contract. Or at least, I'd tried to seduce her. It had backfired. Sort of. But I'd gotten my rocks off a time or two in the process, so consolation prize and all. Thing was, I wasn't cool with second place, and my consolation prize had skipped town and taken her delectable little pussy with her. I wasn't okay with that.

Shit. *Why* wasn't I okay with that? Over the years, I'd built up a wall to keep the crazy out, and, bit by bit, she'd been chiseling away at it and making me *feel* things. I shivered, the horror of that thought prancing down my spine like a thousand tiny Cassidys doing their victory dances.

Don't get me wrong, the whole "feeling things" didn't mean I'd fallen in love with her or anything. No, the things she'd made me feel were the same emotions I'd left behind the night I'd watched a man get his head blown off right in front of my eyes. I'd just been a kid, but living in Detroit had been a game of survival I'd been forced to learn early on. Feelings equaled weakness. And it wasn't like I had parents to shelter me from all that bullshit, either. My folks couldn't give a shit whether I lived or died. Hell, they probably would have preferred I'd died because at least then they could collect some sort of check on me.

With a frustrated growl, I shook the fucked-up situation with my parents out of my head because thoughts like those wouldn't further my goals in life. They were behind me. That life was behind me. I'd been moving forward since the day I became a man at the ripe old age of nine. Having no mother to coddle you after you'd just witnessed a brutal, bloody murder sort of put things in perspective. No one was going to take care of that little boy but the man he was meant to be. And the only way anyone could ever hurt me was if I gave them the ammunition to do so.

I'd worked hard to make my way in life. And I'd taken every opportunity I could to further my cause, but being handed a contract that had originally been offered to a fucking woman smarted. It was emasculating. Though I had no intention of backing down from the mother of all contracts, regardless of how I'd gotten it, the first thing I needed to do was reclaim my manhood. And at the moment, Cassidy Whalen was holding my balls in her purse.

Once I got them back, I could put her and all the touchy-feely stuff behind me once and for all.

Deer Isle–Sedgwick Bridge loomed before me like a 400-foot iron sentry that would either grant access to my destination or turn into a rolling and twisting amusement- park ride to dump me into the waters of Eggemoggin Reach below. Obviously, the amusement would not be mine. But as luck would have it, I crossed without issue. The steel suspension cables even stayed in place, and I was fairly certain the ominous laughter I'd thought I'd heard had only been my imagination having playtime with the natural creeks and groans of metal on metal. Christ, I needed some sleep before the boulders scattered about the landscape turned into rock people frolicking through blueberry fields.

Rock people did not exist. Just like the bumps in the road were not made by genetically altered super mole spies with ninja reflexes sent to keep track of me, and the sandbar supporting the causeway to Deer Isle would not turn into quicksand to suck me down to Middle Earth. But my phone *was* ringing.

"Shaw Matthews," I answered, grateful for the distraction. My sleep-deprived brain needed to save the neurons still firing some-where inside in order to be able to keep my wits about me when I finally came face-to-face with the little piggy that had gone "wee, wee, wee" all the way home. I had a thing or two to say to her, and I was perilously close to forgetting every one of them.

"Hey, bro! Whatcha doing?" Chaz asked from the other end of the line.

"I can't be sure, but I think I'm driving through one of the seven gates to hell." Actually, I was fairly certain, but my sleep deprivation probably meant my judgment was questionable. "What's up, man?"

"Just wanted to give you a heads-up to tell you that you might want to keep your head down."

What Chaz had just said made perfect sense to me, which was proof positive that I had, in fact, crossed over into an alternate universe. "Do tell," I said, prepared for just about anything at this point.

"The girls and Quinn are catching a flight to Maine to be with Cassidy. It's supposed to be a surprise, so don't say anything to her or Demi's gonna put my nuts in a sling."

"Join the club," I said, still picturing my own boys in Cassidy's purse. I ignored his questioning response and instead opted to move the conversation along. "So why do I need to keep my head down?"

"Because they know you're already there."

Even so, it made no sense. Quinn had been the one to give me Cassidy's flight information in the first place, telling me to go after her. Only because he thought there was something romantic going on, which he was wrong about, but still, it had gotten me the information. Oh, shit. They'd probably figured out I was the cause of their bestie's quickie departure in the first place. Great. The last thing I needed was to have two pecking hens and a feminine, sympathizing cock to add to the little piggy I was already trying to hog-tie and put back in the barn. What was I, Old fucking McDonald?

"All right, man. Thanks for the warning." I sighed. "With any luck, I'll be gone before they get here. I'm leaving first thing in the morning."

"What are you doing there, anyway?"

"I wish I knew. I've been asking myself the same question."

"Well, that's answer enough, isn't it?"

"What? I don't follow."

"Dude, you jumped on a plane . . . Maine . . . girl . . ." his call had some serious breaks in the line.

I pulled back to look at my phone, which was showing only

one bar going in and out. I must have been driving through a dead zone, but I put the phone back to my ear. "Chaz? Hey, man, you there?"

The three beeps in my ear and "Called Failed" screen meant he wasn't. Oh, well. I'd call him back later because if the ocean on the horizon was any indication—and I was pretty sure the compact car I was driving wasn't going to Chitty Chitty Bang Bang into a boat—it looked like I'd reached my destination. Not that Simi had done her fucking job and told me so. *Pfft,* technology.

Popping over the hill and following the main road down to the small village nestled below, I couldn't help but be mesmerized by the simplicity of it all. It was like stepping onto the set of a fictional town in a movie or book. I never knew places like this actually existed, but there it was.

The street corners were not home to Starbuck's or McDonald's. There were no Walmarts or Targets. No shopping malls or gas stations. Not even a traffic light. Main Street was home to a handful of tourist boutiques, one locally owned and operated diner, a convenient store, and a singular bank. But the hustle and bustle was centered on the hub of it all. A dock. A dock loaded down with just about every make and model of truck ever produced in the good ol' U. S. of A.

Just past the opera house—"Wait. They have a fucking opera house?" I asked myself incredulously—I made a left off School Street and onto West Main, where a giant weathered sign in need of a fresh coat of paint told me I'd finally reached my destination. Parking on the side of the road, I turned off the ignition and unfolded myself out of the little windup toy car. How clowns got so many of themselves into one during their circus act, I'd never understand.

Stepping out onto the sidewalk, I stretched and inhaled a deep breath of fresh air. Well, it wasn't so much fresh as it was fishy and sodium based, but it was natural all the same. My lungs must have been too used to the carbon footprints left behind by big-city living because the resulting coughing attack had me scared shitless I'd never breathe again. Once the spasm was over, I took a look around to be sure no one had seen me, but was struck dumb by the scenery.

Fishing boats moved in and out of the bay with a flock of seagulls hot on their water trails. The sound of engines and horns, the call of the birds, and stray shouts between fishermen as they passed one another was almost a lullaby compared to the harsh noise of the city. Islands of all sizes were scattered throughout the bay and beyond like a treasure map inviting exploration. But most impressive was the horizon beyond. It was like a painter's canvas of blue sky the color of a baby's eyes, with streaks of sunlight penetrating marbled white clouds. It was as if the fingers of a young god were playing with toy boats in a tepid bath.

Cassidy Whalen had been born inside a postcard and had stepped right out of it like a two-dimensional character brought to four-dimensional life. Rarely had I ever taken note of the splendor of such things. Maybe that was because I'd always been in a hurry, thanks to the fast pace of big-city living, but something about this backdrop forced me to stop and take notice. Chick'ish moment aside, I was in awe.

I took out my phone to call Ben to let him know I'd arrived and did a double take when I spotted the words NO SERVICE in the top corner where there should've been full bars.

Holding my cell phone in the air, I did a three-sixty. "No service? Is that even possible with today's technology?" I sighed in defeat and shoved my phone back into my pocket. Forget the postcard. I was in the Twilight Zone.

Looking around again, I shook my head at how easily I'd been duped. Like Cassidy, the small town was beautiful and nonthreatening, a succubus luring in its prey with a false sense of security, and then *blammo*! You were under her spell with no choice but to submit to her will until she sucked the essence from your soul and then discarded your rotting corpse. Luckily for me, I'd figured it out way before it was too late, which was a miracle in and of itself, considering my level of exhaustion.

Behind me, the Whalen House stood proud atop an incline that overlooked not only the bay but also the entire town. And I use the word "town" loosely. How fitting that it should be a place the great counselor Cassidy Whalen called home. Obviously, the high and mighty perch from which she passed judgment had been one she'd inherited at birth. I wouldn't be a bit surprised if I walked inside to find her father was the town's judge, jury, and executioner.

If I'd been in my right mind, I would've turned around and made my way back to civilization. But again—thanks to the sleep deprivation—I'd traded out "right mind" for "one hallucination short of a padded cell" a long time ago. The one and only order of business at the moment was to make it inside and into a warm, comfortable bed to capitalize on some much-needed downtime for my brain. After that, I'd say my peace to the she-devil and then I'd make my hasty escape back to some normalcy in San Diego, with my new and very lucrative partnership at Striker Sports Entertainment and an extraordinarily exceptional life.

Yep, everything I'd worked so hard for was just sitting there waiting for me to come live the dream . . . As soon as I could get free of the nightmare.

ABOUT THE AUTHOR

C. L. PARKER is a romance author who writes stories that sizzle. She's a small-town girl with big-city dreams and enough tenacity to see them come to fruition.

Since she's been the outgoing sort all her life—which translates to "she just wouldn't shut the hell up"—it's no wonder Parker eventually turned to writing as a way to let her voice, and those of the people living inside her head, be heard. She loves hard, laughs until it hurts, and lives like there's no tomorrow. In her world, everything truly does happen for a reason.

www.clparkerofficial.com
Facebook.com/CLParkerOfficial
@theclparker

ABOUT THE TYPE

This book was set in Galliard, a typeface designed in 1978 by Matthew Carter (b. 1937) for the Mergenthaler Linotype Company. Galliard is based on the sixteenth-century typefaces of Robert Granjon (1513–89).